PRAISE FOR

The Most Secret Memory of Men

"More than an engrossing investigation into the mysterious author of a cursed book, Sarr's magnificent novel also offers a profound reflection on the resonance of literature in our lives."
—David Diop, International Booker Prize–winning author of *At Night All Blood Is Black*

"Thanks to translator Lara Vergnaud, English-language readers can seamlessly experience Mohamed Mbougar Sarr's pyrotechnic prose. A labyrinth of a novel, *The Most Secret Memory of Men* is as enthralling as it is thought-provoking. Sarr is a writer that comes along once in a lifetime."
—Eric Nguyen, author of *Things We Lost to the Water*

"An aerobatic feat of narrative invention, whirling between noir, fairy tale, satire, and archival fiction in its self-reflexive meditation on the nature of literary legend... There's an element of poetic justice in an homage to Ouologuem winning such approbation from the very establishment that discarded him. Sarr witheringly scrutinizes the cultural Françafrique—a word for France's geopolitical influence over its former colonies—that relegates African fiction to the status of veiled memoir, ethnographic study, or folkloric entertainment. Defying these categories, he delivers a demiurgic story of literary self-creation, transforming the sad fate of an author who stopped writing into a galvanizing tale about all that remains to be written."

—*The New Yorker*

"Brilliantly executed...a rich narrative about art as a lasting marker of ephemeral individual existence. Literary mystery fans will be captivated."

—*Publishers Weekly* (starred review)

"Sarr investigates with keen psychological detail...[*The Most Secret Memory of Men*] justifies itself as the winner of the 2021 Prix Goncourt, one of France's most prestigious literary prizes...a novel of undoubtable prowess."

—*Kirkus Reviews*

"New, urgent questions surface as postcolonial violence is compellingly pitted against the savagery of Western twentieth-century wars...The seemingly melancholy ending...does not cast a shadow over the vitality and jubilation that the novel otherwise evokes."

—*Times Literary Supplement*

"A playful defense of Ouologuem, one laced with rage at a literary establishment obsessed with identity...[an] act of imaginative recovery."

—*The Drift*

"A powerful book, crossed by an epic breath that celebrates the power of literature."
—Alain Mabanckou, author of *Black Moses*

"I thought I'd come to terms with the spellbinding style of this young prodigy of Senegalese literature. That was until I came across his most luminous, vertiginous, and cerebral novel, *The Most Secret Memory of Men*. Sprinkled with flashes of rare purity, this is a high-flying reflection on the art of writing as well as the freedom and solitude it brings to the writer. Here comes an investigation about a cursed author, in which not one style, but many styles are woven together to give birth to a masterpiece of pure wonder. Sarr has written a political, funny, and sensual work of fiction that readers will devour like detective fiction with an esoteric flavor. It's also a compelling journey into the dark pages of History, as well as to the heart of a question that lives in all those who can't live without books: What can literature do while so many events constantly beset us?"
—Blaise Ndala, award-winning author
of *In the Belly of the Congo*

"An ingeniously constructed, ferociously intelligent literary detective novel in the tradition of Roberto Bolaño and Jorge Luis Borges. In *The Most Secret Memory of Men*, Mohamed Mbougar Sarr adds to the West's fascination with canonization, cult books, and their absent authors, but with a resolutely postcolonial twist. His comic, piercing, multifaceted story politicizes the tendency of Europe's literary establishment to tokenize and then erase marginal-ized authors. A brilliant, labyrinthine, highly entertaining page-turner, rightly cemented as a contemporary master-piece by the Prix Goncourt."

—Dimitri Nasrallah, bestselling author of *Hotline*

"The impressive ambition and stunning narrative energy of *The Most Secret Memory of Men* carries all before it."

—*Le Monde*

"The revelation of the literary year."

—*L'Express*

The
Most Secret Memory
of Men

ALSO BY MOHAMED MBOUGAR SARR

Brotherhood

The
Most Secret Memory
of Men

Mohamed Mbougar Sarr

Translated from the French
by Lara Vergnaud

OTHER PRESS
New York

Originally published in French as *La plus secrète mémoire des hommes* in 2021 by Éditions Philippe Rey, Paris, in co-edition with Éditions Jimsaan, Dakar

Copyright © 2021, Éditions Philippe Rey
In co-edition with Éditions Jimsaan

Published by special arrangement with Éditions Philippe Rey, France, in conjunction with their duly appointed agents Books and More Agency and 2 Seas Literary Agency

English translation copyright © 2023, Lara Vergnaud

Production editor: Yvonne E. Cárdenas
Text designer: Cassandra J. Pappas
This book was set in Monotype Sabon
by Alpha Design & Composition of Pittsfield, NH

Robert Bolaño epigraph translated from the Spanish by Curtis Bauer.

3 5 7 9 10 8 6 4 2

Library of Congress Cataloging-in-Publication Data
Names: Sarr, Mohamed Mbougar, 1990- author. | Vergnaud, Lara, translator.
Title: The most secret memory of men : a novel / Mohamed Mbougar Sarr ; translated from the French by Lara Vergnaud.
Other titles: Plus secrète mémoire des hommes. English
Description: New York : Other Press, [2023] | Originally published in French as La plus secrète mémoire des hommes in 2021 by Éditions Philippe Rey, Paris, in co-edition with Éditions Jimsaan, Dakar.
Identifiers: LCCN 2023006273 (print) | LCCN 2023006274 (ebook) | ISBN 9781635423273 (paperback) | ISBN 9781635423280 (ebook)
Subjects: LCGFT: Novels.
Classification: LCC PQ3989.3.M36714 P5913 2023 (print) | LCC PQ3989.3.M36714 (ebook) | DDC 843/.92—dc23/eng/20230515
LC record available at https://lccn.loc.gov/2023006273
LC ebook record available at https://lccn.loc.gov/2023006274

For Yambo Ouologuem

For some time, the Critique accompanies the Work, then the Critique fades away and it is the Readers who accompany it. The journey can be long or short, then the Readers die one by one and the Work continues alone, although another Critique and other Readers gradually accompany it on its voyage. Then the Critique dies again and the Readers die again, and on that trail of bones the Work continues its journey toward Solitude. To approach it, to sail in its wake is an unmistakable sign of certain death, but another Critique and other Readers approach it tirelessly and relentlessly, and time and speed devour them. Finally the Work travels unavoidably alone in the Vastness. And one day the Work dies, as all things die, as the Sun and the Earth, the Solar System and the Galaxy and the most secret memory of men will be extinguished.

—ROBERTO BOLAÑO, *The Savage Detectives*

Book One

PART ONE

The Spider-Mother's Web

August 27, 2018

Of a writer and their work, we can at least know this: together, they make their way through the most perfect labyrinth imaginable, the path long and circular, and their destination the same as their starting point: solitude.

I'm leaving Amsterdam. Despite everything I've learned in this city, I still can't decide if I know Elimane any better or if his mystique has merely grown. It would be appropriate here to evoke the paradox of any quest for knowledge: the more you discover about a little piece of the world, the clearer the vastness of the unknown and of your ignorance becomes; except that equation would only partially convey my feelings toward this man. His case demands a more radical formula, meaning more pessimistic about the very possibility of comprehending a human soul. His resembles an occluded star; it mesmerizes and devours everything that comes near. You examine his life for a time and, pulling back, serious and resigned and old, perhaps desperate even, you whisper: The human soul can't be understood, it won't be understood.

Elimane sank into the depths of his Night. The ease of his farewell to the sun fascinates me. The willing embrace of his shadow fascinates me. The mystery of his destination haunts me. I don't know why he stopped speaking when he had so much left to say. But mainly, it pains me that I can't do the same. Encountering someone who's gone silent, truly silent, invariably prompts reflection about the meaning—the necessity—of your own words, as you suddenly wonder whether it's all just worthless babbling, linguistic sludge.

Time to shut my mouth and pause this diary. The Spider-Mother's stories tired me out. Amsterdam emptied me. The path of solitude awaits.

I

T.C. Elimane offered the African authors of my generation, who can't be described as young for much longer, the chance to tear each other limb from limb in pious and bloody literary jousts. His book was both cathedral and arena; we entered it as if entering a god's tomb and ended up kneeling in our own blood, offered as libation to the masterpiece. A single page was enough to assure us that we were reading a writer, a hapax, one of those celestial bodies that only appear once in the literary heavens.

I remember one of the many dinner parties we spent with his book. The discussion grew heated, and Béatrice—the sensual, dynamic Béatrice Nanga who I hoped would one day asphyxiate me between her breasts—had said, ever combative, that only the works of true writers merited venomous debate, that they alone boiled the blood like wood alcohol and that if, in an attempt to conciliate that flabby, spineless creature we call general opinion, we avoided the impassioned clashes they provoked, we were doing a dishonor to literature itself. A true writer, she had added, sparks fatal disagreements among true readers, who are forever at war; if you're not willing to fight to the death for an author's carcass, like in a game of *buzkashī*, then fuck off and go drown yourself in that warm puddle of piss you take for quality beer: you're anything but a reader, much less a writer.

I had backed Béatrice Nanga in her dramatic charge. T.C. Elimane wasn't classic, he was cult. Literary mythos is a gaming table. Elimane sat at that table and laid down the three most powerful trump cards there are: first, he chose a name with mysterious initials; then, he only wrote a single book; finally, he disappeared without leaving a trace. So, yes, it was worth sticking your neck out in an attempt to grab hold of his carcass.

It was possible to doubt whether a man named T.C. Elimane had truly existed at one time, or to wonder if that was a pseudonym invented by an author to mess with (or escape) the literary world. No one, however, could have disputed the powerful truth of his book: after reading the final page, violent, pure life would come coursing back through your veins.

Knowing if Homer was a real person, yes or no, remains an interesting question. But in the end, it changes little of his reader's marvelment; for it is to Homer, whoever or whatever he was, that the reader owes thanks for having written *The Iliad* and *The Odyssey*. Likewise, the person, hoax, or legend behind T.C. Elimane mattered little; it was to that name that we were indebted for the work that changed our perspective on literature. Perhaps on life. *The Labyrinth of Inhumanity*: that was its title, and we went to its pages like manatees straight to the water's source.

In the beginning, there was a prophecy and there was a King; and the prophecy told the King that the earth would grant him absolute power but demand, in return, the ashes of old men and women, to which the King agreed; he imme-diately started to burn the elders of his kingdom, before scattering their remains around his palace, where, soon, a forest, a macabre forest, grew, which would be called the labyrinth of inhumanity.

II

How did we meet, this book and I? By chance, like everyone else. Though I haven't forgotten what the Spider-Mother told me: chance is always merely a fate unknown to us. My first reading of *The Labyrinth of Inhumanity* is very recent, just over a month ago. But to say that I knew nothing about Elimane before that reading would be wrong: in high school, already, I knew his name. It was listed in *The Reader's Guide to Negro Literature*, one of those ineradicable anthologies that have been used as reference books for schoolchildren in francophone Africa since colonial times.

It was 2008, my junior year at a military boarding school in northern Senegal. Literature was beckoning, and I developed the adolescent dream of becoming a poet, a completely banal ambition when you're discovering the greatest among them and living in a country still haunted by Senghor's cumbrous ghost; in other words, a country where a poem remained one of the most reliable tools in the arsenal of seductions. It was an era when you could pick up a girl with a quatrain, memorized or made up.

Accordingly, I began to immerse myself in poetic anthologies, in dictionaries of synonyms, rare words, rhymes too. Mine were terrible, interspersed through wobbly hendecasyllables full of "tears bereft" and "skies dehiscent," of "hyaline dawns." I parodied, perverted, plagiarized. I frenetically leafed through my *Guide to Negro Literature*. Which was where, alongside classics of black literature, between Tchichellé Tchivéla and Tchicaya U Tam'si, I first stumbled upon the unknown name of T.C. Elimane. The corresponding commentary was so distinctive from the rest of the anthology that I lingered on it. The entry read (I kept my textbook):

T.C. Elimane was born in Senegal. He received a scholarship and moved to Paris, where, in 1938, he published a book whose fate proved unusual and tragic: The Labyrinth of Inhumanity.

And what a book! The masterpiece of a young African Negro! A first in France! The novel ignited the kind of literary quarrel for which that country alone has the aptitude and the appetite.

The Labyrinth of Inhumanity *counted as many supporters as it did detractors. But though there was talk of prestigious prizes destined for the author and his book, a mysterious literary scandal stopped the rumors cold. The work was pilloried. As for its young author, he disappeared from the literary scene.*

Then the war broke out. After 1938, no one heard from this T.C. Elimane again. His fate remains a mystery, despite some interesting hypotheses (on this topic, see, for example, the short but edifying account by the journalist B. Bollème, Who Was the True Negro Rimbaud? Odyssey of a Ghost, *Éditions de la Sonde, 1948). Besmirched by the scandal, the publisher took the book off the shelves and destroyed all its remaining copies.* The Labyrinth of Inhumanity *was never reissued. Today, the work is unobtainable.*

It bears repeating: this precocious writer had talent. A touch of genius perhaps. It's unfortunate that he used it in service of a portrait of despair: his bleak book nourished the colonial vision of Africa as a place of darkness, as violent and barbaric. A continent that had already suffered so much, that was suffering and would continue to suffer, was entitled to expect its authors to paint a more positive picture of it.

Those passages immediately sent me down Elimane's dusty trail, or rather, his ghost's trail. I spent weeks trying to find out what became of him, but the Internet didn't tell me anything that the textbook hadn't already. There were no photos of Elimane. The few sites that mentioned him did so in such an allusive way that I quickly understood they didn't know any more than I did. Nearly all of them spoke of a "shameful African writer from the interwar period" without noting what, exactly, was the source of his shame. I wasn't able to learn more about his book either. I couldn't find a single account that explored it in depth; no studies or dissertations on it existed.

I mentioned the book to a friend of my father's, a professor of African literature. He told me that Elimane's fleeting existence in French letters (he made sure to emphasize "French") prevented his novel from being discovered in Senegal. "It was written by a eunuch god. People sometimes talk about *The Labyrinth of Inhumanity* like it's a sacred book. The truth is that it didn't inspire a religion. Nobody believes in the book anymore. Maybe no one ever did."

My search was limited by the fact that I was at that military boarding school in the middle of the bush. I stopped looking and resigned myself to a simple and cruel truth:

Elimane had been erased from literary memory, but also, it would appear, from all of human memory, including that of his compatriots (though everyone knows that it's always your compatriots who forget you first). *The Labyrinth of Inhumanity* belonged to the other history of literature (which is perhaps the *true* history of literature): that of books lost in a corridor of time, not cursed even, simply forgotten, and whose corpses, bones, and solitudes blanket the floors of prisons without jailers, and line infinite and silent frozen paths.

I pulled myself away from that sad history and went back to writing love poems in my shaky lines of verse.

In the end, my only major discovery, on an obscure online forum, was the long first sentence of *The Labyrinth of Inhumanity*, seemingly the sole survivor of the book's obliteration seventy years prior: *In the beginning, there was a prophecy and there was a King; and the prophecy told the King that the earth would grant him absolute power but demand, in return, the ashes of old men and women*, and so on.

III

———

And now here is how *The Labyrinth of Inhumanity* came back into my life.

Following my first encounter with Elimane in high school, some time went by before I found myself contending with him again. Of course I had thought about him, but only on occasion and always with a touch of sadness, the way you remember stories that are unfinished or unfinishable—an old friend lost, a manuscript destroyed in a fire, a love rejected out of fear of finally being happy. I passed the baccalaureate, left Senegal, and moved to Paris to continue my studies.

Once here, I briefly resumed my research on Elimane, without success: the book was still impossible to find, even among booksellers who supposedly had impressive inventories. As for B. Bollème's opuscule, *Who Was the True Negro Rimbaud?*, I was informed that it hadn't been reissued since the mid-1970s. My studies and life as an immigrant soon steered me away from *The Labyrinth of Inhumanity*, a phantom book whose author appeared to have been a mere flick of a match in the deep literary night. And so, little by little, I forgot them.

The course of my studies in France led me to a dissertation on literature that quickly began to feel like an exile from the writer's Eden. I became a lazy doctoral student, rapidly diverted from the noble path of academia by what was no longer a passing temptation but a desire as pretentious as it was certain: to become a novelist. They warned me: You might never succeed in literature. You might end up bitter! disappointed! marginalized! a failure! Yes, it's possible, I said. The relentless "they" insisted: Maybe you'll end up suicidal! Yes, maybe, but life, I added, is nothing more than a series of "maybes," a slip of a word and yet it can carry so much. I hope it holds my weight but tough luck if it gives way, in which case I'll get to see what lives or rots below. And then I suggested that "they" go to hell. I told them: No one ever succeeds in literature, so you can take your success and shove it wherever you like.

I wrote a little novel, *Anatomy of the Void*, which I published with a fairly small press. The book was a flop (seventy-nine copies sold the first two months, including the ones I bought out of my own pocket). And yet one thousand one hundred and eighty-two people had liked the post I put on Facebook to announce the pending publication of my book. Nine hundred and nineteen had left a comment. "Congratulations!" "Proud of you!" "Awesome, bro!" "Bravo!" "An inspiration!" "Thank you, brother. You do us proud," "Can't wait to read it, *inshallah*!" "When's it out?" (even though I had included the publication date in the post), "How can I get it?" (also in the post), "How much does it cost?" (same), "Interesting title!" "You're a role model for our youth!" "What's it about?" (this question embodies the Evil in literature), "Can I order it?" "Is there a PDF?" et cetera. Seventy-nine copies.

I had to wait four or five months after the novel's publication for it to be rescued from the purgatory of anonymity. An influential journalist, a specialist of so-called francophone literature, reviewed it in twelve hundred characters, including spaces, in *Le Monde* (the "Africa" section). He voiced a few reservations about my style, but his final sentence stuck me with the formidable, dangerous, actually maybe even diabolical label of "a francophone African writer full of promise." Granted, I had avoided the terrible and fatal "rising star," but his praise was no less murderous. It was enough to earn me, as a result, a certain kind of attention in the literary world of Paris's African diaspora—the Ghetto, as it's affectionately called by certain shit-talkers, including me. From that moment on, even people who hadn't read my work, and undoubtedly never would, knew, from a tiny review in *Monde Afrique*, that I was the umpteenth new young writer to arrive, dripping with promise. At the festivals, meet and greets, literary fairs, and salons to which I was invited, I became the obvious addition to those irradicable roundtables titled "New Voices" or "The New Guard" or "New Writers to Watch" or whatever else was supposedly new in literature but that, in reality, already seemed so old and tired. The minor buzz reached Senegal, my country, where people began to take an interest in me because Paris had, which served as an imprimatur. From that point on, *Anatomy of the Void* got talked about ("talked about" not meaning read).

All the same, the novel had left me unsatisfied, unhappy perhaps. Soon I felt ashamed of *Anatomy of the Void*—which I wrote for reasons that I will explain later—and, as if to purge myself of it or bury it, I began dreaming of another great novel, which would be ambitious and decisive. I just had to write it.

IV

And it was precisely that, write my great masterpiece, that I had been trying to do for one month when, one July evening, unable to think of the first sentence, I escaped to the streets of Paris. I wandered, on the lookout for a miracle. It appeared to me, on the other side of a bar window, when I recognized Marème Siga D., a Senegalese writer in her sixties whose every book had caused such scandal that, for some, she'd come to be viewed as an evil Pythia, a ghoul, or an outright succubus. I, however, saw her as an angel: the black angel of Senegalese literature, which would have otherwise become a deadly cesspit of boredom in which float, like listless specks of shit, those books that inevitably open with descriptions of an eternal sun "casting its rays through the foliage," or the sight of that one-size-fits-all storybook face with its "prominent" cheekbones, "Grecian" (or "broad") nose, and "protruding" or "imposing" forehead. Siga D. was saving contemporary Senegalese literature from pestilential embalmment in clichés and expressions that had been sucked dry, devitalized like old, rotten teeth. As it happened, she had left Senegal to write a book whose sole offense to moral sensibilities was radical honesty. That had earned her a cultlike status—and a few legal proceedings, which she always attended without a lawyer.

She usually lost them. But, she would maintain, what I have to say is right here, in my life, so I'll keep on writing it, and to hell with your pathetic attacks.

So, I recognized Siga D. I entered the bar and sat near her. Apart from us, there were three or four customers spread out inside. The rest had gone to the terrace in search of some air. Siga D. was alone at her table, perfectly still. She looked like a lioness lying in wait for her prey, hidden in the tall grass, tearing apart the steppe with big, yellow eyes. The seeming coldness of her demeanor clashed with the fieriness of her works, the memory of which—sumptuous and pelean pages, pages of flint and diamonds—cast doubt in my mind, briefly, that this impassive woman was the one who had written them.

At that exact moment, Siga D. moved her arm to push up the sleeve of her grand boubou. Through the gap in the garment, a matter of seconds, I glimpsed her breasts. They loomed as though at the end of a tunnel or maybe a long waiting room, a waiting room of desire. Siga D. had written memorable paragraphs about those breasts, blazons worthy of the most torrid anthologies of erotic texts. And so there I found myself before a chest enshrined in literary posterity. Countless readers had imagined that same ample bosom, and many had developed robust fantasies accordingly. I summoned my own. The arm dropped and sent the chest back into hiding.

I took my courage in one hand, threw back my drink with the other, and then I approached Siga D. I introduced myself, Diégane Latyr Faye, I said that I loved her writing, that I was overwhelmed to see her in person, that I found her personality fascinating, that I was impatient to read her next book, in short, the muddle of formulaic praise that her admirers must have showered on her at every encounter; then, seeing her look of annoyed politeness, the kind people get when they want to send away a nuisance without having to tell them, I went for broke and brought up her chest, which I had just glimpsed and would have liked to see again.

She blinked in surprise; a breach formed, I dove in: Your breasts are truly sublime, Madame Siga.

"Did you like what you saw?" she said calmly. "Yes, I liked it very much and I want more." "More?" "More." "Why?" "Because I'm hard." "Seriously, Diégane Latyr Faye? Doesn't take you much, young man!" "Yes, I know, Madame Siga, I've been obsessed with your breasts for so long, you have no idea." "Stop being so formal, stop calling me Madame Siga, it's ridiculous, and also, lose the hard-on, let the air out, *mënn na la jurr*, I could be your mother, Diégane." "*Kone nampal ma*, then suckle me like a mother," I responded, like when I was a teenager and girls would reject my advances (or fail to understand my hendecasyllabic poems), judging, because they were four or five years older than me, that they could have given birth to me.

Siga D. looked at me for a moment and, for the first time, she smiled.

"Ah, so the kid's quick on the draw, huh? The kid talks a big talk, huh? You want to suckle. All right. Follow me. My hotel is a few minutes away. *Inshallah* the kid gets to suckle."

She started to rise, then paused. "Unless you'd prefer that I *nampal* you here and now?"

This offer was made concrete when a second later she pulled the neck of her billowy boubou low on her chest; one heavy breast, the left, sprung from the loosened top. "You want?" said Siga D. "Here it is." The revelation: the large medallion of her areola gleaming; a brown island amid an ocean of abundance in lighter hues. Siga D. watched me, head tilted to her right, impassive and seemingly indifferent to everything else. She could have easily played up the shock value, the crudeness almost, of her gesture, but quite the opposite: this wanton voluptuousness was displayed with restraint, which I even soon deemed elegant. "Well? You want it or not?" She grabbed her breast. She massaged it slowly. After a few seconds, I said I'd rather suckle in the privacy of the hotel. "What a shame," she responded in an alarmingly gentle tone, and she put away her breast before standing up. The smell of cinnamon and myrrh filled the air. I paid. I followed her.

V

———

We reached the hotel where she was staying for the few days she was in Paris to attend a symposium dedicated to her writing. But this is my last night here, she told me as she called the elevator. I'm going home tomorrow, to Amsterdam. So it's tonight or never, Diégane Latyr Faye.

She entered the elevator, a terrible smile on her lips. As we rose to the thirteenth floor, I plunged, toward utter ruin. Siga D.'s body had known, done, tried everything: What could I offer her? Where could I take her? What could I think up? Who did I think I was? Those philosophers who extol the inexhaustible virtues of erotic inventiveness never had to deal with a Siga D., whose mere presence wiped away my sexual history. How should I go about it? The fourth floor already. She won't feel anything, she won't even feel you enter, your body will liquefy against hers, it will trickle down and be absorbed by the sheets, by the mattress. Seventh. You won't just drown inside of her, you'll disappear, disintegrate, crumble, she's going to obliterate you, and the pieces that are left will drift into the clinamen of the ancient materialists, Leucippus, Democritus of Abdera (whose only equal when it comes to philosophy was Empedocles), not to mention Lucretius, the noble expositor of the pleasure-seeking Epicurus exalted in *De rerum natura*. Tenth. Boredom, deadly boredom, that's all you can promise her.

It was warm, I broke into a cold sweat, and Siga D. could have sent me flying with a flick of her fingers, with a single breath, like a fragile spikelet. To boost myself, I thought about the Rabelaisian suckling to come, about the literary bosom. But instead of helping, that image set me to obsessing about an even greater weakness: my hands struck me as absurdly harmless and small before the writer's breasts, worthless hands incapable of desire; stumps. As for my tongue, I didn't even dream of using it: the poetic teats had already tied it in knots. I was fucked.

Thirteenth floor. The elevator doors opened, Siga D. walked out without looking at me, turned left, and, for a few seconds, I could no longer hear her footsteps, which were absorbed by the thick carpeting in the hallway; then came the sound of a bolt opening at the touch of a magnetic card, before the silence returned. I had remained in the elevator, where I finally released the gas I had been holding in since the first floor to protect my dignity. I considered flight. Though flight wasn't the right word, given that, we both knew, I had lost before the battle even began. If I had left, it would have merely been the sad but predictable conclusion to my defeat, the consummation of my foreshadowed trouncing. The elevator was called to the lobby. The doors began to close. I stopped them at the last second and walked out, driven less by courage than by an obscure desire to experience a crushing vanquishment.

So, I made my way down the hallway. A door had been left ajar, allowing that same aroma of cinnamon and myrrh to escape, as either invitation or warning. I didn't push it open, as though the door was in fact the gateway to hell. I waited there, dumb and motionless. The hallway light eventually switched off. I took one step forward; it came back on; I crossed the threshold. A room in pastel tones welcomed me, luxurious and impersonal. For a second, through the large sliding door that opened onto a balcony, I saw Paris sparkling. The sound of water: Siga D. was taking a shower. I breathed: a little respite before the moment of truth.

I was struck less by the size of the bed, improbably large as it was, than by the kitsch factor of the painting proudly hanging above it. Any artist who so superficially enhances (meaning disfigures) the world shouldn't be allowed to keep on living, I thought. I looked away, flopped onto the gigantic bed, and sent my thoughts on a suicide mission to the ceiling. Several possible scenarios of what was to come were playing out in front of me. They all ended the same way: I would step over the balcony railing and leap into the void, to the sound of pitiless laughter coming from Siga D., who hadn't sensed a thing. She emerged from her shower fifteen minutes later. A white towel, which came to her thighs, was knotted at her chest; another was wrapped around her head like a sultana's turban.

"Oh, you're still here, huh."

From the tone of her voice, I didn't know if this was a cold observation, an unexpected discovery, a devastatingly ironic comment, or even a question. Any of those options could have harbored terrifying innuendos. I didn't answer. She smiled. I watched her go back and forth between the bedroom and the bathroom. Siga D.'s body was clearly that of a mature woman who had never retreated from either pleasure or pain. Hers was a beauty entangled with suffering;

an immodest body, tried and tested; a body without harshness but one that wasn't frightened by the harshness of the world. It sufficed to see it, truly, to understand it. I watched Siga D. and I knew the truth: this wasn't a human being I had before me, but a spider, the Spider-Mother, whose vast composition was interwoven with millions of threads of silk but also of steel and maybe blood, and I was merely a fly mired in that web, a fascinated and fat, green-hued fly, caught in Siga D., in the lattice and density of her lives.

Then passed those long minutes during which certain women, after their shower, do a thousand things that appear to be of the utmost importance, without anyone knowing exactly what. She eventually sat down in the armchair in front of me, still covered by a single towel. It inched up, I saw her upper thighs, then her hips, and, finally, her pubic mound. I made no attempt to look away and stared at her bush for a moment. I wanted to see her Eye. She crossed her legs, and the memory of Sharon Stone abruptly paled in my mind.

"I bet you're a writer. Or an aspiring writer. Don't act so surprised. I've learned to recognize your kind at first glance. They look at things like they all contain some profound secret. They see a woman's vagina and contemplate it like that's where the key to their mystery is hidden. They aestheticize. But a pussy is just a pussy. There's no need to drool out your poetry or your life philosophy while you feast your eyes on it. You can't live in the moment and write it at the same time."

"Of course you can. That's what it means to live as a writer. Make every moment of life a moment to write. See everything with a writer's eyes and..."

"There's your mistake. There's the mistake every guy like you makes. You all believe that literature fixes life. Or completes it. Or replaces it. You're wrong. Writers, and I've known many, have always been among the most mediocre lovers I've ever encountered. Do you know why? When they have sex, they're already thinking about the scene the experience will turn into. Every caress is ruined by what their imagination is doing or will do with it, every thrust is weakened by a sentence. When I talk to them during sex, I can almost hear their 'she murmured.' They live in chapters. Quotation marks precede every word they say. *Als het erop aan komt*—that's Dutch, it means 'at the end of the day'—writers like you are stuck in their make-believe. You're permanent narrators. It's life that matters. The work only comes after. The two don't mix. Ever."

An interesting and debatable theory to which I was no longer listening. Siga D.'s towel was now almost undone. She had uncrossed her legs. Her open towel revealed nearly her entire body: her stomach, her waist, every inscription on her skin...Only her breasts remained hidden by two final bits of towel. As for the Eye, I could see it clearly, and it was out of the question that mine blinked first.

"Look at you. You're thinking up sentences this very second. Bad sign. If you want to write a good novel, forget it for now. You want to fuck me, right? Yes, you do. I'm here. Focus on that. On me."

She rose from the armchair, came closer, leaned her face over mine. Her towel came completely undone; her chest emerged; she pressed it against mine.

"Otherwise, get out of here and go write another little shit novel."

I found the provocation kind of juvenile and threw Siga D. onto the bed. The expression on her face (triumph, pleasure, defiance) filled me with raging desire. I began kissing her breasts. I gave it my all and managed to get a few moans out of her, or more precisely, protomoans. At least that's what I told myself. Real or imagined, they galvanized me. I, the fly, was near the center of the web, near the lethal and obscure center of the Spider-Mother's home. I wanted to slip toward the Eye. But just then she stopped me and rolled me onto my side like a child; with humiliating ease and a burst of laughter; she stood and began to put her clothes on.

A wave of intense anger rising inside me, I wanted to have another go. But knowing how ridiculous I surely appeared in that instant held me back. I shut my mouth and kept it shut. Then Siga D. began to sing slowly in Serer. I stretched out to listen and, little by little, the room, which until then had exuded icy comfort, became alive and sad and populated by memories. The song spoke of an old fisherman readying his small boat before confronting a fish-goddess.

I closed my eyes. Siga D. finished getting dressed as she hummed the last verse. The boat sailed off across the calm ocean and the fisherman scanned the horizon with hard, glistening eyes, prepared to face the mythical goddess. He didn't look back at the shore, where his wife and children were watching him. At the very end, *Sukk lé joot Kata maag, Roog soom a yooniin*, "His pirogue passed behind the ocean, and God was his only company." The instant Siga D. stopped singing, a terebrant sadness filled the room.

It persisted for several seconds, and I could almost feel its heft, make out its smell, when Siga D. invited me to sit on the balcony, where we would both feel better. She had brought some excellent weed from Amsterdam, which she packed herself, with the indolent nimbleness of habit, into a large and rather intimidating joint, of which I'd never seen the like, which we smoked as we discussed serious things and frivolous things, the thousand masks of life, the sadness at the heart of all beauty, a truly enormous joint, and quality weed. I asked her if she knew the rest of the story about the fisherman and the mythical goddess.

"No, Diégane. I don't think there's any more to it. One of my stepmothers, Ta Dib, used to sing it to me when I was a child. She always sang it that way."

Siga D. had paused briefly, then told me that there didn't need to be any more to it because everyone, *als het erop aan komt*, knew the end of the story, which could only conclude in one way. I agreed with her. There was only one possible ending. The gleam of the joint between my fingers went out just then. In all my life, I had rarely felt so relaxed. I looked up at the sky, a starless sky veiled by something—not a procession of clouds, no, another expanse, vast and deep, that looked like the shadow of a gigantic creature flying over the earth.

"It's God," I had said. I stopped talking for a moment before resuming, in a calm, low voice (I don't think that I ever again experienced the unprecedented and unjustifiable sensation that I had then, the sensation that I was within reach of the Truth): "It's God. He's very close tonight, in fact, I don't think He's been this close to us in a long time. But He knows. He knows that coming would destroy Him, once and for all. He's not well armed enough yet to confront His biggest nightmare: Us. Man."

"So you're one of those people who turn into metaphysician-theologists when they smoke weed," murmured Siga D.

More silence, then she said, "Hang on." She went into the bedroom, rummaged through her purse, and returned with a book in her hand. She sat back down, opened the book at random, and said, "We can't end this night without reading a little literature, without sacrificing a few pages to the god of poets," then she began to read: three pages were enough to send shivers through my whole body.

"I know. It's better than a joint," she said, closing the book.

"What the hell was that?"

"*The Labyrinth of Inhumanity.*"

"Impossible."

"Sorry?"

"Impossible. *The Labyrinth of Inhumanity* is a myth. T.C. Elimane is a eunuch god."

"You know Elimane?"

"I know of him. I had *The Reader's Guide to Negro Literature*. I looked for that book for...I..."

"Do you know the history of this book?"

"*The Reader's Guide* said that..."

"Forget *The Reader's Guide*. Did you look yourself? Yes, you must have tried. But you didn't find anything. Obviously. No one finds anything. Except I almost did. I got close. But the path is winding. Long. Sometimes deadly. You search for T.C. Elimane, and a silent precipice suddenly opens beneath your feet like an upside-down sky. Like a gaping, bottomless mouth. That abyss opened before me too. I tumbled. The fall came...the fall..."

"I have no idea what you're talking about."

"...and I lived through it. Life took unexpected directions, my thread got lost in the sands of time, and I no longer had the courage to keep looking."

"For who? For what? And first off, how did you get the book? What proves that this is in fact *The Labyrinth of Inhumanity*?"

"...I never told anyone what I lived or almost lived with him. It's always felt like a blind spot in my life, the invisible horizon..."

"You smoked too much."

"...but also the spot I see the clearest, the looming horizon...and if I can pick up the thread of that story, I'll have gone farther than I ever have into the foreign land that's inside of me and which he inhabits..."

"You're out of your mind."

"...and I will have descended into the heart of what I really have to write: my book about Elimane. But for now, I'm not ready. As for the circumstances in which I got this book...It's not a story that I can tell you, Diégane Faye. Not today, in any case. Not yet."

Siga D. stopped speaking and turned her head toward the city, but it was obvious to me that she saw none of the glimmers of light popping up here and there, like a constellation of precious gems, across the center of Paris. Her gaze was directed inward, toward the glimmers or twilights of her past. I didn't attempt to pull her from the melancholy of remembering. The opposite: I let her sink into it, trying to gauge, from the shadows of her eyes, how far she had slipped into memory. And even though she was drawing further away in time, the Spider seemed closer to me, more present, more real. She was silently spinning the wheel of the past, creating obscure, complex, and beautiful patterns that appeared to reopen the same wounds they depicted. Suddenly I felt like I was being swept along by her memory, her thoughts; they radiated outward, so intense that they seemed to burst from her physical shell and penetrate, ravish any nearby presence. I understood, after a few seconds spent beneath that heaviness (a chaotic and irresistible heaviness, invisible but palpable: the heaviness of a concentrated thought from which you're trying to glean a little meaning, perhaps some truth), I understood that I was a spectator to something I had previously believed must only ever be staged within oneself, relegated to the secret theater of the mind, reserved for mystical experiences, and only possible in a symbolist painting or a nightmare: *I was watching an introspection*. Another soul was inviting mine inside her, directing her gaze at her innermost depths, and preparing to judge herself without mercy. It was an autopsy where the coroner was also the corpse, and the sole witness to this vision, to this sensation that could have been described as beautiful or hideous, beautiful and hideous, was me.

"He's a ghost," said Siga D. suddenly, and in her voice I sensed the voices of all the Siga D.'s she had encountered in her memory. "You don't meet Elimane. He appears to you. He goes through you. He turns your bones to ice and burns your skin. A living illusion. I felt his breath on the back of my neck, his breath rising from among the dead."

I simply looked at the sleeping city, it was my turn, and as I contemplated Paris, it occurred to me that this evening seemed a lot like a fucking dream. I told myself I should be prepared to wake up at any moment on the busted couch in

the apartment I shared with Stanislas. That was more prob-
able than standing here, on the balcony of a luxury hotel,
in the company of a great novelist who had a copy of *The
Labyrinth of Inhumanity.*

"Here," said Siga D.

She handed me the book. I suppressed a shudder.

"Read it, then come see me in Amsterdam. Take care
of it. I don't know why I'm offering you this gift, Diégane
Latyr Faye. I barely know you, and yet I'm giving you what
is undoubtedly the most precious thing I own. Perhaps we're
meant to share it. Our meeting was unusual, it came about
through odd detours, but it led here: this book. Maybe it's
chance. Maybe it's fate. But the two aren't necessarily contradictory. Chance is merely a fate unknown to us, a fate
written in invisible ink. Someone told me that once. She
might not have been wrong. I think that us meeting is life
revealing itself. And that's exactly what you should always
follow: life and its unpredictable paths. They all lead to
the same place, the same destination for all of us, but to
get there, they take routes that can be beautiful or terrible,
paved with flowers or bones, night roads we often travel
alone, but where we have the chance to put our souls to the
test. And also... it's so rare to meet someone to whom this
book says something. Take care of it. I'll wait for your visit
to Amsterdam. Write me once you've decided, so I can get
organized before you arrive. I'll leave you my contact info
on the inside cover. Like this. There. Take it."

That's when I told myself: You're going to wake up
now, when you touch the book. I held out my hand, ready
to open my eyes and see the backdrop of my living room.
But the scene continued: I was holding *The Labyrinth of*

Inhumanity. It had the sobriety of a different era: a white background on which appeared, from top to bottom, the author's name, the title, and the publisher (Gemini), framed by an anthracite-blue border. On the back, I read two sentences: *T.C. Elimane was born in the colony of Senegal. The Labyrinth of Inhumanity, his first book, is the first authentic masterpiece from a Negro from black Africa who confronts and honestly depicts the madness and beauty of his continent.*

I had the book in my hands. I had already dreamt of this moment and was expecting it to prompt something different; but nothing happened, and when I lifted my head, Siga D. was watching me.

"Go, go read. It'll take you a while. I envy you. You get to discover this book. But I feel sorry for you too."

She didn't hide the sad shadow that flickered in her eyes. I didn't ask her what she meant by that last comment and slid *The Labyrinth of Inhumanity* into the back pocket of my jeans after a tentative thank-you. Siga D. said that she didn't know if I should be thanking her or cursing her. I retorted that perhaps she was being slightly overdramatic. She kissed me on the cheek and said, "You'll see."

And thus the fat fly emerged from the web. I came home to a thick silence that was nonetheless punctuated by belligerent, conquering breaths: Stanislas was snoring. He was a translator from Polish and had been working for several months on a new version of *Ferdydurke*, his illustrious compatriot Witold Gombrowicz's masterpiece.

I went to my bedroom with what was left of a bottle and played some music on my phone, a personal selection of songs by Super Diamono, my favorite group. I felt the book in my pocket, took it out, studied it for a moment. I couldn't claim that I hadn't believed in its existence: there had been nights when I'd belonged to the book, utterly and unabashedly, nights when I had recited the whole thing in one sitting without ever having read it; but there had also been many others when its existence was reduced to less than a myth: to its mere shadow, to a fragile hope. That goddamn labyrinth! Yet here it was: the object of obsessions that I'd dismissed as juvenile and forever dead was rising from the bloody ruins of my dreams.

Super Diamono was playing, and Omar Pène's voice of molten obsidian was sailing toward day on the calm nocturnal sea. In its wake slid the peaceful and glorious "Moudjé," a memento mori in the form of a unique gem, forged in the lava of twelve minutes of jazz. *Da ngay xalat ñun fu ñuy mujjé*, it said, remember our end, think about the great solitude, contemplate the promise of twilight, which will be held for everyone. A reminder as formidable as it was essential, as old as time, but whose dizzying gravity I felt like I was realizing for the first time in my life. And so it was after surrendering myself to this abyss opened by Diamono and Pène that I began to read *The Labyrinth of Inhumanity*.

It was still dark although moody indigo was already spilling over the edge of the horizon. I read; the night perished without a cry; then I read again and the bottle emptied; I almost opened another one but then changed my mind, and continued to read while listening to Diamono songs, until every star had disappeared into the ray of light piercing through my window and every shadow and every wounded silence and Stanislas's snoring and the oldest song of lament on this sad earth and everything I thought I knew about Man had faded away; then, long after the sun had risen and my playlist had ended (though the silence that follows Pène is a poetic testament to Pène), I fell asleep, prepared to discover in my slumber a delirious transfiguration of that night's events, to awaken in a world that would appear unaltered at first glance, but where everything, beneath the surface, beneath the skin of time, would be forever changed.

Those were my first steps, after my evening in the Spider's web, onto the circle of solitude along which glided *The Labyrinth of Inhumanity* and T.C. Elimane.

PART TWO

Summer Diary

July 11, 2018

Diary: I'm only keeping you for one reason: to record the extent to which *The Labyrinth of Inhumanity* has left me a poorer man. Great works impoverish us and must always impoverish us. They rid us of the superfluous. After reading them, we inevitably emerge *emptied*: enriched, but enriched through subtraction.

When I woke, around one p.m., I read the entire book again, sober, without the drugs, without Siga D.'s magnetic presence. The experience was just as shattering, and I remained in my room, destroyed, unable to move. Around four, my roommate came in to make sure I wasn't dead. I claimed a migraine to justify my lethargy. Stanislas, who knows what he's talking about (he has Polish blood), gave me a host of tips for recovering from a hangover. Even one caused by a book? What book? I handed him *The Labyrinth of Inhumanity*. This is what you're reading right now? Yes. This is what's putting you in this state? Maybe. Because it's good or bad? Not waiting for my answer, he opened it at random. Two, three, four pages read. He stopped. I gave him a questioning look: Well? He said: It's got style. I wish I could keep reading but I have a political GA. I said: Are the anarchists finally going to take power? He said: No, topple it. I said: And after? He answered: Give it away. I retorted: To who? He asserted: The people. I asked: Who are the people?

The translator left without telling me who the people were. Then I read the book again, to the point of exhaustion. But the book itself is inexhaustible; it's gauging me, gleaming like a skull in a cemetery night. *The Labyrinth of Inhumanity* ends with a promise: something to follow, something that I might never read.

I'd simply need to call Siga D. to find out the whole story. But I won't take the easy route just yet. The book will show its true colors. I can still see the Spider-Mother's sad look when she gave me the novel. I can still hear her words: I envy you but I feel sorry for you too. I envy you means you will descend a staircase whose steps sink into the deepest regions of your humanity. I feel sorry for you means when the secret nears, the staircase will be lost in shadow and you will be alone, stripped of the desire to go back up, because the book will have shown you the vanity of the surface, and incapable of going down because the night will have buried the steps leading to revelation.

I closed the book, then I began writing in you, Diary.

July 12

This morning, routine visit to the Senegalese consulate, the academic scholarship office, to renew mine. It's good until next July. After that expiration date, I'll have to figure something out: find a real job, or resume and complete my dissertation, or live on the street, or become the lover of some rich bougie old lady who adores the mysteries of Africa and will support me on their behalf, or write a book about personal regression disguised as a handbook for personal development. Or drop dead. Until then, long live the charitable Republic of France, which provides for all the necessities of my survival!

Next, I went to the library to take a look at noteworthy publications from 1938. I found an exceptional literary, poetic, and philosophical French cohort: Bernanos, Alain, Sartre, Nizan, Gracq, Giono, Aymé, Troyat, Ève Curie, Saint-Exupéry, Caillois, Valéry...Nothing less. But not a ghost of a T.C. Elimane or a *Labyrinth of Inhumanity*.

Back home, I ran into Stanislas and couldn't help bringing up the book again. He asked me what it was about. I wasn't expecting the question, which incidentally I hate. I thought for a second, then, since I had to answer, I said something grandiose, sentences rife with capitalized words, something like: It's the story of a man, a bloodthirsty King; this King is seeking Power and is prepared to commit absolute Evil to obtain it, but he discovers that even the paths of absolute Evil lead him back to Humanity.

After my lyrical peroration, the translator looked at me for a minute, then said: That doesn't mean anything. I'm going to give you some advice: never attempt to say what a great book is about. Or, if you do, the only possible response is "nothing." A great book is only ever about nothing, and yet, everything is there. Don't ever fall into the trap of wanting to say what a book that you think is great is about. It's a trap set for you by the general consensus. People want a book to necessarily be about something. The truth, Diégane, is that only a mediocre or bad or ordinary book is about something. A great book has no subject and isn't about anything, it only tries to say or discover something, but that only is already everything, and that something is also already everything.

July 15

France won the World Cup and the country celebrated its second star beneath a sky brimming with them. I watched the game with Musimbwa, then we went out to eat at a little African restaurant where the food was decent, the service mediocre, and the mood set by an old kora player whose repertoire was limited to one long and repetitive Mandingo ballad.

Musimbwa is the former occupant of the "promising young African writer" seat. He's D. R. Congolese, three years older than me, and his body of work already amounts to four books that were immediately applauded by the Ghetto and critics from the outside world. After the success of his first novel, he quit his job as a bartender to dedicate himself to literature, like a nun to God.

I remember being skeptical at first, hating him even, when he shot into the literary universe like a raw aerolite, collecting prizes, admiration, and laurels with a detachment that verged on either humility or arrogance, I couldn't tell which. That Musimbwa is just trending, I'd think, and he'll only be the hot new thing long enough to get burned, like so many others whom our day and age eventually put back in their place after the sacramental coronation. I, of course, hadn't read a single sentence he'd written at that point. Once I did, my jealousy turned to envy, then envy to admiration, and sometimes that admiration morphed into total despair at my certitude that I would never have his talent. I hold him without contest our primus inter pares, the best of our generation.

When *Anatomy of the Void* was published, he was the first writer to talk about it, without knowing me. His response to the novel was enthusiastic, he went on to recommend it, and even though his prescription didn't carry the same weight as the tiny review in *Monde Afrique*, his words, the words of a writer, held the most value in my mind. We met, and our friendship was forged by shared readings, and rejections, minor disagreements, similar interests, healthy emulation, friendly (and necessary and virile and sometimes tempestuous) rivalry, proximity in age, endless strolls amid the motley, surprising train of night. But more than anything, our friendship was built on the same desperate faith we placed in the entelechy of life that literature incarnated for us. We in no way thought that literature would save the world; we did, however, think it was the only way to save ourselves.

So, I was eating with him after the game and soon enough told him about my guy.

"Come again?"

"T.C. Elimane?"

"No, can't say I've ever heard of him. And the book? *The Labyrinth of Humanity*, is that it?"

"*The Labyrinth of Inhumanity!*" I cited and recited the first lines: "In the beginning, there was a prophecy and there was a King; and..." Nothing doing, Musimbwa didn't know it. I wanted to tell him the story of the book, or the marginal bit that I knew at least. But I quickly realized it wouldn't be so easy: this was a cannibalistic tale, and its teeth were gnawing on me from the inside. The story is simultaneously impossible to tell, to forget, to silence. But what do you do with something that can't be forgotten or told or reduced to silence? Did Wittgenstein write anything about that? He said that what we cannot speak about we must pass over in silence; okay, sure, but if we can't speak or remain silent or forget, then what do we do, Herr Wittgenstein? I have no idea, but I know this: the things a man can't forget or speak about or silence will cause him suffering and eventually kill him, and I had no desire for either. So I said what I knew, not a lot in the end, but once I stopped speaking, I felt neither relieved nor sad, more like every part of me ached, inside and out, as though this fragment of existence weighed tons, a millennium, and that the mass of its age had collapsed upon my very being as I was trying to tell its story. After my account, Musimbwa, with the gravity of confession, said he had never believed in cursed literary geniuses who wrote while seeking the heart of silence, or the bottom of oblivion. He let a few seconds pass, then, looking out the window, as though he wasn't addressing me but the night, some invisible creature of the night, he continued:

"Trying to destroy yourself in your work isn't always a sign of humility. Even a desire for nothingness can be vanity...But hang on, have you already read this *Labyrinth of Inhumanity*? I'm assuming not. You said the book has been impossible to find for decades."

"I found it."

I told him about my night with Siga D., then took the book out of my pocket and handed it to him. Musimbwa looked at me for a moment, as if to reassure himself that I wasn't playing a bad joke on him, before taking it. I told him I was going to wander around while I waited for him to read it. He opened the book immediately.

I left him and went to kindle the Parisian night, its incandescence, its rivers of beer, its pure joy, its pure laughter, its pure drugs, its illusions of inhabiting eternity or the moment. But very quickly the party blues set in, splenetic and oppressive. I've never been able to revel for long. More often than not, shared jubilations, celebrations en masse, great exultant fervors end up burying me beneath a desolation that has no way out. No sooner would I enter a state of inebriation or joy than their flip side would rear its ugly head. As a result, I never celebrated long enough for the sadness of things to be spared me: the sadness before the party, the sadness after the party, the sadness of the party that will inevitably end (a moment as horrible as the instant a smile fades from a face), the bit of sadness felt by all humanity, with which we each fight like a shadow and as best we can. Sometimes I made the best of this inevitability. Other times, I simply ignored it and rushed with heedless fury into the circle of dance and fire. Most often, though, my inner low tide would prevail. That was the case this night. I sat on a bench, with no other goal than to rise from it as intact as possible, or even just to rise at all. Next, I took a deep breath and slipped very easily, like a suppository, into the prelubricated asshole of the world—you take the Pascalian experiences you can get.

Literature appeared to me in the guise of a woman of terrifying beauty. I told her, in a stammer, that I had been looking for her. She laughed cruelly and said that she didn't belong to anyone. I got on my knees and begged her: Spend one night with me, a single wretched night. She disappeared without a word. I set off after her, full of determination and arrogance: I'm going to catch you, I'm going to sit you on my knee, I'm going to force you to look me in the eye, I'm going to be a writer! But then that terrible moment always comes, en route, in the middle of the night, when a voice rings out and strikes like lightning; and it reveals to you, or reminds you, that desire isn't enough, that talent isn't enough, that ambition isn't enough, that being a good writer isn't enough, that being well-read isn't enough, that being famous isn't enough, that being highly cultured isn't enough, that being wise isn't enough, that commitment isn't enough, that patience isn't enough, that getting drunk off pure life isn't enough, that retreating from life isn't enough, that believing in your dreams isn't enough, that dissecting reality isn't enough, that intelligence isn't enough, that stirring hearts isn't enough, that strategy isn't enough, that communication isn't enough, that even having something to say isn't enough, nor is working tirelessly enough; and the voice also says that all of that might be and often is a condition, an advantage, an attribute, a strength, of course, but then the voice adds that in essence none of those qualities are ever enough when it's a question of literature, because writing always demands something else, something else, something else. Then the voice stops and leaves you to your solitude, en route, with the echo of something else, something else that rolls along and then away, something else in front of you, writing always demands something else, in this night without the certainty of dawn.

Two hours later, I was still twitching. The ordeal was coming to an end. I mustered the strength to shake myself off like a wild animal in from the rain and peeled myself from the metaphysical marinade of the bench. I returned to the African restaurant. The kora player was running his never-ending scales. Musimbwa was growing roots at the same table. He had a handful of pages left to read. I ordered a strong espresso and waited. Twenty minutes later, he looked up at me with eyes both frightened and impressed, then he said, Well, shit, what comes next? I told him that as far as anyone knew, nothing. A long, sad shadow spread across his face, and I didn't know if it was cast by the painful incompleteness of *The Labyrinth of Inhumanity* or its suspended beauty. We stayed like that for a moment, silent and serious. The restaurant owner apologized for having to close soon, the kora player put away his instrument, Musimbwa paid, we left.

In the street, after we had been walking without a word for two or three minutes, Musimbwa suddenly told me, elated, as though he'd just had an epiphany, that we absolutely had to get our peers to read *The Labyrinth of Inhumanity*. It would liberate us. I didn't respond, but I may as well have: a massive yes vibrated through my silence.

Though why continue, why attempt to write after a millennium of books like *The Labyrinth of Inhumanity*, which gave the impression there was nothing left to add? We didn't write for the romanticism of the writer life (now a caricature of itself) or the money (that would have been suicidal) or the glory (an outmoded currency to which the modern age preferred celebrity) or the future (it never asked for anything) or to transform the world (it's not the world that needs transforming) or to change life (it never changes) or to make a difference (leave that to the heroic writers) and not as a celebration of free art either (which is an illusion because art always pays for itself). So what was the reason? We didn't know, and maybe therein lay our answer: we wrote because we knew nothing, we wrote to say that we no longer knew what to do in this world except write, without hope but without facile resignation either, with obstinacy and exhaustion and joy, our only goal to finish the best we could, meaning with our eyes open: take it all in, don't miss a thing, don't blink, don't turn a blind eye, even at the risk of pulling an Oedipus, try to see everything, not the way a witness or a prophet sees, no, but in the way of a sentinel, the sole, trembling sentinel of a run-down, doomed city, who nonetheless continues to scrutinize the shadows from which the flash of lightning announcing his death and the fall of his city will shoot forth.

We next discussed at length the occasionally comfortable, often humiliating, ambiguities of our status as African writers (or writers of African origin) in the French literary milieu. Somewhat unjustly, and because they were obvious and easy targets, we then piled on our elders, the African writers of previous generations. We blamed them for the curse hanging over us: the feeling that we couldn't, or weren't allowed (same thing), to say where we came from; then we accused them of getting themselves stuck in a box, a box that was in fact a trap, a cage, a snare, a noose, which required that they be simultaneously "authentic"—meaning different— but nonetheless similar—meaning comprehensible (again, in other words: marketable in the Western context in which they were maneuvering); our aim was good, meaning merciless, and we couldn't stop once we were doing so well, so we bemoaned the fact that some of our elders had fallen into the slave hold that was complacent exoticism, while others had stumbled into autofiction, where they were incapable of transcending their tiny lives, and those same forerunners, enjoined to be African but not *too* African, in obeying these two equally absurd imperatives, forgot to be writers, which was a capital offense, serious enough that we continued our cross-examination as the smell of their blood grew stronger, and we maintained that they had never risked venturing to the poetic fringes, even briefly, and we reproached them for becoming caricatures of themselves and for being led off course by their barren pretensions of "commitment," not to mention the Parnassian and borderline bourgeois aims of your basic writer, and we pointed a finger at their lifeless realism, which was content to reproduce the world without interpreting or re-creating it, and we scorned their egotism hiding behind the artist's right to freedom, and we beheaded by the dozens those predecessors who had written countless novels that by their banality were an insult to literature, and we delivered death sentences to the ones who had given up on collectively asking what it meant to be in their literary situation, powerless to create the conditions for innovative aesthetics in our texts, too lazy to use literature as a tool for (self) reflection, too in thrall to literary prizes, to flattery, to fancy dinner parties, to festivals, to paychecks, to the circuit in an attempt to approach (or poach) acceptable literature, their reading skills too poor or their camaraderie too strong to read each other's work and bravely say what didn't work, too craven to dare to break tradition via the novel, via poetry, via anything at all: diaries, F; essays, D−; science fiction and detective novels, double F; theater made out much better, thankfully; but letter collections, F, F, F, a vast fuck all, as though questions about their lethally ambiguous venture, the problematics of riding two horses with one ass, left them cold; ah yes, our elders, so often honored so often celebrated so often rewarded, so often described as the new blood of francophone literature, yes, those elders, golden generation my ass: we placed their work beneath a harsh light, we brought it near the fire and straightaway the precious metal melted, revealed to be nothing more than plywood, sticky sludge between our fingers, and we saw that many of their books were worth less than had been said or hoped, we saw that the writers who stood the test of time could be counted on the fingers of one of Master Yoda's hands, we saw that they had only published the nice little books expected of them, we discovered that they made us their heirs but had bequeathed us nothing, that they had all written believing themselves free, even as strong irons encircled their wrists their ankles their necks and their minds, ah, those glorious elders, yes, yes, but were they the only guilty ones? we suddenly, dramatically, rhetorically, asked ourselves, had there been extenuating circumstances? we magnanimously mused, and so we called their ignoble accomplices to the witness stand: first up, some of their African readers, whom we immediately felled with a terse verdict: worst readers in the world, who don't read, who are lazy, caricatural, and intransigent as only a minority can be, always avid to be represented when they are in fact unrepresentable; then came their Western (let's just say it: white) readers, many of whom read our predecessors as an act of charity, wanting to be entertained or told of the vast world with that legendary African exuberance, those Africans with rhythm in their souls but also in their pens, those Africans skilled at weaving tales in the moonlight, those Africans who don't complicate things, those Africans who can still pull at your heartstrings with their moving stories, those Africans who haven't yet succumbed to the smug navel-gazing in which so many French authors get bogged down, ah, those wonderful Africans, with their colorful, much-loved books and colorful personalities and big smiles full of big teeth and hope; then a detachment of critics (academics, journalists, culture reporters) advanced to the scaffold, and our guillotine fell just as heavy on its lithesome neck: the most boring criticism on earth, clinging to its *thoughts provoked* and *questions raised*, narrow, generalized tunnels in which books trundled along like cattle, some of which suffocated to death beneath the weight of concepts, the blubber of jargon, the insipidness of subject matters; and this was how, beneath a peaceful sky, a bright, near-nival sky, the assorted heads of our writer-elders, their readers, and their critics, all origins and skin colors combined, came to be floating above ours like a grim constellation or a flock of small starlings, and it was only at that moment, dripping blood, steaming with blood like barbarians of yore in the midst of a reddened and abruptly silent battle plain, only at that moment, wearied and still a little drunk with violence, looking around at the ground strewn with the corpses of those who had ceased to be writers and others whose reading skills had increasingly deteriorated, supposing that they had ever known how to read at all, we felt guilty for having been so cruel: Who were we to direct such tough, uncompromising, and categorical criticisms against the men and women without whom we wouldn't have existed? Who, to claim that we were in no way indebted to the predecessors to whom, all the same, we owed an immense and unpayable debt? Who, who, who, we repeated in an infinite echo, even though we knew the answer, who? Well, simply some young idiots who had only just ventured into literature and thought they could do whatever they wanted; newcomers who would soon be old-timers, fated to be ripped apart by hungry upstarts, since that's how the world turns, yes, that was the way of the world and we were nothing to it, apart from specks of dust in the infinity of literature, we knew that, so then, our consciences asked us, why were we so arrogant, so pretentious, so unfair when undoubtedly we weren't any better than they? And our response was: because we were tormented, like all writers no doubt, by the idea of finding nothing and leaving nothing, and fundamentally we were criticizing ourselves, we were expressing our own fears of never being good enough, because we felt like we were in a cave with no way out and we were scared of dying there, trapped like rats.

We moved to another bar, where on the terrace we continued discussing the book. We parted ways with the tenuous promise to meet at my place or his, a few days later, to introduce T.C. Elimane to the other African writers of our generation.

July 23

Among our literary cohort—I'm referring to the young guard of African writers living in Paris—my favorite, apart from Musimbwa, was Béatrice Nanga.

Of course, there was Faustin Sanza, a Congolese giant whom I took, the first time I saw him, for a herald of the Apocalypse. Except that Faustin was far more terrifying: he was an unknown poet. Five years earlier he had published a seventy-two-page work, *The Barbaric Badamier Tree*, an epic poem written in dactylic hexameter (with trochaic caesura) and full of forgotten terms. That appetite for rarities wasn't a superficial quality either. A poet who uses archaisms out of affectation can be quickly spotted: it's like women in bed; you can tell right away when they're faking (I think). *The Barbaric Badamier Tree* didn't get read. Sanza was wounded by the experience, not because readers had ignored him—on that front, Sanza was satisfied even, considering that a poem with more than one hundred twenty readers was suspect—but because he no longer believed in the poetic word. Nothing can be said. That's what he would say. After that, he sought truth in his first love, the pure abstraction of mathematics, which he taught at a high school. All he ever wrote anymore were reviews, often to cogently and elegantly and cruelly destroy countless literary poseurs. His critical model is Étiemble.

(I remember the article he wrote after the publication of *Black as Ebony*, the latest book by William K. Salifu, one of the best-known writers of contemporary African literature. Two decades earlier, he had published *The Melancholy of Sand*, a magnificent novel that earned him global recognition. It was translated into forty languages, including Silbo. Hollywood bought the rights immediately after its publication. Vargas Llosa and Rushdie, Toni Morrison and Coetzee, Le Clézio, Susan Sontag, Wole Soyinka, Doris Lessing: each and every one of them had hailed *The Melancholy of Sand* as a masterpiece. Even the irascible and brilliant Naipaul himself admitted that he never thought he would one day read a novel of such depth penned by an African.

Two years later, Salifu published a second book. Given how catastrophically bad it was, the most magnanimous readers ascribed it to an accident: after all, even the masters fail sometimes. But then two other novels, just as appalling, came out in rapid succession. Salifu's popularity diminished as fast as he published: he was suspected of having resorted to a ghostwriter for his first book. Salman Rushdie posted a laconic, murderous tweet, which was retweeted by Stephen King and Joyce Carol Oates. Old, Nobel Prize–winning Naipaul snickered and made a comment that began "I was surprised by the quality of the first book from the African writer Salifu" and ended, a few cruelties later, abiding by the ancient principle of *in cauda venenum*, with "Literary mediocrity is like nature: pitchfork or not, it always comes back, even if you were able to hide it long enough for one book." Granted, Salifu's books, increasingly indigent, indigestible blends of thriller and romance, were still being read: no one had forgotten the sumptuous *Melancholy of Sand*; but fewer and fewer people took him seriously. I read each of his new books in the hope of rediscovering the beauty of the first one, or at least a trace of it. But the splendor of *The Melancholy of Sand* appeared to have forever vanished.

Amid the chorus of standard and hypocritical high praise for Salifu's latest novel, from those who no longer needed to read an established writer to laud him, Sanza published a harsh review. Rocked the pirogue. Everyone took a hit: poor Salifu and his *Black as Ebony*, of course, but also the journalists and critics who had stopped evaluating books in favor of listing them, enshrining the notion that all books are equal, that the subjectivity of taste is the sole criterion of distinction and that there are no bad books, just books that people don't like; plus the writers who refused to subject their work to any literary or creative standards, content instead to produce flat copies of real life that necessitated zero sustained effort on the part of the omnipotent and tyrannical abstraction we call the "Reader"; plus the masses of readers who looked to books for easy enjoyment and entertainment, constructed from simple emotions molded into simplified sentences—the kind, said Sanza, that rarely exceeded nine words, were only ever written in the present indicative, and did away with all subordinate clauses; plus the editors, slaves to the market, who were preoccupied with generating and selling predefined products rather than encouraging literary originality. Old criticisms, but ones that Faustin Sanza skillfully revitalized. Obviously, he wasn't spared himself; the offended parties retaliated swiftly and robustly. Elitist! Reactionary! Snobbish! Idiotic! Essentialist! Bitter! Intolerant! Holier-than-thou! Reductive! Fascist! Highbrow! Over the top! Jealous! Cerebral! Hypocritical! But Sanza took every blow with the same courage with which he had dealt his.)

In the group, there was also Eva (or Awa) Touré, a Franco-Guinean influencer about whom there's both a lot to say and very little. Eva Touré crusades for all the righteous moral causes of our time, on top of being an entrepreneur, a self-empowerment coach, a diversity model, a galactic example. Obviously, as was to be feared, and since literary incontinence is one of the most widely spread diseases of our time, she couldn't stop herself from writing. And thus emerged from the darkness *Love Is a Cocoa Bean*, which I consider to be a methodical negation of the very idea of literature. The novel is soporific and dull and it was a huge bestseller. It's worth noting that with her two hundred thousand followers on Instagram, Eva had at her disposal a faithful audience, for whom anything that emanated from her represented a divine unction. That vast and fanatical readership, ready to die for her, forced the bravest of critics to stand down. Even Sanza, to avoid enduring the social media cyclones of shit that the goddess's disciples unleashed upon any heretic who examined her work with any perspective, gave up on publishing the review he'd written of *Love Is a Cocoa Bean*.

So there were those two, but most important there was Béatrice Nanga. Musimbwa and I were of the opinion that, of all of us, she had the most distinctive literary style. I should add that none of us had slept with her, at least as far as I knew, though it became apparent during our discussions that all we wanted was to be able to. Béatrice Nanga is thirty years old and has a son whose custody she shares. She's originally from Cameroon. I couldn't tell you if she's beautiful, but she emanates a thick, sensual aura at all times. The sweeping tessitura of her voice paralyzes me at the cellular level. The sight of her curves sends my blood flowing in the wrong direction. She's written two erotic novels: *The Holy Ogive*, a title taken from a sentence in *Irene's Cunt*; and *Diary of a Pygophile*, which I read wholeheartedly and one-handedly. Béatrice is a fervent Catholic. One day she told me her favorite sexual position was the "cubist angel" and that one day we would try it. All my searches for the position led nowhere. There is a Dalí sculpture with that title, but its pose is implausible in terms of sex. Maybe Béatrice made it up? Maybe the cubist angel is a bluff? Who knows.

That's the group. I've never sensed any awareness of or desire for a collective aesthetic venture; we're not a movement; each of us walks alone toward our literary destiny; and yet I feel as if there's something invisible firmly linking us, forever. I couldn't say what. Perhaps the vague impression that we're heading toward disaster. Perhaps the inchoate feeling that we need to reinvigorate our literature, and soon, or endure the humiliation of being forever designated as its killers, or worse, its gravediggers (killing is simple, but burying...). Perhaps the redoubtable prescience that some among us will face off with the beast of literature in prolonged battle, while others get lost or give up on the way. Perhaps the silent realization that we were unhappy and unmoored Africans in Europe, even if we pretended to be at home wherever we were. Or perhaps the only thing that links us is the certainty (or hope) that it might all end in an orgy one day.

So, yesterday, after we had exchanged all the literary gossip and happily lingered on topics of zero consequence and mild erudition, Musimbwa brought up the real reason for our gathering: Elimane.

Sanza was the only one who even vaguely knew his name. Musimbwa asked me to tell his story, which I did before a half-fascinated, half-bewildered audience, then, in the silence that followed, he began without preamble to read *The Labyrinth of Inhumanity*. And for three hours Musimbwa read without tiring. When he was done, the astonishment lasted for a long, silent minute, then the debates started with a roar. We debated with rage and with outrage. We told untruths. We crossed our hearts.

The discussion was harsh, passionate, uncompromising, and it pushed deep into the night. I thought to myself that a world in which you can still debate a book like that, into the late hours, wasn't lost after all, though I was well aware that there was something profoundly comical, vain, and ridiculous, perhaps even irresponsible, about a group of people discussing literature for an entire evening. Conflicts were raging, the planet was suffocating, the nobodies with nothing were starving to death, orphans were contemplating their parents' corpses; there were all those people living tiny lives alongside the microbes, alongside the rats, sewer people fated for a pestilential eternity of clogged and squalid pipes; there was real life; there was a whole ocean of shit outside, and we, African writers whose continent was swimming in it, were discussing *The Labyrinth of Inhumanity* instead of doing a single damn thing to rescue it.

One night, after we had worn ourselves out analyzing the true value of Senghor's poetry, I confided in Musimbwa the feeling of shame that sometimes niggled at me when I saw us talking about literature as if our lives depended on it or as if it was the most important thing on earth. After a brief pause, my friend told me: I understand what you're saying, Faye, and sometimes I have the same feeling. Of being shameless, a little dirty. He stopped for a few seconds before adding: And also, a person could argue that we only talk about literature so much because we can't produce it, or because our literary universe is empty. There are countless so-called writers who turn out to be more gifted at criticizing literature than actually writing it, countless poets who hide the impoverishment of their creations behind scholarly annotations, literary references, citation fever, empty erudition . . . It's true, Faye, it really is: spending our evenings talking about books, discussing the literary world and its little *comédie humaine* might appear suspect, unhealthy, boring, sad even. But if writers don't talk about literature, by which I mean if they don't talk about it with every fiber of their being, as practitioners, as lovers, as raving lunatics, as if they're haunted and possessed, if those writers for whom literature is the be-all and end-all, even if the be-all and end-all sometimes disguises itself as an anecdote or as futility, don't, then who will? It might be an unbearable, obnoxious, and elitist notion, but we have to accept it. This is our life: we attempt to create literature, yes, but we also talk about it, because talking about it keeps it alive, and as long as it's alive, our lives, even if they're pointless, even if they're tragically comical and insignificant, won't be completely wasted. We have to behave as if literature were the most important thing on earth; it just might happen, rarely, but even so, that someday it will be and someone will have to bear witness. We're those witnesses, Faye.

His words weren't always enough to comfort me, but I kept them close.

We continued to debate. Musimbwa and I thought the book was masterful; Béatrice deemed it too smart; Sanza couldn't stand it, though he conceded some flashes of brilliance; Eva Touré didn't say much, but I saw in her eyes that she didn't think much either. Around three a.m., she asked us to pose for a group selfie that she immediately posted on social media with the hashtags #writing #newgeneration #reading #staytuned #literarydinner #labyrinth #empowerment #Africa #auboutdelanuit #bookaddict #nofilter #Evafamily.

The evening came to a close, but we saw each other again several times in the subsequent days, at someone's place, or a bar, to exchange our thoughts about the book and to share our writerly dreams.

July 31

Diary, tonight I did the thing I dread most in the world: I called my parents. My mother: Is something wrong? Me: No, everything's fine. The mother: Really? The son: Really. Her: You're calling just like that? Him: Yes, to catch up. My mother: Anh, Latyr, that's what worries me. Are you sure you're okay?

When we do a video call, my parents, sitting side by side, hold the phone in such a way that only part of each of their faces appears on the screen. I find myself before the parental face reunified. Its signs of age pained me, and I wanted to turn off the video. But that wouldn't have changed anything; their voices had aged too: deep cracks in the walls of time. I promised myself, like I always do, to call them more often. And yet I knew I wouldn't. I would continue to call them only on rare occasions. My mother never failed to point out, jokingly, my weak sense of family. Bitter jokes: they bore a silent accusation. My father never said anything on the matter, which said everything. Neither of them could understand my long periods of silence. And yet it struck me as simple: I was performing the duty that many children have had to fulfill in regard to their parents at one point in their lives: the duty of ingratitude.

But there was also some naivete at hand, the kind that had me believe that my parents would be available to me always and forever. The reason I constantly put off the moment when I had to give them a call was perhaps that I was sure, with blind confidence, that I'd see them soon, and that therefore it wasn't necessary to contact them every day, since the day I would rejoin them for good would arrive quickly. A day that was a mirage in the desert of exile. And so every call postponed, under the illusion of a soon-to-come reunion that would justify its cancellation, marked in reality a greater distancing. I've reached the terminal stage of immigration: I no longer simply believe in the possibility of return, I am convinced of its imminence and persuaded that I can regain the time spent far from my loved ones. That tragic hope is as life-sustaining as it is lethal: I pretend to believe that I'll go home soon, that everything there will be unchanged and that I can *make up for it*. The dreamt-of return is a perfect novel—in other words, a bad novel.

Something is dying. The world I left disappeared as soon as I turned my back on it. I thought, having lived there and having buried my childhood there, like a treasure, that it had become indestructible solely by the grace of that gift. I believed in its eternal loyalty to my past existence. Nothing was more chimerical: the world I once loved didn't sign a pact of fidelity. No sooner had I gone than it started to recede further down the tunnel of time. I contemplate the ruins, and what saddens me in these moments isn't the fact that this world was destroyed: this world was alive, meaning mortal; what grieves me is that it was destroyed so easily when I thought I had given it the resources to hold on.

Exiles are obsessed with geographical separation, with physical distance. Yet it's time that forms the core of their solitude; and they cast blame at the miles when it's the days killing them. I could have abided to be a continent away from the parental face if I was certain that time would pass over it without harm. But it's impossible; wrinkles inevitably dig in, eyesight weakens, memory fails, disease threatens.

How can we bring our lives closer together? By writing? Write makes right: here I'm summoning the gemellity, the fortuitous homophony, of these two words that incarnate the supposed power of the pen. Still, can writing lessen our internal distance? As of now, the divide is growing, indifferent to the Word and its enchantments.

For some who have left, it's best they never return, though that may be their deepest desire; if they did, they would die of sadness. I missed my parents, but I was scared to call them; time went by; and as sad as I was not to hear them telling me what was happening in their lives, I was equally terrified by the idea that they would tell me, because I knew deep down what was really happening in their lives. It's what happens in every life: they were nearing death. I didn't call them, and that caused me great pain; I called them and that caused me pain as well, perhaps even more.

My parents wanted to talk to me about a thousand things, happy or annoying little nothings, about my unruly younger brothers, about the tense political situation back home. But I didn't have the heart to listen to all of it. As for the only topic that matters, they remained silent. They pretended, and I pretended too. A fool's game. With a little coolness and lots of cowardice, I cut the call short.

August 4

My roommate, who refused to frequent our writers' coterie (he found our mentality too bourgeois), finally read *The Labyrinth of Inhumanity*. His verdict was terse: "hard to translate," which by his criteria amounted to the highest praise.

He asked me questions about the book and the author. I told him what I knew. The story intrigued him, and he told me I should visit the press archives. If I was able to gain access to certain newspapers from 1938, I might, he thought, be able to find out something. I told him that when I came to Paris eight years earlier, I had already tried to access old newspapers in search of traces of *The Labyrinth of Inhumanity*. In particular, I had been hoping to read the investigation by Bollème (Brigitte) mentioned by the *Reader's Guide* in its T.C. Elimane entry. All my attempts had ended in failure. Though I had discovered, in regard to Brigitte Bollème, that after a long career as a literary journalist for *Revue des deux mondes* and publishing a few monographs, she had sat on the jury for the Prix Femina, over which she presided from 1973 to her death in 1985.

"Okay," said Stanislas after listening to me, "but now that you've published a book that got mentioned by a big paper, the press archives might open more easily to you, no?"

"No. Outside of the African Ghetto, I'm not at all known as an author. The press archives don't care that I'm a promising young African writer who got a review in a famous newspaper. As an African writer, I have no literary renown in the outside world."

"And is that what you want? To attain literary renown in the outside world?"

Yes. No African writer established in France will admit that publicly. They'll all deny it, adopting a rebel pose for good measure. But deep down, it's a dream harbored by many of us (for some, it's THE dream): induction into the French literary world (which it's always helpful, in said posturing, to mock and shit on). It's our shameful secret, but also the glory about which we fantasize; our servitude, and the poisoned illusion of our symbolic elevation. So yes, Stan, here's our sad reality, the pathetic contents of our pathetic dream: recognition by the mainstream—the only recognition that counted.

But because that was too desperate, too cynical, too bitter, too inexact (or, the contrary, too true), I decided not to tell the translator any of that and merely said the following, which was no less exact:

"I just want to write a good book, Stan, a book that would exempt me from writing other ones, that would liberate me from literature, a book like *The Labyrinth of Inhumanity*, know what I mean?"

"Yeah, I do. But you guys, meaning you African writers and intellectuals, best watch out for certain kinds of recognition. Obviously, France will end up crowning one of you, to ease its bourgeois conscience, and sometimes you do see an African who makes it or who's held up as a model. But deep down, believe me, you lot are and will remain foreigners, whatever the merit of your writing. You're not from here. Though it's also been my understanding, and stop me if I have this wrong (in that moment, I had the thought that when someone says *stop me if I'm wrong*, it's probably already impossible to stop them), it's also been my understanding that you weren't really from your countries of origin anymore. So then...from where?"

He paused, and it wasn't to let me answer. He was thinking about what he had just said or what he was going to add, and in any case he quickly resumed:

"I know, of course, that some of you call yourselves citizens of the world...Universal writers! Universality, huh... An illusion maintained by people who brandish it like a medal. They place it around the neck of whomever they want. But if they put it around your neck, it's to hang you. If they don't, begging for it with tears streaming down your face won't change anything. Nothing is universal except hell. Burn the medals. And the hands holding them. Rip off the last tatters of the colonial era and expect nothing! Set the old ideas ablaze! Down to the embers, to the ashes, to the death! Write with gasoline!"

"Everything you're saying might be right, Stan. But African writers are aware of all that. We're human beings, not political heroes or ideologists. Every writer should be able to freely write what they want, wherever they are, whatever their origin or skin color. The only thing that should be demanded from writers, whether they're African or Inuit, is talent. Everything else is tyranny. Bullshit."

Stan looked at me for a few seconds, a smile of commiseration on his lips. I knew what he was about to say, which is exactly what he did a second later: "You're naïve."

August 5

Diary, it was an eventful evening. Béatrice Nanga invited Musimbwa and me over for dinner. We found her the same as always: a powerful woman, as the cliché goes.

"I only wanted to see you two," she said as she opened a bottle. "Sanza and Eve Touré are interesting, but with you guys, it feels different. You know what I mean, right?"

I said yes a little distractedly: all my attention was focused, as it was every time I went to Béatrice's place, on the large crucifix that dominated the living room. I looked at Jesus, and the same thought that always came to me when I saw him like that, on the cross, absorbing all of man's evil, struck me again: *He's wondering what the hell he's doing there.* I'd had several dreams in which I questioned him: Two thousand years have gone by since you suffered and perished on that cross, Lord, it's to honor you, but you've seen the results; so now I ask you: *Would you do it again?*

No response. We sat down to eat. Béatrice served her *ndolè*, and soon enough we began discussing what we ought to do with *The Labyrinth of Inhumanity*. She thought it wasn't right to keep it within our pretentious circle of young writers, and that we should try to get it republished so the general public could discover it. Musimbwa opposed the idea. They argued. I didn't take sides.

Over dessert, the mood lightened, and Béatrice put on some music. Ritualities, spiritualities: first we surrendered to the galvanic tremors of the barely nubile night, green as a young mango. Then everything softened; the moon ripened, ready to fall from the sky. Time became diaphanous, its arms draped around us, and the hours, vestibules for sumptuous dreams conditional on our staying awake. Inside the apartment, fewer and fewer words were spoken. Soon all that remained—between the clinking of midnight drinks or flimsy laughter rising from the street, and in the few seconds of impeccable prose that separated two songs—soon all that remained was archaic speech: breaths and glances, slowness and the brush of a hand, suspended encouragements, summons, ripostes, concealed signs, languages in await of Language; soon all that remained was the lucidity of inebriation. I might have heard the sound of a breaking glass, knocked over by a body (mine?) as it danced. Then there were no more hours; this—*this*—was the true night.

What had to happen happened: the lady of the house proposed or suggested (unless she demanded, I'm not sure anymore) that we fuck. But not here, she said. Christ is here. Come on. And she turned around and headed to the bedroom. Musimbwa took a few steps after her, like a somnambulant dog. I didn't move. He stopped, turned back toward me, and divined my intentions.

"Don't be an idiot, man. Not now. Come on. We're finally going to see the face of the cubist angel. We're going to paint it a new portrait. We'll finally know if it's called

Michel or Jibril or Lucifer. An incredible ménage à trois is waiting for us. Come on."

I shook my head and sat down to show that my refusal was irrevocable. Musimbwa seemed to hesitate for a split second, then said, in a tone that was part advice, part threat: "Faye, women sometimes forgive a man who forces the opportunity, but never a man who misses one."

"Rocco Siffredi?"

"No."

"Robert Mugabe."

"No."

"I know: DSK!"

"Nice try. But no. Talleyrand."

He then went toward his destiny in Béatrice's bedroom, and I remained alone in the living room, sinking into the armchair, drunk and slightly sad, thinking that I knew nothing about Talleyrand except that he had been limp as a dick and supposedly quite witty; a few minutes went by and I felt like changing my mind and joining them, but my pride held me back: it would have been ridiculous, shameful in fact, to walk back my decision, a decision that staked my honor and my word, and I had already spoken; so I stayed put, and an instant later, I began to hear, at regular intervals, though never at the same moment, Béatrice sighing and Musimbwa yowling, and from that I deduced that the foreplay had commenced. Then all I could hear was Béatrice moaning, and her flesh (her powerful thighs, to be precise) suffocating Musimbwa, who still managed, from time to time, to extricate his head from the vise and fill his lungs with air before diving back into the unknown, gleefully lapping up Béatrice's liquid reserves, and all that was quite

clear to my ears, and before my eyes: their two bodies arousing each other, their breaths increasingly short and abrupt,
the thin layer of sweat and the salt crystals on their skin,
yes, I saw all that in spite of myself, so then I told myself
that I needed to fight, that I had to pull myself together and
think about things that would absorb me so fully that I
would escape the sounds coming from the bedroom, a reso-
lution that seemed to provoke my friends, because I had
barely begun searching for a topic in which I could bury my
mind when Béatrice started to wail and Musimbwa to pant
and the bed to creak and then came the sound of flesh
smacking together like two slippers when you clap one
against the other, oh shit, I said, it's starting, and from that
moment on I tried to concentrate on finding a subject that
could distract me or prompt reflection, but nothing worked,
every veil I attempted to draw over my mind was ripped
apart like rolling papers by the noisy presence of Béatrice
(who was now ululating) and Musimbwa (who was shouting, in Lingala, poetic obscenities of which I understood a
few words he had taught me: *Nkolo, pambola bord oyo.
Yango ne mutu eko sunga mokili...*); in any case, they're off
to a good start, I thought, they have a nice rhythm going,
not monotonous at all, varied but still attainable, but you
need to get a grip, Diégane, you need to distract yourself, try
to read, for example, immerse yourself in a book, why not,
and that's when I was tempted to read *The Labyrinth of
Inhumanity*, to lose myself in it, by which I mean seek refuge in it, but I reconsidered, because I knew it was a lost
cause: I wouldn't have been able to read with that noise, all
the more since it wasn't diminishing, the opposite, in fact, it
was gaining in intensity: the sound of physical lovemaking,

the cantilena of young, vigorous bodies, the thrumming
engine room of state-of-the-art fuck machines, and I could
hear that noise, there was no way I couldn't hear it, Béatrice
trumpeting and Musimbwa yelping *Bomanga, Béa, Bomanga*
and me wishing I wasn't like this, always too shy, too complicated, too reserved, too detached, too cerebral, too
Edmond Teste, too entrenched in my proud, foolish solitude, so I closed my eyes, resolved to suffer through it,
resigned to waiting for the moment to pass and be done
with, because this too shall pass, everything flows, everything is in flux, *πάντα ῥεῖ*, said the sage Heraclitus, so be it,
I told myself, just close your eyes and wait for *panta rhei*,
but as soon as I shut my eyes, like a child hiding beneath a
blanket, a powerful idea, or desire rather, came to me: I
needed to kill them, I needed to enter the bedroom armed
with a knife and bury the blade in that body, because there
was quite clearly now only one body in the bedroom, formed
by a powerful desire from which I was excluded and that I
therefore needed to stab, expertly and patiently and carefully, like a professional killer, there at the heart, and the
belly, and the aorta, and then once more at the heart to be
certain that this nasty, tenacious organ that inflicts such
harm on man would cease to beat, then the genitals, and the
torso too; of course I would have been careful not to touch
the face, for the face is sacred territory, a temple that no
violence must desecrate, the Face is the sign of the Other,
the image of their anguished injunction sent out, through
me, to all Humanity (there was a time when I read a bit of
Levinas), but I would stab that body everywhere else until it
stopped climaxing or it climaxed to death, carried by the
sublime transports of *la mort douce*; this, then, was the

impulse I had to deliver myself from the noise torturing me—Béatrice was lowing and Musimbwa was lowing too—and, in fact, look how divine providence provided for my lugubrious plans, a large knife had been left on the sideboard in the kitchen, I merely needed to grab it to regain control of the situation, and I began to smile at the thought of what was going to happen, I devised complex and macabre scenarios worthy of the best "true crime" headlines, but then, at the very instant I was about to stand and fetch my weapon, I felt a nearby presence, something alive: I opened my eyes again and saw Jesus Christ moving on the large cross hanging on the wall, and out of reflex, even though I'm not Christian, even though I'm a full-fledged Serer animist who believes first and foremost in the *pangool* and in Roog Sene (*Yirmi inn Roog u Yàl!*), I crossed myself and I waited, oddly enough I wasn't afraid, merely a little surprised, but I believed in apparitions and in the physical manifestation of transcendence, so I waited for Jesus to remove all his nails and come down from his cross, which he did with great elegance and agility given the circumstances, then he sat on the couch across from me, lifted the diadem of bloodied thorns hanging over his eyes, and looked at me with his gentle, blue gaze, a haven in which I immediately took refuge; and still the headboard was furiously banging against the wall, *To liama ti nzala ésila, Nzoto na yo na yanga, etutana moto epela, maman,* but I stopped paying attention because the only thing that mattered was this being before me, and without opening his mouth, he spoke to me, he spoke to me through the *vox cordis* and this eased all the misery in my soul, crushed into nothingness my murderous impulses, my pain, my pathetic jealousy, my solitude;

his sentences were simple but profound and could only have been spoken by him, and I listened to them despite the loud cries that rhythmically followed the sound of buttocks being slapped, I listened to Christ and tried to absorb his teachings, his parables, which any writer would have loved to write; he spoke at length, then paused, and we both checked on the bedroom; the grand finale seemed imminent, and it was no longer possible to distinguish who was doing what amid the high-pitched chorus of howls and shrieks; I looked at Jesus and for a split second, I thought I glimpsed in his eyes the desire to go into the bedroom too, but I must have imagined it or been possessed by the devil during that split second, especially since the Son of Man said in the following third that he had to go, that other lost souls required his presence; then he rose, his divine light blinded me, I asked him if he needed help getting back on the cross he'd occupied for two thousand years, I offered to give him a leg up for example, but he laughed (God, Christ has a beautiful and soothing laugh) and he said: I think I'll make it, and indeed he did make it, he managed to recrucify himself on his own, don't ask me how, I have no idea, but he did, after all he's capable of astonishing things, in any case he nailed himself back up as I watched, and at the very moment that Béatrice and Musimbwa reached the summit in a torrent of thunder and lightning, Christ, before his face regained its pained, impassioned, and two-millennia-old expression, looked at me and said (this time he opened his mouth): *I'd do it again.*

With those sublime words, without giving me a chance to ask him other questions (I'd have liked for him to clarify the art of transubstantiation, for example, or describe the view from the top of Golgotha), he left, and a horrible emptiness filled the apartment, the harrowing emptiness of a world that God has just abandoned. How much time passed during his visit? It's impossible for me to say, the same way I couldn't say how long I remained in the chair, silent and motionless, after his departure. No further sounds came from the bedroom. Perhaps the body was already asleep. Or dead. We'll see, I said. Then I got up, I grabbed *The Labyrinth of Inhumanity*, and I went home.

August 6

Foggy awakening. Musimbwa called me in early afternoon. We discussed the evening, and as I expected, he asked me why I hadn't joined them in the bedroom. I said the *ndolè* had made me queasy, he responded that I was lying, and that I should learn to think less and fuck more, to which I responded, I'll think about it, then we fell silent. I almost brought up the cubist angel but thought better of it, certain that Musimbwa would refuse to reveal any details whatsoever. Instead I changed the subject by asking him if he had any contacts high up at the press archives. He promised to put me in touch with someone in the next few days, then said: "I'm not sure I want to know who this Elimane was anymore. You should never get too close to the artists you love. Admire from afar, in silence: elegance is what's needed. Don't you think? *The Labyrinth* is enough for me, incomplete or not... But I understand that you want to find him. I think I've finally figured it out."

"What have you figured out?"

Musimbwa said: "I figured out that, in reality, by looking for whatever came after this book, you think you're looking for literature itself. But look for literature and you'll always end up chasing a ghost. Looking for literature just means you're looking for trouble. Trust me, Faye: looking for literature means…it means…" but he didn't finish his sentence, he ended in a rush or with sadness or annoyance with "anyway, whatever."

I didn't press him, and we talked about other things before hanging up. I then decided, after lengthy hesitation, that I wouldn't write to Béatrice. I wouldn't have been able to explain to her how, at a certain degree of alchemy, lovemaking becomes a tragic oath. Two bodies speak to one another, hear one another, recognize one another, then, unintentionally, without even noticing, they silently pledge their mutual fidelity. But because nothing is as unfair as love, sometimes only one of the bodies makes that unbreakable oath. Of course, the breakup eventually occurs; and then the pledged body finds itself alone, bearing the weight of its word given to a memory. It inherits an oath cumbersome as a corpse, of which no friend can help dispose in the middle of the night. The oath-bearer wanders from one body to the next with its burden, never finding peace, and soon loses all hope of ever doing so. Its partners only exist in comparison with the vanished ideal. And these encounters, because the oath-bearer expects disappointment, inevitably offer it. Indeed, there comes a time when the awareness of that certain disappointment prompts it to renounce all new experiences; but more than the awareness of that disillusionment, it is the terror of being an oath-breaker, of betraying a vow it swore to a body that has perhaps already forgotten it, that keeps the oath-bearer on the dock, paralyzed, as the ocean of desire spreads before it, calling. Even alone, it still fears being unfaithful. To describe his mother's love, which he never found in anyone else, Romain Gary spoke of a promise at dawn. For carnal love, if you ask me, there's sometimes an oath at night. I swore it to another woman over a year ago.

No, I wouldn't have been able to explain that to Béatrice Nanga. She would have vomited her laughter in my face.

That woman is gone. Her seal is powerful, and I don't know how to undo it. Since she left, all female bodies terrify me. And even my deepest fantasies yield before her unrelenting ghost. As long as I wanted to sleep with Béatrice, my body begged for it. And yet, once the occasion arose, that's all it took for my body to remember its past loyalty, and switch off.

I met her in a cliché of a Parisian setting: the park bench in a square, off Boulevard Raspail, at the foot of a monument of Captain Dreyfus bearing a broken sword. A cluster of pigeons was milling at her feet. She was tossing them crumbs from her sandwich, and the only way I could think to start a conversation was to say, "Excuse me, but the city has rules against feeding the birds." She looked up at me, eyes full of the most magnificent disdain. Her disdain didn't bother me, since I could finally see her whole face. I weathered a fitting comeback and immediately launched into the banalities that open the breach for a conversation. At the time I was reading Kundera's latest novel. One of the characters explains that men, when seducing women, who are often more intelligent than they, would benefit from being nondescript rather than exhausting themselves, and making fools of themselves, by trying to be brilliant at all costs. I applied the lesson and never attempted to impress her. I was careful not to bore her either. The path between the two is narrow and winding, dark and dangerous, but it exists. I took it and employed all my agility not to stray off course.

She left a few minutes later. I didn't know her name or her telephone number, but was betting we would see each other again. It wasn't the first time I'd noticed her in that square near my university, where I often went to read. I was counting on the fact that it wouldn't be the last. Three days later, in the same place, she was the one to spot and hail me from the bench. The conversation was longer, less defensive, and this time, when we parted ways, I knew her name: Aïda. We didn't exchange telephone numbers until much later, when chance was no longer enough to ensure our encounters in the square, which increasingly resembled dates, or the hopes thereof.

The standard, near-banal stages of the prolegomena of a potential relationship followed. The first dinner allows you to gather basic biographical information about the other. I found out that she was a photojournalist, a specialist in urban uprisings and civic resistance movements; she learned that I had been dragging out a literary thesis for some time. She was mixed-race—Colombian father, Algerian mother—and the youngest of three children. I was the eldest of five. She was vegan; I swore by steaks served rare. She voted communist; I lived with an anarchist. She wanted to become a foreign correspondent; me, merely a writer. The feverish exchange of text messages continued, unflagging, at all hours of the day. Then there was the second dinner (vegan), the first shows of modesty, the first silences, the first big laughs, maybe the first serious moments. The first kiss can happen here. Not in our case. Our game was to make ourselves wait. Then the first confessions. Who said I miss you first? It was me. She adroitly replied: Me too, but let's take it slow, no quicker than the music. First concert. First holding of hands before the large stage at the Fête de l'Huma, the famous music festival, with Manu Chao's blessing. *La vida es una tómbola*, he sang, and as I listened,

I idiotically thought, yes, it's true, *la vida es una tómbola*, and sometimes you win a miracle: the smell, the body that moves and brushes against us, the voice of a woman humming, Aïda, whose presence at your side at that moment had no justification, nothing, not luck or merit or hope, not even the most indulgent of dreams. Then, our first kiss, slow, perfect in that nothing had forced it apart, it having reached maturity. It lasted a whole verse, then we latched onto the chorus in progress, as if nothing had happened, whereas everything had happened. "Me Gustas Tú," the last song of the show, ended as night and a vertical rain fell. We didn't need to speak to say that the concert had been amazing, to revive the sensation of the kiss still prickling our lips, to ask *Where we going?* as we took the RER B. We boarded knowing where we were going: toward each other, without a word but in an intense conversation of interlaced fingers and hints of smiles so loaded that any sentence that attempted to carry their weight would have broken. We went to her place. I remember her drenched hair, wetting her face, and mine, when we made love, no, we *invented* love, ours so explosive that it shot off blazing fragments that circled us like rings around a planet.

True ontological transformations aren't as frequent in the course of a lifetime as is believed. I've experienced two, and reading *The Labyrinth of Inhumanity* was only the second. In terms of mystical crises, Pascal had his Night of Fire and Valéry his Genoa Night; for me it was the first night of lovemaking with Aïda. No one will ever dim the glimmer of its truth within me; the veil of time itself will fail. That night, I kneeled in the light and I swore an oath. I promised my soul's fidelity to another. I did it alone.

August 10

I spent the day at the press archives, which an influential acquaintance of Musimbwa's had been able to get me into. My phone was taken away at the entrance, but I took notes. I read B. Bollème's investigation, a copy of which was available there. Then I reread *The Labyrinth of Inhumanity* in light of what I learned about it from the reviews of the era and from the journalist's investigation.

———

Gemini Editions recently published an astonishing debut novel whose author is said to be colored, an African from Senegal. The book is titled *The Labyrinth of Inhumanity* and its author calls himself T.C. Elimane.

Let's be honest: one wonders whether this work was written by a French author in disguise. Colonization may well have performed miracles in education in the African colonies. Still, are we meant to believe that an African could have written like this in French?

Therein lies the mystery.

In any case, what is *The Labyrinth of Inhumanity*, which is hopefully the first book of many, actually about? The novel recounts the story of a bloodthirsty king, a black Nero of sorts, who [...]

Now it remains to be seen who is hiding behind that strange name, T.C. Elimane. If it turns out, improbably, to be one of the Negroes from our colonies, that will be reason enough to start believing in the powerful magic they are said to possess.

B. BOLLÈME
La Revue des deux mondes

August 11

Silence may have been Elimane's response to the whole business. But what kind of writer keeps quiet?

———

La Revue des deux mondes noted, in yesterday's edition, the release by a small emerging publishing house of an "astonishing debut novel whose author is said to be colored, an African from Senegal."

A dubious use of the passive voice in our mind: this admirable book that is *The Labyrinth of Inhumanity* is the masterpiece of a black man. The work is African down to its marrow [...]

For Mr. Elimane is clearly *both* a poet and a Negro [...] Beneath the seeming horrors described in the novel lies, in reality, a profound humanity [...]

This author, who, as his editor Mr. Ellenstein told us, is barely twenty-three years old, is going to make a name for himself in French literature. Given his youth and the astounding brilliance of his poetic vision, it would appear that we have before us, if we may, a kind of "Negro Rimbaud."

AUGUSTE-RAYMOND LAMIEL
L'Humanité

One year ago, I knew the felicity of days, the plenitude of weeks, the ardent jubilation of great beginnings. I saw myself falling in love and prayed that the fall would last forever. Aïda warned me, just in time according to her, of the risk I was taking. But of course, that "in time" came too late. I had already long been in love with her when she told me she couldn't allow herself the luxury of an attachment. She said: My work will take me somewhere else, maybe for a long time; I'll leave.

It was honest and therefore cruel. I loved her with the rage of a child unable to find the language for his emotions, an anger whose object—her or me—I wasn't sure of. Because every day spent with her, or every night, might have been the last, I lived them with elation, sorrow, and sometimes, though I fought the feeling, hope: hope that she would stay with me rather than go somewhere else in the world to photograph the sparks of a revolution. The greatest revolution of all is happening before your eyes: I'm falling in love with you, look. She brushed me aside; I brushed myself off, and refused to give up.

One day, hopeless or crazed by hope, I said the three fatal words. Nothing, not even a cautious "me too," not even a brutal *moi non plus* in response. Aïda didn't respond, and I knew it was unfair to hold it against her: I had accepted that in this matter, reciprocity was not guaranteed. I even think, if I'm being completely honest, that deep down I liked the uncertainty of the wait. Maybe I was just one more masochist of love. I was playing a game of tennis on the court of sentiments with an invisible partner. I sent my "I love yous" over the net. They disappeared into the darkness on the other side; I didn't know if they would be returned to me— and it was precisely that agonizing doubt that prompted a vague feeling of pleasure. For uncertainty doesn't equate to despair, and it was possible that Aïda's silence, like the primitive chaos, could, with a few words, birth a spark of life. I had enough balls. I served again. I was ready for a marathon match.

It didn't happen. One night, Aïda announced that she was going to Algeria, her native country, where a historic revolution waged by the people was rumbling. Suddenly we had six months left to live. I learned this the way you learn that a cancer too advanced to be treated has been detected. That was the night I began to secretly write *Anatomy of the Void*. A love story, a long farewell, a breakup letter, an exercise in solitude: all those things at once. For three months I wrote, and we continued seeing one another. Why? The thought that she was in the same city I was but that I wouldn't see her was more unbearable to me than the thought of our impending breakup. I loved to love her, I loved to love, *amare amabam*, I loved myself loving her, I loved her seeing me love her. The dizzying *mise en abyme* of an existence abruptly reduced to one of its dimensions. This wasn't a reduction but a concentration of my whole being, which was entirely devoted to a single thing. If someone had asked me in that moment what I did in life, I would have responded with proud and tragic humility: I'm a lover and nothing more. My body was already promised; blind servitude was inevitable.

Anatomy of the Void practically wrote itself, and very quickly. I sent it to the small publisher. They responded three weeks later, to my great surprise (since they always took at least three months to respond), that they wanted to get the book out as quickly as possible. Three days before Aïda's departure, I published *Anatomy of the Void*. I had dedicated it to her. That didn't hold her back. She left to cover the revolution in Algeria. I asked her, before her departure, if we could stay in touch. A Bartlebyian response: she would prefer not to. Even if we didn't admit it, she explained, keeping in touch would mean continuing to hope that, one day, a relationship would be possible. And she didn't want us to prevent ourselves from finding love elsewhere, from loving other faces. Hers was the one I wanted, but out of love, or weakness, I respected her decision. She deleted her social media accounts and shut down her email address, told me that once she was on the ground she would change her number and that there was no point in my writing her. I said yes to everything. It had always been her leading our waltz. And then one day I found myself alone on the dance floor, with the ghost of the music and the memory of my partner gone in the wind. There was no gradual creep into solitude, for which no one is ever properly prepared; I was thrown immediately into the deep end. But I had sworn an oath.

August 13

Elimane had been a sort of first man who, banished from paradise, could only find refuge in that same paradise, but on its hidden face. Its other side. But what is the other side of paradise? Hypothesis: the other side of paradise isn't hell, but literature. Meaning: Elimane's only choice was to die (or resuscitate?) by writing after being killed as a writer.

———

One would need to be a socialist wag in the vein of Auguste-Raymond Lamiel to see the work of a "Rimbaud," even a Negro one, in *The Labyrinth of Inhumanity*. The book is the slobbering drivel of a savage who, taking himself for a master pyrotechnist of a language whose subtle fire he inadequately controls, ends up singeing his wings.

[…] The savagery of the Africans isn't only in our minds: we could see it at the front, during the Great War, in those brave but terrible phalanxes of Negroes who horrified the Germans and the French alike. And we see it again in *The Labyrinth of Inhumanity*. We were already somewhat terrified by Africa. Now, we are truly repulsed. Colonization must continue, and the Christianization of those wretched, damned souls with it. Otherwise, we'll find ourselves with even more books by this pen.

[…] Every one of these graceless pages reveals that civilization has not yet penetrated the veins of those pickaninnies, who are good for nothing more than pillaging, feasting, skirt-chasing, burning, drinking, fornicating, tree-worshipping, killing […]

ÉDOUARD VIGIER D'AZENAC
Le Figaro

August 14

Sanza invited us to his place tonight. I went without really wanting to, thinking about the vanity of what I was writing, the lie of what I was writing, the chasm between what I was writing and life. Siga D. had been right: from the perch of my speeches about what literature was or should be, I took off soaring above the world like a falcon in majestic flight; but those flights were only for show, not combat; entertaining, circensian exhibitions in lieu of fights to the death. I was sheltering behind literature as if it were a windowpane or a shield; and on the other side stood life: its violence, its horns, its battering ram to the gut. I needed to come out of hiding and face it, prepared to absorb the knocks and maybe dole out a few. It was going to take a bit of courage; no haggling, no tricks, no deals; courage alone. That was the price.

At Faustin Sanza's, I didn't participate much in the discussion, which I found insipid. Béatrice barely said hello to me, then nothing else for the rest of the evening. Everyone's minds appeared to be elsewhere. Sanza tried to throw a few controversial assegais, but they slid right off our armor of indifference and boredom. Eva Touré didn't take a single photo for Instagram. Everything was off. We cut the evening short. Béatrice gave me a death stare before leaving in an Uber. Eva called her personal taxi. Musimbwa and I walked. On the way, I told him what I had discovered in the press archives. He asked me if I would go to Amsterdam. I said that it was likely.

"All this merits a book," he said. "You know that. I'd have liked to come along, join the adventure, but I can't. I've done a lot of thinking these past few days. There's another book in my mind. I'm going back to the DRC. I'm not sure I'm ready, but I have to go."

I know that, in that instant, I should have said something serious or comforting or beautiful, or simply a joke that would have lightened the weight of the moment, but nothing came: my lips remained shut and the moment kept its weight of silence. We were each heading toward our own book.

Musimbwa rarely talked about his home country. I only knew that he had fled the war, as a child, with an aunt who passed away last year. He had never told me about the circumstances of his escape, about his parents, about his life before France. One day I asked him why he never spoke directly about his past. I'll never forget his response:

"Because I only have unhappy memories of Zaire. I spent the happiest moments of my life there. But thinking about it always makes me unhappy. Remembering those moments confirms that not only are they gone, they're destroyed forever, and an entire world with them. I only have unhappy memories of Zaire. Bad ones, yes. But good ones too. What I mean is that nothing makes a man sadder than his memories, even when they're happy."

I never dared bring up that period of his life again. Still, I sensed that it contained the keys to the enigmas in his work. All his books, for example, include a deaf character, or powerful metaphors for deafness. He never expanded on the subject, but my intuition told me that, when it came to Musimbwa, *everything was there.*

We were still walking. He was the one to break the silence: "What made you become a writer, Faye? Can you identify an event about which you would say, thinking back to it, there's where writing began for me?"

"It's hard to say. Maybe my reading. But I don't know if that counts. I don't have a powerful origin story. Not like Haruki Murakami, for example. Do you know the story about the incredible way that he became a writer? No? He's at a baseball game. A ball slices through the air, pure harmony, Murakami watches the ball's perfect trajectory, and as he does he knows what he has to do, what he has to become: a great writer. That ball was his literary epiphany, his sign. But I didn't have a ball. I didn't have a sign. Which makes me want to say that my origin as a writer lies in my reading, I think. What about you? Do you know why you became a writer?"

He said yes. But we had reached the intersection where our paths diverged, and he couldn't (or wouldn't) tell me more about the origin of his calling. He simply asked me what the next stage of my search would be. I answered that I didn't know exactly, even though it was likely that I would visit Siga D. soon, in Amsterdam. He was planning to leave for the Democratic Republic of the Congo in one week. He wanted to return with the least amount of preparation possible. See where the wind takes me, basically, he told me, smiling. But his smile saddened me a little.

We promised to meet up one last time before he left, to drink like never before and read our favorite poets and novelists. That was the only way, we had said, that two young writers who had become friends and were on the cusp of embarking on the unknown could exchange a proper goodbye. I think, however, that we knew in our guts that the literary farewell–cum–drinking spree would never occur. We only pretended to believe in that promised evening to make the end of this one easier to bear. He and I would call each other, of course, but we wouldn't see each other again for a very long time. Whenever our reunion came, we would be different men. Perhaps even, we would have only just become men.

———

For several days, people have been saying that the now-notorious *Labyrinth of Inhumanity*, penned by Mr. Elimane and published by Gemini Editions, is an illustration of African civilization. Ideological adversaries whose respective readings of the book differ on every point agree at least on this: the book is African. If you ask us, however, that interpretation couldn't be more wrong: the book is anything you like, except African.

We were expecting more tropical color, more exoticism, more insight into the purely African soul [...] The author is well-read. But where is the true Africa in all of this?

This book's great weakness is that it is not Negro enough. And it is unfortunate that a manifestly talented author preferred to limit himself to a vain exercise of style and erudition rather than let us hear what would have been of far-greater interest: the throbbing beats of his continent. Let's hope they reverberate in his next book, which one would expect to be the denouement of *The Labyrinth of Inhumanity*.

TRISTAN CHÉREL
La Revue de Paris

August 15

What can we truly know about an author?

———

Given the many differing reactions prompted by The Labyrinth of
Inhumanity, *I wanted to speak with Charles Ellenstein and Thérèse
Jacob, the two young editors who founded and run Gemini Editions,
which published the controversial novel.*

BRIGITTE BOLLÈME: People are saying that *The Labyrinth of Inhumanity* was written by an author in disguise...

CHARLES ELLENSTEIN: People in Paris say lots of things. For that
matter, it's often you journalists saying them. Not everything
is true. All authors wear disguises. But if you're referring to
the rumor that the book wasn't written by Elimane, but by
an established author using an alias, it's ridiculous.

BB: Why?

THÉRÈSE JACOB: Because he exists. Elimane exists.

BB: Is he really African?

TJ: He's African, from Senegal, like it says on the back on the
book.

BB: He's reportedly the same age as you two, or just about...

CE: Let's not exaggerate. He's a little younger. In any case, the age doesn't make the writer.

BB: Where is he? Why isn't he here with you?

CE: He's a solitary person. What's more, he knows that the fact that he's African would expose him to all manner of comments, and not the most obliging.

BB: The novel is arousing lots of heated interest in the press, notably because its author is such a unique and mysterious figure. You have to understand, we need proof that it is indeed this T.C. Elimane who wrote it… His silence casts a suspicious shadow over his work.

TJ: Elimane is aware, and it's a risk he's willing to take.

BB: In that case, could you at least tell us a little more about him? What does he do? How did you meet him? What is he like? Where does he live?

CE: We met him in a café last year, by chance. It's a café we frequented often, and we would always see Elimane at one of the tables, furiously writing, not paying attention to anything or anyone. It was clear that he was a writer. It's the kind of thing you can sense. One day we engaged him in conversation. Elimane is a mistrustful man, whose confidence is not easily gained. But we became friends. He eventually had us read what he was writing. We liked the manuscript. That's how this whole book venture began.

BB: What does he think of all the hoopla around his book?

TJ: I don't get the impression that there's all that much. Regardless, he doesn't pay attention to it, as far as I know. That's not what interests him.

BB: What interests him?

TJ: What should interest every writer: writing. Reading and writing.

BB: And is he truly African? I'm sorry to insist, but please understand that for our readers, it's quite unusual for an African to...

TJ: ...write like this?

BB: ...to write at all. And receive so much attention in the small literary world. For that matter, did you know that Auguste-Raymond Lamiel dubbed Elimane the "Negro Rimbaud" in *L'Humanité*?

TJ: He's certainly free to make that comparison, and to own it.

BB: Can we hope to see T.C. Elimane anytime soon?

CE: It all depends on him. But I'd be surprised.

The interview ended there. It's hard to say what to take away from all this. Charles Ellenstein and Thérèse Jacob are both trying to keep the identity of their mysterious friend a secret. Therein lies the paradox: we know a little more about him, but his mystery remains intact.

B. BOLLÈME
La Revue des deux mondes

August 18

What can we truly know about a work?

———

In reading certain remarks about *The Labyrinth of Inhumanity,* little doubt remains: the color of the writer's skin is what bothers people. His race is at the heart of the scandal. Mr. Elimane arrived too early in an era that's not yet ready to see blacks excel in all domains, including art. Perhaps that time will come one day. Who's to say? For now, Mr. Elimane must act as a brave forerunner, and an example. He must show himself, speak up, and prove to all racists that a Negro can be a great writer. We will offer him our fullest and most loyal support. Our columns are open to him.

LÉON BERCOFF
Mercure de France

August 19

I wrote an email to the Spider-Mother. I was ready to come see her in Amsterdam. She replied immediately: *I'll be waiting for you, Diégane Faye.*

I bought train tickets—thank God (France!) for scholarship money—for the following weekend.

Then I searched for photos of Brigitte Bollème on the Internet. Most of them were from the 1970s, which is when Bollème, an influential juror for the Prix Femina, and well into her sixties (she was born in 1905), was at the height of her career as a literary figure and journalist. In the photos, Brigitte Bollème is always looking straight at the camera, like she wanted to send a message to the future through that frank gaze.

———

The Labyrinth of Inhumanity, or the True Origins of a Hoax
Henri de Bobinal
Professor of African Ethnology, Collège de France

I made several trips to Africa, and more precisely to the colony of Senegal, between 1924 and 1936. It was during one of these trips, between 1929 and 1934, that I discovered and studied a strange people called the Bassari. I spent enough time with them to confidently state the following: T.C. Elimane's book is a shameful rewriting of one of the narratives of Bassari cosmogeny. The novel's plot borrows the key elements of this people's foundation myth, which it blends with fictional episodes. I heard the myth in 1930.

It recounts how an ancient king established the Bassari kingdom. This cruel and bloodthirsty king would burn his enemies and sometimes his own subjects. He would then mix their flesh with manure to plant trees whose fruits rendered him more powerful. It didn't take long for those trees to become a vast forest, and for the king to have enough fruits to reign eternal. One day, as he was walking alone through the forest, the lord encountered a woman (or a goddess: the word is the same in the Bassari language) whose beauty captivated him. The woman-goddess disappeared into the forest; the king followed but eventually got lost. He wandered for years, amid the trees that had grown thanks to his grisly fertilizer. This forced the king to confront his past crimes, since from every tree the soul of a person burned alive spoke to him. The king teetered on the brink of madness, but then, at the instant he was about to die, after having listened to each tree tell its tale, the woman-goddess reappeared and restored his reason and his life. Together, they reemerged from the forest. The king believed he had been gone for years; but once out of the forest, he returned to his court, where his subjects told him he had only been gone four or five hours. The king then understood that the gods had been testing him. He married the woman-goddess and renamed his people the "Bassari," a word that means "those who venerate trees."

I shared this extraordinary myth with Marcel Griaule and Michel Leiris when they visited Bassari lands in 1931, at the head of the famous Dakar–Djibouti ethnological expedition. They were fascinated. Incidentally, Leiris loosely cites me in *Phantom Africa*.

The troubling similarities between this myth and Mr. Elimane's book are quite clear. It's obvious that he borrowed this narrative and changed almost nothing. That is called plagiarism. He may have done so with noble intentions (e.g., an introduction to Bassari culture), but in that case, why not mention this people, who are perhaps his own? Why did he write as if this story was solely the product of his imagination or his talent?

I therefore appeal to Mr. Elimane's integrity. If he has any left, he would do himself credit by publicly issuing a mea culpa. He won't emerge untarnished, but somewhat redeemed, surely. And the Bassari people with him.

Henri de Bobinal

August 21

Stanislas and I were eating lunch at a Pakistani place when he said to me, as he finished his samosas:

"I forgot to tell you something. Yesterday, I was leafing through Gombrowicz's *Diary*. It was the early '50s. He was living in Argentina at the time, which maybe you knew. There's a note where he writes: 'Sábato introduced me to an African writer who just got here. An odd guy. I'll see if his book is worth anything. Sábato gave it to me.' Two pages later, he's read the book in question. And he writes: 'Finished the African's book. It's a joy to get lost in his *Labyrinth* (even if it is inhuman), despite all the unnecessary virtuosities of the teacher's pet who's read everything.' It might be a coincidence. Maybe he's talking about another book, by another African. But still: *Labyrinth...inhuman.* Is there a chance that...Do you know if your Elimane spent time in Buenos Aires in the '50s?"

"I don't know. I don't know yet. But Siga D. must. She'll tell me."

———

Henri de Bobinal's article confirms it: the Elimane affair is nowhere near over. As a matter of fact, intrigued by his ethnologist colleague's response, Paul-Émile Vaillant, the tenured chair of literature at the Collège de France, contacted us after reading Mr. Elimane's book.

This scholar was surprised to find "literary plunder" within the work, both subtle and blatant. He discovered, braided into the text, rewritten sentences originally penned by European, American, and Eastern authors of the past. No major work appears to have escaped this rewriting, from antiquity to the modern era [...]

Mr. Vaillant of course condemned this methodology, but he also stated that he was impressed by the author's ability to place all those book fragments end to end, blending them into his own prose and the narrative of an original story, without this ever rendering the text incomprehensible.

ALBERT MAXIMIN
Paris-Soir

August 22

Musimbwa's last day here before his return to the DRC. He called me and I understood immediately: he was experiencing the sudden fear that constricts your chest the night before a major departure. His apprehension, however, reassured me: it indicated that his imminent trip responded to a true *summons*. He told me he would have liked to bring the *Labyrinth* with him, then he wished me good luck on my quest for T.C. Elimane. I thanked him, then begged him not to write the umpteenth book about *the return to the native land*. He promised to stay away from the squalid morass that exile opens at the feet of all writers who believe they are going home. We had a good laugh, then that was it. We said goodbye. We hung up.

After that I turned on my computer and began to type out *The Labyrinth of Inhumanity*. I tracked the words closely, like a hunting dog, a detective, a jealous lover. I was a scribe shadowing Elimane's writing down to its molecular core. I didn't copy the text. *I wrote it*; I was its author, the same way Borges's Pierre Menard was the author of the *Quixote*. Four hours later, I was done. I emailed the file to Musimbwa with the words "for the road." He responded right away: "You're crazy, man, but thanks." Then I went out to eat at the African restaurant. The kora player was covering the latest number-one hits. That saddened me and I was surprised to find myself, as I ate my *mafé*, missing the old, monotonous Mandingo ballad.

———

There's no way around it: T.C. Elimane, whose book we enjoyed immensely, is a plagiarist. Nevertheless, we maintain that we are dealing with a very talented writer, regardless of what imbeciles like Vigier d'Azenac may think. After all, isn't the whole history of literature one of sweeping plagiarism? What would Montaigne have been without Plutarch? La Fontaine without Aesop? Molière without Plautus? Corneille without Guillén de Castro? Maybe the real problem is the word "plagiarism." Things would have unfolded differently, no doubt, if it had been replaced by a term more literary, more scholarly, and much nobler, in appearance at least: innutrition.

The Labyrinth of Inhumanity reveals too many of its borrowings. That is its sin. Being a great writer is perhaps nothing more than the art of knowing how to conceal one's plagiarisms and references [...]

AUGUSTE-RAYMOND LAMIEL
L'Humanité

August 23

I dreamt about Elimane last night. He asked me: What are you doing here, on this path orbiting solitude and silence, what are you doing here? I know that I responded with something beautiful: a spiritual, desperate phrase, the kind you only find in a dream, or at the end of a letter by Flaubert, or on the lips of certain Senegalese taxi drivers when, stuck in heavy traffic, between a vulgar obscenity and a gob of spit out the window, they proffer luminous philosophical maxims. It was that kind of phrase, I just know it. Of course I'd forgotten it by the time I awoke. Which made me miserable the whole day.

———

Gemini Editions has just withdrawn all copies of *The Labyrinth of Inhumanity* from sale. It also announced that after compensating a number of the plagiarized authors, it will be filing for bankruptcy.

Charles Ellenstein and Thérèse Jacob, the two founders of the publishing house, have yet to say anything about T.C. Elimane, who, despite the fact that he is the subject of the scandal, has maintained his distance and his deafening silence. [...]

Within the literary world, the hoax is proving to be as entertaining as it is troubling: for a time, it worked. Experts were taken in. In a way, T.C. Elimane cast doubt on their credibility, their reliability, and, perhaps, their erudition.

The matter will be all the more troubling if T.C. Elimane indeed proves to be African. In which case, he will have dealt a resounding affront to the custodians of a culture that claimed to civilize him.

Let's hope that the truth about this affair will one day be brought to light.

JULES VÉDRINE
Paris-Soir

August 24

Stanislas left to spend a few days in Poland. He still has family there. He asked me to keep him posted about my research on Elimane.

Since I was alone, I invited Béatrice Nanga over for dinner. What I feared would happen did: she accepted. She arrived, and those first few minutes were unbearable, silent as a grave but less peaceful. She asked me if I'd heard from Musimbwa. No, and you? No. I hope he arrived safely. Me too. More silence. I refilled our drinks. I emptied my glass just as quickly. Should we eat? Yes. I served the food. She tasted it and said nothing. I took refuge in the bottom of my bowl. But there was no point pretending: we needed to talk, and the talking might hurt. Rip off the Band-Aid, as they say. I attacked, sword drawn:

"So you're mad at me for not coming into your bedroom last time, Béa?"

"You're not the only red-blooded man on earth," she snickered. "And the man who did come in that night was blessed by nature, not to mention he knew what he was doing. You must have heard me." She stared into my eyes with a look intended to be cruel, that she believed was cruel, but that struck me as merely sad. "But I'm mad at you, yes. It wasn't only about bodies or desire."

"What was it about, then?"

She launched herself at me like a torpedo.

"You never back up what you think. You're always talking about nuance, about complexity. Do you really believe that's what it means to be intelligent, to be mature, to have a thought? You go back and forth on everything, whether it's the most serious subject in the world or the most ordinary. You want something. And a second later, you don't. You believe and you doubt in the same sentence. A life full of maybes! What do you want? No one ever knows what you're thinking. For you, the world is a long tightrope over a deep abyss. At first, yes, when I saw that you weren't coming that night, I was mad at you, I was disappointed, because I had wanted to sleep with you too, and you said that you wanted to as well. But when I think about it, it's your general attitude in the world or toward the world that's frustrating. What matters to you? What desire drives you? What are you faithful to? Even when we're debating *The Labyrinth of Inhumanity*, you act indifferent, as if what really interests you is watching us get riled up. But where the hell is your fire? I'm mad at you for going through things and people like a ghost through a wall. People get attached to you, for a while you seem to get attached too. But one night, you leave, they wake up, your spot beside them is cold and they don't know the reason for your leaving or where you went. They only know that you won't be coming back. People aren't experiments, they're not specimens under a microscope, I'm not a fucking lab rat, Diégane. People aren't literary fodder, forever at your disposition, they aren't sentences-in-the-making that you compose in your mind with an ironic smile. Do you know what Musimbwa has that you don't? You're alike in a lot of ways, but he can see people. He's down on earth with them. He screws when it's time to screw, drinks when it's time to drink, offers comfort when he can, isn't afraid to open up, to make a mistake. He's a man. And a better writer for it. He's warm. But you, you're cold. Blind to people, blind to the world. You take yourself for a writer. And it's killing the man inside you. Do you get it?"

She said all that without taking a breath, like she was giving a performance, but I could tell that every word came from her gut. Her voice had trembled, I'd sensed the tears. When she stopped talking, I looked out the window at the night sky. I suddenly felt very tired, and I sighed.

"Maybe you're right."

"That's all you can think to say?"

"There's nothing else to say. You're right."

"You really don't get it."

At that, she stood and gathered her things. I'm sorry, Béatrice. She didn't respond to those words, which in any case I had only said in my mind. She turned around and left.

I went onto the balcony and looked down. That night my street, normally animated, was empty. All I could see was Béatrice's shadow receding, and the sight of it made me want to cry.

August 25

Aïda, on our last night together, had said to me in her characteristic style (curt and biting):

"I read *Anatomy of the Void* yesterday. I wanted to talk to you about it before I left. Sorry if I sound harsh. I'm flattered that you dedicated your first published book to me. But it's obvious you're not a writer yet. Or rather: you don't know what kind of writer you want to be yet. I can't find you anywhere in your book. You're missing. You don't haunt it. It doesn't haunt you. There's no evil or melancholy. The book is too pure. Too innocent."

I responded that I found the idea of writing to capture or represent evil pretty pretentious. True evil, I said, isn't written, it's done. It's actions that are needed, Aïda, not words, not books, not dreams: actions. Aïda said nothing. I continued by saying that I wrote neither out of melancholy nor to attain it. I wrote, whatever she might think, to find the last road of innocence on earth.

Aïda smiled but said nothing more, which allowed us to dedicate the little time we had remaining to sex rather than words. Hers lingered in my mind all the same.

Today, more than one year after that conversation, I'm

tortured by the idiocy of my answers. Evil's the big question. Innocence has no place in literature. Nothing beautiful is written without melancholy. It can be manipulated, distorted, stretched into pure tragedy, or transmuted into infinite comedy. Anything goes when it comes to the variations and combinations offered by literary creation. You open a hatch of sadness, and literature sends up a big laugh from the hole. You enter a book like it's a lake of black, icy pain. But at the bottom, you suddenly find yourself at a party: the joyful ambience of sperm whales tangoing, seahorses zouking, turtles twerking, giant cephalopods moonwalking. You always start with melancholy, the melancholy of being human, and any soul that can penetrate to the core of that feeling, and make it resonate in each and every one of us, that soul alone will be the soul of an artist—of a writer.

I'm writing these bold, chaotic words on the train taking me to Amsterdam. Siga D. is waiting for me. I brought *The Labyrinth of Inhumanity*. I also have my notebook, with everything I jotted down at the press archives. As early as tonight, or tomorrow, I'll know more. But about what? About whom? *The Labyrinth of Inhumanity*? Its hypothetical sequel? Elimane? Siga D.? Myself?

Perhaps what we're all looking for, my dear Diary, is never truth as revelation, but rather truth as possibility, the gleam at the bottom of the mine in which we've been endlessly digging without a headlamp. What I'm chasing is the intensity of a dream, the fire of an illusion, the passion of what's possible. What is there at the bottom of the mine? More mine: the vast wall of coal, and our axe, and our mandrels, and our haws. There's your gold.

I look up: there's no shining star that I might follow; there's only a shifting, sometimes stormy sky, ever silent, spinning above the world. The star maps no longer allow themselves to be read: the sky is a labyrinth too, and it's no less inhuman than the labyrinth of the earth.

First Biographeme

Three notes on the essential book

(Excerpts from T.C. Elimane's diary)

You'd like to write one book and one alone. If you're being honest, you know there's only one that matters: the book that begets all the rest, or the one that is their culmination. You'd like to write the book-slayer, the work that will kill the others, erasing those that came before and dissuading any tempted to emerge in its wake, to cede to such folly. In one act, abolish and unify the library.

But any book that strives for perfection dooms itself to failure; and it's within the lucid vision of that imminent failure that the ardent heart of the endeavor beats. A desire for sublimity, the certainty of nullity—this is the equation for creation.

The dire aspiration of the essential book is to encompass infinity; its desire, to have the last word in the long discourse of which it is the most recent phrase. But there is no last word. Or if there is, it doesn't belong to the book, since it doesn't belong to Man.

———

With what ink is written the book whose aim is absence? With what language does a work unfold once it has revealed its ambition to be silence?

A void of ignorance. A void of stupidity. A void of fear. Except that the void is in fact a never-ending suicide. And it's always during the split second between each act of self-annihilation that the writer, if he seeks refuge here, feels the blinding and fatal blade of intuition and clairvoyance:

The essential book is written in the language of the dead;

The essential book is recorded in the time of oblivion;

The essential book adheres to nonpresence (neither presence nor absence).

At this moment the void slits its own throat, and in the mute cry sparked by the blade cutting into flesh, you think you hear something fall from its twitching, pollarded head: a final hypothesis, terrible and terribly calm:

The essential book cannot be written.

———

On the path to the essential book, the temptation to remain silent is sometimes as useless as the temptation to speak. Empty cenobitism kills, and for the same reason, just as surely as energetic jabbering: both believe they are making the essentialness of their book dependent on a posture taken in regard to words or the world, when it stems from submission to an interstitial language. To unleash the inner earthquake, you must find the fault, and weaken it.

You grasp the truth of all this: if it's merely a matter of gratifying the mysticism of solitude, through muteness or speech, but without giving it any substance, or better still, truth, immediate death is the better option. Some withdrawals are empty, some company is hollow. Certain heavy silences carry nothing, just as words meant to be decisive collapse in on themselves, their foundations trembling at the crucial moment, when the time comes to support the true heart of things. Armed with silence or with words, advancing toward the truth, toward the essential book, requires courage above all.

Will you have enough, to begin your book now that the shadow of your father no longer haunts you? Will you have his courage, the courage to write what you carry in your heart? Stop this diary here, and begin your book: enter The Labyrinth of Inhumanity.

Book Two

PART ONE

Ousseynou Koumakh's Last Will and Testament

I

—

The bedroom: you haven't entered yet but it's already puking its guts in your face: the smell of old age and disease and the frailty of a body shedding all modesty as the end nears. I only knew my father as an old man. I hated him all the more because of it, the same way I hated that bedroom he hardly ever left in the final years of his life. He and it eventually became one. I think about the old bastard and, before his face appears, that smell is the first thing I sense. I see it. I touch it. The smell grabs hold of my insides, wrings them. Only then does it take flesh, and that flesh becomes my father's face. He forced his smell on me while he was alive; he's still inflicting it on me from his grave. Rank breath. Viscous phlegm. Urinary incontinence. Anal secretions. Perfunctory hygiene. The whole of it inevitably rotting. My father was blind, but he's the one who was unlookable. That's the way I always knew him, from my childhood to that night when he summoned me. It was 1980, I was twenty years old, he was ninety-two.

I had knocked six times on the zinc door to his bedroom, per the rule. Three times first—wait—three more times. If he still hadn't responded after that last volley, you left: he was asleep or busy. You'd need to come back later. That was the law of the house. Only my father's wives could break it. Mame Coura, Yaye Ngoné, and Ta Dib permitted themselves to enter my father's bedroom at any moment, to change him or tidy up. The three took turns at my father's bedside with a devotion long incomprehensible to me. To make sense of it, I used to tell myself, during my childhood and adolescence, that they bustled into that filthy bedroom less to keep it clean or care for the dying man inside than to check whether he was still alive, each hoping to announce the good news to their co-wives. I would imagine their hushed conclave after one or the other's excursion:

"Well?" Yaye Ngoné would say, her voice shaky with hope.

"Not yet," Mame Coura, who had just left him, would helplessly reply. "He's still breathing."

"I'll go check later," Yaye Ngoné would add after taking a few seconds to digest this new disappointment. "Perhaps God will have spared him this needless suffering…"

"God hears you," Ta Dib would conclude. "God hears us."

(But God didn't hear anything, because God had burst his own eardrums to survive and save his mental health.)

For a long time these made-up stories helped me justify the three women's attitude toward my father. But maybe I have it wrong. Maybe I'm attributing to these women I didn't really know a rationale with no basis in their experiences, which wide chasms separated from my own. It's possible that they simply loved him. After all, he was their husband: the gate to their heaven, as tradition had beat into their skulls since birth. Mame Coura, Yaye Ngoné, and Ta Dib were my stepmothers. They raised me because my mother, a few minutes after giving me life, lost hers.

But I'm back at the bedroom threshold. Three knocks. Wait. Silence. Three more knocks. A prayer that he was asleep or dead, and that I wouldn't get a response.

"Come in."

Out of luck. I took a deep breath, then removed my sandals at the door and entered. A small hurricane lamp cast its dim, dirty light across the room. In reality, it only lit up the area directly beside the bed. Beyond that circle lay the shadows of another land. Here was the rotting bastard. I can still see him wrapped up in his blankets, in his pestilence, not moving, like a recumbent statue. Was he still fully aware of his surroundings? Did his sense of smell still function, or had it finally been blunted by repeated exposure to that sickening odor? A few seconds after I entered his lair, he moved to prop himself up on his elbows. He moaned from the effort. All the weight of his ninety-two years gone by had left him wizened in his bed, which was suddenly too big for the athlete of imposing stature he once was. He pushed the covers down to his skinny thighs. In the half light I made out his gaunt profile, his weak, bare chest, his slumped shoulders, the prominent outline of every rib. He briefly tilted back his head, which, seeing his neck so fragile and devoid of strength, I feared would detach under its own weight. A strong whiff of urine struck me when he turned to the side where I was standing. I instinctually brought my hand to my face to plug my nose. For a second, forgetting that he was blind, I was scared he had seen me. He extended one dry, knotty arm toward the end of the bed, and grabbed a large tinplate pot half-filled with sand. His spit bucket. He cleared his throat. I looked away to avoid seeing what was coming. Pointless, since the sound gave me an idea of the deep and glairy expectoration that followed. I heard the pot being set on the floor, and only then looked back at him. His eyes, empty but open, were already waiting for me.

"Do you find me repulsive, Marème Siga?"

Speaking had become difficult for him. When he attempted to say something, his mouth would twist into a grimace that would have been comical if it hadn't transformed his face into a mirror of the suffering and weakness that can befall anyone—including me—tormented and at times degraded by advanced age. Looking at this man, at my despised father, at his pained rictus, I saw my future face.

"I disgust you, is that it?"

This time his tone was more aggressive. I didn't respond and tried to withstand his dead gaze. It was the only part of him that expressed any vitality. His eyes hadn't seen anything since his younger years. But when he opened them and set his gaze on you, Diégane, you'd be hard-pressed not to tremble. Everything else was crumbling beneath old age and the stench, but that gaze held, it held in the midst of that corpse. My father's pride taking its last stand against the ruins of the rest of his body. His mouth twisted again, but the aggression had disappeared. Replaced by something akin to sad, resigned gratitude:

"Yes, I disgust you, Siga. But unlike the others, you no longer have the hypocrisy to hide it. I don't need my eyes to see that."

He lay back down. Relieved to be freed from his gaze, I inhaled the room's acrid smell, which burned my throat. My father's breathing was labored. A slow wheeze rose from his chest.

"Mame Coura said you wanted to see me."

"Yes," he said. "She told me that you would like to continue your studies in the capital, now that you've passed your exams. I won't stand in your way. There'd be no point. Sooner or later, you'll go. Sooner or later," repeated my father, "you're going to leave. I've known that since the day you came into this world. I read your future, and so I know. You can go whenever you like. I've already relayed my instructions to Coura. She'll give you some money as soon as you're settled. We have some family in the city too. You can live with them. They've been informed. But I wanted to tell you a few things before you go. You're my last child, the only one I had with your mother. You came into the world when I was old enough to have easily been your grandfather. And yes, that age difference didn't help us. But that's not why I was so distant. There's another reason. I want to talk to you about it before you leave. I know we won't see each other again in this life."

Nor in any other, I hope, I had thought to myself. I distinctly recall thinking that, Diégane, and I still think it.

Siga D. stopped talking. It was approaching two o'clock in the morning. One hour earlier, I had rung at the Spider-Mother's door, guided by my GPS. When Siga D. opened, I remained frozen on the steps for several seconds. The memory of our last night together had rooted me to the ground like an oak. She quickly alleviated my discomfort with a joke, before kissing me at the corner of my mouth, very simply. Then she stepped aside. I brushed against the literary bosom as I entered.

"What I want," I had said immediately, "is to spend the rest of the night hearing everything I have yet to know about T.C. Elimane. Everything that you can tell me."

She had teased me for my ambition and my rush. We sat down in the living room. She made me tell her about things that I considered to have no real urgency, the progress (what progress?) of my second novel, for example, before finally agreeing, as I jittered with impatience, to bring me into her father's bedroom. She had warned me: it's a long story, you need to be patient, but it begins in this bedroom.

The Spider-Mother was still silent. I had already glimpsed her father's shadow in some of her writing, but it was something quite different to come face-to-face with him that night and brave the smell. Now I could see him, lying on the couch at the foot of which the tinplate pot filled with sand awaited his viscous humors. Siga D. was watching him, eyes blazing. She resumed:

"Few writers remain faithful to their hatred for their parents. In books where they settle their scores, or simply examine a difficult parental relationship, a bit of love always appears eventually, a bit of tenderness that slows the pure momentum of their pure violence. What a waste! Life is offering them an undreamt-of gift, and they chuck it all away because of the idiotic sentimentality we have for our progenitors. What a miserable waste! My hope is that I'll continue to hate my father, and that I won't waver. He certainly never did. He deprived me of his love until the end. He deemed me unworthy of it. That was his lesson, and I learned it well. If I stop hating my father, what of him will remain in me? It's his great legacy. It's my heritage and I must prove myself worthy. You can count on me, Ousseynou Koumakh. You can count on my hatred for a long time still, dear father."

On the couch, in lieu of a response to his daughter's words, a violent cough shook Ousseynou Koumakh's sickly body, but he didn't have time to grab the spit bucket. Viscous, russet saliva surged from his chest and was expelled with such force that it crashed at Siga D.'s feet. She didn't move, and continued:

"Maybe you think that I don't love you because you stole your mother's life, is what he said to me. I'm not distorting things, I responded, those are your exact words, aren't they?"

Siga D. continued: "No, I'm not distorting anything, that is exactly what he said to me: Maybe you think that I don't love you because you stole your mother's life. And actually, Diégane, that is what I thought. My father had taught me very early on that I needed to treat Mame Coura, Yaye Ngoné, and Ta Dib like my mothers, though none of them were, since my true mother, my progenitor, died a few minutes after I was born. He told me so in a cold, accusatory tone. I was six years old, and from that day forward, I told myself that the reason he didn't love me, that he punished me, that he didn't speak to me, that he treated me differently than his many other children, was because I had taken my mother's life. Mine hadn't been enough. I'd needed to steal my mother's life too, to be satisfied. I clung to that explanation for years. It was cruel, perhaps, but had the advantage of being simple and credible enough to justify my father's distance, his harshness, his deliberate refusal to respond to my childish games, my childish mischief, my solicitations, to anything that I made up or did to earn his undivided attention, not his tenderness, which he dispensed as frugally as a skinflint, but merely his simple, ordinary, undivided attention to my existence. Sometimes I succeeded: he would violently scold me or give me an unsparing beating, and those days were some of the most reassuring of my childhood. Those were days when he saw me, when he remembered that I existed and showed me his nonlove with a vengeance. I clung to that violence, because it allowed for the rare physical contact I had with him. And so I exaggerated my insolence. I tested his limits. I broke his rules. I cultivated my bad manners. My unabashed tongue. I fought. I stole. All that so he'd see me. He would hit me. I would go further. I would provoke him. So he'd see me. Hoping he'd show his lack of love for me. Sometimes he'd beat me within an inch of my life. The neighbors didn't bother coming to my rescue anymore. In the village, they thought I was possessed, and if my father, reputed to have healing powers, couldn't fix me, nobody could. My stepmothers didn't understand the reasons for my behavior. They did everything to compensate for my mother's absence; sometimes they even treated me better than their own children (which caused my half siblings to see me as the black sheep of the family), they tried to remedy my condition as a motherless child. But all their efforts were futile: I carried my mother's death inside of me, I was that death, since I owed her my life. My father reminded me of that often, so often that, even in my happiest dreams, it wasn't the sun that rose, but another star: my mother's head, floating without a body in the sky. I wrote in my first book that my mother had taught me solitude. It's true. But paradoxically, I could never be alone. She's there, deep inside me. I swallowed her so I could live. I've always felt her in my gut. That was what connected me to my father. And there was no getting rid of it. Not his indifference cut with hate, or my stepmothers' attempts to calm my wild nature. It was impossible. From my very first wail, I was destined for this: to be hated by my father for costing so much. At least that's what I thought, until that night. And that's what I told him. I said: Yes, that is what I think. I think that you never loved me because my mother had to die for me to live."

"You're wrong," I thought I heard the father moan from the couch, though Siga D. was still talking. "I loved your mother, but God alone took her life. I knew that she would die, and I accepted that fate. I saw it. But I also saw what you would become. And that, I had a harder time accepting."

"What does that mean?" I asked Siga D.

"It means, Diégane, that my father hated me before I even came into the world, because he had divined what my life would be."

"Divined?"

"He claimed to have visions, sometimes. Nocturnal revelations of sorts. I never believed it. I was the only one who didn't. The whole region, the whole country even, knew of him and would come see him to have their futures told. That's how he made his living, by telling people their futures and offering them prayers and mystical advice. Politicians. Business leaders. Wrestlers. Betrayed women. Cuckolded husbands. Spinsters. Welfare cases. The sick. The crazy. The powerless. All kinds would come by the house to speak with the great and powerful Ousseynou Koumakh and leave bearing his prayers or amulets. But best believe that even soothsayers end up as worm fodder. Look at him, in his stench, so weak, so human, so vulnerable. Did he see that too? Can soothsayers see their own end, their own miserable end? Just look at him!"

On the couch, the ghost of the father was slipping away, and I turned away from that sad image as Siga D. laughed.

Once her laughter faded, she continued with even greater determination, seemingly electrified by that burst of rageful hilarity.

"He told me: I saw what you would become, and all that was revealed to me was proved true. You're becoming in reality what you were in my dream, and I won't forgive the universe for that: giving me a daughter that reminds me of everything I hate, everything I thought I had forever left in the past. At that moment, I forgot the smell, the dying, the bedroom. I was clinging to the wheezing voice coming out of my father's body. Then he told me... (Siga D. paused for a second, as if to cement the most crucial details of the account she was preparing to give. I closed my eyes. A voice began to speak. I didn't know if it was Siga D. or her father, who from the couch wanted to tell his own story himself. I didn't know if we were still in Siga D.'s living room, in Amsterdam, or in her father's rank bedroom. Though why did we necessarily have to be in a specific place, where an identified voice was talking to us, at a clearly defined moment? We always find ourselves, in a story—but perhaps, more broadly, at every moment of our existence— between voices and places, between the present, past, and future. Our greatest truth is more than the simple sum of those voices, times, places: our greatest truth is what runs ceaselessly and tirelessly between them, in a dual movement of back-and-forth, recognition and loss, dizziness and assurance. I didn't open my eyes and the voice was speaking.)...you're like them. I knew before you were born that you would be a source of unhappiness, that you would take your mother's life and make mine a living hell by reminding me with every breath that you would be nothing like me, but like them. How is that possible? Ask the blood! Ask the flesh! Ask the mystery of genes, which travel through time and with two distant points along their long course designate ancestry and progeny, forebears and heirs! Everything begins with the great forebear. Everything begins with Mossane."

II

———

Everything begins with Mossane. Everything begins with her choice. After the events I'm going to recount to you, I asked Mossane my question again, across from the cemetery, beneath the mango tree. She'd long since sunk into a world of solitude and shadow and silence. But I still asked her my same eternal question: Why him?

That day, once again, I spoke with no hope of an answer. It had been a very long time since I'd stopped addressing the question solely to Mossane. It was directed at God as well. Though, more than anyone, it was directed at myself. Every man on earth has to discover his question, Marème Siga. I don't see any other purpose for our presence here. Each of us has to find our question. Why? To obtain an answer that will unveil the meaning of our lives? No: the meaning of life is only unveiled at the end. You don't look for your question to find the meaning of your life. You look for it so you can confront the silence of a pure and uncompromising question. A question for which there can be no response. A question whose only goal is to remind the person asking it how profoundly enigmatic their life is. Every being must look for their question in order to brush against, if only briefly, the dense mystery at the core of their destiny—which will never be explained to them and yet occupy a fundamental place in their lives.

Men die without finding their question. Others identify it late in the course of their lives. But I had the luck and the misfortune to find the form of my question rather young. Delivered for the rest of my days from the anguish of looking for it, I was burdened at the same time with another kind of anguish: being forever haunted by the silence that followed my questioning. But this silence isn't a void; it is always filled with the tumult of endless hypotheses, possible answers, and immediate doubts that arise.

Why him?

That day, once again, I had been expecting Mossane to react to my question like she always did: an ironclad silence that let nothing in and nothing out. My question had become a ritual. A greeting. It operated like a shibboleth whose meaning was only known to two people in the whole world—us. After it was asked, we would each sink, side by side, into our respective worlds. Me in mine, full of memories, pain, humiliation, rage, and incomprehension. She in hers, which had remained a complete mystery to me ever since she shut herself inside a few years earlier.

Yet I knew she heard me. That certainty is what brought me back to her, tirelessly, every morning. Yes, of course, she gave no sign that she heard me or even noticed my presence. I couldn't see her, but her image was clear in my heart. She would stare, unblinking, at the graves. The corners of her mouth didn't wrinkle with bitterness, compassion, or even annoyance. Motionless, silent, as distant as another planet: that was Mossane. It was as if the cemetery before us had already welcomed her. But I knew that she heard me each time I asked her my question. I knew it. How? Because her question, the question of her life, was the same. We were linked by having the same question as punishment and solution: Why him?

For a long time Mossane had been living naked beneath the old mango tree in the cemetery, without uttering a word. I sat down beside her, as usual, and placed a small bundle of food near her. I had stopped bringing her clothes: she never put them on. One day (years earlier), I had forcibly dressed her. She took off the clothes and ripped them up as soon as I left her.

In the early days of her silence, I tried to keep her home with me. In the evenings, I tied her to a bed to keep her from running off. She would cry the whole night. She'd let out mournful howls, making it sound like she was being subjected to some sickening form of torture. After a few days, I was forced to let her go. She was still talking a little at the time. Seeing my determination to keep her close, she told me: Not all sick people want to get better, not everyone knocked to the ground wants to get back up, because getting back up sometimes guarantees them another fall, deadly that time, not everybody wants to return to a normal life that sometimes has nothing on death. I'm not interested in getting back up, it's a daydream, a dangerous illusion. I don't want to be saved, Ousseynou. I don't want to come back. Let me go.

In the end, it was those words, Mossane's terrible nighttime cries, and her repeated escapes to the same spot, the old mango tree across from the cemetery, that helped me make up my mind. I didn't have the power to hold her back. And so I watched, in an impotent rage, her progressive descent into madness.

After she had begun to slip away, I was tormented by my inability to keep and save her, even against her will. I swore to myself that I would never again lose a loved one without fighting harder to save them. I resolutely resumed my study and exegesis of the Koran and my initiation into traditional mysticism. In those two forms of knowledge, I was seeking the strength of healing, the secrets of second sight, the power of revelation. A few months later, I went to a neighboring village, where a Sufi mystic had agreed to complete my religious training. He initiated me into the mysteries of all that can only be perceived by the eye within, the sole eye I had. I learned to see and read the world in an invisible light. Time no longer held any secrets from me. It opened behind me. It opened before me. And I was able to follow its winding road far in both directions. I acquired the necessary knowledge to assuage all human wounds. Wounds of the flesh, of the mind, of the being. Upon my return, one year later, I had become he who soon the whole country would know by the name and title of Sheik Ousseynou Koumakh, *yal xoox lé*, Sheik Ousseynou Koumakh, the knowledge-bearer.

Mossane was still there, beneath the mango tree, motionless before the graves. I knew what she was waiting for. But I also knew that what she was waiting for wouldn't come. I tried to draw her back using my new knowledge. I failed: she had ventured too far into shadow for me to have the slightest chance of bringing her out alive. And since it was too late to rescue her from her world, I chose instead to accompany her through it. This was in 1940, if I remember correctly. It had been two years since Mossane had slipped into the large chasm that had opened inside her.

I resigned myself to spending my life apart from her. I finally decided to turn to other women. It was easy enough to find them. My reputation as a healer and a man of God had begun to spread beyond the village's borders. Some families considered it an honor and an opportunity to offer me one of their daughters in matrimony, despite my advanced age. For them, as I well knew, such a union represented a form of insurance against bad luck, disease, or certain calamities from which my prayers would have protected them. That's how I soon came to marry Mame Coura at the end of the year, when she was only eighteen years old.

I could have been the father of any of my wives. I could have sired Mame Coura, Ya Ngoné, Ta Dib, and your own mother, Siga. My love for them was stronger for it, because I loved them doubly. I loved them as wives and cherished them as the daughters they could have been. Becoming a husband and a father at a late age was a blessing: I was spared certain youthful missteps. I lived those experiences with the maturity of a man who had already deeply loved a woman, and for whom paternity held no secrets. My recent initiation had also granted me mental serenity and wisdom. Mossane was the sole perturbance.

I had given up on a life with her, yes, but not on sensing her nearby. And so, even married, even after fathering my first children, even though I was close with my wives, I would go find Mossane every day beneath her mango tree. And every day, her proximity brought me the same happiness and the same pain. She was a living wound inside of me, and I liked to pick at it. I didn't want it to scar over. I wanted it to keep hurting, forever raw. That's the reason I went to her every day, with my happy and sad memories alike, with my disappointed hopes, and my eternal question.

Before I left for my initiation with the Sufi sheik, Mossane would sometimes speak, between episodes. She did so clearly and coherently enough to be understood. She could even, on rare occasions, maintain a perfectly lucid conversation. Those occasions would lead us to believe that she had decided to come back. But she never came back. Which would become apparent when, a quarter of an hour after that flash of lucidity, she sank deeper into debilitating confusion or morbid silence. Every gleam of reason had a price: a steeper fall back into darkness.

When I returned from my initiation, Mossane no longer said anything. The villagers informed me that she had stopped speaking a few days after my departure. Ever since, Mossane had maintained her silence before the graves. Blind though I was, I could see her, in my darkness. Nothing could have made me forget her beauty. Her image was a gift my eyes gave me before I lost them. Even now, though many years have gone by, I still see her.

The aura I had gained in the village spilled over onto her. People believed that she possessed some kind of power and that I sat beside her for mystical reasons. Even children, ordinarily merciless with the feebleminded, left her alone. You'd never see her running through the village to escape a group of cruel kids chasing her, armed with stones and insults. She had aged, I sensed it. Her hair was turning white, and deep wrinkles were etched into her face.

But the passing time wasn't the main assailant. It was suffering. An internal suffering, which only went after the flesh once it had completely eroded the soul over many years. And yet I was certain that Mossane was still beautiful. Barring the natural fear inspired by her state, many men would have already tried to have her. She displayed her naked body in sight of everyone. But no one dared approach, and even less so touch that body. People said that she was protected by the dead. They called her Mossane, the lover of the dead, or the madwoman of the mango tree.

I was the only one who could approach Mossane without her screaming. It wasn't because I had a mystical aura, as the inhabitants of our village used to say. I had no hold over her. Quite simply, she recognized me. I was the last link to an era that explained her present, our present. But most importantly, I'll say it again, we had the same question. The oldest elders in the village, the ones aware of our story, knew part of our secret. We formed an odd couple beneath that mango tree: a naked madwoman and a blind sorcerer, side by side, across from a cemetery. That was enough to scare off the gossips and interlopers.

But let me get back to that one day I keep mentioning. It was 1945. Mossane had been in her world for almost eight years. It was 1945, yes, that's right. I remember it well. They were saying the war would end soon. Information was coming in from afar, carried by the wind. And that day, that infamous day, like every other day for eight years, I asked Mossane my question: Why him? I heard her move, then I felt her hand in mine. I wasn't surprised by her reaction: that night, in my sleep, I had seen her come back. God had sent me a sign. And Mossane had in fact come back. She had agreed, one last time, to come back, to answer.

III

You'll hear Mossane's answer later, Marème Siga. What I want to tell you now concerns something else, the origin of my unlove for you. Though these two stories are one and the same. The first time I put my hand on your mother's belly when she was carrying you, there was a blinding flash in my head. And in that shower of light, I saw your face between theirs. You hadn't been born yet but I already knew you would be on their side. They were coming back in you.

I never knew which of the two of us was older. According to my mother, I came out before him. But in our culture it's said that time is reversed when twins enter the world: the child who comes out of his mother's belly last is considered to be the elder. When we were children, Mère Mboyil always told me the same story: Ousseynou Koumakh, your brother let you come out first to make you happy, he was acting like a big brother who wanted to be nice to his little brother. Assane Koumakh came into the world nine minutes after you, you are therefore younger by nine minutes. That's what my mother would say. I never shook off the feeling that Assane Koumakh, my twin brother, stole more from me than those nine minutes. He took away the possibility, my right, to exist outside of his shadow.

We were born in 1888. Let me note—though perhaps you know already—that I wasn't born blind. I could see. For the first twenty years of my life, I could see. But that's another story that will come later. So, we were born in 1888. We didn't know our father. He died while fishing, in the jaws of a large crocodile, the terrifying legend of which colored our entire childhood. Our mother, Mboyil, your grandmother, had been carrying us for six months when our genitor, nobody knows why, went fishing alone in the most dangerous part of the river. That was the monster's territory. Mboyil never really spoke to us about our father. And the rare times that she let herself mention him, I always detected, though she tried to hide it, relief at his absence. It was as if she was grateful to the enormous crocodile that reigned over the river for taking away our father. Nothing had remained of his body. There was therefore no grave at which we could have paid our respects, at least during the first few years of our lives.

At the end of 1898—so we were ten years old—a group of men, including the man who raised us, went on a three-day expedition down the river. The goal of the hunt was to kill the crocodile terrorizing the region, and to which people attributed all the unexplained deaths and disappearances in the area, even when they hadn't occurred on the river. But a scapegoat was needed: it was the crocodile. The men organized a river campaign and, following a fierce and violent struggle, were able to kill the monster. Three hunters were killed and devoured; two others amputated (one lost an arm, the other a leg). But the animal was killed in the end.

The man to deliver the mortal blow was our uncle Ngor, Tokô Ngor, as we called him. He was the one who, following levirate law, had raised us and taken us in, along with our mother, after the death of our father, his older brother. He and Tokô Ngor had been very close. Once we were old enough to understand such things, Tokô Ngor told us that our father's death had brought him tremendous grief. But what grieved him more, I thought, was knowing that the crocodile was still alive. For ten years, he harbored a tenacious resentment toward the animal, which he tried to kill on his own many times, risking his life. This time, he succeeded. When he returned, avenged and victorious, I sensed, even though I was a child, that he had changed. He seemed like a sick man healed after many years of suffering. But more importantly, that night I understood that I had gotten it wrong: what had grieved Tokô Ngor the most all those years wasn't that the crocodile had still been alive; it was that his brother had no grave where he could mourn him.

After their triumphant campaign against the saurian, an impressive male specimen measuring nearly twenty feet long and weighing one ton, the hunters had to divide its enormous carcass. Some of the men wanted a swath of its hide, a few, its teeth or eyes, and others, simply its meat. But Uncle Ngor only wanted one thing: the animal's innards. Nothing, he said, remains of my brother's body, but he was inside this animal's stomach. It's the stomach I want, and everything inside of it. The others agreed. He eviscerated the beast and buried its entrails, not in the cemetery (such a thing wasn't possible; you don't bury the contents of a crocodile's stomach in a human cemetery) but at the foot of the mango tree across from it, the mango tree beneath which Mossane, years later, would go to sit. Mossane didn't know this story, which everyone had forgotten, and I had never told her. But I'm telling you this right now, Siga: when I went to join Mossane, it wasn't for my father. I never knew him. I went for Mossane alone. But I hadn't forgotten, even thirty years later, that the mango tree was also a grave. The grave laid for my father (his name was Waly) by Tokô Ngor with the stomach of a crocodile in which his body had been digested and disintegrated a very long time before.

Tokô Ngor and our mother raised Assane and me like two little princes. We were both loved, but we didn't love each other. In any case, I didn't love my brother. I think the feeling was mutual, whatever he claimed. In front of others, he acted the protective, loving older brother. He would feign, when we were being watched, a bond that in reality didn't exist. As soon as we were alone, his true nature reemerged: he'd lose interest in me, look down on me, and only speak to me to humiliate or mock me.

We had nothing in common. Physically, of course, we were true twins, similar in almost every way. But every personality trait opposed us, created distance. I never felt the intense, symbiotic connection attributed to twins. Assane showed every sign of being a seductive child. He charmed, laughed, listened; he was gregarious and played his part with exuberance and visible delight. He sought the approbation and admiration of adults. He had the fascinated obedience of the other children our age. He was the favorite, the leader. I was more taciturn. Withdrawn. Anxious. Moody. I had none of my brother's light, his natural poise, his cheerfulness. From an early age, I suffered in secret from the incessant comparisons people would make when they saw us. Checkers was the only thing I was able to best him at. For everything else, he was the strongest, the quickest, the wiliest, the smartest, and the bravest.

A few days after the burial of the crocodile stomach, our uncle Ngor gathered us together with our mother. He said that it was time to start thinking about the future.

"You both," said Tokô Ngor, looking at us in turn, my brother and me, "you both have started at the Koranic school here. That's important. You need to understand Islam, which is an essential part of what we've become. You also need to understand our traditional culture, which was here before Islam. But more than that, you need to see what's happening. You need to think about your future. And what's happening is that this country is going to belong to the whites. Maybe it already does. It's sad to say, but they have control over us. They got what they wanted, by force and by ruse. Maybe we'll get free, but for now, those who come from *Kata maag*, from behind the ocean, are here. I have the feeling this will last for a long time. I won't be here to see the day when they leave for good and we turn back into what we were. Maybe even you two, as young as you are, will already be long dead, and that day still won't have come. Maybe that day will never come and it's impossible to go backward in time to turn back into what we were. After all, man can't go against the current of history the way some fish go against the river current; he can only descend toward the great delta, the very tip of his destiny, before flinging himself into the great sea. We will be something else. Our culture is stricken. The thorn is in its flesh and there's no way to take it out without dying. But we can live with the thorn and leave it in our body, not like a medal, but like a scar, a witness, a bad memory, like a warning against future thorns. There will be other thorns, in other forms, in other colors. But this one, this thorn, is now part of our great wound, meaning our life."

Uncle Ngor paused and looked up at the sky. I had no idea what he was talking about. He continued:

"One thing is certain: we must prepare ourselves for this future in which we will never be alone again, never again like before. I discussed this often with Waly, your father, God rest his soul. This was his most fervent wish: that his future children, or one of them at least, go to the *toubabs'* school, not to adopt their ways, but to learn to defend himself when they say that not only is their way of seeing the best way, which is debatable, but it's the only way, which is wrong."

All this muddled together in my head. I didn't see where he was going. Uncle Ngor paused again and looked at us with a grave expression:

"Do you understand?"

"Yes," said Assane.

To avoid looking like an idiot, I lied: "Yes, Tokô Ngor."

Our mother must have sensed my confusion, and, gently, like she was measuring the weight of her words and through tenderness attempting to lighten them, she said: "What your uncle means, *néné* (the affectionate nickname she gave us), is that one of you has to go the white man's school."

I cast a terrified glance at my uncle. He had his usual serious demeanor, and was probing us with his eyes. I then turned to look at Assane. How could he be so calm when they were telling us something so terrible?

"So you have nothing to say?" asked Uncle Ngor.

"I don't want to go," I sobbed.

"All right, then I'll go," said Assane as soon as I quieted. "I'll go to the white man's school."

A few seconds passed, then Tokô Ngor said:

"Praise be to Roog Sene. This is how your mother and I see things: Assane Koumakh, you will go toward the outside world in search of other forms of knowledge, and you, Ousseynou Koumakh, you will stay here, and protect the knowledge of our world."

That night, I wrestled with the most conflicting of feelings and I couldn't sleep. On one hand, I was happy to be rid of my brother, since he had to leave, but on the other, I had the foreboding sense that his departure heralded great misfortune. A breach was opening in our world, and we didn't yet know what might enter through it, or what might exit.

IV

—

I need to make this fast. My chest is hurting me. You hear it rattling, don't you?

The years that followed were happy years for me. Assane was gone most of the time. He was studying at the white man's school, in the big city up north, and living in a dormitory run by missionaries. He only came home when the rainy season began and left once it was over. The rest of the year, I was alone with Uncle Ngor and my mother. I was free to love them fully, free of my brother's shadow. When my mother said *néné*, I knew she was only addressing me. That feeling of being the sole recipient of her affection, in that precise moment, brought me enormous joy. I was the only face in the photo. Assane was excluded. As he grew older, his temperament didn't change. The opposite: the education he received at the white man's school amplified his taste for seduction. But he had new weapons.

He was one of the first in the village to go to the white school in the big city. Whenever he returned, he was the main attraction. He spoke of the city. He described the whites and their customs. He hinted at their knowledge and their marvelous secrets. He cultivated elegance, eloquence, coquettishness. He interjected French words into our language, which gave anything he said, however insignificant,

an air of importance. The others were fascinated. As a
child, Assane was gifted and curious. The French school
turned him into an adolescent and then a young man who
was educated, cultured, and sure of himself. But most of all,
the French school (this was its mission, after all) turned him
into a white man's Negro.

In 1905, Tokô Ngor died of septicemia after a nasty and
poorly treated ankle injury. But before he departed, he told
us that he was proud of what we were becoming: Assane
Koumakh, a man educated by Western learning, and me,
Ousseynou Koumakh, a good fisherman, solid and responsible, anchored in our culture. He tasked us with taking care
of our mother. But Mère Mboyil only survived him by one
year. In 1906, a common fever took her away too.

Once again, Assane and I were alone on stage. I hoped
that the deaths of our uncle and our mother would bring us
together, that our joint sadness would reunite us. A dashed
hope. Ngor and Mère Mboyil's deaths caused Assane great
pain, as they did me. But he endured it alone, in his way,
and so did I. We shared nothing but an unshareable grief.
The gap between us deepened. It was no longer measured
in minutes but in worlds. Our differences were compounded
by a form of deep, mutual animosity. I felt like he was distancing himself from the world in which he had been born;
he thought that I was shutting myself inside of it. Soon any
dialogue became impossible. After my mother's death, he
would barely even greet me on his periodic returns to the
village.

When he wasn't immersed in the many European books
he always brought home, he was indulging in the easy
pleasures made available to him by his education and the

admiration it aroused. He started drinking. He abandoned religion. In fact, he told me he had converted to Christianity at the missionaries' school and was now called Paul. I told him that was his business, but that I didn't know any Paul. He would always be Assane Koumakh to me. He forgot our ancestors. I never saw him go to Uncle Ngor's grave or my mother's. He preferred chasing girls. Or rather, they were the ones—some, at least—chasing him.

In our age group, only a few resisted him. The wildest and most beautiful among them, the one girl he failed to impress, was Mossane. And for that reason, he liked her. For that reason, among others, I liked her too. Mossane was two years younger than us, but she seemed three years older. When she emerged from childhood, her beauty had erupted like the sun revolting against a thousand-year dictatorship of the night. She was a woman, already fully a woman, while we were straggling at the end of adolescence. Assane and I weren't the only men who wanted her. I can say without fear of error that all the able-bodied men in the village desired her. At that time her magnificence was a subject of daily conversation. Mossane played off it. She knew she was beautiful; she felt desired, envied, coveted. She had learned to behave like a fantasy, meaning like a dream you think is in reach but that recedes like a horizon you're running toward. Playing off her charms is how she learned what it meant to live freely. Mossane didn't belong to anyone; therefore everyone thought she would be theirs. I thought so too.

What was it that attracted me to Mossane, someone who seemed so immodest, so defiant, so untamed, so daring—everything I wasn't? It wasn't your basic attraction for a person whose nature I thought was the opposite of my own.

What I loved about Mossane, first off, was what she *didn't* seem to be. What I imagined her to be *on the inside*. Maybe I fell in love with the idea I had of her. But isn't that what we often fall in love with, in others? Then you get to know them. And either the idea you had of them is right—and you love them even more for matching it—or the idea differs, and your love for that person thrives on that sense of surprise, that challenging strangeness.

I loved Mossane. But I wasn't the only one. For two or three years, I had to be patient, show my worth, seduce her, methodically and mercilessly eliminate the other competitors. In 1908, there were only two of us left: my brother and me. The indifference he initially inspired in Mossane is what motivated him to intensify his efforts at seduction. He was a conqueror, and his sole obsession the territory resisting his conquest.

I had time and location on my side. When Assane Koumakh went back to the city, I took all the time necessary to seduce Mossane, who lived in the village. I made patience the sole instrument of my courting. I didn't attempt to impress Mossane or promise her pipe dreams. I showed her who I really was, in my barest truth: modest, lacking privilege and wealth, nothing to my name apart from my worries, my silences, my doubts, but also a few moral qualities, my attachment to our land, my simple honesty. I didn't have my twin's talents or intelligence. But I felt like I had something that he didn't, which might also have value in a life. As for Assane, whenever he came home he would monopolize Mossane. He smothered her with presents, used his honeyed tongue to get her dreaming of the big city, and taught her to count and read in the language of his new white teachers.

In Mossane, the two worlds that we incarnated, opposed in every way, once again faced off.

At twenty-two, I went blind. It happened while fishing. I was alone that day, and I found myself on an arm of the river feared by most of the fishermen for a very simple reason: it was the spot where the crocodile who killed my father had once lived. The animal's legend had survived its death. Certain rumors said the beast had offspring, which a few fishermen had glimpsed. Other rumors had it that the crocodile was in truth one of the spirits that inhabited those waters, and that it was impossible, even when it had been killed, to kill it. The women who washed their laundry on a wharf had heard, supposedly, its disturbing wails. None of this had been confirmed, though. It might well have been that another crocodile lived there, but I didn't think it was related to the one Uncle Ngor chopped up in front of us to pull out its insides. I believed (I still believe) in the water *pangool*. I was attached to our traditions. I was a fisherman. And every fisherman around here knows that sometimes you see supernatural things in the water.

And so I found myself in those waters full of myths and memories. I was about to toss my net when something, something enormous, collided with my boat. The impact was so hard and abrupt that I lost my balance. I fell into the water. For a few seconds, it felt like I was being dragged into the depths by an invisible force. There was nothing enormous around me, silt was darkening the water, but after a few seconds I could see that I was there alone with that powerful force pulling me toward the bottom.

I understood. Today was the day. I thought about my uncle Ngor, and the words he said to me when he taught me to fish when I was ten or eleven: "The river always tests those who brave its waters, Ousseynou Koumakh, one day or another. When it tests you, you'll think you're dying, you'll be frightened, you'll be tempted to fight, but don't forget: in that moment, the water is like a swamp, and every panicked movement will push you deeper into the mud, so don't struggle."

"What will happen if I struggle, Tokô Ngor?"

"The water will deem you unworthy and kill you."

And so I didn't resist, I surrendered to the water. I closed my eyes and fell asleep. I had a long dream in which I saw, in turn, my uncle, a monstrous creature with the body of a man and the head of a crocodile, my mother, and Assane. I spoke to them, or else we merely exchanged a glance or a smile or a thought. Impossible, however, to remember the conversations I had, even though I know they were important. Mossane also appeared in that dream at the bottom of the river, in a divine image. She was naked, and I looked at her for a long time wishing I was the water so I could envelop her body in a caress and slip inside the deepest part of her.

When I awoke, I was on my boat again, as though nothing had happened and I had never left it. A single thing had changed: I could no longer see. This took me a few seconds to realize, after which, very naturally, I accepted it. That was the price of me surviving an ordeal that, I understood, should have killed me. Some elements of the dream I had in the water became more or less clear. It seemed obvious, for example, that the man-crocodile was the hybrid incarnation of my father and the saurian that had devoured him. Despite the darkness, I managed to get back to the village.

I knew that nothing else would befall me in those waters. When the villagers saw me, they were convinced my tumble overboard had been caused by the ghost of the legendary monster or its offspring, and that in exchange for my survival, it had taken my eyes. They might have been right, but I didn't care what they said. All that mattered to me was knowing whether I still had a chance with Mossane despite my new handicap. When I found her, she had already heard about my misfortune (the village was small, and rumors traveled fast). She said: "You'll never see again."

"I'll never see you again," I responded.

She laughed and said that it didn't change anything, that she would be my eyes from then on.

"I'll never see you again," I repeated.

It was then that sadness and rage at my blindness came over me for the first and only time since the ordeal. I broke down in tears.

In the years that followed, we became so close that I believed I had bested my brother in the contest for her affection. She came to see me every day, and helped me tame the darkness. She didn't give herself to me, but was dedicated all the same. Assane would return occasionally. I don't know if it was because he felt sorry for me, or because his face was now hidden to me, but at the time, I found him more bearable. He had passed the baccalaureate and was studying to become a teacher. He said he wanted to return to our village one day to teach all the children here. In the city, he lived in a small house in the white quarter that the colonial administration had given him following his outstanding exam results. He said he wanted to become a writer. As for me, I became a maker and mender of fishing nets. Business was good, more or less. I saved some money. In 1913, on my twenty-fifth birthday, I asked Mossane to marry me.

"I can't, Ousseynou. Forgive me but I can't marry you."

"You let me down... What about our promise?"

"Your promise. You made it to yourself, and you made it alone."

I accused her of duplicity. She told me that she loved me enough to not have to marry me; that for that matter, she didn't want to marry anyone for the time being; that there was nothing for her here, in this village; that she wanted to go to the big city up north, to discover something else.

"Discover what?"

"Other possibilities in life."

"Go to him," I said furiously. "He at least won't ask you to marry him. He only wants your body. And you'll give it to him. That's what you want, that's what you've always wanted. To turn your back on all tradition so you can be free to better embrace and justify lust. He understood that and twisted your mind with his stories about the whites. You're not free. You're nothing but a Negress who's turned her back on her own, a girl without honor."

Mossane left me at those ugly, bare-chested words. She left without saying anything back, which was worse than if she had responded to my insult in kind.

For a time, I heard nothing from or about her. My brother stopped returning to the village. I assumed that meant they were living together in the big city. The thought of it began to torment me. I would spend entire nights imagining them, a happy couple amid the lights and dreams of the city. I imagined their bodies intertwined, and that image was killing me even as it refused me the facility of death. I would find myself screaming in the middle of the night, at times cursing Mossane, at others begging her, like a child, to come back.

I was tempted several times to go looking for them, of course. But I was a prideful man. Mossane's absence had me in a state of near madness. Still, my brother's satisfied smile, the smile that I imagined on his lips if he were to see me at his home, pitiful and beseeching in my solitude and my sadness, the idea of that smile, Marème Siga, was unbearable. Better to die a madman than grant him that pleasure. For all that I loved Mossane, I couldn't humiliate myself like that. What would I have said to her after the venomous words I'd spat at her before she left? Apologize? That wouldn't have erased the words. Words can't go against the current of time to prevent their own birth either. I regretted saying them. But deep down, even in that moment, I still thought them: Mossane was deluding herself with the illusion of freedom. She was an African woman who thought it was enough to live provocatively and smoke in public to be like the white women that Assane showed her in magazines. She thought she could be like the female characters in the books my brother read and translated to her. She was weaving dreams out of air. But I loved her that way. I was torn between jealousy, pain, solitude, pride, and love. That was when I started asking myself: Why him?

V

———

One day, three or four months after Mossane left, the pain was too great, and I gave in: I set out for the big city. It was completely foreign to me, and I didn't know where Mossane and my brother were living, but I went anyway.

I arrived after a day and night of travel. The city was animated and noisy. All around me I sensed an energy that was chaotic and generous, furious and beautiful, that could exhaust a man to death or bring a corpse back to life. Wrangling a bit of change, a child loitering in the street agreed to guide me. I placed my hand on his shoulder and we began to walk. He asked me where I wanted him to take me. I told him to head toward the white part of town. The stench of garbage and rot kept my stomach turning, though the smell of the sea, when it penetrated the dense urban chaos, brought occasional relief. I was mesmerized. As I made my way through the city, I forgot the point of my visit and let my surroundings flood over me. The child walked at my rhythm, pleased to have made some money for doing nothing more than accompanying a blind man. We walked through *marchés* where vendors and customers, police officers and criminals, dogs, donkeys, sheep, and cats coexisted. The smell of meat. Then of fresh-caught fish. Hints of spices. Sea salt in the wind. And again, garbage dumps and wastewater. And the voices, the conversations: serious, gay, bawdy, philosophical.

They'd chat for a while, pray for the ancestors to ward off the rough rainy season that had been forecast, praise Serigne the miracle-maker, who was soon to arrive in the city, describe the ass-shaking of a much-vaunted Salimata Diallo, then discuss the upcoming wrestling match, some spirit that had dragged a child out to sea, the sacrifices that needed to be made to the goddess so she wouldn't take others, the romantic sagas of the white governor who had been found drunk, his mustache interwoven with the pubic hairs of a local *dryanké*, divine mercy, the inevitability of man's destiny. In one square, I could hear, between animated arguments, the dry thud of checkers smashing down on a board. I paused for a while to listen to the squabbles, jeers, challenges, and promises of retaliation. I was reminded of my former passion for the game.

The sirens of an ambulance or a police car. Bustle. Curses, commentary. We stopped. A fire? A robbery? No, a man had been arrested, a magnificent vagrant who appeared to be as hated and feared as he was idolized. A woman told me to join the crowd that was going to liberate him. I responded that my path didn't lead that way. She tsk-tsked like a shrew and called me a coward, lamenting, with a tongue fierier than a green pepper, that there were no more men. Or else they were getting softer and softer. Sissies! Peacocks! Women-men! Weaklings! Where are the virile and the brave? The men of yore! May they come to our aid as we liberate the prince of our city! I responded that I wouldn't be of any use to them: I was blind and I wasn't from around there. She asserted that in life, a man, especially if he was young like me, didn't need eyes or to be from somewhere. Oh yeah? Yeah, *Silmaxa*, that's what I'm telling you! Wherever he is, wherever he's from, all a man needs to work and to fight are his balls. I got distracted during the conversation and let go of my young guide's shoulder. He slipped into the crowd. As it started to move, I asked the shrew, on the move too, where I could find the white quarter. Cross the bridge and head north! And once night falls, you better watch out, monsieur "not-from-around-here"! Watch out? For what? For whom? Her answer was lost in the commotion.

A good Samaritan agreed to bring me across the bridge. We reached the colonial quarter. Another world. Silence, order, calm. I could hear myself walking on pavement. I also began to hear the *toubabs*' language. And in their voices, I sensed serenity. Serenity and nothing else. I was on their territory, this was their home—and for a long time to come. Tokô Ngor had told us... I tried asking around, but none of the *toubabs* who spoke our language could help me at first. Nevertheless, I persisted. Eventually a few spoke of an African who had recently started teaching, and who lived with his wife farther north of the island. Nobody knew his name, but when anyone said that they'd seen him before, I asked if he looked like me. Some said yes without hesitation, others responded no, not at all. That was the only lead I had, and I planned to follow it through. As evening approached, I succeeded in finding the man's house. There was a guard in front of it, someone from our parts. He responded coldly to my greeting, and when I asked him if Assane did in fact live there, told me there was no Assane there. With some difficulty I was able to recall the Catholic name that Assane had told me he now went by.

"What do you want with Moussé Paul?"

"I'd like to see him. I'm family. He's my brother."

"*Sa Waay*, Moussé Paul doesn't have a brother."

"I'm telling you he does! Can't you see that we resemble each other like the two half-moons of one ass?"

"Maybe."

"That's more like it!"

"Not so quick. Not all ass cheeks look alike. A butt crack isn't a mirror."

"We're twins!"

"Maybe, brother. But Moussé Paul has never mentioned a brother to me. In any case, he's not expecting visitors. I can only let in the visitors that are expected."

"You're telling me that now it's necessary to announce your visit to a family member before you can see them?"

"That's how it is here. You have to let people know. To be sure they'll be home. Right now, you see, he's not here. If you had let him know, you'd have come at the right time."

"I'll wait for him inside."

"No, you need to leave."

"I'll wait here then."

"Out of the question!"

"How's that?! You can't be serious! The road doesn't belong to you or your father or your great-grandfather. It doesn't belong to your Moussé Paul. It doesn't belong to the *toubabs*. You know the popular saying: *mbedd mi, mbeddu buur la*. It's the king's street, and in the street, everyone is a king. I'll wait if I feel like it."

"I know, *mbokk*, but you need to leave. I don't want any trouble, and neither do you."

"His wife!"

"What about his wife?"

"Her name is Mossane."

"And? You're not telling me anything I don't know."

"You can tell that I know them. I'm not lying. I'm his brother. Tell Mossane I'm here. My name is Ousseynou."

"*Saa Waay*, leave or I'll make you leave. You can't see me, but believe me, I can lift you off the ground with one arm, and one arm only."

"Mossane knows me!"

"Madame Mossane isn't here either. They went on a trip with two of their *toubab* friends. I'm watching the house until they return. That's the truth."

"When will they return?"

"They didn't tell me that."

I remained silent for several minutes, not knowing what to do. I didn't have the luxury of staying in the city long. I had my affairs in the village, and even if I could have remained there a while, thanks to the money I had saved, I knew the city wasn't for me. I felt prey to some impalpable menace. Noting my abruptly pensive mood, the guard again urged me to leave. I felt a violent surge of anger warming my chest. It wasn't directed against the watchman, but against myself, my stupidity, the pathetic spectacle I was making of myself. What had I truly hoped to accomplish by going there? Why had I come to humiliate myself? Was the love of a woman who had chosen another worth all that? Where were my dignity and my honor? I cursed Mossane and Assane and left without a word to the sentry.

It was getting colder, and I could sense, within my darkness, that shadows were slowly eating away at the day. I heard a call to prayer in the distance. It was too late to get back to the train station and return to the village. I needed to find a place to sleep. But I knew no one. So I crossed the bridge again, this time without help, and headed for the outskirts of the city. I had heard that I could find a cheap bed there. Someone pointed me to an inn. Modest price. Basic amenities but decent. It even included dinner, which I ate with little appetite. I was about to return to my room when the manager, handing me back my key, asked me point-blank if I wanted some company. Without thinking, I said yes. I even requested whichever girl customers asked for most, the most expensive one. I paid up. At the time, I thought I was doing this out of sadness or hopelessness. Now, I know that it was mainly out of anger. I wanted to pass that anger on to someone else. A prostitute will do nicely, I told myself. The one who came that night endured my rage. I penetrated her cruelly and violently. Before she left I asked her name. Those were the first words I spoke to her.

Her: Salimata. Me: Salimata what? Her: Salimata Diallo. Me: So it's your ass everyone in town is talking about? Her: Yes, it's mine, and now you know why. Me: Very true.

She left. I expected to have trouble sleeping, but I fell into a deep slumber. The next day, I felt guilty for having sex with Salimata Diallo. I returned to the village somewhat ashamed, and accepted that I would no longer hear from Mossane or my brother. Which, in a way, brought me relief. I resumed my life here.

A few months later, the war broke out, and France charged into the fray. Of course it dragged along its little house dogs too. Our country, the most docile of the litter, included. I remember when the black French deputy came from Paris, accompanied by white officials, to find men who wanted to fight for France, the motherland. He came all the way here, to the village. He spoke and I felt like I was hearing Assane, but a more clever, more seductive version. He promised things to anyone who would go fight for the *toubabs*. Glory, the gratitude of the republic, medals, money, land, riches, eternity in a heroic heaven, oh how he promised and he did it well and many believed him.

But they didn't say a word to me. An invalid wouldn't have been of any help to them. They needed men with eyes to see the bullets, to see the enemy, to take clear aim at his head and shoot him dead, but also eyes to see their friends fall, and to cry when they were alone in the belly of the earth, where all aid was impossible, wondering why they had to die for a country that wasn't even their own in an absurd slaughter. Many men from the village, from my generation and older ones, believed the black French deputy and his friends. They went to war and left behind children and wives.

Then came that evening at the end of 1914. I'll never forget it. I was about to perform the *timis* prayer when I heard footsteps in the court.

"Who's there?"

"It's me."

I would have recognized his voice anywhere.

"What are you doing here?"

"I came to see you."

"Who's with you?"

No response.

"Who's with you?"

"It's me, Mossane."

Her voice, however, had changed. It had lost its former youthfulness and combativeness. Another pause, a terrible pause. We were the three points of a triangle of bitter memories, of questions without answers, of loathing and love. We knew we were linked and we hated each other for it. Assane spoke: "I need your help, Ousseynou."

I snorted. He immediately said: "You can laugh, of course, it's your right. In your position, I'd have laughed too. After everything that's happened, it might feel unreal that I'm asking for your help."

"It's mostly ironic."

"True. But I'm still going to ask for your help because you're my brother. I wouldn't do it if I had a choice."

"I don't care that you have no choice. I'm not your brother anymore, Assane."

"Whether you like it or not, whether I like it or not, we are brothers. Blood flows from a spring more distant than the flesh. It flows from the spring of a faraway past, and its torrent carries along a history in which we're not alone. The link between us doesn't concern us alone."

"I don't see who else it might concern. What do you want? No long speeches. I need to do my prayers."

"I'm going to France. I'm going to war."

"And? That's your path, not mine."

"We're expecting a child."

I said nothing, stunned, and after a few seconds, my brother continued: "Mossane and I are going to have a child. I want to leave them with someone I trust, until I return. You and I never got along. Maybe we never loved each other. But if there's one person to whom I can entrust my greatest secret, knowing that it will be well kept, it's you."

"You're a hypocrite, Assane Koumakh."

"Believe that if you like. But answer me: Can you take care of Mossane and my child during my absence?"

"You're a hypocrite, that I knew, but you're also irresponsible. How can you go fight for France and leave your wife and child here?"

"I'm fighting for this child too. Not only for France. By fighting for France, I'm also fighting so that he or she will grow up in a world at peace."

"Don't pretend you're fighting for the child. You've never fought for anyone. All that matters to you is yourself, and that the French acknowledge you! Stop trying to ease your conscience: admit that you prefer France over your flesh and blood. At least have the courage to say it. And did she believe you when you told her that? Huh, Mossane? I'm talking to you now. Did you believe it, when he told you he was going to fight for your child's future? He's lying! And you're going to let him leave like this?"

"I'm not lying."

"He's abandoning you both."

"I'm not abandoning them."

"Let Mossane speak!"

"I'm the one who came to see you."

"She's here too, and she's the one carrying the child."

"Let's go, Assane," said Mossane. "I told you."

I sensed a great frailty in her voice. I didn't recognize it. In the preceding months, every time I thought of her, a deep, dull anger had burned inside me, devouring me. Since she left, I had been dreaming of the day I would get the chance to blanket her with my hate, the day when I would be able to unleash, without restraint, the disgust she inspired in me and the violence into which my disappointment at losing her had transformed. That day had finally arrived. Mossane was there, in front of me. But hearing her so weak, so resigned, it wasn't rage that came over me, but pity.

"For once in your life," I said, "think of others, Assane. Think of the life of your child."

"I have to go to France," said my brother.

"Why?"

"Out of duty."

"You know nothing of this war. It's not your fight."

"Yes, it is. It's everyone's fight, even if it seems far away. It's yours too. It'll be quick."

"How would you know?"

"The *toubab* officers say so. They know."

"They're not Roog. They know nothing!"

"France is going to win quickly with the help of its African sons and brothers."

"Sons and brothers? No: you mean slaves. You'll all die for France. And it will forget you."

"I won't die."

"Don't challenge the future. You can't see what it holds."

"I'll come back for the child."

"It'd be better to stay for the child."

"I already enlisted. I'm leaving. I'm going to northern France. That's where I'll be."

"I couldn't care less where you'll be. No matter what, it will be far from your child. What kind of man are you?"

At that Assane let out a harsh laugh. Then he said: "Don't judge me, Ousseynou Koumakh. Contrary to what you think, you know nothing about me. You believe that you know who I am, that you understand what drives my heart. You understand nothing. You can't penetrate men's souls. What you think to be the whole truth is merely one fragment among a thousand fragments. You're one shadow among a thousand shadows cast. You don't know what I've had to sacrifice these last few years. The paths I took are stained with mud. And anyone who claims to follow me will be as well. Don't judge me. Your court of conscience isn't..."

"Keep your fancy phrases and your lectures, Assane. I do judge you. Yes, I'm judging you because I know you. I know you better than you know yourself, and always have. You're a despicable man. I think you know that too, deep down. Or maybe you truly don't. In which case, in all sincerity, I hope you realize it as late as possible, once you've lived a long life. Because on that day, you might no longer have the capacity that you have now to stand yourself."

At that moment, Mossane began to cry, and Assane didn't respond. I heard him whisper a few words to her, which I couldn't make out, words of comfort, no doubt. The village, as though it wanted to add to the drama unfolding in that courtyard, blanketed us with dense silence. Mossane was still sobbing. Then my heart spoke. I said:

"Mossane can stay if she wants. But Assane, if you decide to go to fight in this war, you'll leave tomorrow as soon as possible. You already know the house: there are two free bedrooms. Pick one and get settled."

Then I returned to my bedroom and did my prayer, which I extended with a long meditation, during which I asked God to guide me. When I reemerged, almost an hour later, Mossane was alone in the courtyard.

"Where's Assane?"

"He left so he wouldn't miss the last taxi-charrette that goes to the city. He wanted to say a few final things to you, but his boat departs the day after tomorrow. He needed to get back to the city tonight to prepare for his trip. I'm to tell you goodbye for him and thank you."

"I don't need a thank-you from him, and I don't care whether he tells me goodbye or even if I ever see him again. He's not the one I'm helping. As for you, I don't want your thank-yous. Or your apologies."

"I don't want yours either."

I remembered the bare-chested words I had said to her before, and I felt ashamed. We made a pact in the silence that followed. I returned to my room, torn between anger, shame, and joy. Mossane had come back. But she had come back carrying the fruit of her and Assane's love. Why him?

VI

——

Four months later, in March 1915, the child was born. His father, before he left, had asked, if it was a boy, that Mossane give him Tokô Ngor's middle name, his never-used Muslim name: Elimane. It was a boy. I gave him his traditional name. Madag. Elimane Madag Diouf.

As you may have guessed already, Assane never saw his son. He didn't come back from the war. We never heard from him. No one knows what became of his body. He surely got lost in time and in History. Like so many others that the Great War ground to dust, swallowed, erased. I think about him sometimes and I feel nothing, not anger or pity. Even my contempt has faded. I don't miss him. I didn't love him when he was alive. I didn't love him dead. Our lives, intertwined as they were from the very start, advanced in opposing directions. He was a man blinded by his love for France, a love greater than any other he felt inside himself. It ended up consuming him. I think he knew from the start that he wouldn't be coming back. I even wonder whether he secretly wanted to die. What more fitting way for him to become white than to die in a white man's war, on white land, from a white bullet or bayonet blade? His dream couldn't come true in this lifetime, and so he needed another one—a life in the skin of a white intellectual; that, to him, was the summit of existential achievement. Not being a father, not loving Mossane, but being an intelligent white man who reads or writes books. And so he went to his death willingly, in the hope, perhaps, of reincarnating as his dream. Sometimes I wonder how he met his end. I wonder what his final thoughts were. Did he think about our childhood, about Tokô Ngor, about Mère Mboyil's voice as she called us *néné*, about me, about Mossane, about the white missionaries who educated him, about the son he had abandoned and would never see? Did he die alone? Violently? Did he suffer? Did he have time to realize he was dying? I don't wonder all that out of empathy for Assane. I wonder because I'm fascinated by people's final moments. Only then can we assess, have a worthwhile regret, make a sincere confession, only then can we take a truthful look at ourselves. The moment our lives slip away is when they belong to us.

I won't linger on Elimane's childhood, or my life with Mossane in the years after. The weeks that followed Mossane's return were very hard for both of us. We were living in the same house, but were separated by deep chasms, the kind dug by resentment and the wounds of the past. Then time did its job. Elimane Madag arrived. I found myself in the same position with him as my Uncle Ngor had with us years earlier. I was responsible for my brother's progeny.

Did I love Elimane? I still don't know. Some days, I would hear Assane's voice in his infant babbling. And on occasion, in his pure laughter, I even *saw* Assane. He radiated innocence, but at times all the hatred I'd felt for his father would eclipse him. Can you hold a child responsible for a past he's never known? Is he the inevitable heir to the events that preceded him? Can he be blamed for the mistakes of his forebears? Blamed for being the living trace of who his ancestors were, the custodian of what they did? Most men would respond no to these questions. They would be right, no doubt. And yet, I have doubts. I had doubts. When I touched Elimane wrapped up in his swaddling clothes, I would wonder, though he was just a baby, why wouldn't he be anything like his father? Why should he be absolved of the past? Was he completely new, with no connection to his history? Assane used to say that blood came from a distant source whose current surpassed individuals. Wasn't Elimane linked to Assane by more than simple filiation? There were days when I answered yes: Elimane was the fruit of Assane's desire. Before becoming his flesh and blood, he had been an idea in his mind, or at least the horizon of Assane's carnal obsession for one woman. Some profound part of what my brother once was had settled inside of Elimane like silt on the bottom of a lake, the lake of blood. Elimane, even if he contested it, even if he took different paths, would continue his father's history. He could even hate him later, consider him to be the most despicable man there was: that still wouldn't take away the part of Assane inside of him, a part that's not only physical but also mythological—a part of the void from which every man emerges. Once again, my uncle Ngor's words came back to me: what he had said about the thorn of white civilization planted in the flesh of our civilization, with no way to remove it, was true of Assane and Elimane as well.

Elimane would drag Assane's shadow and memory with him everywhere he went. He was that memory, he was that shadow. And for that alone, I knew he would always remind me of my brother. He would never be rid of him. None of us can rid ourselves of our history when it's the shameful kind. It can't be abandoned in the middle of the night like an unwanted child. You fight it, you're always fighting, and the only way to win is to keep fighting, to accept it, acknowledge it, endlessly try to designate it, name it, flush it out of hiding where it's gone to draw you closer. Does what I'm saying strike you as horrible? You're allowed. You can think that telling a child that the shadow of his forebears will forever be cast upon him, even if he kills or forgets them, is awful. You can think that, Siga. But deep down, you know I'm not wrong. You of all people should understand that. You may have imagined killing me, and wanted to kill me, you can even kill me in the books you'll write—you might not believe in my premonitions but I saw that you'll write books later on, books in which you'll kill me with your words—but I'm here and I'll always be here. I'm your thorn. Take me out and you'll die. And even dead, I'll still be here.

Elimane wouldn't escape Assane. Neither would I. Neither would Mossane. It was going to be a struggle for all of us to keep those two faces from merging into one in our minds. Elimane would suffer his whole life. There. That's what I thought the first time I heard him crying in his mother's arms.

So, did I love him? Yes, off and on. I cared for him more than I hated him. Because yes, I hated him, at times, when I heard him playing in the courtyard or talking to his mother. But I did love him. I loved him because I loved Mossane. The months of anger hadn't changed my feelings toward her. The opposite, in fact; the period during which I had hated Mossane hadn't destroyed my love for her, but rather shown me its necessity, and the deep reasons behind it. By threatening destruction, that interlude of disappointment revived my love. And so I decided, for and with Mossane, to raise Elimane as best I could.

We agreed to tell him the truth about his father once he turned seven. We did as we'd said. It was all the easier since Elimane proved to be an exceptionally alert and quick-witted child, curious and intelligent, precocious and attentive. In all those respects, he resembled his father, who had revealed similar aptitudes at a young age. But Elimane didn't display his talents with the sole aim of seduction. Unlike his father, there was a profound sadness inside him—I noticed this early on—that accompanied his impatient intelligence. He was a playful, energetic, and sociable child, but he also craved solitude and shadow in a way his father never had. He would gladly play with other children, talk like them, laugh like them, make mischief like them. But there always came a moment when he would disappear into the brush around the village, or remain inside the house despite his mother's encouragements to go out. In that sense, he was already a bit odd: his cheerfulness was contagious, and vivacious, the glimmers of an uncommon wit already apparent; but from a very young age, he also knew how to let the silence take over. I didn't need to see him to know or feel that. He merely had to speak to me, on certain days, for me to sense that inclination immediately. We forget that children have their own melancholy to carry, and for better or worse, they may feel it more intensely, for at that stage of life, nothing is felt halfway: the world comes rushing inside us with all its force and through every portal of our still-tender souls. It wreaks its havoc without regard for our age, before retreating just as violently. Then comes the time during which we learn to understand, to flee, to shut down, to pretend, to trick, to heal more quickly. Or to die. Still, time remains the perennial teacher. But it takes time to learn from time. Children are only at the beginning of theirs.

At the beginning of his time, Elimane already sensed all that. Maybe he understood it. Or so I used to wonder when, on occasion, he'd ask me about darkness, life in the absence of light, perceptions of the world, recognizing things, the sharpened use of other senses, the memory of preserved images, what I remembered of his mother's face. One day he said to me:

"Tokô Ousseynou, who's worse off: the blind man who's never seen, who's blind from birth, or a blind man like you, who went blind after having seen? What's worse: never having seen and desiring sight, or having seen?"

I thought about it for several days but couldn't decide. I asked his opinion.

"I think the unhappier man is he who has seen, Tokô Ousseynou."

"Why? Because he's seen the beauty of the world and he feels its loss, and loss or regret is more painful than desire?"

"No," he replied. "He's unhappier because he sees in his memory that there is beauty in the world. But he doesn't know that what he remembers no longer exists because the world changes. Every day has its own beauty. But the main reason the blind man who has seen is unhappy is because his memory keeps him from imagining. He dedicates so much energy to not forgetting that he forgets that he can reinvent what he's seen, and invent what he will never see again. And a man without imagination, blind or not, is always unhappy. But you're not like that. You've seen, but you still know how to imagine things to see."

He must have been about ten at the time. He was a precocious boy. Mossane was devoted to him. I had feared (or maybe hoped, deep down) that she would hate her son. That like me, she saw Assane in him and would reject him for that reason. That seeing him would remind her that his father had abandoned them both. It was mostly her he had abandoned. He had left her alone, pregnant with their child, to go fight halfway across the world, in the country that he loved more than her and their future child. He had preferred to die there rather than live here with her and Elimane. But Mossane loved her son madly. Her intense maternal devotion came in part from the desire not to abandon Elimane to his father's history alone, the history of a man who had turned his back on them.

As for Elimane himself, I never really knew what he thought of his father. Did he hate him? Did he wish he'd known him? Was he indifferent? He never brought him up around me. I don't know whether he did around his mother. In any case, as far as I was concerned, Elimane never asked any questions.

Up until his tenth birthday, in agreement with his mother, I taught him the fundamentals of the Koran, but also the foundations of our traditional culture, where Roog Sene is the supreme spirit and the *pangool* the spirits of our ancestors. Those two cultures had formed me, and I wanted him to understand them. As usual, he was curious about both currents of knowledge, whose rudiments he learned with enthusiasm and impatience. I imparted to him the kinds of knowledge that are typically only acquired at manhood. I taught him many things, things that you can't imagine. But he absorbed them so quickly, asked so many questions, and forced me to think as well...He wanted to go further, ever further. He backed me into corners. It was as if, as young as he was, he was looking for something. As if he was rushing to learn and digest new knowledge in search of an answer, a secret. I wonder whether he came into the world with his question, Marème Siga. I really do. As a child (and later, a teenager), he was in a hurry. Thirsty. Waiting, but also poised to strike. Something was boiling inside him. That something was rising over his mind's horizon, and he wanted to reach it quickly. I was certain he had already lived several lives before this one. But unlike other people, he hadn't forgotten any of what he had learned in those previous existences. That's the impression he always gave me.

When he was ten, against my wishes, Mossane enrolled him at the French school. A mission had been established in a village a few miles from ours. You no longer needed to go to the city to find a white man's school, which, after Assane's experience, I had come to view as hostile. I no longer simply feared their teachings. I hated them—which is perhaps the ultimate form of fear. What the *toubabs* had made of Assane, or encouraged in him, led me to believe that such an education would inevitably destroy in us Africans the deepest parts of our being. That the school would uproot everything that, for ten years, we had tried to sow inside Elimane. But inexplicably, Mossane would hear nothing of it. Was it Assane's desire? She told me no, that she was the one who wanted her son to also receive a Western education. The evening we fought about it, one of the rare occasions I had felt anger toward Mossane since her return, I remember accusing her of sending him to the same slaughterhouse where Assane died. So you've lost your memory, is that it? Look what they did to Assane! Look what they did to you! She gently responded that Elimane wasn't Assane. That's when I understood that, in a way, Mossane was trying, through Elimane, to get even with Assane, to erase his memory. She wanted to steer Elimane down the same paths, and prove to my brother that his son could follow them without being splattered with mud.

Elimane displayed exceptional abilities at the French school. The missionaries that oversaw his education were so impressed by the speed with which he absorbed their lessons that one day they came to see us. They wanted to congratulate us, but also to ask where he had acquired his gift for learning, memorization, reflection. I let Mossane answer. I knew what she would say. And indeed, she spoke at length about Assane, who had been just as gifted. It was his genes, she told Father Greusard, the parish priest who ran the mission. He had come all the way to our home on his moped, flanked by an interpreter. When Mossane spoke about Assane, I understood that there was a part of her that would remain eternally linked to him. This saddened me, but I tried not to let anything show. Did she see that I was hurt, despite my efforts to maintain my composure? I don't know, but immediately after talking about Assane and his genes, she added that I had taught Elimane, before he started school, about the Koran and animist culture. That, she said, had opened his brain, had made it permeable to knowledge. Father Greusard congratulated me, but I sincerely believe that all the merit belonged to Elimane. I remember that Mossane was jubilant that night, beaming with pride for her son. I, however, was overcome with worry after Father Greusard's enthusiastic visit. I couldn't avoid seeing what my nephew was becoming: a product of the Western school, less alienated than his father, perhaps, but just as thirsty for the knowledge he was discovering and the seductiveness of the French language. Elimane spent a great deal of time at Father Greusard's home, which had a large library. That fascinated Elimane Madag, and once he learned how to read, Father Greusard used to invite him over regularly.

Allow me a brief digression: you might be wondering if Mossane and I got married in the meantime. We didn't. She never wanted to get married. But in 1918, when the war ended and we still had no news of Assane, I asked her if we could share a bedroom. She agreed. In 1920, she got pregnant. But the child she was carrying didn't survive. It was a stillbirth, which was common in the villages back then. After that, all our repeated attempts failed. I was saddened not to be able to have a child with the woman I loved. Mossane was sad too, but she found some consolation in Elimane's education. She told me that if we couldn't have a child, we needed to accept it, and added that she wouldn't be opposed to me taking another wife in order to have children of my own. I told her the problem might come from me, that I might be the one who was sterile. Mossane told me no, that she'd known since birthing the stillborn baby that something had moved inside of her. At that time, I didn't feel like I could marry and love a woman other than her. Despite her insistence, I decided not to take another wife and tried, like Mossane, to find my happiness in her and her son, since they were the family that fate had given me.

And so life went on, its rhythm set by Elimane's scholarly exploits. He soon became one of the favorites in the village. He had inherited intelligence and presence from his father; beauty and calm strength from his mother. And from me? What had he gotten from me? Other things. Other knowledge.

VII

—

In 1935, at the age of twenty, after passing the baccalaureate (with, said Father Greusard, scores never seen from a native), Elimane was offered the chance to go to France to continue his studies. He asked our opinion. I opposed his leaving. Once again, I saw his father's hand and shadow. But Mossane encouraged him to go. I couldn't talk her out of it. She appeared so happy about what her son was becoming that I didn't dare share my fears. Father Greusard had connections. He handled everything, and succeeded, by insisting on the exceptional character of this African whom one might compare to a young genius, in securing him a spot at a prestigious boarding school. He also got Elimane one of the few scholarships the colonial administration allotted to remarkable natives. It would allow him to live comfortably. He was to prepare for the entrance exam for the most prestigious French school at the time, one that produced intellectuals, thinkers, writers, presidents of France, and professors. Elimane's eyes, Mossane told me, shone whenever he mentioned it. From then on, it became clear that he had to go. Like his father.

Elimane left us near the end of the rainy season, in 1935. The night before his departure, we spent the evening together in the courtyard. Mossane was singing softly. I sensed that Elimane wanted to say something. Or wanted us to say something to him. Maybe he was realizing, for the first time, that he was following in his father's footsteps, and that he was reaching the stage where Assane had lost his way. Maybe he wanted to ask us what he should do, what was going to happen. Was he afraid of ending up like his father? I don't know. He said nothing. Mossane stopped singing. The night—I felt it—was deep, inhabited by a great and beautiful sadness, unless that sadness was simply my own.

"Go in peace, son. Remain the man that you are and everything will be fine. Don't forget where you come from, or who you are. Don't forget the mother you're leaving behind."

"Yes, Tokô Ousseynou, I promise."

He was holding back tears. I decided not to say anything more, to avoid making an already solemn moment any heavier. A moment later, he said:

"Mother, I'll come back. I won't lose myself there. I'll come back and you'll be proud of me."

"I know, Eli. You'll come back and I'll wait for you. I'm your mother. You're going to be a great man. I've dreamt it many times. But you'll come back."

She finished her song, and we stayed there without saying another word until tiredness set in. Assane's face was floating above us, and it was by turns smiling, troubled, hard, bloodied, serene, tender, enigmatic.

His first year living in France, Elimane wrote to us. It wasn't often, but every two or three months we received a letter. He would tell us about his life in Paris, describe the people he met, the astonishing things he saw, the friends he'd made, the whites and the Africans he encountered. He also told us about the entrance exam he was preparing for, and his studies, which were difficult but enriching. Father Greusard, who received the letters, would bring them to us and have them translated by his interpreter. Mossane would hold on to the letter and sometimes spend hours looking at it with an expression both happy and sad, even though she couldn't read very well. She took the letters with her.

Starting in 1937, there were fewer and fewer letters from Elimane, and soon, none at all. After a few months with no word, Mossane went to see the missionary and begged him to write to her son on her behalf. He did, but Elimane didn't respond. My heart tightens when I think about those months, because I know that that was when Mossane began to waste away. In the face of Elimane's abrupt silence, she felt like she was reliving Assane's disappearance and silence, though he had never written at all. This was the start of Mossane's tragedy (and part of mine): Assane and Elimane, the man she chose and the son they had together, had both left. For all their differences, they shared the same fate, to leave and not come back, and the same dream too: become learned men in the culture that subjugated and abused their own.

What possible explanation can there be? A personal failing, built into their genes? The powerful seductiveness of white civilization? Was it cowardice? Self-loathing? I don't know. And that ignorance is at the heart of the whole saga. The white man came, and some of our bravest sons went mad. Beyond mad. Madly in love with their own masters. Assane and Elimane were among those madmen. They left Mossane, and she began to lose her mind in her turn.

You're starting to see where I'm going with this, Siga. I'll tell you again: you were in your mother's belly, I put my hand on that belly, there was a bright flash in my mind. Within that light I saw your face between theirs: Elimane's and Assane's. The ones who left. I knew before you were born that you would follow them. That your fate would lead you far from our culture. I saw that you, too, would seek intelligence in the language spoken by the French. You would become a writer. It's not because your mother died while giving you life that I didn't love you. It's because when you came into the world you reopened my rawest wound and my most painful memory. You were the third cursed member of the family, heir to the two men who caused me the most pain on this earth. The truth is I don't hate you; I fear you. You frightened me even from your mother's belly. You were a harbinger of new tragedies. Assane may have been right. The mysteries of blood defy all logic and go beyond individual reasoning: you are my biological daughter, but in spirit, Siga, in spirit and in your heart even, you belong to Elimane's blood, to Assane's blood. They had already destroyed my family. They had destroyed the woman I loved. And you—I knew this—would do the same thing: you would destroy something or someone. There. Now you know.

Then the voice went quiet for a while. I kept my eyes shut. I was back in Amsterdam. Several small boats were gliding down the canal. The inebriated revelers aboard were bellowing a chant I recognized: it belonged to the repertory of Ajax Amsterdam fans and was dedicated to Johan Cruyff, the greatest soccer player in the country's history. The voice resumed. I followed it into the past.

I'm almost done, Marème Siga, grant me your attention for a few more minutes.

It was 1938, and Elimane hadn't written in over a year. We'd received no news of him, and the letters that we had had Father Greusard write went unanswered. It was as if he'd vanished. Then we began to imagine the worst: he was dead. Mossane sank further inside herself. More and more often, I'd hear her speaking, crying, praying, muttering to herself. At night, she would wake up in the middle of a nightmare, drenched in sweat, repeating Elimane's name. Her fall had begun, and it seemed unavoidable.

In August 1938, something happened. I heard the putt-putt of Father Greusard's motorbike. A few seconds later he entered our courtyard, out of breath. Mossane wasn't there. I was mending an old fishing net.

"He wrote," he said (after a few years here, the priest had begun speaking our language).

"Who wrote?"

"Elimane. Our Elimane. Your nephew."

I was speechless for a moment.

"You have the letter?"

"Yes. But it's not just a letter, Ousseynou. He wrote something else. He wrote a book."

"A book?"

"A book!"

"Like the ones in your library?"

"Yes!"

"Where is this book?"

"I have it right here."

"The letter too?"

"Yes. Do you want me to translate it for you?"

"That won't be necessary. We'll ask one of the students from your mission. Our neighbor's son reads your language very well. He'll help us. Thank you, Father Greusard."

"What about the book? That student might not be able to perfectly translate the whole thing. I can come back and do it for you, if you like."

"Yes, but not today. Another day, if you can. Today, we'll just read the letter."

"As you like...Our Elimane is becoming a great man, Ousseynou, he's becoming a giant. Tell his mother that her son is becoming a great man."

Father Greusard handed me the letter and the book, then left in a rush. I fondled these two objects that were meant to bring me relief and joy, but which filled me with grief. So, Elimane was alive. He was alive and had sent no sign of life. He had become a writer, had taken the time to write all those pages, and not a single one to his mother for one year. I can still feel the warm knot of anger in my chest at that moment. I made the decision not to say or show anything to Mossane. It was an easy decision to make, even though it had serious consequences. I don't regret it, despite everything it brought about. I'd do it again. If I had to do it again, I would still hide her son's letter and book from Mossane. Knowing that he was alive, that he had written a book during all that time without sending one word to her, knowing all that, in the state she was in, would have been the end of her. So I hid Elimane's novel among my personal affairs. It wasn't the moment for him to resurface in our lives, which he had already wounded by disappearing. I could have burned the book or ripped it apart and gotten rid of it forever. So why didn't I? Because I sensed that it was a very powerful object. I sensed that Elimane had put part of his soul in it. But mostly because the second I held the book in my hands, I knew that it would still have a role to play in our lives. I wasn't sure what, but I knew that. So I hid the book in a place where nobody would ever be able to find it. As for the letter, I destroyed it on the spot, not bothering to find out what it contained. In destroying the letter, in hiding the book, I'd had the impression I was protecting Mossane.

I never found out what was in that book. Father Greusard had a bad motorbike accident a few days after his visit and was taken to the city, where he was treated for many months before succumbing to his head injuries. He was the only person in the village besides me who knew that Elimane had written that book and sent a letter. He hadn't told Mossane. She never found out. I had decided not to mention any of it, and took Elimane's continued silence as reassurance that I had made the right decision. Even after the book was published, he didn't write. He gave no further sign of life. I even had doubts as to whether he was the book's author. Maybe it was another Elimane. Maybe ours had met with a terrible fate a long time ago. Or maybe, simply enough, he had decided to break the promise made to his mother the night before he left. Instead of coming home, as he had pledged, maybe he had quite simply chosen another life, elsewhere.

Mossane's state deteriorated in early 1939. Lunacy tightened its grip on her. She began spending her days beneath the mango tree. She would stare at the cemetery where we had buried our stillborn child. She told me once that she was thinking about that child—it had been a girl. But I also knew that when she stared at the cemetery, she was thinking about Assane and Elimane, whose bodies had disappeared. In truth, by staring at the village cemetery, she was trying to offer them a mental cemetery, an imagined grave for the two bodies she had so loved and who had abandoned her. Her mind was their shared tomb. In the middle of 1939, I left for my initiation by the Sufi sheik just as another war, said the news, was breaking out in Europe. My personal war was here. I had to wage it against Mossane's madness. I decided to try to take care of her on my own. You know the rest of the story. My failure. The mango tree. My regular visits. My question. Mossane's silence.

I'm coming back to that day in 1945. Mossane had put her hand on mine. She had reemerged to answer me. I'd seen it in a premonitory dream. I'd waited. I had been waiting thirty years for her to tell me why she had chosen him, *him*, rather than me. She said: "You're the one I chose. The proof is that I'm here, and you're here too, Ousseynou, with me. But I'm tired. Come back tomorrow and I'll tell you more. I'm tired today, I need the earth to shake."

I was so stirred by the sound of her voice—which I hadn't heard in at least five years—that I didn't want to upset her by asking all the questions jostling around in my heart. I hadn't understood what she said about needing the earth to shake, but it didn't matter. I went home. I returned the next day. Mossane was gone. I looked for her everywhere, for days and days. She had vanished. Some of the villagers, who lived not far from the mango tree, said they had seen her at night, going into the cemetery. They never saw her come back out. But that version seemed too much like the beginning of a legend for me to believe it. I kept looking, but after a few weeks (I even returned to the city), I had to come to terms with her disappearance, which marked the moment one chapter of my life came to a definitive end. It took me a very long time to accept that Mossane was gone. I never grieved for her. I was never able to and I never wanted to. Every night for over thirty years, I've hoped to hear her walk through that door. I'll probably die still hoping. I met your mother years after Mossane's disappearance. You were born fifteen years after she left the shade of the mango tree. In my darkness, all I see is her. And though I loved and still love Coura, Ngoné, and Dib, though I loved your mother, in my dreams it's Mossane who appears. I see her the way I saw her so many years ago, in the water, when I lost my eyes. She's naked and smiling. Some nights, I cry. Some nights, I'm angry at her. I wonder where she went. I also wonder what she would have told me if she had been there the next day, like she promised. But ultimately, it doesn't matter. She gave me an answer.

I wanted to tell you all this. I know you'll leave, toward your destiny, and that I probably won't ever see you again. You needed to know this before we parted ways. I'm not asking you to...

"I don't forgive you," I told him, gathering what was left of my courage. "I don't forgive you for damning me from my mother's belly to be unlovable. I see you and I hate you. With every ounce of my being. I hate you. As a child, I wanted so badly for you to love me that my hatred now is just the flip side of that dead love. My curse is that I did love you, deep down. But nothing remains of that love that you never reciprocated. Explaining all this to me changes nothing. I despise you even more. I don't forgive you."

He responded calmly: "I'm not asking for your forgiveness, Marème Siga. I just want you to know. I wasn't able to love you for the reasons I gave you. You can blame me for the rest of your life if that's what your heart tells you. I wouldn't blame you. In your position, I'd probably have hated me too. But remember: even if you hate me, I'll always be here. That's all. I just have to give you one thing. It's my last will and testament. Your inheritance. After this, you can leave. So can I."

Then, said Siga D., my father stuck his hand under his pillow and pulled out a book. He gave it to me without a word, and said nothing more. That's how I got *The Labyrinth of Inhumanity*. The copy I gave you is the one my father had been keeping among his belongings since 1938. And since that night in 1980, since that confession, I've carried the book with me. The book written by Elimane Madag, alias T.C. Elimane, my cousin.

I opened my eyes. The Spider-Mother was staring at the couch. Her father's body had stopped moving. Soon it began to gently fade, and eventually disappeared entirely, with a wheeze, carrying into the shadows his faithful spit jar filled with sand and saliva.

Second Biographeme

Three cries as the earth shakes

...and also what's with everyone asking me questions as if I didn't have enough worries to deal with as it is, I'm getting a little annoyed but not for real, just so we're clear, because deep down, down in my hole, it actually suits me, what I mean is I don't mind the earth's question, it gives me a chance to make it move, I know talking about this will make it move, though I don't know why it seems so important, but anyway, that's the earth's business, I stopped asking myself why things are important to people or things, they are, that's all, everyone lives with whatever it is that stirs their hearts and it might seem incomprehensible to others but it's not up to them to decide what's important or not, nobody is anybody else, everyone is everyone, everyone, all while seeming like everyone else, is only, first and forever, themselves, none of us are inside someone else's heart or mind, and all the better actually, especially for the mind, I think that that's where the worst of it happens, what happens in the mind is chaos, in mine in any case, and I imagine that in other minds things aren't any tidier, even if everyone pretends to be perfectly stable and sane, which makes me laugh because I know, believe me I know, that all it would take is for me to take a good look at them and then the jumble in their minds would slip down to their eyes and once it's there nothing can stay hidden, the eyes are indiscreet, can't hope to hide anything there, but anyway, I'm getting away from the earth's question, I'm going to answer it without trying to understand why this is the question driving it, even though I have an idea, I'm going to answer and hope that the earth moves, which would do me lots of good, and so I answer *I don't know* to the earth's question, and sure enough, it began to shudder, which proves that I know it well, I knew that it would get upset and tremble, but I like when there's trembling around me, it's when the world trembles that I feel good: my vision clears, like all of a sudden someone put those things on my nose, glasses I think they're called, and they fix your sight, to make a long story short this is how it goes, the world moves and things fall into focus, they fall back into my rhythm and the beating of my heart, the world doesn't move and it's only my body that trembles and then everything shifts, but I know that it's not reality that's shifted, it only shifted because I did, yes, I'm the first to shift, everything stirs inside of me, I'm a bodyquake of varying magnitude, it depends on my mood, and I can't find harmony and stability again unless the earth shakes, from anger or cold or laughter or thirst or joy or sickness or tears or excitement or anything it wants, the earth needs to tremble so that I can live, otherwise it's the nothingness that awaits me, when the earth is still, my body alone trembles and it's the nothingness that looms, but to be honest it doesn't bother me, nothingness is less frightening than they say, but you shouldn't stay there too long, because behind the nothingness there's something else even more frightening, but I don't know its name, I don't think there's a word for it, for that thing that comes after nothingness and that I'm afraid of, I'm not ashamed to say that, and if I want to steer clear or push it back then I have to provoke the earth like I've just done by answering its question, and it works, it started to quake so I kept going, *I don't know*, but it doesn't matter, not knowing doesn't matter at all, and I don't want to know; all that counts is that...I think, I don't know...but is it really so important? it's me that counts, the rest isn't important, for him, it's me that counts, me, his mother, it's me that counts, as for the father, it has no real importance, he'll choose whom he wants between the two, Assane or Ousseynou, Ousseynou or Assane, it's not important, it's almost the same thing. even though they're very different, what counts is me, Mossane, the mother, his mother;

...it's rumbling, I feel better, I feel better, the quaking goes all the way down, the roots tense like bowstrings, I feel better, I'm myself and no one else, the leaves of the mango tree sway above me and gently whisper, you are you and entirely you, Mossane, whom everyone desires and whom no one dares approach anymore except for him, but I don't know if he's here for himself or for me, to get an answer to his question or to ask me mine, but no matter, he's here, he never left, he's trying to save me without knowing from what, so he comes and we sit in silence and each think about the past, about our choices, about all the what-ifs that can torment us, what if we had done this instead of that, and what if I had said this instead of that, what if what if what if, and enough already, it leads to regret, to straying into the impossible dream of fixing the past and going back in time, which can turn a person bitter, but I don't want bitterness, I have pain and I have waiting and that's plenty for me, I want to enjoy this rumbling of the earth because when the ground gets angry everything inside me calms, everything returns to order, everything moves and everything stops moving, I see clearly, so I look at the cemetery, which stopped scaring me a long time ago, the cemetery where I know my place lies, my place already prepared, my grave already dug, and I would have taken it a long time ago if I wasn't waiting for new news, I'm a slave to the waiting and nobody should be a slave to that, nobody should have to wait for something that left with no possible date of return, maybe with no possible return at all, but I'm still waiting, I've been waiting since, let's see, oh to hell with it, how boring, how deceptive it is to claim you can calculate the waiting, which for that matter isn't measured in hours days months years but in units of measurement of the decomposition of the soul: existential falls, spiritual apocalypses, mental and moral extinctions, one after the other, while you wait, or because you're waiting, and yet I'm still alive, well-known to the nothingness, fighting what's behind the nothingness and that which has no name, or if it does I don't know it, I'm still alive, living inside my silence, it's surprising how falling can take so long, and more surprising still to see how alive people can be as they fall, but I don't know if I'll hold on for much longer, I don't think so, but it will happen when it happens, in any case, I hold the keys to my fate, and it's because I know that I can go at any moment, take a bow whenever I want, that I'm still waiting, but the out is there, available, it's simply that I don't want to waste it, I'm saving it for the day when I can't go on, when the pain becomes unbearable, and on that day all I'll have to do is get up and take a few steps to enter the land of the dead, where someone is waiting for me too, a small being of light and innocence, they're waiting for me too, so why should I stay here and make them wait when I know how fatal waiting can be, why, I know why, I'm waiting because I love, it's as simple as that, I'm waiting because I love and hope to be loved in return even if there's nothing on the horizon of this long wait, a blank line that I'll stop watching one day so I can finally free myself, and on that day, I'll enter the cemetery and take my place and no one will ever make me suffer again, and no one can ever say that I didn't wait, in fact I'll have gone to the very bottom of the waiting, the bottom of the thirst that all the water on earth couldn't have quenched and that could only be appeased by the single drop of a person or thing coming back, though I can sense a vast desert stretching between that drop and me, but tonight is a peaceful evening, I don't want to think about all that, the earth is moving and I see clearly, I feel good, I feel better, all because I told the voice beneath the earth that I didn't know who Elimane's father was, it really is so easy to annoy men, you just have to tell them that you don't know, that it doesn't matter that they want to know and that it's your life that counts, tell them that and they go mad, little matter if you're telling them the truth or playing on their nerves, they go mad and tremble and rumble, and it feels good at the bottom of the bottom, at the bottom of the hole where I've been waiting alone for so long;

. . . but is it true that I don't know, is it really true that I don't know who the father is, of course not, one knows these things, I think, or feels them, in any case I'm sure, I know who his father is but I won't say anything because it's me that counts, anyhow it's the past and things are just fine as they are, everyone in this story thinks this is the way it is, and all the better, Elimane thinks that Assane is his father, Assane thinks that Elimane is his son, Ousseynou thinks that Elimane is his nephew, Elimane thinks that Ousseynou is his uncle, Ousseynou thinks that I'm a slut who betrayed him to give myself to Assane, who left certain of continuing his line, and I look at all that and I know the truth, but I tell the earth that I don't know, otherwise it won't rumble, and if it doesn't rumble life gets a little complicated, so I tell it what it doesn't want to hear, which suits me fine, but deep down I wonder why the whole damn world is meddling in my life, Ousseynou asking me why him, the earth asking me who's the father, enough with your questions, leave me alone, is that too much to ask, leave me alone already, I'm Elimane's mother and that's all that counts for him, that's what I told him before he left, he told me he'd come back but he didn't come back and I'm waiting for him, because he's the one I'm waiting for, not Assane, whom I loved, of course, just like I loved Ousseynou, but the one I'm waiting for, obviously, is him, the one that the one thinks is his son and the other his nephew, when it could be the opposite, in any case, he inherited something from each of them, but no one knows, and that's what drives the earth mad, rumbling, and rumbling, for my enjoyment, which is so great that one day I might tell the earth the story of how that night when Ousseynou was standing in front of our home in the big city, I heard his conversation with the guard, whom Assane, before he went on the road with the missionaries, had told not to let anyone in, I had been alone at the house for two days and was bored to death, so when I heard Ousseynou in the street, when I recognized his voice, I almost shouted his name and ran to meet him, but I remembered how we had parted ways, the harsh words he flung in my face, a Negress who'd turned her back, a girl without honor, those exact words, I never forgot them and I'll never forget them, so when I remembered those words, I held back, even though I wanted to see him, to talk to him, to ask him how he was doing, to tell him that I loved him but that I also loved his brother, and that I had wanted to spend time with Assane after staying with him, Ousseynou, all those years in the village, I wanted to tell him that I didn't want to choose between one or the other, and that I wanted both of them equally, because both of them had something I was looking for, but no man can hear that, they want to possess a thing completely or not have it at all, they want your whole body for themselves alone, so I decided not to say anything, then a thought occurred to me, and very quietly, while the guard was trying to get rid of Ousseynou, I took advantage of his being distracted to climb the wall surrounding the house and get onto the neighboring road, I was still young and strong and agile, the guard didn't see anything because his back was to the courtyard, Ousseynou didn't see anything because the poor man can't see anything, so I got outside and I waited for the watchman to chase off Ousseynou so I could follow him discreetly, from a distance, with the help of the falling night, then he walked through the city in the twilight and I followed him, he didn't seem to know where he was going, which surprised me, because the blind always give the impression, even when they're groping along, of knowing exactly where they're going, but I followed him, and several times I told myself that I ought to catch up and talk to him, but something held me back, and I remained at a distance, waiting for my chance, which presented itself when I saw him enter a run-down hotel on the outskirts of town after walking quite a ways, I waited a few moments, then I went inside too, I didn't see him, I asked the manager where the man who'd just come in was, he told me that he was eating and said, *What do you want with him*, so I decided to go for it, I looked around and the place looked like a whorehouse in disguise and the man himself looked like a brothel owner disguised as a hotel manager, so I went for it and told him that I needed money and that the man, meaning Ousseynou, had stopped me in the street and suggested that I join him if I wanted to make some cash, which I had agreed to after a brief hesitation, which is why I had arrived a little bit after him, but the manager didn't seem to really believe my story, or if he believed it, didn't intend to let my plan unfold like that, so he told me that it wasn't a *maison close*, unless I was paying, so I told him I would give him half of what I made if he set everything up for me, which he agreed to do after pretending to hesitate, then he said, *You're young and you've got a body on you, he'll love it*, he told me to wait in front of the hotel, that he would come find me when it was settled, so I walked out and I waited in the night, like a real streetwalker, I watched the people passing by cast me glances bursting with desire, except desire was mixed with disgust, with themselves or with me, I didn't really know, but in any case one thing was certain, which is that people found me attractive, they wanted me, a man even told me, *Salimata Diallo in the flesh*, I said not at all, he told me I had her same thighs and slid away, telling me that one day he'd ride those thighs, it was strange, because I felt incredibly ashamed and at the same time regal, proud like never before, I felt like a holy prostitute, a divine, sacred whore, necessary to the salvation of damned souls, and I was about to start psst-psst-ing the passersby when the man, I mean the hotel manager, came back and told me, *We're all set, he ate a lot, drank a lot, go finish him off*, we agreed on a price, he's in such and such room, I thanked him dumbly and went to such and such room, I knocked, Ousseynou said, *Come in*, I went in and I saw his body on the bed, naked, ready, in the dark, I could barely make out his face, he didn't say anything but I could tell that he had rage inside of him, I told myself it wasn't the moment to talk, that he didn't need to talk and neither did I, I wanted something else, so I got undressed, I joined him on the bed, and he threw himself at me with rage and fury, he wanted to possess me, to take me away from myself, but he had met his match, he wasn't the only one lost and looking for an outlet for his anger, so I let everything that I had been holding on to explode too and we made love like it was a battle, but within that urge I found a truth, the truth of a lost bond, we battled in that bed until it was soaked with all our liquids, I thought he would recognize me, but he had never been with me, and besides he was so enraged that he didn't even recognize my voice when I moaned, or my smell, or my hands, in truth he was completely blind, not just his eyes, but his whole being, but I didn't let him dominate me, I answered back until we collapsed, exhausted, panting, I watched him in the darkness as I caught my breath, he was handsome, I wanted to talk to him but there was nothing to say, so I got up, I got dressed, and before I left, he asked me my name, I don't know why, and spontaneously I gave the name that the passerby had said, the one that suddenly popped into my head, *Salimata, Salimata what*, he said, *Salimata Diallo*, I said, Salimata Diallo, whom I didn't know but whose wide hips, similar enough to mine to breed confusion, had been noticed by a man who did know her, Ousseynou asked me if it was my ass that every man in town was talking about, I answered, *Yes, and now you know why*, and then I left before he could recognize my voice, but deep down I think that he wouldn't have recognized it even if I had talked to him for the whole night, I left and fled that hotel without even taking my money, I went home, surprising the guard who hadn't seen me leave but who saw me come back, I told him it wasn't a big deal, that I was a bird and that I could fly, which he seemed to believe, opening wide his frightened, superstitious eyes, and so I came home and waited for Assane, he returned the next day, and upon his return, like a good little wife who missed her husband, I gave myself to him, and three months later I found out I was pregnant and that the child had been conceived on one of those nights I had slept with the two brothers, I told Assane that I was expecting a child and he was wild with joy, certain that he was the father, even though he told me a few days later that he was going to war and would have to leave me and the child here, for our own good, which I understood, that's how he was, how Assane was, he loved France, so I didn't blame him, I let him go, he thought the war wouldn't last long, that invincible France would win, thanks be to God, and that he would return soon to witness the birth of his son, but I knew he would never come back, that one way or another he would stay in the country he loved and that he was willing to die for, so I let him go, all that mattered then was my child, and even when Assane took me to the village to leave me with his brother, I told myself that it was the child that mattered, and I held strong when Ousseynou scorned me because it was the child that mattered, I held strong when he wanted to kick us out of his home, which I also understood, and I held strong when he agreed to keep us, my baby and me, that night after Assane bid me goodbye in a touching way, asking me to take care of the child until his return, telling me the names he wanted the child to have when he or she came into the world, I agreed to all of it, and Assane left, sad but happy to leave, and I stayed with Ousseynou, and the child came into the world and was named Elimane Madag, and he was my child, and his father had no importance, Assane or Ousseynou, it was of no importance, the only thing that mattered was that I love him, that I loved him, as if I had conceived him on my own, and I did *conceive* him on my own, I loved him and he knows that, wherever he is on this earth right now he knows that I loved him and that he has a mother who's waiting for him, even if he forgets it sometimes, deep down he knows that I'm waiting for him, and my love for him is more important than knowing the identity of his natural father, I know who it is, and I'll only tell him if he asks me, him, my son and nobody else, not even the earth's masculine voice, certainly not, I have to keep telling the earth *I don't know*, so that it rumbles, and trembles, and so I'll be okay and see clearly and find the strength to finish this waiting that can never end, my little Elimane, where are you and what have you become, Eli, come back, like you promised me, come back before I go take my place in the cemetery across from the mango tree;

PART TWO

Sought and Seekers

I

It had been a long time since Siga D. had said anything.
I had the feeling the silence might stretch into dawn, and
maybe I even wanted it to. There was a fault line in every
version of this story, from which erupted an existential
question that shone so brightly it blinded any who claimed
to see it. Ousseynou Koumakh, Tokô Ngor, Assane Koumakh, Mossane, Elimane... All these figures of an abruptly
opened past were moving before me in a choreography as
complex as it was fascinating.

Had they been aware, in their time, that this dance was
for the future? Or, more precisely, had it ever crossed their
minds that one day, long after their deaths, their lives would
become the obsession of other lives? I thought about the
look on Brigitte Bollème's face in her photos; a look that
seemed to be addressing posterity. Had the protagonists of
the story I'd just heard been concerned, the way Bollème
was, with sending signals to the future?

I told myself: Of course not, Diégane, obviously not,
don't be stupid: fundamentally, even if appearances always
suggest otherwise, even if his existence always propels
him forward, toward the unknown, no man *thinks* about
the future. Our deep preoccupation is with the past; and
even as we head toward the future, toward what we are to

become, it's the past, the mystery of what we were, that troubles us. This isn't some sort of morose nostalgia. It's simply that between these two questions that mask a similar anxiety—*What will I do?* and *What have I done?*—the latter is more serious: all possibility of correction, of another chance, is eliminated. In *What have I done?* another bell tolls: *This can never be undone.* It's the question asked by the good man who commits a crime in a fit of rage, and who, after the act, lucidity restored, holds his head in his hands: *What have I done?* This man knows what he did. But his real anguish, his real horror, comes from also knowing that he can't undo, can't fix, what he's done. The past, because it makes man tragically aware of the *irreparable*, the *unfixable*, is what troubles him the most. The fear of tomorrow always carries the hope, even faint, even when we know that it might and probably will be dashed, of what's possible, what's doable, of an open door, a miracle. Fear of the past doesn't carry anything but the weight of its own anxiety. And even remorse or repentance aren't enough to alter the irrevocable nature of the past; quite the contrary: they are the very confirmation of its eternalness. You don't only regret what was; you also regret, even more so, what will forever be.

So no, I thought: All these shapes aren't bustling around for the present, Diégane, for this moment when you're watching them without necessarily having understood the message they didn't try to send you. They're worrying about their past actions. They lived, and the weight you're placing on their shoulders concerns you alone: your desires, your questions. Elimane, Mossane, Ousseynou Koumakh, and Assane Koumakh didn't ask you for anything. You're the one chasing them through time and not the other way around. People think, as if it's a foregone conclusion, that it's the past that returns to inhabit and haunt the present. But it could be that the reverse is just as true if not more so, and that it's us relentlessly haunting those who came before. We are the true ghosts of our history, our ghosts' ghosts.

"I've tried several times to make a book out of all this," said Siga D. suddenly. "But I have yet to succeed. Maybe because it's too close to me, too personal. How ironic, for a writer who has built her entire body of work on personal experiences. But I'm in no rush. I'll write the story one day. Or you'll write it, why not."

Siga D. paused. She might have been waiting for my reaction, but I said nothing. Did she mean to imply that it was I—because I wrote novels—who should write it? Was she asking me to write it? Was she asking me if I planned to write it? She probably assumed that was why I had come to see her. After a moment, she continued:

"My father died three days after telling me his story in that rotting bedroom. I remember the whole household in mourning, the courtyard filled with tearful faces, and the sounds of fake or sincere crying, my stepmothers inconsolable or pretending to be, my brothers and sisters adrift. And me, secretly, I was jubilant. I read *The Labyrinth of Inhumanity* for the first time. I read it beneath the mango tree across from the cemetery, almost like I wanted, in that spot, to absorb part of the history that had spawned the book. I read the book a great many times. Always with excitement. Always with surprise. But nothing I experienced later was comparable to the shock of my first readings. I felt as if Elimane, through this story of a king so greedy for absolute power that he burned people alive, was telling a more personal story. His. The story of his family, of our family. The book was speaking to me. Just like any essential book is always speaking to us. My father was buried. I didn't go to his grave. I think that I would have cried. So I fled. I said my goodbyes to my stepmothers. I think they knew I would never come back. The bridges had been burned. Then I left for the capital. Free at last. Ready to fight. The only object worth anything among my belongings was that book. I enrolled at the university, majoring in philosophy. After living with a maternal uncle for a few weeks, I managed to find a room on campus. I didn't have the money to pay for it. But it didn't matter. I was thirsty for the world. I wanted to squeeze and suck it down to the last drop of life. I jumped in headlong."

"This is when you experienced what you wrote about later in *Elegy for Black Night*?"

"Yes."

She paused again. I was thinking about the book, Siga D.'s first, which had announced her as a writer. Among everything she'd written, it was my favorite. It was what prompted the prolonged outrage over her work, which is still viewed as scandalous by much of Senegalese society. In *Elegy for Black Night*, Siga D. told the story of Marème, a young philosophy student with a destructive sexual appetite who was also immensely lonely, obsessed by her desire to love or be loved, gripped by a deep attraction to death. She wanted to reach the unreachable through the bodies successively pressed against her or in her various romantic relationships (this striking blurring of cold sex and the ingenuous, painful quest for love is the source of the book's terrible ambiguity and by extension its beauty). It's unclear whether that quest was meant to elevate or degrade her, intensify her life or extinguish it. Marème seemed to want all that at once, everywhere, at school, in men, in women, in solitary pleasures and in the streets of the capital, where her reputation as sex famished attracted many: not only strangers, outcasts, down-and-outs, curious onlookers, partyers, and libertines, but also media, political, and religious figures, who hid the debauchery of their secret and peccaminous lives behind grand sermons about virtue. She described how the sexual impoverishment of her society—which she portrayed as frustrated, diseased, lost in the chasm between what it claimed or wanted to be and what it really was— was reflected in the mirror of her body. She wrote about her fall from grace, how she was expelled from college after an important professor turned customer for a night—and who had been unable to get hard at the crucial moment (obliging her to pleasure herself as he tried unsuccessfully to raise the dead)—had accused her of corrupting the campus and turned her in. She wrote about her aimlessness without, her aimlessness within. Her first suicide attempt. She wrote about how a stranger whose face she merely glimpsed before losing consciousness and whom she would never see again saved her as she was bleeding out, in the middle of the night, in a deserted street. She described how she searched for that stranger's face in every face she came across after leaving the hospital. She wrote about her solitude and her bouts of madness. Her second suicide attempt, except that the Atlantic wanted none of her and spat her out. She was committed at Dalal Xel. She spent three months behind its white walls, among the men and women dressed in white, the schizophrenics, the feebleminded, the possessed, the dispossessed, swinging like a pendulum between total annihilation and pure joy. She left, returned to Dakar. The whirlwind swallowed her back up. She evoked her terrifying hallucinations and deliriums in the city streets. She spoke of the stubs of charcoal she collected to write, at night, on the walls of the capital, her poetic trances: words gleaming like the first sparks of a poetic inferno, smoldering metaphors in which life burned beings alive. Chaos—not disorder, but chaos—reigned in her mind, where torrents of sentences long as boas rained down. She drowned herself in that diluvian hailstorm of antediluvian words, words far older than she, that emerged steaming, as if just forged, from her belly, though she knew they were only steaming because they'd remained too long beneath the embers. Her own words were older than her stomach and her story, older than the stories of all the stomachs that carried themselves from the Night to her night. They were syllables orphaned by language, and waiting for her language. She embraced the boas and learned theirs. She hissed her hatred for any infringement on pleasure. She hissed her desire for another world, where she'd never set foot but nonetheless glimpsed every night in her dreams. In her throat burned her intact, powerful thirst for love. She recounted her struggle against the temptation to obliterate herself. She wrote about how a woman much older than she, a poetess who came from far away, from Haiti, and who was working as a senior civil servant in Dakar, had found her one night, as she was preparing to write one of her images with her stub of charcoal. The poetess said she'd been looking for her for a long time; she admitted to scouring the city for several weeks in search

of the person who'd blanketed it with such raging, pure
lava. She wrote about how they formed a friendship, about
her curiosity toward this woman, who called her *corazón*
and who was as beautiful as the melancholy of a summer
evening. She mentioned the long nights they spent writing,
talking, sometimes saying nothing and, more rarely, getting angry with each other. Confiding as well. Loving each
other in a way long forgotten. She recounted the starless
night when, at her place, the Haitian poetess had told her:
"Today is a black night above the city, the way life is a black
night above or around us, but you wrote its black beauty
in *kërin*, in black charcoal, an elegy to the black night, and
that was the solitary star I followed to find you, *Corazón*."
She recounted how the poetess, before leaving Dakar (she'd
been summoned for other duties, in the United States), had
offered to help her resume her studies, not here, but elsewhere, in Paris. She wrote about how it broke her to be separated from this woman who had saved her from madness the
same way the stranger in the narrow street had from death.
They parted ways with an oath: remain faithful, individually and together, to their unabashedly poetic connection,
meaning open to any manifestation of a word that told no
lies, a word that didn't betray the most essential, a word
brave enough for every battle, even if every battle ended in
defeat. She wrote about the departure of the Haitian poetess and the verses she left her as a farewell. And how, a few
months later, she left too, for Paris, where the poetess had
helped her find a spot at a university and a small room, the
rent paid for one year. She wrote about all this bluntly, casting a harsh gaze at Senegalese society but an even harsher
one at herself. And this—self-inflicting the intransigence it

had reserved for her—is what that society will never be able to forgive her for. She broke the rules of *masla*, that reserve and honed tactfulness through which harsh truths in our society aren't said but implied, and sometimes concealed for the sake of public honor. Siga D. had spoken plainly, without *masla*, not in the shadows but in broad daylight, beneath the piercing noontime sun. When her first book was published (in 1986), few people saw it for what it really was. *Elegy for Black Night* was the beginning of Siga D.'s rift with her society. It endures. It deepened. Siga D. has never gone back. I think she'll die without ever returning. But at the core of all her writing, even though she found other settings, other images, other passions, lie those of her country.

"What I didn't say in that book," continued Siga D., "is that I had a third savior. Along with the stranger in the street and the Haitian poetess, there was Elimane. At least there was his *Labyrinth of Inhumanity*. There were periods when I would read it every God-given day. I knew it by heart, and that's the reason I could live in hell. There are a few ways to get through hell, and one of them is to learn a book by heart. That's what I did. I could have chucked it after, I knew it so well. But I kept it, like a talisman. I had lost everything, and those losses eventually became part of my wealth. But my most precious possession, by which I mean the thing I couldn't lose again, was *The Labyrinth of Inhumanity*. It became the part of me that couldn't be shared. Elimane was my lover and I introduced him to no one, not even the poetess from Haiti, a woman to whom I felt connected by something deeper than intimacy. The book was my secret, my cherished treasure, it couldn't be known, seen, loved by anyone but me. In the midst of the fits of lunacy, the temptations at the edge of the sea, the insomnia, the inebriation, all that pitiful and sublime solitude, on a mattress made of rubbish and wrested from the dogs, lying beneath a sweaty body for a few coins, tunneling my way through madness, I would open or recite from the book yet again. And so: it was impossible to die. Even when I sliced open my veins, I knew that death didn't want me. Sprawled in my blood, I spoke those sentences that were a part of me. I wasn't surprised when the stranger saved me. I'm convinced that the stranger was Elimane. It was him, or his spirit, who was summoned by the words I whispered at the threshold of death. The face I glimpsed could have been his. I'm not sure. At the time I'd never seen him. But I remember the sensation of being in his arms. Of being in the arms of a man you love, a man you know."

She stopped talking and closed her eyes, perhaps to remember that sensation of the body of a stranger who isn't.

"Yes, it was him. It could only have been him," she continued gently, with certainty, opening her eyes. "His book went with me everywhere. Elimane was my cousin. My blood. His history was also my history. We were linked by something more profound than a text. It was a confession. Or a family psychoanalysis. He was talking to me. Elimane was talking to me. I knew what he was talking about. And that's why I clung to his voice. And then, like you are now, I started to wonder what had happened to him, where he'd gone, what he did and saw and endured and kept quiet and hid. That kind of man doesn't just disappear like that. Or maybe he does. Maybe all men can disappear like that. But is it so easy to believe in a disappearance that leaves nothing behind? In a pure vanishing? I didn't. I still don't. A presence lingers after any departure. Or maybe the true presence of a being or thing only emerges once it's gone. Don't you think? I don't believe in absence. I only believe in the traces that remain. Sometimes they're invisible. But you can follow them. I already knew what Elimane had left behind in my father's memory. But I was convinced that he existed in other memories as well. I was certain he'd been present in other lives. It was a question of finding them. Tracking them down and finding them. Deep down, Diégane, as deep as it gets, I know this: I didn't agree to the Haitian poetess's suggestion that I finish my studies for her, though I loved her, or for myself, meaning to escape my country. No: I agreed for Elimane Madag. That's who I was looking for when I came to France in 1983, after three years of drifting and silent tottering atop a high cliff with my stubs of charcoal in the streets of Dakar."

II

———

A few weeks after her investigation was published, as she stared at her confidante's grave in the grip of emotions whose intensity surprised her most of all, Brigitte Bollème told me she had asked herself, precisely, in the cemetery of that small village, beneath a dingy late-autumn sky, whether the deceased had told her the truth.

"I'd never considered the truthfulness of her account until that exact moment. You must be asking yourself why the question suddenly came to me then, years after my interview."

Obviously, Brigitte Bollème wasn't talking to me, Diégane. She was talking to herself. But I had wondered too, as I watched her, why it was that Brigitte Bollème had only questioned her primary source's word when she was standing at her grave, after the publication of *Who Was the True Negro Rimbaud?* After all, that's Journalism 101. In that instant, in response to Brigitte Bollème's comment, here's what I thought: it's because your primary source had just died and because you were realizing at that very moment that no one else, to your knowledge, could tell you about Elimane. Yes, that's exactly what I thought, Diégane: that Brigitte Bollème was confronting the terror of the definitive silence that would henceforth surround Elimane's life, since the last person to hold it in her memory had just passed away. In my mind, that justified why she was suddenly according such importance to the veracity of that final account...

"But that has nothing to do with the question of the account's veracity," I said to Siga D. "Wondering whether that woman told the truth is unrelated to the realization that she was the last person to have known Elimane in his lifetime. Bollème must have understood that, right?"

"You're wrong," replied Siga D. "The two truths are connected. In any case, they struck me as connected in that moment. The woman who had just died was the last person in France to have spent time with Elimane. That meant that what she said would forever pass for the truth. Maybe she'd lied about some elements of their shared history. Maybe she had had some regrets. Maybe she would have corrected her version of events. But she was dead. None of that would happen, there'd be no more regrets, no more corrections. Her account of Elimane was frozen for eternity. Bollème had put it in her report. And that account, even if it wasn't entirely true, would stand as the truth for posterity. Both you and I now know, Diégane, that it's not true, that Elimane's life went on, and that other people knew him. We know that his life didn't come to a halt in 1938. But the 1948 Brigitte Bollème, the one standing in front of a grave, couldn't know that. The investigation she'd just published was overwhelmingly based on secrets confided to her. If they were proven false, her efforts would be worthless. I think that's what was tormenting her."

"I understand," I said. "Maybe you were right."

"Well, actually, I was wrong. In any case that's what Brigitte Bollème made me understand that day. After a long pause, she told me: It's 1985, young lady. I published my investigation in '48...or was it '49? No, '48. For that matter, have you read it?"

"Yes. I found an old copy in the back room of a second-hand bookshop."

"Ah yes, that must be the only place you can find it any-more...It's an investigation that was of no interest to anyone. By '48, everyone had forgotten about Elimane, or didn't want to hear about him anymore. The only wit-ness died a few days after my article was published. It was 1948, yes, early November, 1948. She let herself die, I'm sure of it. It was only when you wrote me a few days ago to request a meeting that I thought back to that morning, in the cemetery, in front of her grave. Why was it only at that moment that I asked myself whether she had told me the truth? Until I received your letter, I didn't have an answer. Now I do: when I listened to her confession, I was seeing a woman in pain. And I believed, because of that pain, that she was telling, and could only be telling, the truth. At no moment during the interview did I think to myself that she might be lying or skirting around the facts. She was in too much pain. But it was mostly that her suffering seemed too pure to beget a lie. And it was only before her grave that I thought, there's no inherent correlation between pain and truth; it's not because we're in pain that we tell the truth, whether it be about the nature of our pain, its cause, or its consequences. Sometimes we even twist the truth because of our pain. It was only before her grave that I thought, this woman, voluntarily or not, might have twisted the truth. Maybe she died believing she'd spoken truthfully when she had merely expressed her pain. That's what I was thinking that day at the cemetery. That's what was saddening me as I looked at her grave. It had started to rain. I was remembering the day we'd spent together, when she told me the true story that connected her to Elimane. The true story of *The Labyrinth of Inhumanity* and its curse. Or rather: what she believed to be the true story. Not long after, I would discover that my intuition at the cemetery, which prompted that sudden doubt, was not entirely unfounded. But I'm the only one who knows what happened next. I didn't write it anywhere or tell anyone. I could have expanded on my investigation. I should have. But I didn't. First of all because nobody gave a damn about the whole thing. Then, because I was scared to talk about it. I suppose that you're here to find out what I know."

"And was that true?" I said. "Is that why you went to see Brigitte Bollème in 1985?"

"Unlike you, Diégane, I'm not really fascinated by Elimane the writer. It's the man. I know that for you the two blend together. Not for me. We've already had this conversation, let's not repeat it. I was looking for the man, him, and not for whatever came after *The Labyrinth of Inhumanity*, like you are. The plagiarism scandal didn't interest me much. What interested me about him, what drew me to him, was his silence."

"His silence is the main mystery for me too."

"Maybe. But I don't think it's the same silence, Diégane. I'm talking about his silence toward his mother, his family. He didn't keep his promise to Mossane. I wanted to know why. I wanted to know why he never came back and never sent news to his mother and his uncle, meaning my father. The reason behind his chosen, radical exile—that's what I was looking for. I was writing *Elegy for Black Night*, and every day the absent figure of Elimane haunted me a little more intensely. I decided to go looking for him. And I immediately came across the name Brigitte Bollème. I looked for her investigation, I found it and read it. Then I wrote to her. I didn't lie. I told her that I was Elimane's cousin, and that I was researching him."

"And?"

"And so I said: Yes, Mrs. Bollème."

"Brigitte."

"Yes, Brigitte. That's why I'm here. To find out what you know."

She looked at me curiously, almost amused, and said: "I never thought I'd meet a relative of Elimane's. I didn't know he had any. It's not a subject he ever broached with anyone, as far as I know."

Siga D. asked me if I remembered the details of *Who Was the True Negro Rimbaud? Odyssey of a Ghost*. I confirmed that I did, and that I had with me some notes I'd taken at the press archives. Siga D. continued her account:

"As she said that, Brigitte Bollème stood and walked over to her bookshelf. I can still see her, a little hunched with age, but as elegant as always, dressed in the style she'd been known for: velvet pants, linen blouse, and a silk scarf knotted around her neck. She had the same short hair, and the same foppish accessory dancing between her fingers, a long and slender cigarette holder that had borne witness to every battle waged by the avant-garde after the war, every excess, every contestation and contraction of Europe's attempted rebirth. And her eyes, a deep metallic gray...She radiated a charisma that you don't often see nowadays. She grabbed a slim book from the shelf and handed it to me.

"'Would you mind reading this? I know, you've already read it. You said so. All the same, I'd like you to read this investigation for me. I haven't looked at it in years. There are details I can't remember anymore.'

"I took the book. Brigitte Bollème sat down and lit a cigarette. Then I read her her own investigation."

III

Who Was the True Negro Rimbaud? Odyssey of a Ghost
By B. Bollème

Ten years ago, the French literary world was roiled by a momentous scandal that everyone today appears to have forgotten. Which is understandable: in the interim, there was the war. All the same, the autumn of 1938 was marked by a strange literary affair—that of *The Labyrinth of Inhumanity* and its author, T.C. Elimane.

Here is a brief recapitulation: in September 1938, an author from Senegal published *The Labyrinth of Inhumanity* with Gemini Editions. The book was astonishing on every level: its subject, its style, and its author, a twenty-three-year-old African of whom no one had ever heard. His talent prompted a famous critic to dub him a "Negro Rimbaud" of sorts. The book elicited both accolades and criticisms. This went on for several weeks, until a man named Henri de Bobinal, a professor at the Collège de France and an explorer and ethnologist specializing in sub-Saharan Africa, published a newspaper article in which he accused T.C. Elimane of having plagiarized the founding myth of a Senegalese ethnic group to write his novel. This incriminating article was followed, a few days later, by revelations from a Paul-Émile Vaillant, a professor of literature who was also at the Collège de France. He revealed the presence in the novel of innumerable borrowings from major literary texts. This second article heralded the beginning of the end for *The Labyrinth of Inhumanity* and its author; it soon emerged that the book, in part at least, was a mix of original writing and a subtle patchwork of quotes. Multiple lawsuits were filed against Gemini. The publisher pleaded guilty, reimbursed the money owed, and closed down shortly before the shadow of war began to loom over our country and the world. Throughout the whole affair, T.C. Elimane didn't make a single statement to the press. He disappeared with his book without anyone knowing who he was, or even if he existed. The war came; the scandal surrounding the book was forgotten.

I didn't forget, however, and decided to find its author. His editors didn't respond to my queries. People said they had left Paris after the lawsuits.

In early 1939, it occurred to me to visit the milieus frequented by Paris's black students and intellectuals. Their silence throughout the controversy around Elimane's book had surprised me. After all, they had ways to make their voices heard, in several interwar journals. I am thinking notably of *Légitime défense*. I managed to get an interview with Léopold Sédar Senghor.

He admitted his "distaste for that dreadful novel, about which ridiculous things were written in the papers." I asked him which things. He responded, with melodious diction in which you could hear every punctuation mark: "I suggest you ask Professor Henri de Bobinal about the Bassari, about whom he claims to be a specialist. What Professor Bobinal says about them may be true, but there's a problem: the Bassari are not from Senegal. It's unequivocal. Therefore, either Professor Bobinal never went to Senegal and isn't familiar with its ethnic groups, which would be shameful, or he did go, but is mixing up the people he studied with the Bassari, which would be even more shameful. In either case, there's confusion; I'd call it pure confabulation. For that matter, I don't understand why Mr. Elimane, who's been very quiet indeed, has yet to bring this deception to light."

In shock, I went to the Collège de France the very next day. I was hoping to meet with Professor Bobinal and confront him with Senghor's assertions about the Bassari. To my great surprise I was informed that Bobinal had died in the tail end of 1938, a few weeks after his article was published, of a sudden heart attack.

Paul-Émile Vaillant, however, the other Collège de France professor involved in the matter, was still alive. He was the one who had revealed the literary plagiarism within the text of *The Labyrinth of Inhumanity*. I told him what Mr. Senghor had said about Henri de Bobinal. Professor Vaillant then told me what he knew. I consider his account to be crucial: "Mr. Senghor is right. Bobinal's article on *The Labyrinth of Inhumanity* was dishonest. In the final years of his life, Bobinal adopted a myopic, racist discourse, for all that he had long loved and defended Africa's indigenous cultures. Such contradiction is the profound mystery of man. Bobinal was beside himself over the publication of that African's book. So he made up the cosmogonical Bassari myth supposedly plagiarized by the author. He confessed his scheme to a friend in common, who shared it with me after his death. Bobinal lied. The true incidents of plagiarism are the ones I discovered and revealed:

literary plagiarism. That said, despite their existence, I remain convinced that Mr. Elimane is a writer."

These were the revelations Paul-Émile Vaillant shared with me. Hearing them, I thought back to Mr. Senghor's question: Why didn't Elimane and his editors, knowing that Bobinal's article was pure invention, issue a public reaction? What secret was hiding behind T.C. Elimane's silence that was terrible enough that he preferred calumny over innocence?

That's what I wanted to find out. But the war came, and it quickly become impossible, under those conditions, to do anything. The war and the Resistance dragged me away from my obsession with Elimane.

It wasn't until the beginning of this year, 1948, that I was able to resume my investigation into *The Labyrinth of Inhumanity*. After a few weeks of searching, I managed to locate, in Paris, one of Gemini's three employees, an André Merle (the other two were Pierre Schwarz—deported to Dachau—and Miss Claire Ledig, the publisher's secretary, whose head was shaved on liberation for horizontal collaboration). André Merle was the accountant at Gemini when *The Labyrinth of Inhumanity* was published. When I explained the purpose of my visit, he informed me that no one at the publishing house, apart from Charles Ellenstein and Thérèse Jacob, had ever seen Elimane. I told him I had no idea where to find them.

At that point, Merle revealed that the last time he'd seen his former employers at the Gemini offices, they'd been fighting. Ellenstein had been insisting they leave Paris, because the city was no longer safe for people like them, meaning Jews. Thérèse Jacob wanted to stay in the capital, not flee. Finally, Ellenstein was able to convince her to go. I asked Merle if he knew where to. This was his response:

"They mentioned the two small towns where they had country houses: Cajarc, and Tharon, in the Lower Loire…"

I didn't hesitate for a second, and set out for Cajarc. The department of Lot had been part of the free zone at the start of the occupation, unlike the Pays de la Loire region, which teemed with Nazis until May 1945.

I therefore gambled that a Jewish couple would have had a better chance of surviving in Cajarc than in Tharon, and found myself in the beautiful valley of Lot a few days after my conversation with André Merle. It only took me two days of asking around, however, to learn that although Charles Ellenstein and Thérèse Jacob had lived in the village at the start of the war, they hadn't stayed there together until its end. One of their neighbors told me they had separated in 1942. Charles had been gone since then. Thérèse ended up leaving as well, but only after the war, in 1946. This neighbor of course didn't know where either of them might have gone. "They were a very secretive couple the whole time they lived here," she told me. "They were polite, but didn't say much to other people. I don't even think they said much to each other."

After three days I left Cajarc and decided to go to Tharon, in the hope of picking up Charles Ellenstein and Thérèse Jacob's trail there.

It was late winter. The air in Tharon, cold and biting, stung the flesh. Pushed along by the ocean wind, it circulated in gusts unimpeded by the town streets. I quickly found an inn and asked the proprietor if he knew of a Charles Ellenstein or Thérèse Jacob. He told me no, but added that if I was looking for someone there, I should head toward the *marché*.

I dropped off my things and set out immediately to scout the area, which would have made a perfect setting for a seaside crime novel. And wasn't I living a sort of detective story, completely absorbed by a literary investigation shrouded in mist into which the writer had disappeared, leaving no trace?

I crossed the herbaceous dunes lining the beach like ramparts and descended toward the sea, which was bordered (or surveilled) by elevated fishing huts that resembled miradors. The sun was setting. I remember thinking: This is how T.C. Elimane disappeared from the world, without a sound, like a sunset in the ocean. A blanket of fatigue settled on my shoulders. Rather than going around to every port brasserie in search of Ellenstein or Thérèse Jacob, I decided to return to the inn and rest. My investigation could begin tomorrow. I ate dinner and before going to bed, reread a few pages of *The Labyrinth of Inhumanity*.

I woke up around four and couldn't fall back asleep. Around five, I decided I would watch the sunrise. There was already one person on the dock. I said hello. She turned swiftly toward me, a little surprised, no doubt. There wasn't much light, but I recognized her right away: it was Thérèse Jacob. I know that she recognized me too. Still, we both remained silent. It was only once the sun had risen that she said: "You found me."

Her voice wasn't as I had remembered. It was gentle, pacified almost, whereas I recalled her speaking quickly and nervously. I turned to look at her. Her face, in contrast, was still young and beautiful, though her cheeks had hollowed.

"Hello, Miss Jacob. So you remember me."

"I remember you, Mrs. Bollème."

"Call me Brigitte, please."

"I remember you, Brigitte. I remember the unpleasant interview you conducted with Charles and me about Elimane. I assume you're looking for him. But I'm the only one left."

She was seized by a violent coughing fit that lasted several minutes. She told me her lungs were a little fragile, and added that we would be better off indoors, in the warmth. I took those words as an invitation and followed her. She coughed a few more times, less violently, on the way. After a ten-minute walk we reached a small bungalow, painted blue. We sat in the living room and I asked her if I could record our conversation. She had no objection. I set up my equipment, a small tape recorder that I almost always carry with me, then took a more careful look around.

"This was Charles's parents' house," she told me, bringing in coffee and *kouignettes*, the local pastry. "They both died here. Charles was their only child."

"I see. And Charles? Where is he?"

She sat down across from me and lit a cigarette before answering: "Charles is gone."

"Gone? What do you mean by that?"

"I simply mean that he's gone."

I restrained myself from reacting to that piece of news. It was Elimane who interested me; Elimane and not Ellenstein and Thérèse Jacob's private life; Elimane and his book alone. So I decided not to press when it came to Charles Ellenstein. I lit a cigarette too, my first of the day, and, for a few moments we smoked in silence.

"I knew one of you would come eventually. So it's you. I bet you're still possessed by *The Labyrinth of Inhumanity*. You'll never be free of it. It's not so easy to escape. Elimane..."

She paused then. I asked if she minded if I took some notes, in addition to the recording. With a vague gesture she made it clear that she didn't really care, and finished her sentence: "Elimane is a demon. He possesses. But he himself is possessed."

She broke off again. I didn't prompt her. The confession had to come from her, at her rhythm.

"Do you remember the circumstances in which Charles and I claimed to have met him?

"What you said in your interview? The meeting in a bar? Yes, I remember."

"You're remembering a lie. Charles and I didn't meet him in a bar, by chance. The first time we saw him was at one of Paris's best high schools. He was twenty years old, had just arrived from his country, and was about to begin his college prep year in literary studies. At the start of every school year, some former students who had gone on to the École Normale Supérieure would come to encourage the new arrivals. Charles and I were among the former students invited that year. We were just starting out in the publishing world. Naturally Elimane was one of the star attractions of the new class. We were seeing more and more black students in Paris. But the phenomenon was still rare at our old school. Everyone wanted to hear him speak, to find out what he was worth, to form an opinion of him or see if he corresponded to a preexisting one.

"The new students were asked to introduce themselves. They took the floor one by one, but everyone was waiting for Elimane. When his turn came, his voice was clear and distinct in the sepulchral silence. He said, 'My name is Elimane. I'm from Senegal. I want to write.' Those three sentences echoed like pistol shots across the school's inner courtyard. The silence persisted a few more seconds, then a murmur rose from the students, the teachers, the former students. The murmur was jumbled, indecipherable. Some people seemed shocked that he spoke our language. Others repeated his name like a talisman or an incantation: Elimane... Elimane... A few were wondering where (or what) Senegal was. But his last sentence was the most important: I want to write. There was something pure in those words. They would have sounded ridiculous and pretentious in the mouth of any young womanizer barely out of adolescence and already imagining himself as a Stendhal or Flaubert. It's not a sentence you say casually, especially not in a literary preparatory class like that one, where students often discover that it's not because you can turn a phrase that you'll become a semblance of a writer. But when Elimane spoke those words, I'd felt in my gut that it wasn't simply vanity. He was going to have to prove it, stay the course, withstand the mocking that would soon begin (a Negro, a creature barely higher than a primate on the ladder of civilization, who wanted to write!). But in his voice and his gaze, there was... there was a fire. Charles and I sensed it.

"His first year, he boarded at the school. Charles and I kept tabs on his progress, and it quickly became clear that he had no need to, as they say, become acclimated to his new environment. It was as if he had always lived there, as if back home, in Senegal, someone had prepared him. The teachers we spoke with told us he was extremely well versed in literature and philosophy. Where did he get it from? Was he one of those African sorcerers who came to mind, in Europe, as soon as the dark continent was mentioned? One thing was certain: thanks to his knowledge and his maturity, he found himself head and shoulders above his classmates, which earned him as much hatred as it did admiration.

"One day, shortly before the fall break, Charles told me that we ought to be frank with him. So we went to see him.

"'We're publishers,' Charles said. 'We wanted to see you again because we haven't forgotten what you said, "I want to write." Do you still want to?'

"I added, 'We'd love to read your work if you have something, a manuscript.' He gave us a long look before giving us the address of a brasserie, around Place Clichy, where, he told us, he wrote on his rare outings.

"'I'll be there every afternoon, after three, during the break.' he said.

"Then he stood, told us goodbye, and he left.

"On the very first day of the break, we found him there. And for nearly the entire duration of the holiday, we met at that restaurant, in Place Clichy, always at the same time, in the afternoon. We weren't friends yet, but that's where our first real conversations took place.

"Elimane never really wanted to tell us about himself, his family, his life in Senegal, how he had become so cultivated. All that interested him was the present. And the present was his book. At first he didn't want to tell us about it either. He would say he wanted us to read it when it was ready. I remember him as very calm, very gentle, except when we debated literature. Then he'd get fired up, twitching like a predatory animal, a bull in an arena. By the end of the break, I think we had become friends. He and Charles had grown particularly close. They discovered they shared literary tastes, though their debates about certain authors were epic. Some evenings, when I was tired, Charles would meet Elimane alone, and come home very late. We formed a trio of friends, but I could tell they understood each other a little better. There was a kind of symbiosis there, but I wasn't jealous of it at all. When school resumed, we continued to see him on occasion.

He told us his book was coming along. We didn't rush him, but were eager to read it.

"The incident that started everything happened during the summer. He told us he wanted to go to the north of France, without specifying the reason. Charles suggested that we both accompany him. I had other plans, other inclinations. But Charles was bent on going with him, at least for part of the trip.

"He left with Elimane and was gone for several weeks, four or five, before coming home."

"Now do you know the purpose of that trip through the north? Where did Elimane go? What did they do during those weeks?"

"When he returned, I asked Charles, but he was evasive, as if he had promised not to reveal what they had done. I pushed, and Charles eventually told me. That's when I understood why talking about his trip with Elimane was hard for him. He felt like he had betrayed our friend's confidence."

"What did he tell you?"

"He said, 'Elimane was looking for his father's body. He was a Senegalese *tirailleur* who disappeared during the Great War, in northern France.'"

"And do you know if they found it?"

"I have no idea, Brigitte. Charles didn't tell me much. He simply said that they had combed several villages in northern France near where there had been front lines and combat zones during World War I. Notably in the departments of Somme and Aisne. That's all. I sensed that whatever happened during that monthlong trip belonged to them alone. So I let them have it. I didn't ask Charles any more questions. We spent the rest of the summer break together, in Cajarc and

Tharon. Elimane had already gone back to Paris. We met up with him again in September."

"And he didn't tell you anything either, about this father he was looking for?"

"No. But I truly hope that he found something. Maybe the reason Elimane came to France was to find his father. Maybe he was simply looking for his history. In any case, that quest released him from it. It gave him the impetus he needed to write the novel he was dreaming of writing. Yes: I think that *The Labyrinth of Inhumanity* was born that summer."

Thérèse Jacob paused, suddenly pensive, as though she had succeeded in formulating and understanding a truth long hidden within her.

"And then?" I asked after a pause.

"Then he stopped prepping for the entrance exam for the École Normale. He said he wanted to write, and nothing else. That decision baffled and saddened his teachers, who had believed that he would get in. Elimane didn't re-enroll the following year, and managed to find a job as a construction worker. Of course we offered to let him stay with us; we had a little extra room. But he said he wanted to get by on his own, friends though we were. The site foreman, who was a sleazy guy, offered to rent him a run-down room off the books. Elimane agreed. That moment marked the beginning of the happiest period we ever spent together. After abandoning his studies, Elimane found a new rhythm. In the mornings, from six to noon, he worked at the construction site. Then he wrote in the afternoons, after a nap. We would meet up at night, in a bar or at our place. That seemed to suit him. We could tell that he was eager for experiences, for freedom, for new people, for traveling, for extraordinary things. He wanted to experience the myth of Paris—the city of artists, revelry, intoxi-cation. After much discussion, Charles and I decided to intro-duce him to a world that he didn't know yet."

She paused, as if she wanted to force me to ask the obliga-tory question, which I immediately did:

"Which one?"

"The libertine world."

With that, Thérèse Jacob looked at me with a glint of defi-ance in her eyes. She might have been expecting a reaction, some judgment. I didn't even blink.

"Charles and I weren't married," she finally said. "And ours was a very open relationship, governed by nothing apart from pleasure. We had been regulars in libertine circles for a few years. It was a universe of secrets, masks, and shadows. Peo-ple weren't interested in your résumé, or even your identity. They just wanted your company on their erotic journey."

I kept my mouth shut. She continued:

"We didn't know much about Elimane's private life, by which I mean his sex life. Charles may have known a little, since they were closer. But I definitely didn't. I wasn't aware of any girlfriends, or boyfriends for that matter. All he had, it would appear, was literature. So one evening, at our apart-ment, we told him, holding nothing back, about that part of our life. Afterward, he reflected for a bit, then said he was in. We began inviting him to our 'special' parties. He immediately became the star attraction. In those circles, the ultimate plea-sure came from the newest thing, unfamiliar flesh, the thrill of the unknown. Elimane, on top of offering all of that, was African. Even in that world, though it was full of educated and cultivated people, you couldn't escape the stereotypes about Africans and their sexuality. He quickly developed a reputation as an excellent lover. Everyone would ask for him. They all wanted to get a taste of Elimane, to see if the gift attributed to him was true."

"So you and Charles formed a threesome with Elimane?"

Thérèse Jacob was silent for a moment, then she said: "Yes. I was reluctant at first, but Charles wanted to. It excited him, it always had, to watch another man make love to me. And I think that the idea that Elimane would be that man excited him even more."

"Why is that, in your opinion?"

"I don't know. Maybe because he saw him as a kind of twin. That's just a hypothesis. I don't know."

"And why were you reluctant?"

"I felt like it would end up destroying us. But I'll come back to that. Elimane was an incredible lover, attentive, imaginative, ardent, indefatigable and eager, rough when it was needed, gentle when necessary, and there was a heightened intensity to everything he attempted. The way he'd look at you during sex made you feel like he was entrusting you with his soul. He knew how to do certain things... things that not many men know how to do... or dare. Or imagine doing. It was like...yes...it was like he transformed during sex into a gentle wind, or hot water, or warm water, and he'd come in through your belly, through your intimate parts, through your entire body. He flooded you. And the water would rise sky-high. Charles had a kinky imagination, he loved to stage erotic scenes. He would invent scenarios, either between us or with others, that everyone who participated in the debauchery found incredibly arousing. He'd always had that gift, beneath his demeanor of a respectable editor whose sole concern was capital-L literature."

She doubled over just then, racked by another coughing fit. I gave her something to drink. Once she'd recovered, she said: "Thank you...Let's move on. I'm guessing you're not all that interested in what I've told you about Elimane's sexual exploits..."

"On the contrary. Everything interests me."

"In that case, listen carefully to this next part. In the beginning of 1938, Elimane was able to move to a nicer place. The first time he invited Charles and me over, he told us he had finished writing. We were as surprised as we were delighted, as you can easily imagine. We were so eager... That was the night he read us *The Labyrinth of Inhumanity*."

For a moment, a long moment, she sank back into her memories, then said:

"Extraordinary. I found the text extraordinary. I found Elimane's reading extraordinary. Everything. At the end, when I looked at Charles, he had tears in his eyes, and I knew we wouldn't change a thing in the manuscript, not even a comma."

"You didn't detect the plagiarism?"

"I'm getting there. No, not in listening to it. The text had us in thrall."

"And Elimane didn't say anything."

"No. It was only a few days later, while rereading the manuscript he had given us, that Charles and I had some doubts about a few passages. The ones whose authors were the most apparent. We checked and were shocked to discover the borrowings, but also to see how he had managed to blend them into the flow of his text. Once I got over my surprise, I was even more admiring of *The Labyrinth of Inhumanity* and Elimane's genius—and yes, I dare to use that word. You have to be a genius to write an entire book with fragments of what other people have written. At least, you have to be incredibly skilled at patching things together. Charles was more circumspect, however. He recognized the virtuosity of the writing, and he recognized that the story was one of a kind, but he couldn't shake off the idea that the whole thing was theft, a dishonest sham. It was a singular book, never before seen, deeply original, but at the same time it was also a compilation of existing books. For Charles, that ambiguity was intolerable. When we saw Elimane again, that same night, we had our first big argument. Charles admonished Elimane for pillaging literature; Elimane responded that literature was nothing but a game of pillages, and that his book proved it. He said that one of his goals had been to be both original and not, since that was one possible definition of literature and even of art, and that his other goal had been to show that anything could be sacrificed in the name of creative perfection. They argued all night. Charles didn't agree with anything Elimane said, and was all the more upset since he couldn't deny that the book had its own beauty, and was more than a pale reflection of the works it contained. He said that he would never publish the book as it was, and then Elimane said, 'So be it. I'll publish it somewhere else.' As for me, at first I didn't say anything. I let the cocks fight it out. But fundamentally, I agreed with Elimane. When I finally said so, Charles flew off the handle and yelled that he wasn't surprised, that Elimane had made me crazy. I think that he was a little jealous of Elimane, even though he was his best friend."

"And then?"

"After a few tense days and much debate, Charles and I invited Elimane over. Charles told him he was happy to publish the book, on the condition that we put the direct citations in quotation marks, and the rewritten passages in italics. Obviously Elimane refused. Charles made a desperate attempt to get him to agree to a preface or foreword, a disclaimer to explain his method. Again, Elimane angrily rejected the idea. He said that nothing was worse than a book that explained itself, that warned the reader, that gave hints on how it should be understood, or absolved for being what it was. He lost his temper and walked out. Charles and I followed him down the street. When we caught up with him, Charles said that, in the end, he wanted to give it a try."

"Why did he change his mind, in your opinion?"

"I don't know. Maybe he was thinking about the long road Elimane had taken to get there."

"And how did Elimane react when Charles told him in the street that he would publish him?"

"He started crying like a baby. That was the only time I saw him overcome by his emotions. Charles cried too. We went to the brasserie where we'd met up the first time, in Place Clichy. We celebrated, then we went home and the three of us had sex—passionate, drunken, happy sex. Elimane thanked us for our trust, and that same night he told us that he would publish *The Labyrinth of Inhumanity* under the name T.C. Elimane. T for Thérèse, C for Charles. He wanted to put the initials of our first names next to his. Three months later, we published *The Labyrinth of Inhumanity*. A few days later, you were the first person to talk about it in *Revue des deux mondes*. You know the rest."

"That's just it: I don't. How did Elimane react to the articles in the press? I'm not talking about Bobinal or Vaillant's articles. I simply mean the other reviews."

"They made him very unhappy. During that period, he holed up in his tiny apartment, saddened and deeply affected. He was destroyed by what your colleagues and you yourself wrote about *The Labyrinth of Inhumanity*. He said that you didn't understand, that none of you understood, that everyone, even those who defended him, had misinterpreted the book. He believed that his critics hadn't read the book, or, worse in his mind, had read it the wrong way, and that not knowing how to read correctly was a sin."

"And yet at the time there were rumors swirling that his book was of great interest to the jurors of the Goncourt prize."

"True. J.H. Rosny, president of the jury, liked the novel's supernatural dimension. But people said that the other Rosny, the younger brother, wasn't convinced. Lucien Descaves found the book audacious, perhaps overly so. Dorgelès, who had fought alongside the Senegalese *tirailleurs* in the war, and respected them, made it known that he would support the book. Léon Daudet apparently told one journalist: 'The only thing I don't like about this book is that its editor, Ellenstein, is an Israelite!' Léo Larguier described the writing as horrendous. Francis Carco thought it had style. Pol Neveux thought it had none at all. But, yes, they were discussing it."

"And in spite of that Elimane was still sad?"

"He didn't really care about the Goncourt. Every time we saw him, he would repeat over and over that no one had understood him, and that that was a crime. We felt powerless. It was clear to us, despite everything we tried, that he was inconsolable. It was at that point that you wrote to Charles and me, asking for an interview. Obviously, Elimane refused to do it, but he wasn't against us meeting with you."

"But what was it that aggrieved him, exactly? That we hadn't seen what Professor Vaillant saw later—the plagiarism? The rewritten passages? The virtuosity of his writing?"

"Even now, ten years later, you don't understand. What pained him was that he wasn't seen as a writer, but as a media phenomenon, as an exceptional Negro, as an ideological battlefield. In the press, hardly anyone talked about the text itself, his writing, his creation."

"Excuse me, but you and Charles also viewed him as an exceptional Negro..."

"That's not true," she said in a hard voice. "We saw the exceptional writer in him, not the black savant. Unlike you lot. To you, he was just a circus freak. You put him on display, not as a talented writer, but the way you would display a man in a human zoo. Like an object of demeaning curiosity. It was because of that as well that he couldn't show himself. You killed him."

"Henri de Bobinal and Paul-Émile Vaillant are the ones who killed him. They're the ones who spotted the plagiarism. By the way, did you know that Bobinal's article was..."

"...a web of lies? Yes, I know. I also know that Bobinal is dead. When his article came out in '38, we immediately went to see Elimane. He told us that the professor was lying, since the Bassari were not a people of Senegal. Bobinal had invented that myth. Charles wanted to write an article to refute Bobinal's, but Elimane refused. He said he preferred to maintain his silence, and nothing would get any further reaction out of him. We'd gone to see him at night. It was thundering. We told him he was being selfish, and that he wasn't the only party involved: we, his editors, his publishers, were in the firing line too. Charles said he was going to write an article, whether Elimane liked it or not, to vindicate the book, the company, all of us. He couldn't bear the idea that a lie would destroy Gemini without us putting up a fight. Elimane of course tried to talk him out of it. The discussion got heated, and it came to fisticuffs. Elimane was winning—he was huge. Charles was gutsy but he didn't stand a chance. I yelled at them to stop, they didn't listen, thunder was rumbling outside. It all happened very quickly. At one point, when Charles was on the floor, half knocked out and forehead bloody, Elimane said, 'I'm going to stop all of this. I have to.' He looked at me, a look that contained so many things, so many pleas and prayers, so much pain, and tears too, and love, but he said nothing, and he walked out into the storm after grabbing a few things. That's the last time I saw him."

I let a few seconds of silence pass before asking: "You didn't see him again after that argument? Ever?"

"No. Though I did hear from him, much later. That night, the night they fought, we stayed in the apartment after he left. It was his apartment. I tended to Charles, patched up his wound. He told me that the whole thing was stupid beyond belief, that it was madness. He cried and said it was his fault and that he never should have dragged Elimane into this writing business. I hated him in that moment. I hated his weakness, but even more than that, I hated his condescension and his arrogance. He had to have been arrogant to think that Elimane wouldn't have written without him. But I said nothing, and we stayed at the apartment, waiting for Elimane to come back. He didn't return that night. Or the following day. We went home. The days went by, and Elimane was still gone. The concierge told us he hadn't seen him in over a week. We began to fear the worst. We looked for him in every conceivable spot: cafés, bars, parks, bookstores, places we had gone together and that he'd liked. We checked all the libertine clubs we'd taken him to. Not a trace of him. He'd vanished. We were on the verge of filing a missing person report when Vaillant's article came out. That was the final nail in our coffin. He lambasted the actual instances of plagiarism and put the blame squarely on us. The press jumped into the fray, and the courts quickly intervened. Some of the plagiarized authors' heirs demanded compensation. For Charles and me, that was the worst part of the scandal. We received threatening letters from all over, we were found guilty in court, crucified in the public eye, we were held responsible for everything, since no one saw hide or hair of Elimane. Because the writer himself was invisible, people went after his publishers. We were forced to close Gemini after destroying all the copies we could find of *The Labyrinth of Inhumanity*. We took them off every shelf and out of every warehouse. We cleared our backstock. Whatever capital remained was used to cover our legal costs, reimburse the heirs who had filed lawsuits, and pay our three employees. After that, there was very little money left. We closed Gemini, sold the small apartment we were living in, and left Paris at Charles's urging. We went to Cajarc, in Lot, to ride out the storm. I couldn't stand it, first because I hated our house there, which I had inherited from my parents, and then because I felt like we had abandoned our dreams in Paris, along with our youth. And Elimane, of course."

"You didn't hear from him at all during the legal proceedings?"

"Not once. We were so overwhelmed and in such a rush that we stopped looking for him, at his apartment or anywhere else. We simply wanted to get out of that hell. He didn't come to court, he didn't write us. He remained invisible. I thought he was dead. I even told myself it would be better if he was: his death would at least explain his silence."

"Where was he and what was he doing during those weeks of proceedings?"

"I don't know. He didn't tell us when he did write us."

"When did he write you?"

"Two years later, early July, 1940. We'd been living in Cajarc for over a year and a half, and we knew we wouldn't be leaving anytime soon because of the war. Of course we had tried writing him at his address. But our letters were never answered. Then, one day, his letter arrived."

"What did he say in that letter?"

Thérèse Jacob didn't answer right away. She looked at me for a few seconds, then said: "It's personal."

"Please, Miss Jacob, I…"

"Don't push it, Brigitte. And enough with the 'Miss Jacobs.' Call me Thérèse. That letter is personal. All I can tell you is that it ended with these words: 'Now that it is finished and remains to be finished, I can finally go home.'"

"Go home…to Senegal?"

"You don't understand. It was wartime. France was occupied. It was impossible for him to go back to Senegal at that point. 'I can finally go home' could only mean one thing: I'm going to start writing again."

"And what did he mean by 'it is finished and remains to be finished'?"

"That he was going to leave again once he had done his time."

"Done his time?"

"Yes; for his crimes: Elimane was condemned, in 1938, by everyone, including you, to not being understood. 'It is finished' means 'in the end I understood that not only is being understood rare in literature, but also that you should do everything to not be completely understood when you're a writer. Now I can write freed from the fear of not being understood, since I no longer want to be.' That's what it meant."

"Once again, that's your interpretation."

"You're free to come up with another one."

"Did you keep the letter?"

"If I did, I wouldn't show it to you."

"Did you respond?"

"No. Elimane didn't include a return address. And anyway, Charles and I were busy surviving in Cajarc, at the beginning of the war. Those were hard years. I didn't like the house in Cajarc, like I said. It's a house where I had bad childhood memories. But what made life more difficult was my growing anger at Charles. I wished I were in Paris. Or anywhere else, other than Cajarc. But he would say that Paris was a massive death trap, and that it was best to wait in the country for a while, and try to find networks of a possible resistance. And there were some, it turned out. We were about to initiate contact with them when Charles left. One day, in 1942, he left without warning. When I woke up, he was gone. Two days later, I understood where he went, once he wrote me. Regardless, he didn't come back. The only letter he sent me from whatever front he was at was also a farewell letter of sorts. I think Charles wanted to redeem himself. He wanted to redeem himself in my eyes, but also in his own. I think that in the end he blamed himself for abandoning Elimane. Charles didn't tell me because he knew I wouldn't have let him go. Not without me, at least. In the single letter he sent me after he left, he told me that if I went three days without receiving another letter from him, it meant he was dead. He never wrote again. I understood. There was nothing I could do. So I hid out in Cajarc until the end of the war. I helped the Resistance in my own way. And in '46, two years ago, I moved here, to Tharon. I miss Charles. I loved him. Spare me your condolences. Let's keep going. And what about Elimane, right? Did I love him? He wasn't a lovable man, Brigitte. I don't mean that he was impossible to love. A quiet violence radiated from him, and it was hard to know whether you wanted to extinguish that violence, share it to ease his load, or run away from it, and cast it as far away as you could."

"So you haven't heard anything else from him since his letter in July 1940?"

"Nothing. But several times, after Charles left, I had the feeling that Elimane was nearby, observing me. Surely a figment of my imagination. He had to have died during the war, like Charles. Over time, I came to understand that the letter he sent us in July 1940 was a goodbye."

I said nothing. A long pause went by, then she looked at me: "There you have it, Brigitte. I think that's all I wanted to tell you. For me too, in a way, everything is finished."

After those words, Thérèse told me that she was tired and in pain from her cough. The interview was over. I thanked her and returned to the inn. I spent the rest of the day and the whole night writing and transcribing the first draft of this account, not sleeping, barely eating. Two days later, I went back to Thérèse Jacob's home to have her read it. She told me that it didn't interest her, and that I could do what I wanted with it. She told me goodbye. My stay in Tharon was over.

Back in Paris, I conducted a little more research. For example, I found proof of Elimane's remarkable high school trajectory between 1935 and 1937, and I discovered his full name, under which he had been listed in the foreigners' registry at the prefecture of Paris: Elimane Madag Diouf. But I essentially added nothing to Thérèse Jacob's account, which is what you're holding in your hands.

It might be that this investigation is a total failure. "Who was the true Negro Rimbaud?" asks the title. But do we know, by the end of this report? Do we know who Elimane Madag Diouf, a.k.a. T.C. Elimane, really was, now that we've reached this final page? I'm not so sure.

Granted, one might know a little more about his arrival in Paris, and his life here, at a certain period, during which he wrote and published *The Labyrinth of Inhumanity*. That's surely fairly significant in itself, given the total mystery surrounding his life. We also know a little about how he wrote that novel, engendered by countless others, in an entirely deliberate way.

It's not my role to judge the man or the work. Posterity will handle that, if one day it's still interested in *The Labyrinth of Inhumanity*. We know a little more about how Elimane experienced this turbulent period. We know something about his morals, his temperament, his mind. We know that he was brilliant and haunted by books. But is all that enough to tell us who he was deep down?

Since 1940 and the letter that Thérèse Jacob claims to have received from him, Elimane hasn't shown any sign of life. Many things, terrible things, as we all know, occurred in our country after 1940. Perhaps Elimane was swept into the current of those tragic events. But it's impossible to know. Nothing says that he's not alive, somewhere, here, and that he'll read this investigation with a slight smile, maybe at this very moment. Nothing tells me that he didn't go back to Africa. One thing is certain, and Thérèse Jacob said it: he found his true country in literature; maybe the only one.

As I write the final lines of this investigation, I'm thinking of him, wherever he is. And I'm also thinking of his friends: Thérèse Jacob and Charles Ellenstein. This account is dedicated to them.

Third Biographeme

___

The end of Charles Ellenstein

1

He's on his way to Paris, but of course Charles Ellenstein doesn't know where Elimane might be (or even if he's still living in the capital). Most critically, Ellenstein has no idea what's waiting for him. He's caught wind of a few rumors. But Charles Ellenstein, by temperament and culture alike, doesn't believe those rumors. He has faith in the restraint and intelligence of Man. But the rumors he's heard are neither restrained nor intelligent: they're repugnant.

In any case, Ellenstein isn't *really* Jewish. He's not practicing. His interest in the Torah and the Talmud is limited and strictly academic. Like Thérèse, his Jewish identity doesn't obsess him, nor does it shape his worldview; he doesn't talk about being Jewish and in fact hardly ever thinks about it, though the anti-Semitic climate of recent years has saddened and even outraged him. In reality, Charles is only reminded of his Jewishness by others, who hear it in his name; and when they mention it, Ellenstein responds, smiling, that he's Jewish, but only as an afterthought.

Charles Ellenstein is thinking about his friend. They parted ways without a proper goodbye. Which he regrets. This is the reason he's come back to Paris, to fix the past (Ellenstein is among those men who think this is possible). He's here for Elimane, but he's also here for Thérèse, and a little for himself.

A few days earlier, in Cajarc, he was beset and paralyzed by a feeling of guilt like never before. Charles Ellenstein had told himself he couldn't stay there anymore, hiding like a coward, with Thérèse, who had hated him ever since they fled, always giving him that terrible look. He made the decision, without discussing it with Thérèse, to return to Paris alone. The smuggler who helped him clandestinely cross the demarcation line between the free zone and the occupied zone told him he was heading to certain death.

July 1942: soon it will have been four years since Thérèse and Charles saw Elimane. He'd responded to just one of the letters they sent him. That was in the summer of 1940: a sort of farewell letter that he had concluded with these words: "Now that it is finished and remains to be finished, I can finally go home." The last time they saw him, that epic stormy night when everything went sour and almost ended in tragedy, had been at Elimane's place, in the room he rented on the top floor of a building not far from Place de la République.

That was his last address known to Charles. So that's where he planned to begin his search.

2

He'd steeled himself (though no one can properly steel themselves for disappointment), but all the same Charles is vexed and distraught when he learns that Elimane no longer lives in his former building. The concierge (the same as before) tells him that Elimane left, he's positive, before the war. Ellenstein asks if he knows where he went. The concierge replies that the African never was very talkative, though he had gleaned that he was moving to the south of Paris, near Porte d'Orléans. It's a meager piece of information, proven by nothing, but it's all Ellenstein has, so he decides to follow what can't rightly be called a lead, but rather a rustling in the underbrush of a dense jungle.

He crosses the city on foot, and is forced to stop several times to catch his breath. His heart starts racing as soon as he takes a few steps, and Ellenstein, who's still young and in good health, wonders if it's the change of air that's causing this perpetual shortness of breath. He eventually hails a bike-taxi, and a strapping type with huge shoulders, powerful legs, and little to say, but who knows Paris well, takes him to Porte d'Orléans. As he watches the city stream by from the back of the cart, Charles Ellenstein begins to understand the cause of his racing heartbeat. He closes his eyes. His heart is beating almost normally now, but it soon seems to him that this return to a more regular rhythm has opened the door to an even greater sense of anxiety. It's not only the fact that he doesn't recognize the city that is putting him in this state, it's also, mainly, the feeling that the city doesn't recognize *him*. Or the opposite: the vague feeling that it absolutely recognizes him, that every street has identified him and every building is watching him. The entire city is whispering his name, and that's what frightens him. He tries to master his fear. It only subsides once he finds himself alone. He manages to rent a room in a hotel, Hôtel de l'Étoile, on Rue du Couëdic, a few minutes' walk from Porte d'Orléans.

Once he's somewhat calmer, Ellenstein decides to write to Thérèse to reassure her and explain where he is, as well as provide the reasons for his sudden departure. Further on in the letter, he also summarizes his first day in Paris, tells her he misses her, and shares his plans for the following day (essentially, walk around Porte d'Orléans and maybe stop by city hall, in the hope of stumbling into Elimane's shadow). At the end of the letter, he confides to Thérèse that while crossing occupied Paris, the city filled with German officers and soldiers, plastered with Nazi signs and swastikas, almost empty of people and spangled with yellow, he had the feeling that he was *meant*—he hesitated at length here, between meant, wanted, and might, and finally chose "meant" for its ambiguity—to die.

Then he makes up his mind, fear in his gut, to go mail it. But outside the city has stopped whispering his name and his terror recedes. He goes to bed and that night dreams of his father. Simon Ellenstein, standing in the central aisle of a synagogue, was talking to another immediately recogniz-

able man: the Führer himself. Charles Ellenstein couldn't
understand their conversation: they were speaking a strange
hybrid tongue, a kind of German-Arabic mixed with
Hebrew, which, aided by the Hitlerian theatricality and
sweeping crescendos, became a deafening, unhinged pro-
peller, its blades tinged with red. Simon Ellenstein, however,
spoke calmly and firmly, while being remarkably sparing
with his movements, the complete opposite of the frenetic
Führer. Charles struggled to determine (in the dream at
least, for when he thought about this once awake, it struck
him as obvious) if the contrast between these two oratori-
cal and existential styles gave the scene a comic quality or a
tragic one. A few feet from the two duelists, on one of the
benches, a third man appeared to be praying, or sleeping, or
simply dreaming. From behind, Ellenstein thought he recognized him. He went closer. When he walked between Adolf
Hitler and Simon Ellenstein, neither noticed him, as if he
was an invisible guest. He took a close look at his father
and found himself agreeing with his mother, who used to
say they had the same jawline. He did not, however, linger
on the Führer's face, which resembled the Führer's face in
every way and held no surprises. He then left them to their
quarrel and advanced toward the man seated farther away.
There was no longer any doubt: it was him, Charles. But
once he reached the man, instead of his own face, he saw
Elimane's. He also saw that he wasn't asleep: he was dead.
Overcome by fear, Charles wanted to scream, but suddenly
his father's voice rang out (in French): Charles, there's nothing more you can do for him. Then Hitler added (in the
hybrid language Charles intuitively understood): There's
nothing more you can do for yourself.

Charles wakes up, drenched, troubled for another few seconds; then he tells himself it was just a nightmare, and that he doesn't believe in nightmares any more than he does rumors. He drinks a glass of water and falls back asleep. The rest of his night is peaceful.

3

Naturally, as the reader, who knows how life is, will have guessed, Charles Ellenstein doesn't run into Elimane by chance the following day. He does, however, in the early afternoon, have an encounter he wasn't expecting. He's sitting on a public bench on Rue d'Alésia thinking that coming to Paris might have been an absurd or suicidal idea when a woman, after walking past, doubles back. She stops in front of his bench and says, "Mr. Ellenstein?" He looks up but doesn't recognize her. In fact he's certain he's never seen her before, even though, on her end, the woman is sporting a complicit smile that indicates or suggests that they know one another. He tries to stir the sludge of his memory in search of her face. Futile. The woman says, "Charles, is that you?"

"Yes, but... I'm sorry, but..."

"Have I changed all that much? It's me, Claire. Miss Ledig."

Charles Ellenstein wavers another half second, then, quite naturally, Miss Ledig's face matches up with her name, and the memory returns. He finds it unforgivable that he could have forgotten what this woman, who was the secretary at Gemini for several years, looks like. He apologizes profusely, tells her she hasn't changed (which is untrue), and that he was lost in his thoughts (which is true). He offers to buy her a drink to fully redeem himself, she agrees because she's running a little early. She suggests he accompany her to a nearby brasserie, where she has a date soon. They go; it's a few minutes away. She orders a tea, him a beer. They inevitably talk about Gemini, the glory days when the company was stable and turning a profit despite its small size and demanding but (or consequently) limited editorial ambitions. The shadow of *The Labyrinth of Inhumanity* looms over the conversation, yet neither Ellenstein nor Claire mentions it. He asks her if she found another job after Gemini shut down.

"More than a job, Charles, I found a man. I might be getting married."

Charles Ellenstein congratulates her. Miss Ledig thanks him half-heartedly, a little embarrassed. Charles notices and asks her why. She hesitates before answering: "My fiancé is . . . Well, you'll understand, I'm sure you will, you're a man with an open mind . . . he's . . . he's a German officer. But he's not like the others!" she adds hastily, almost imploringly.

Charles Ellenstein can't think of what to say for a few seconds, then he replies: "These things happen. I'm not here to judge you."

They both remain silent, until Ellenstein asks her if she's heard from Pierre Schwarz or André Merle, her former colleagues at Gemini. Claire says no. Then, to forestall any further awkwardness between them, she asks her former employer what he's doing there: "I thought you'd decided to leave. Are you living here again?"

"No, I did leave Paris. I only came back yesterday. I'm staying in a little hotel close by, the Hôtel de l'Étoile, on Rue du Couëdic."

"Ah, I know it well. I tried to get a job there after Gemini closed, but another hotel ended up hiring me."

"I see...I came back to Paris because..."

As she had a moment before, he hesitated before continuing:

"I came back because I'm looking for Elimane."

"Elimane?"

"Yes, you know, the author of *The Labyrinth of Inhumanity*, remember...I know you never saw him, but..."

"No, I never saw him. But Josef did. Josef definitely saw him. That's what he told me."

"Josef is the German officer you're seeing?"

"Yes, that's him. He met Elimane. And I'm certain that without his book, Josef might never have spoken to me."

Charles Ellenstein finishes his drink. Claire begins telling him the story. After Gemini closed, she found a job at the reception desk of a fancy hotel near Montparnasse. She's been working there barely three months when the war breaks out, and after the Germans penetrate the French front in 1940 and are nearing Paris, she decides, unlike many of her colleagues, to stay. She stays because she likes her job, but also because she has nowhere else to go. The hotel is quite nice. And soon enough the occupiers requisition it. They use it to lodge officers: handsome officers with shiny boots, impeccable uniforms, and thick epaulets with gold stripes, officers as elegant and proud as Greek archons on parade. Among them is Captain Josef Engelmann, one of the princes of the German general staff in Paris. He's an avowed Francophile who visited Paris several times before the war, and is well versed in French poetry. He reads it in the original, though the meaning of certain words and images eludes him, notably in works by the poet he considers superior to the rest, ranking him even above the poetic, sacred constellation formed by Lautréamont, Baudelaire, and Rimbaud: Mallarmé.

Nonetheless, Engelmann's military prowess and bravery during the French campaign leave no room for doubt as to his devotion to the *Vaterland*. He distinguishes himself, in fact, by a determination and cruelty in combat that is interpreted as a desire to dispel, through violent, rageful acts, any suspicion of him. Once France is defeated, he returns to being a gentle, sensitive aesthete. After hurrying through his administrative tasks, he spends his time reading, searching for rare texts, and strolling through this city he loves. He's a rather solitary man, one who prefers the company of books to that of people. Still, he can be spotted at the occasional social event, talking to Ernst Jünger, to whom he's often compared, though he lacks and incidentally doesn't desire his aura and prestige. He's not a writer and isn't tempted to become one. Reading and enjoying poetry is enough for him.

Engelmann notices Claire Ledig, whom he sometimes sees at the hotel reception. He interceded on her behalf when his superiors wanted to replace her with a purebred German. Engelmann did so by emphasizing that Claire Ledig, born in Alsace before the Treaty of Versailles, has never forgotten those German roots, even though she has perfectly reintegrated into French society. Moreover, she speaks German as well as she does French, which represents, again according to Engelmann, an indisputable advantage given the context: she could be a precious ally for the regime. He likes Fräulein Claire; nevertheless, his somewhat old-fashioned sense of courtship long holds him back. But one day, Captain Engelmann is returning from one of his strolls with a book he bought from a collector for next to nothing. At the reception, he asks Claire, in perfect French (though the conversation continues in German, a German just as lucid), if she's heard of this book he just bought, the reading of which completely enthralled him.

"It was *The Labyrinth of Inhumanity*," says Claire, "our *Labyrinth of Inhumanity*. Imagine my surprise when I saw the title, and the Gemini logo again. Josef must have thought he'd triggered some painful memory, or that he had expressed himself poorly, when he saw the expression on my face. But I recovered quickly and told him the reason for my reaction. He was just as astonished by the coincidence. But what fascinated him most of all was the story behind the book, the way the plagiarism had been done, the fact that no one ever saw Elimane, the fact that his identity remains unknown. He also explained to me that the story recounted in the book itself was a powerful allegory for the quest for moral and aesthetic elevation through purifying fire. I must confess, Charles, that I hadn't read the book yet, and so I couldn't discuss it that day with Josef, but I listened to him talk at length about literature. After that conversation, we saw each other every day, and he admitted that he had been waiting for a gallant opportunity to approach me without appearing uncouth, and that *The Labyrinth of Inhumanity* had provided one. He brought up the book often, and his fascination for its subject and its fate. He didn't believe that Elimane could have been a Negro, and was leaning toward the hypothesis of a literary hoax. He asked me questions about you, about your relationship with Elimane, about where you lived (which I couldn't tell him, since I didn't know). I think he believed that you had orchestrated the farce. One night, a few months after we met, he came back to the hotel quite upset and told me: 'I found him.' 'What? You found whom?' 'T.C. Elimane. I found him.' 'Really?' And then Josef said some things that were rather strange and frenzied, which I didn't understand, but regardless, he said that he had found Elimane by chance, like a Mallarméan poem, like in one throw of the dice, that they had talked for six hours straight, that Elimane, to Josef's great surprise, was in fact a Negro, but he was also Igitur, who descended the staircase of the human mind, who went to the very depths of things, Igitur, *mein Liebchen*, who had drunk the drop of nothingness missing from the sea, Igitur, then, who withdrew into the night. But the greatest miracle is yet to come: Elimane is writing it, Claire, *mein Schatz*, I saw him writing the Book, the one with which the world must end. That's what he said, more or less. I guessed that my Josef, so robust and solid, had a bout of fever, I touched his forehead and it was burning hot. I tended to him, he fell asleep, and, upon waking, the first thing he said was that he wanted to introduce Elimane to the leaders of the Reich, for he held the secret, the key to the solution, the remedy to all that ailed them. Meanwhile he was the one ailing, and remained bedridden for three days. But he asked me to read *The Labyrinth of Inhumanity* to him because he found it soothing. That was how, by reading it for my beau, I finally discovered the book. It's awful, but you want to read to the end, it gives you no choice. When he regained his strength, Josef immediately returned to the spot where he encountered Elimane, where he had seen him writing, a café, I think. But Elimane was gone, God knows where. For a few days, Josef was near out of his mind. He was mad with rage at having lost Elimane's trail. Thankfully, time's marched on. He's doing better. Sometimes he'll mention Elimane again and that Igitur, about whom I know nothing, but he's doing better. He doesn't understand how he got that fever. Sometimes he'll stop at that bar, in case Elimane comes back. But Elimane is never there. He vanished."

Claire stops speaking. Ellenstein looks at her for a few moments, mind blazing. He finally says: "When did all this happen?"

"It'll be six months soon."

"Here, in Paris?"

"Yes."

"Do you know the exact place where Josef encountered Elimane?"

"In a café. But I don't remember the name. Josef told me and I've forgotten it. Hold on, though…He can tell you himself. I see him coming. He's who I was waiting for."

Ellenstein turns around and sees Josef Engelmann enter the room. He has an imposing presence. It doesn't come from the uniform, but further away, from the inside. The café customers watch him without hostility, with admiration, even. They're likely thinking that he's only a soldier in appearance, and that deep down he's an artist. Claire stands. They kiss and say a few words in German. Then Claire switches back to French, and smiling at Ellenstein, tells the German officer: "Allow me to introduce Charles, an old friend. You know him without knowing him. And now he knows you too."

Ellenstein stands. The two men shake hands with no show of excessive virility. Captain Engelmann says, "It's a pleasure," though he's not sure (he looks at Claire) he knows this gentleman.

"Charles is my former employer, T.C. Elimane's publisher. The publisher of *The Labyrinth of Inhumanity*. We were just talking about it."

The two men maintain eye contact. They know that, from this moment on, they're linked.

"You can't imagine how delighted I am to meet the man who published T.C. Elimane," says the German. "I'm intimidated even. I envy you. Being the first person to lay eyes on that text is a privilege."

"Thank you, Captain. It would appear that you had the privilege of meeting Elimane recently."

"Yes, indeed," replies Engelmann, "I did have that distinct honor, Charles. Call me Josef."

Josef Engelmann grabs a third chair, orders a beer, and sits down with Claire and Ellenstein. They chat and get acquainted for a while, before Ellenstein asks the German officer where exactly he met Elimane. Engelmann tells him the address. Ellenstein recognizes it immediately: it's the restaurant where Elimane, Thérèse, and he met for the first time, in Place Clichy. The German officer intuits that Ellenstein hopes to find Elimane there and hastens to say that he tried to find him again at that same restaurant but that Elimane appears never to have returned after their meeting. He adds that all the regulars of said brasserie told him that's how Elimane was—he would disappear, sometimes for months, and then reappear one day. Ellenstein confirms this, but secretly he's thinking: If you didn't find Elimane again, Captain, it's because he didn't want to see you again; he didn't disappear; he's hiding, and all the bar customers who know him are helping him hide. But he'll want to see me. I'm his friend.

Ellenstein is certain the restaurant owners will recognize him and tell him where to find Elimane. This thought lifts his mood and gives him renewed hope.

Soon Ellenstein, Engelmann, and Claire Ledig stop talking about Elimane and broach other topics. The German is widely cultivated, and draws on this rich font of knowledge with modesty and finesse. Ellenstein tells himself that the rumors truly are bullshit, this captain is the irrefutable proof. After an hour of conversation, Charles stands up to take his leave. He wants to make his way to the little bar where he believes (no, is sure) that Elimane can be found. He kisses Claire and thanks her for recognizing him. He then extends his hand to Engelmann, who squeezes it with a vigorous grip.

"Lovely to have met you, Charles. Eisenstein, isn't it?"

"Sorry?"

"Eisenstein. That's your last name, right?"

"Ellenstein."

"Ah, yes, my apologies. Ellenstein, that's it. Though that's still a surname that...by all indications..."

Charles guesses the rest of his sentence, which for that matter can be read in the German captain's eyes.

"...is Jewish, yes," says Charles. "I am Jewish...(he lets a brief moment pass—a whole world in fact—before continuing)...but only as an afterthought."

After two or three seconds of suspended time, they all roar with laughter, especially the captain. Once the laughter abates, Engelmann says: "That Jewish sense of humor! An afterthought! Though, after all, it is possible. Rare, but possible. But don't you worry: others are thinking about it for you."

Ellenstein says, "Yes, I would imagine"; Claire looks down; Josef Engelmann laughs loudly again, alone. He finally releases Ellenstein's hand. Claire immediately takes her former employer's arm and whispers: "Don't worry, Charles. Josef isn't like...you understand...like all the others...like the real...well, you know, all those rumors. The stories about the camps, the roundups that are coming, the deportation of Jews...Nonsense. *Nicht wahr*, Josef?"

"*Ja, genau, mein Schatz! Das ist absolut lächerlich!* Ridiculous and absurd."

Claire Ledig looks at the German captain with love and trust. The German captain looks Charles Ellenstein straight in the eyes and smiles. Ellenstein smiles too, not knowing why, perhaps simply out of politeness. He tries to pay, but Engelmann insists on treating him. "I can at least offer you that," he says. Ellenstein gives in, thanks him, and leaves.

He immediately goes to the bar whose address Engelmann provided him, to find Elimane. But he's not there. The manager, who recognizes Charles, explains that Elimane, with all the Nazis prowling the streets, ventures out less and less often. "His skin," he says, "you understand...He doesn't want to take the risk. But I can find a way to give him a message from you. I don't know where he lives, but he still stops by once in a while, discreetly, when there's hardly anyone here."

Ellenstein waits for hours and hours in the restaurant, in Place Clichy. Elimane doesn't show up. Ellenstein resigns himself to leaving, but first, he writes a note. In the letter, he tells Elimane that he'll wait for him there every day after six p.m. He also says that he misses him, that Thérèse misses him, and that he regrets how things ended between them. He concludes by mentioning Claire Ledig and Captain Engelmann. I never would have thought, he writes, that I'd be thanking a German officer, in this day and age, but it's thanks to this Engelmann, whom, I believe, you've already met, that I now have a chance of finding you here, my friend. Ellenstein then leaves the letter with the manager, returns to his hotel, and begins to write another letter, this one intended for Thérèse Jacob.

(The reader, as perceptive as ever, knows that Ellenstein never wrote that letter to Thérèse Jacob or, if he did, he destroyed it when he realized that the shadows, dark but for two silent flashes of light, were knocking at his door. They had waited patiently, hiding, for him to return to the Hôtel de l'Étoile. The reader also knows how—and where—Ellenstein met his end. But despite the night and the fog, despite the two flashes shrouded in darkness, Charles Ellenstein didn't give up any names, any addresses, any secrets.)

4

By the time I got to the end of the report, said Siga D., Brigitte Bollème hadn't moved, eyes shut, in so long that for a few seconds I thought she had fallen asleep as I'd read to her. I was about to cough when she said, without opening her eyes:

"There are a few nicely phrased lines, but as a whole, the investigation is an utter failure and poorly written. Wouldn't you agree?"

I remained silent. She opened her eyes, looked at me, and said:

"I'm a terrible interviewer. I'd been thinking about Elimane for ten years, and when I tracked Thérèse Jacob down in 1948, in Tharon, I didn't ask her any of the questions that I should have. A no-good interviewer, truly. Luckily, nobody else will ever read my report, and nobody else still cares who T.C. Elimane is."

"Then she began to laugh hysterically, and honestly, Diégane, I had no idea how to react. So I watched her laughing at herself, at her investigation that she deemed a failure, or at the fact that there was nobody left, in 1985, who knew who Elimane was."

"And what about you?" I asked Siga D. "Did you think the investigation was a failure?"

"No, I wouldn't say that. I wouldn't say failure, more like incomplete. There's no such thing as an exhaustive investigation, at least not into a man's life. There are only fragments. Placed end to end, they might cover a very large stretch of life, but there would still be gaps. It's life itself that rejects the investigation's claim to be all-encompassing. Here, I'm referring to the external manifestations of a life, the ones that can be the subjects of inquiry. Because psychological shifts, the life of the mind and soul, our inner enigma, can't, by their nature, be investigated. They can only be confessed, or deduced, or assumed. But as for understanding them... Brigitte Bollème covered one part of Elimane's life. And I knew some of his childhood, thanks to my father. We had two pieces. Many were missing. But her investigation wasn't a failure. I didn't think so."

"And did you ask her why she said she thought it was a failure?"

"I didn't get the chance. I wanted to. But as soon as she stopped laughing, she said: 'Nobody else cares who Elimane was, except you, of course. And me, a little. But I'm at the end of my life. I now concern myself with lighter things. I'm finally able to, after being pursued by Elimane for so long.'"

"Pursued?"

"I reacted the exact same way to that word, Diégane. I said, 'Pursued?' At that Bollème stood up and left the room. A few minutes later she came back holding another book. It was *The Labyrinth of Inhumanity*. I recognized it immediately. Two envelopes had been tucked between the pages. Bollème sat back down and told me: 'In reality, if I'm being honest, I don't really know who was pursuing whom. You'll tell me what you think. A few weeks after my investigation was published, I received a letter from the city hall of Saint-Michel-Chef-Chef, which is the municipality that includes Tharon. I understood, of course, even before opening it, that it concerned Thérèse Jacob. She was dead. Untreated pneumonia. That's how I found out. I thought back to her coughing fits. The city hall was requesting that I pick up a few personal items she had left me. Yes, me. That was the real motive for the letter. So I went back to Tharon, or more precisely, to Saint-Michel-Chef-Chef. Thérèse Jacob had left me two small envelopes. A municipal employee handed them to me, and before I left to return to Paris, I asked if she had been buried in the town cemetery. In fact, she had. She'd made arrangements. So I went to the cemetery, where it didn't take me long to find her grave: a gray, sober headstone, the ground around it still turned up and damp. She had been laid to rest beside a cenotaph that I guessed, even before reading the engraved inscription, she had had erected in Charles Ellenstein's memory. It was at that moment, as I already told you, as I looked at that grave, that, for the first time, I questioned the veracity of Thérèse Jacob's account. Elimane left so few traces that I had clung with all my strength to the only one I could find. But now Thérèse Jacob was dead, and it was only then that I began to have doubts. Though if I'm being sincere, I don't believe that I really had doubts. I was simply thinking that I should have asked more questions, forced her to say a bit more, to be more specific. When I was with her, I had behaved like a fascinated child who's being told a wonderful story, and not like a levelheaded and critical journalist trying to get to the bottom of an old affair. I stayed at the cemetery for a long time, until the rain roused me from my troubled, trance-like contemplation of the graves. Then I left. On the train back to Paris, I didn't look at what was inside the envelopes, which I clutched against my stomach. I only opened them once I was home, alone, at night. One contained a letter, the letter Elimane had sent to Charles and Thérèse in July 1940, and which she had refused to show me. I set it aside to read later.

"'Then I opened the second envelope, and pulled out a black-and-white photo: in the foreground, far to the left, there was a young man partially turned away from the photographer, looking to his right. On the right side of the shot, but behind the young man, you could see, in profile, a young woman walking, her long brown hair floating behind her, swept by the wind. She was looking into the distance ahead of her. They were on a beach. Behind them, in the background, was the sea, a little choppy, its waves frothing white. You could also make out, to the left, the tip of a cliff surrounded by rocks. And above all that, an empty sky, no clouds. Based on how the two people were dressed, one would assume it was cold. The woman walking on the beach was Thérèse Jacob, I recognized her immediately. The young man in the foreground was Elimane, I knew it intuitively. The photo had to have been taken by Charles Ellenstein. I flipped it over. There was no date or location given. It had been taken between 1935 and 1938, clearly. I'm leaning toward 1937—the photo gives the impression of closeness or even secret complicity between Elimane and Thérèse, but also between those two and Charles, who was photographing them. All of which leads me to believe that it was a period when their friendship was as beautiful and pure as the sky in the image. Maybe after Elimane had been inducted into their libertine world. Or maybe I'm wrong. I studied the photo at length, fascinated by Elimane's face, which I was seeing for the first time. And actually, that right there, for example, is one of the reasons I think I'm a terrible interviewer: When I interviewed Thérèse Jacob in '48, at no point did I ask her if she had a photo of Elimane. Don't you find it odd that for all those years I searched for a man whom I believed I knew so well that I forgot I had never seen him and wouldn't have been able to recognize him if I ran into him in the street? So, I'm looking at his face. It's a man's face, but it still has a youthful, energetic quality. In reality, I can only see half of it. The other half, because of the sun's angle, is lost in shadow. So, I see one eye, half his forehead, half his nose, part of his mouth. The rest is dark. You can only imagine it. But the visible half is enough to know what he looks like. I'm still looking at his face. Elimane has a strange expression: he's smiling (or scowling), but he also seems intrigued (or amused) by something, or someone, that's drawing his gaze to the right. He's blinking and seems like he was about to speak, unless Charles took the photo just as he said something. Above his right eye, a visible shadow, or hollow, which marks the arch of his eyebrow. It's an expressive face. A handsome face, more than anything. Handsome because it's expressive, handsome because it's eloquent. But in fact, Thérèse Jacob walking is what brings the image to life. The step she's taking, her hair moving in the wind, her gaze at the horizon are what give this image its beauty and mystery. I can smell the sea. I can feel the wind. I can sense the cold. Mainly, I can sense that a few seconds after this photo, Elimane is going to turn around, to look at Thérèse and to look at the sea. And behind the lens, I see Charles, really I do, his blue eyes that are sad even when he smiles, his blond hair slicked back, a cigarette stuck between his lips as he captures the scene.'

"I'm sorry to interrupt, Brigitte, I said, but did you keep the photo?

"'Of course I kept it, young lady. It's inside this book I'm holding right now. This is also where I put that letter I've told you so much about. The photo and the letter are in the two envelopes you see here, tucked between the pages of my old copy of *The Labyrinth of Inhumanity*. You can have them when you leave.'"

"She gave you the envelopes?"

"Yes."

"So you have the photo and the letter?"

"I had both, but now I just have one."

"Be more specific: You have the photo or the letter?"

"Patience. Soon you'll know everything I know, Diégane. At least let me enjoy the small head start I still have over you a little longer."

"Fine. What happened next with Bollème?"

"She gave me the two envelopes and I opened them. Like her, I stared at the photo at length. It was my first time seeing Elimane. He was as Brigitte Bollème had described him, very handsome, young but already mature. There was something about him that I'd seen before, somewhere else. I didn't need to see his whole face to know that there was a vague resemblance, impossible to pinpoint but real, to my father. It was blindingly obvious."

"And? Was it him?"

"What do you mean?"

"Was it really him, the stranger who saves Marème in *Elegy for Black Night*, in the street where she's bleeding to death?"

"It's like you're reading my mind. Not my mind now, but in 1985, when I was looking at that photo for the first time in front of Brigitte Bollème. As I stared at Elimane I asked myself if this was the face that I'd seen between life and death, as the man was carrying me to the hospital. You're bound to find the answer disappointing: I couldn't remember. It was by staring at Elimane's face in the photo that I understood that I'd never seen the face of the man who saved me in the street. I had only ascribed to him certain features. Features that I had also ascribed to Elimane, but that didn't correspond to the ones I saw in the photo. I can't remember. The man who rescued me in the street was Elimane, I'm positive. What I mean is that Elimane's spirit was inside of him. Do you understand?"

"Yes, I do. But I'll let you continue. You were looking at the photo in 1985. And then?"

"Then I read the letter, slowly, very slowly. It was fairly mysterious and sibylline, but everything was understandable. The problem is: it's not because you understand everything that everything is clear. I'll stop you right there, Diégane, I'm not trying to talk in riddles, or mess with your head. It's the letter that was like that. You already know the last sentence: 'Now that it is finished and remains to be finished, I can finally go home.' You understand the sentence, it's coherent enough, and yet it can mean multiple things. Bollème had already mentioned this ambiguity in her investigation, the possibility of multiple interpretations. Should the phrase be understood literally or symbolically? Be read directly or taken as a metaphor? It's hard to decide with Elimane's letter. When you know some of the elements of his life, every sentence becomes ambiguous, everything has a double meaning. It's not a long letter, but I spent several long minutes reading and rereading it, until Bollème said: 'It's unsettling, isn't it?'

"Yes.

"'I had the same reaction that you did,' continued Bollème, 'in '48, at home, when I read it. And from that night on, for a very long time, I had the feeling of being constantly accompanied by Elimane's invisible shadow, or like I was seeing it everywhere. Or looking for it everywhere. I don't really know. But I sensed him there, somewhere, in the city or the world, unless it was only in my mind, but he was there. He was observing me. Sometimes, it would be a gentle warmth whirling around in my stomach and I'd feel protected, invulnerable. Other times, it was a red eye cast on my forehead, and I'd feel the weight of a deadly menace. Sometimes I told myself that he was angry at me for trying, through my investigation, to pull him out of his haven of silence, and other times, that he was grateful to me for having gone looking for him. Until recently, I never had the sense that I was truly alone. It's both an unpleasant and reassuring feeling. It took me time, many years, to get used to his shadow. But the first years were unbearable. One day, when I was looking at the photo again, I thought his eye had moved and that he'd given me a long look, and in that eye fixed on me I heard his voice, against the sound of the waves, and it said to me: "You're next."'

"'Next? Next for what?'

"At this point, Brigitte Bollème paused for a few seconds, then calmly told me: 'Maybe you're next, young lady, maybe you're my replacement. It's possible that's what all of this means. It would be logical, even. Maybe you're his next prey.'"

"What did you say? Did you understand what Brigitte was trying to say?"

"Yes, I understood, Diégane. I understood perfectly. That's why I responded: Let him come. I'm not afraid of him and I'm not afraid of death. I've seen it. I still see it.

"Then Bollème said: 'Then he'll come. Even absent, he'll come.'"

5

Paris, July 4, 1940

Dearest Thérèse, dearest Charles,
  *Neither courage nor folly: braving hellfire wasn't the way
into* The Labyrinth of Inhumanity, *it was drinking the blood
of the damned. What idiocy was mine not to have seen it,
and what blindness, to have looked away when the eye of
the hurricane was descending on you.*
  *But the storm... The diluvian storm was raining down
blood. I sent a black dove out into the night and it came
back to me and said: The earth absorbs blood slower than
water. I understood that I, too, had to drink, to lap like a
wild beast, to take my share if I wanted to reach the heart
of the Labyrinth into which I cast you, abandoning you to
a threat more deadly than the Minotaur's horn. You know
which one... I'm not asking your forgiveness, but I do forgive you. You couldn't have known. I didn't want you to.
Now I see, I drink, I know. I'm with my King, and I heed his
words.*
  *One by one, aside from two pitching on a boat on the
surface, the sinners will be pulled from the lake of Hades.
I'll be with them, though nobody will pull me out since I am
the lake waters. I'll be with them because I, too, am a sinner,*

but I refused to taste innocence when its fruit was offered me, unless I forgot its taste during the Last Judgment being declared in absentia. They never saw me. So how could they have chopped off my head? They decapitated an unknown, some poor, honest man on the gallows of glory as the crowd spat on him. He didn't cry out. He knew—but who was he?—that his blood would open the Labyrinth. I'm with my King, and he hands me his crown so he can rejoin his beloved.

I love you, my friends, I love you. Another, more inhumane, Labyrinth is upon us. The gaping mouth at its center swallows all the sentences in the book, unknowingly swallowing its poison. The essential book is only essential because it kills. Whoever tries to kill it dies. Whoever accompanies it in death lives within.

Now I am the bloodthirsty King, here in my Labyrinth. Let the worthless elders die in my fire. I demand newness. I accept that it's demanded of me. I accept starting over, since starting over is all there is.

All my love to you, dearest Charles, and to you, our heart and soul, dearest Thérèse. Fight the shadows. Stay alive.

Now that it is finished and remains to be finished, I can finally go home.

Elimane

I read the infamous letter four or five times as Siga D. looked on, then I said to her:

"It's crypto-symbolist bullshit. Risible mystagogy. A tasteless parody of a prophet or Meister Eckhart or a Congolese evangelist charlatan planning to expulse the demons inside possessed women by sodomizing them live on Facebook, Bible in hand. T.C. Elimane would have never written this stuff with any seriousness. I don't believe the letter's authentic. Thérèse Jacob wrote it herself. I don't believe it. What crap! Who would write like this to their friends?"

"You're saying that because you don't understand, or worse, because you think you understand without knowing what you think you understand."

"No, I'm saying this because I truly think it's a pile of metaphysical bullshit."

"You can have it."

"I can have the letter? I don't want it."

"Keep it. With time, and by rereading it, you'll understand. Elimane is a writer who can only be understood by being reread. It's true for *The Labyrinth of Inhumanity*. It's true for this letter."

"I'd have preferred the photo."

"It was a nice photo. But I don't have it anymore."

"I'm disappointed. I feel betrayed. This letter is nowhere near the genius of *The Labyrinth of Inhumanity*."

"Elimane knew what he was writing. It might sound like bullshit to you, or arcane, but every sentence in there is saying something specific. However ambiguous or coded. So I'm not going to explain the text to you. I'm not even sure, after carrying it all these years, that I understand it. But there is one detail that struck me in 1985, when I read it in front of Brigitte Bollème."

"Which one?"

"The boat with the two sinners on the lake of Hades, while the rest sink to the bottom. There's something specific there. Who are those sinners, in your opinion?"

"You tell me. I don't understand the letter at all."

"I didn't understand anything the first few times I read it either. But this detail stood out to me. It's the one I grabbed hold of. I mentioned it to Bollème, who told me, speaking slowly: The two individuals on the boat on the surface of the lake of Hades are me and Paul-Émile Vaillant. I was dumbfounded, trying to make the connection between her and Vaillant, attempting to reread the letter in light of that interpretation. Bollème continued: I didn't really understand the letter in '48, when I read it. Apart from a few sentences, it's really quite cryptic. But by rereading it enough times and venturing some guesses, I eventually decided that the mysterious Last Judgment was the whole of the criticisms leveled at *The Labyrinth of Inhumanity* in 1938. This strikes me as rather obvious now, but it took me a while to make the parallel. Based on that, the rest, in that section, becomes clear: the critics are the sinners, and Elimane is the lake in which they drown. I became convinced I was on the right track once I reread my report. Do you know how Elimane, back in '38, referred to people who, according to him, didn't know how to read? No surprise here: sinners. More precisely, he says that reading poorly is a sin."

"Yes," I said, interrupting Siga D.'s account, "but that proves nothing. If you ask me, it only proves that Thérèse Jacob is behind this letter. She's the one who used the word 'sinner' while claiming to be quoting Elimane. And it might be her again using it in this damn letter."

"Wait, Diégane. Wait for the rest. Don't let the letter cloud your thinking. What really matters is what Bollème discovered based on it. So, when she told me all that, I asked her: But Brigitte, why would you and Paul-Émile Vaillant be the only critics not to have sunk in the lake? She responded: I didn't immediately guess that the two survivors were Vaillant and me. It took me months to get there. I only reached that conclusion after rereading every review, every analysis of *The Labyrinth of Inhumanity* published in the Parisian press ten years earlier. Paul-Émile Vaillant had been the first person to understand the structure or the composition of *The Labyrinth of Inhumanity*, even though he considered the book to be a work of plagiarism. But at least he had seen that it was the rewritings or collages of other texts that formed the meat of the book. He had understood that, whereas the others, including myself, had mostly discussed the author, the fact that he was African, whether Negroes can write or not, colonization, and so on. And we mustn't forget that Professor Vaillant never wrote in the press directly about *The Labyrinth of Inhumanity*: he shared his discoveries with a journalist, Albert Maximin. That gets him off the hook."

"And you? What could have gotten you out of it? You have to admit you didn't write much about the text itself either."

"True. And for a long time I wondered about the reason I had found favor with him. Especially since my first review wasn't always tender with the book. Or the author for that matter. I was conflicted. The interview I'd conducted with Ellenstein and Thérèse Jacob wasn't very kind either. I may well have found the reason that, metaphorically, Vaillant had been spared from drowning in the waters of Evil, but where I was concerned, I couldn't see one."

"And?"

"And, young lady, after thinking long and hard, I finally found it. The reason is actually quite obvious. Among all the critics who wrote about the book in the papers, I was the only woman. It might seem like just a theory..."

"...a stupid theory."

"...that Brigitte Bollème didn't disregard, Diégane. She tried to track down every critic and journalist who had written about *The Labyrinth of Inhumanity* when it was published in 1938."

"And so?"

"They were all dead."

"And so?"

"And so listen to what Bollème told me: They all committed suicide between the end of 1938 and July 1940. Only one of them died of natural causes: Henri de Bobinal. *He* didn't commit suicide. He died of a sudden heart attack a few days after writing his misleading article about Bassari mythology, at the age of seventy-two. Apart from Bobinal, all the rest, six men in total—Léon Bercoff, Tristan Chérel, Auguste-Raymond Lamiel, Albert Maximin, Jules Védrine, Édouard Vigier d'Azenac—took their own lives. All dead, young lady. All from suicide."

Bollème paused and looked at me, her face grave. I said to her: You think that...

"No, young lady, no. Let's not talk about what I think just yet. Let's stick to the facts. The facts are there: everyone who spoke about *The Labyrinth of Inhumanity* and Elimane in the press, positively or negatively, to attack or defend them, with the exception of Vaillant (who died peacefully at the age of eight-two, in 1950) and me, died shortly thereafter. One of a heart attack, that's Bobinal, and six by suicide. During that period, no one heard from Elimane. And in July 1940, the same day—the same day: July 4, 1940!—as the last suicide among the six journalists who had written about his book—that's Albert Maximin—he reappeared in a letter in which he alludes to sinners at the bottom of a lake and two survivors. What I think may no longer matter now, in 1985, after all these years. It's just what one old lady believes. I'll tell you later. But what do you think?"

"Yes, what do you think?"

"I told Bollème: Are you sure they were suicides? She said: I checked. They were suicides. I even compiled a report of sorts, where I noted the circumstances of every supposed suicide. I called it the *Suicide / Murder Report*. I'll give you the document, grim as it is. You can do what you want with it. You can even destroy it. Now answer my question: What do you think? I told her that I didn't know, that I didn't have all the elements, and that in the absence of proof, nobody could accuse Elimane Madag. I emphasized the fact that these were serious allegations. I added that all of it, all those suicides, might have been..."

"Coincidence? Chance? Young lady, chance is simply a fate unknown to us, a fate written in invisible ink. Elimane is the link between all those deaths. I don't believe in chance here. I'll be blunt: I think he killed them. That's what I think. Killed. Not directly, no doubt. But I'm certain that he pushed them to suicide. How? Psychological persecution. You're going to think I sound crazy, or that only an old lady would say such things, but it doesn't matter, at my age you can say what you really think, not caring whether you're believed, or judged. Here goes: I think that Elimane had mastered black magic. I've thought it my whole life, not daring to go any further, because I was afraid of dying too, of being tempted by suicide, of seeing him every night in unbearable dreams that would have robbed me of my desire to live. I never actually met Elimane. But like I told you: not a day went by when I didn't sense his presence. He's here. He is. Very close and ever so far. Given my age, I don't have much longer to live. I can say what I want now without fearing death. You can keep all of it, the photo and the letter, and do what you want with it. I don't need them anymore. You know more or less everything that I know about Elimane. If there's anything I haven't told you, it's because I must have forgotten. My memory is a bit shaky. Now you'll have to excuse me, young lady, you make for pleasant company, but I need to get some sleep. You'll learn this one day, but old ladies need their rest. And I'm an old lady who's somewhat unwell; did you know that I'll be eighty years old soon?"

PART THREE

Tango Nights at High Tide

Back then, I was studying philosophy at Nanterre and dancing topless three nights a week in a club, to make ends meet.
The lease for the room the Haitian poetess had rented for
me would be up at the end of '84. The scholarship money
I was getting was barely enough to cover the rest of my
expenses. I had to find another source of income. At the
time, I had a friend from school, a Martinican, Denise, who
was tall and beautiful, with long, slender legs and a nice
ass. She's the one who gave me the tip that summer, when I
mentioned how badly I needed a side job, about the exotic
dancing, which she'd only started doing recently herself.
She told me: "They're looking for girls right now. You've
got the whole package. More even. The pay isn't bad. Your
boobs will drive them wild."

When school resumed, in October of '84, I went to check
out the club, the Vautrin. The owners, a couple in their fif-
ties, Andrée and Lucien, hired me. I started that same night.
It wasn't a fancy place, its customers were solid middle
class. But it paid pretty well for a student. With tips, you
could sometimes make a nice sum of money.

I had my breasts and I wasn't afraid to show them or see
the reaction they got: admiration, jealousy, fantasy, long-
ing, desire, fear, revulsion. People would ask me if they were

real. If I wasn't already naked, I would unbutton my top, slide my bra straps down my shoulders, and push my chest right up to whomever was asking, forcing him or her to meet my gaze. Then I'd observe a three-word silence: "You tell me." Or: "See for yourself."

———

I was the only black girl among the Vautrin's dozen dancers. Denise's complexion was lighter than mine. Therefore, she wasn't considered a true African. Not all the time, at least. She used to say that she felt lost between two colors, swinging from one side to the other of the pitiless epidermal indicator, a line that was in no way imaginary and that distinguished, depending on the day and the stakes, between heaven and hell, beauty and trash, night and day, lies and truth.

During the week we would take turns on four platforms, each built around a stripper pole that went from the floor to the ceiling. A little higher up than the crowd at the bar, we took off our clothes and then it began. In the group, only half really knew how to dance, or made an effort at least. The others were just fine with writhing around like vipers, or raised flags battered by the rain. I belonged to the half that danced well.

Some of the girls, to make extra money, occasionally joined the customers on the second floor, in the Vautrin's private rooms. But not me. After the show, I liked to walk home, in the thick of the night. Sometimes I would stop in on Hafez, a poet like his illustrious Persian homonym, but a poet without a body of work, or one whose work wasn't in any book—and a dealer. We would talk for a bit. He'd remind me of his life philosophy, which can be summarized as follows: reality has no opposite, everything that occurs in the human experience is reality. I was never sure I'd understood. He'd smile without explaining and give me some of his dope. I'd go home, I'd smoke, I'd write. I'd write to the Haitian poetess and I'd also try to write *Elegy for Black Night*.

Those hours of post-dance writing or reading were the only things that made me feel better at the time. They were the only hours that I didn't feel were entirely lost.

Back then, I was studying philosophy at Nanterre, I was stripping at the Vautrin, I was writing to my Haitian poetess, and I was swelling with my first book, which would be born, I could feel it, by cesarean, my belly cut open with an axe. But I was also reading. I continued to read *The Labyrinth of Inhumanity* and I thought about Elimane, my only beacon in that ocean of shit that was my life.

———

At first I couldn't look for him: getting settled, creating habits, kicking habits, rebuilding an entire social network kept me busy. But what mattered was that he stayed in my mind, that he never disappeared. His book was the cornerstone of my library. The first book, soon to be joined by others that I dug out of trash cans or found in public parks, forgotten on a bench, or bought cheap at book fairs and flea markets, or salvaged from people who no longer wanted them. But the whole structure was supported by *The Labyrinth of Inhumanity*. Elimane was the invisible king of that castle. He was sleeping in a secret room and it was on me to go find him, to wake him up, to liberate him.

———

Memories of my years wandering the streets of Dakar haunted me in the form of nightmares and shadows that I struggled to transform into poetic images. And yet the wounds were there, gaping, ready to be used: I merely had to help myself. But whenever I dipped in my pen, the tip came out dry. The months piled up, along with the frustrations, and the failures.

Then, much later, I understood: just because you're wounded doesn't mean you have to write about it. It doesn't even mean you have to consider writing about it. I won't bother bringing up ability. Time heals? Wrong; it kills. It kills the illusion that our wounds are unique. They're not. No wound is unique. Nothing human is unique. Everything becomes terribly banal over time. There's the conundrum; but somewhere in there, literature has a chance to emerge.

———

Because I refused to give private shows in the back rooms of the Vautrin, I quickly become one of its most sought-after girls. Lucien and Andrée didn't force anyone. No really did mean no. But a no, at the Vautrin, only worked for one night; the next day, anything was possible again. Take another shot. Play another round. Let time do its job, cracks slowly emerging in the wall of your principles. The human soul can be turned, after all, and the customers were counting on its thirst, its weakness, its greed.

I still said no. Some people thought it was prudishness, others, a calculation to drive up the price; a few claimed it was because I was frigid. No one saw that it was out of ennui.

Soon, Denise and I were the only ones who refused to go to the private rooms. The two black girls (Denise, in this situation, obviously became or went back to being black) resisting. The exotic fantasy propellers started whirling, spitting out nicknames: *the Black Guard, the Ice Twins, the Old Black Maids, the Unfuckables, the No-thank-you-ma'ams*. There were others, which I've forgotten...Denise and I used to laugh about them. Lucien and Andrée would deliberately schedule us on the same night, knowing that lots of people, apart from the regulars, would come out of curiosity, or to try to unlock the *Black Boxes*—another of our nicknames.

———

The man started coming at the start of 1985, in mid-January. Did he come because of the new attraction we offered? I don't know. The first few times, I didn't see him. It was Denise who pointed him out one night. We were dancing when she made a slight head motion in his direction. That was the first time I saw him: a man alone, in a corner, his back to the room. Afterward, when I joined Denise in our changing room, she said:

"Did you see...? The African prince is back."

"I've never noticed him before."

"You're either really blind or really distracted. First of all, there aren't that many black customers here. And ones like him, white or black, never. He's been coming every night for a week and sitting in the same spot."

I repeated that I'd never noticed him before and that it wasn't all that shocking, since he turned his back to the room and faced the wall. Denise said that attitude alone should have been enough to single him out. That might have been true, but I'd never seen him, end of story.

"The other girls can't stop talking about him," she said. "Fantasizing. He's really rich."

"What makes you think that?"

"Now you're doing it on purpose, hon. Even after getting a look at him, you don't see that he's out of place here? He's a diplomat. Or a minister. He smokes brand-name cigarillos. Maybe he's a president, even. You know, the kind that bring whole suitcases full of cash to the Élysée, or so they say. France's complicated relationship with its former African colonies and so on, you know all that better than me, right? He's an African like you. Just do him, bring me along, we'll stop falling asleep with Shestov or Jaspers and get out of this place. Think about it."

I smiled but didn't answer. I liked reading Jaspers. When I'd looked at the man, I hadn't even noticed that he was black, and even less so that he seemed rich. The only thing that struck me in the brief moment I set eyes on him was his solitude. Though I saw plenty of lonely men drinking in silence at the Vautrin, crushed by their thoughts or inebriation. I could even say that's all there was in that bar. But this man's solitude was different. Maybe my memory of that instant has been transformed by time. I'm not sure anymore. But when I think back, when I think back to the exact moment my eyes saw his back, I see the color of his solitude. I made out an aura floating around him. A halo of milky purple lined with thin green, a green that's hard for me to describe, I'd be hard pressed to list all the different shades of green. But what comes back to my mind is a green, I don't know, maybe a Veronese green. It lasted a few seconds, then I went back to focusing on my dancing, thinking that I must be incredibly tired to be seeing auras around strangers.

When we left, the bar was emptying. I looked at the table where the man had been sitting. He was gone.

———

He stopped coming after that. Two weeks, then three, then five went by and he still didn't show. I teased Denise. I told her that with all their dreaming about the solitary man, all their talking him up, their fantasizing, the girls had unleashed upon him the dark power of the Mouth. The evil eye. Back home, obviously, there was no better way to squash a hope than the Mouth. I explained all that to Denise. You sent the rich African prince running, I joked. You've doomed us to reading German philosophers for the rest of our miserable lives and shaking our asses for eternity around stripper poles at the Vautrin.

———

In February '85, in a fit of madness or lucidity, I burned the pages of my manuscript. I couldn't write *Elegy for Black Night*; or rather, I wasn't satisfied with what I had written. Destruction struck me as the only option for those first drafts. They were missing something. I've always thought that every book published by a writer was merely the sum of every book they'd destroyed before reaching that point, or the result of every book they'd restrained themselves from writing. I wasn't ready for that book yet. So I threw everything to do with it into the fire. I stopped writing for a time, and I began researching Elimane.

Bollème's investigation is the first thing I read. I'd managed to find it at one of the used-book stands along the Seine after many weeks of searching. There was a single copy left.

Then, by scouring flea markets, auction sales, *bouquinistes*, and those little stalls that sell old newspapers, I was able to gather all the prewar periodicals, from 1938 specifically, that mentioned the book. My efforts took all my tips from the Vautrin, but I managed to find and read every article from that period. I knew that Brigitte Bollème was still alive. She was reigning over the Femina jury, crowned twice over, first as a major literary journalist, and second, as a heroine of the Resistance. I wrote her a letter, in which I told her the truth: I was a cousin of Elimane's, I was looking into him, and I hoped that she could help me.

———

The day I sent my letter to Bollème, the man reappeared at the Vautrin. He came in while I was dancing. He was wearing a fedora whose rim hid his face. He walked slowly across the room and again sat in the back. He turned his back to us, as usual, and I couldn't make out his features. But this time I took a good look at him, I noted his elegance, his slow and well-bred manners when he removed his hat and when he placed his coat on the back of his chair. I didn't see the purple-green aura again, but the solitude around him was as dense as before. The chair across from him was empty, ontologically empty: what I mean is that the man gave the impression that there had never been anyone sitting across from him, and that all the chairs in the world across from which he had sat had always been occupied by nothingness. It was like he had reached the end of his solitude and was no longer waiting for anything. Unlike other people, who endure their solitude, secretly hoping that fate or a chance encounter will dispel it, he gave the impression of knowing that solitude was irrevocable, that nothing would dispel it, and that even an encounter would fundamentally change nothing.

Denise had of course spotted him when he came in, and was quick to cast me smiles and winks rich with innuendo and mockery. It was fair game.

At one point, the man stood, put his large hat back on, and walked over to Lucien and Andrée. I watched them talking out of the corner of my eye. I sensed, more than I saw, that they were discussing Denise and me. She hadn't missed a beat of what was going on either. After a brief conversation the man didn't return to his table, but went up the stairs that led to the private rooms, preceded by Lucien. Andrée signaled us to stop dancing and get down from the stage:

"He wants to see you," she said in a voice roughened by three decades of tobacco and alcohol. "Both of you. He wants you to go up. Lucien took him to the last room, number 6, at the end of the hallway. He wants privacy. You're the ones who decide, girls, like always. I know that you've always chosen to say no before. I respect that, and so does Lucien. But if I can give you a piece of advice, and believe me, I know what I'm talking about, I did what you do every night—every night—for twenty years, if I had one piece of advice, it's not to let this guy slip away. And it has nothing to do with the money. He has plenty, that's obvious, but that's not what this is about at all. I think there's something different about this one. Two minutes talking to him is enough to pick up on it. It's your call."

Lucien came down just then and joined us. He said nothing, as usual. He was a taciturn man: he talked through actions and looks. For a few seconds, I observed his. It seemed like he wanted to tell me something, but nothing came out of his mouth.

"Well?" said Andrée.

I looked at Denise. Like her, I was intrigued, but something was holding me back, and I wasn't sure what. Maybe fear that the man's solitude would infect me. Or something else that I didn't understand.

"Well?" repeated Andrée.

I said no. Denise, yes.

I watched her slowly climb the stairs and I thought: God, she's tall and beautiful. I contemplated her long legs, I read the sensual story of her hips, I watched her ass too, an ass in its prime, envied by all the girls, myself included, I followed the sway of her bare shoulders, I lingered on the back of her neck; I watched all of that, and beneath my admiration of my friend's beautiful body, I had a bad feeling. But here, once again, it's easy to reconstruct feelings. Maybe I didn't have a premonition, maybe the only thing on my mind was Denise's sublime femininity as she walked up the stairs to reach room 6, where the man was waiting for her.

I felt tired that night, I asked Andrée and Lucien if I could go home early. They agreed. So I went home, and wrote a letter to the Haitian poetess. But I can't remember what it said.

———

Two days later, Denise didn't show up on campus or at the Vautrin. When I asked if she had let them know she'd be out, Andrée informed me that Denise had called to say she was unwell and would be back once she was feeling better. That night I danced alone. I felt my friend's absence. The solitary man didn't come either.

———

The next day, I found Brigitte Bollème's response in my mailbox. She agreed to see me and suggested we meet at her house one week later.

You know pretty much everything that was said, Diégane. I'll come back to it. But while I was waiting to see Brigitte Bollème, I stopped by Denise's place. I hadn't heard from her in three days, and I was starting to worry.

She lived in the south of Paris, in a small but cozy studio that I knew well. She had invited me over plenty of times, to eat, study, chat, or meet other young people, guys from school, talkative, conceited guys. They would quote philosophers they'd never read, or had read but not understood and probably never would understand. Most of the time they bored me to death. But for one or two nights, when they'd run out of things to say and the only thing left was to fuck, they would do.

I arrived at Denise's apartment. There was no doorbell. Before knocking, I thought I heard singing inside, fading out, the gentle and solemn final words of a song I didn't recognize. I waited in front of the door, not moving, and listened closely. Nothing but silence. Maybe it had been the radio. At least Denise is here, I thought. I knocked three times, then three more after a few seconds without any response. The ritual we used to perform outside my father's repulsive hut had kept its hold on me. Denise still hadn't opened. She's not here, I told myself. Or maybe she's asleep. And strangely that thought lifted a large weight from my chest, as if, all of a sudden, the idea of seeing Denise, even though that was precisely why I'd come, had struck me as incongruous or dangerous. I was about to hurry back down the stairs when the door opened slowly, without a sound, as if of its own free will, as if there was no one behind it. So I watched it swing open like it was being pulled or pushed by a ghost, then I saw Denise, her arm first, followed by one shoulder, and finally her face, or rather, part of her face. The rest of it, like most of her body, was behind the door. I looked at that half of her face for a few seconds, without a word, attempting to smile at her. Though I think that, if I did manage to smile, it must have been a dead man's smile. I couldn't read anything, however, on Denise's half face. A humid draft swept through the landing.

Come in, hon, said Denise. You'll catch cold. She withdrew behind the door entirely to make way for me. All I saw then was the dimness of her apartment. A narrow corridor led to the living room. The windows were closed. Everything appeared normal, nondescript, cold. And yet, in my gut, I was certain that the room would slice through anything that presented itself; that it was a machete with a recently sharpened blade and was just waiting for prey it could chop into pieces. Come in, repeated Denise, invisible behind the door. It's her voice, but I don't recognize it, I thought. My intuition was telling me that turning my back—I don't mean on Denise, but rather on that voice—would have been a suicidal move. Come in, get out of the hall. There was nothing peremptory in her tone. It actually sounded like a prayer, albeit a prayer addressed to the god of Hades. I obeyed and went in. In that instant, I was sure it wasn't Denise waiting for me behind that door, but another presence that I could distinctly sense inside the apartment. I took three or four steps after crossing the threshold, careful not to glance back at the door. It closed behind me. The corridor before me appeared never-ending, stretching out without ever opening onto the bedroom. I turned around, trying to appear as natural as possible. I was prepared to see the cold gleam of a knife blade or the black mouth of a revolver or the noose of a hanging rope.

Nothing of the sort: Denise was alone and wearing a long bathrobe, midnight blue or dark green, which swallowed her lovely curves. She had lost weight, that was clear immediately. I asked her how she was doing. It'll take me a few more days to bounce back, she said, sliding closer. She stopped beside me. I didn't move. She placed her hand on my arm—a hand as cold as a metal glove forgotten outside in winter. Though I saw right away that her eyes were burning. She said: The hardest part's over, yesterday I couldn't move or even open my eyes, there was no fighting the fever, I kept my eyes closed for hours, God, the things that can invite themselves into your mind are awful, I prayed I wouldn't die, the fever slowly broke, a doctor came over and gave me some medicine, I'll be back to normal in a few days, thanks for stopping by, hon. She squeezed her fingers around my arm before taking away her hand (though for a long time after, I could still feel that hand's cold weight). Then she preceded me into the apartment. The corridor had returned to its normal length.

There was a single room that she had split into two sections using a tall Japanese screen. The first was used as a living room and kitchen. The second served as a bedroom;

the shower and bathroom were there as well. I sat on the couch. Denise offered me tea. I told her I would prepare it so she didn't tire herself out, but she insisted on serving me. I looked more carefully at the objects in the room. Nothing had moved since my last visit. And yet the feeling that we weren't alone in the apartment intensified. The presence I had sensed behind the door was there, at that exact moment, and it was altering everything: the order of the books in the bookcase, the number of mugs in the china cabinet, the size of the letters in a poster, Denise's parents' smiles in a photo on the dresser. Everything was struck at its core. Denise was busy with the kettle. I looked at the partition. The person had to be on the other side, in the bedroom space. I sensed the presence, silent and tense, ready to explode at the slightest movement.

Denise caught me mid-inspection and handed me a cup. She sat across from me. For a few seconds neither of us spoke. Neither of us drank either. We were both holding our cups on our knees and looking for a solid object on which to set our eyes, but everything was slipping away. The steam from the tea warmed the bottom of my face, but my hands, around the cup, remained frozen. I eventually took a sip and then began talking about school. I promised Denise I'd pass her my notes from the classes she'd missed, from the prolegomena to Kierkegaard. I told her about *Philosophical Fragments*. When I stopped talking, she didn't ask me about Kierkegaard:

"And the club?"

"The club? Everything's fine at the club. We miss you."

I knew perfectly well that wasn't the response she was waiting for. But she also hadn't asked the real question, which was blazing in her eyes: *Did he come back to his table, face to the wall?* That was what Denise wanted to know, but she hadn't dared say it. For a few seconds, I watched the inner struggle raging inside her. Would she dare ask the question? Would she have the courage to, in spite of the presence behind the partition? At that moment, it was more palpable than ever, piercing the Japanese parapet and filling the whole room. Denise got scared and said: I miss everyone too. A few seconds later her cup slipped out of her hands and shattered on the floor. Tea spilled at her feet. She laughed immediately and said: God, I'm clumsy!

I got up, collected the shards of glass, and cleaned the mess. That time Denise let me. When I got close to her, by her feet, I thought I heard her whisper: Leave. I glanced up at her. Had she really spoken? Impossible to say for certain: she was looking toward the bedroom and seemed to have completely forgotten my presence and the puddle of tea spreading across the tiling. I stood back up. I should have had the courage to go behind the Japanese partition, into the bedroom, to see who was there. But I didn't. I was terrified. I told Denise I was going to let her get some rest. She seemed relieved, though thinking back on it now, I might say that what flashed across her gaunt face in that instant wasn't relief, but despair, or a cry for help. But I'm not sure. I told her I hoped to see her again very soon. My voice surprised her, and she started. I gave her a goodbye peck and headed to the exit, forcing myself not to run.

Still, I turned back around before opening the door. Her eyes were trying to tell me something, but I was too scared to know or guess what. I left. As I began down the stairs, I thought I heard from the apartment the same voices, the same echoes of that fading song I'd heard before entering. I told myself that I was crazy and didn't turn around.

———

Two days after that visit to Denise I met Brigitte Bollème. I left her house with the letter and the photo of Elimane. But I also left with the grim document Brigitte Bollème had told me about. Do you remember? The document in which she noted the circumstances of the literary critics' deaths. Can you imagine? She was so convinced that it was Elimane who'd driven them to suicide that she gathered all their bios together. This is it: the *Suicide / Murder Report*. Do you want to read it? Some of the entries are concise and allusive, like telegrams, almost. Others were painstakingly written. Several blend both styles. I don't know why. Here.

———

Léon Bercoff (*1890–April 14, 1939*): Son of Russian-Jewish immigrants. Majored in philosophy. Abandons teaching degree due to World War I (12th Cuirassier Regiment). Journalism after that. Writes for various Parisian magazines and newspapers in the interwar years. Literary commentary, philosophical analysis. Mid-1920s: switches to politics. Stops commenting on literary and philosophical texts. A Dreyfusard successor from the start, he clashes with Maurras and Bourget. Fervent denunciation of anti-Semitism in France. 1927: B. writes several articles. Possible, in light of what happened next, to interpret them as prophecies (or premonitions) of the Holocaust.

Labyrinth of Inhumanity. At first Bercoff stays out of the debates. Then, after my interview with Ellenstein and Thérèse Jacob, B. reacts. He demonstrates his zeal for justice and hatred of racial persecution. Deplores the press's fascination with anecdotes and biographical details, to the detriment of the text and literary work. Deems my interview biased and mediocre. He concludes his article by supporting Elimane. He encourages him to defend himself.

Beginning in late 1938, B. suffers from intense migraines. Hospitalized following frequent fainting fits (early 1939). Returns to work, seemingly healthy. On April 14, 1939, after writing in his office (an essay: a serious philosophical refutation of *Mein Kampf*), he is found dead at his desk by his nine-year-old son. A revolver bullet in his mouth. No letter.

Tristan Chérel: On March 2, 1939, around 12:30 a.m., Tristan Chérel (Brest, 1898) leaves the conjugal bed. He claims an urgent need to smoke. One hour goes by. He doesn't come back. His wife then gets up to look for him. She finds him in the garden of their small house. He's spinning slowly, hanging from the branch of a tall birch tree.

Formal testimonies: Chérel: energetic man. Enjoyed life and the sea. Also traveling. Unfortunately, *The Labyrinth of Inhumanity* didn't transport him. Disappointed. In his article, he expresses frustration at not having seen more of Africa, which he had largely exoticized. Reproaches Elimane for indulging in a vain stylistic exercise with no meat to it. For not showing enough of the life and landscapes of the dark continent. Insufficiently Negro for him.

Cremated. Remains spread by his children and his wife on a beach in Finistère.

Auguste-Raymond Lamiel (*July 11, 1872–December 20, 1938*): The horrors of the World War I trenches cemented Auguste-Raymond Lamiel's belief in human folly. But rather than succumb to a despairing, pessimistic life philosophy, Lamiel found motivation for a relentless combat, which he waged his whole life, against anything that could create divisions between men. A graduate of the École Normale, a socialist, a humanist, and a dogmatic pacifist after the Great War, Lamiel was best known for his virulent anti-colonial stances, which he defended with passion and panache on the pages of *L'Humanité*, the newspaper to which he contributed from its founding by Jaurès, whom he counted among his friends.

Fed on classical culture (he had an *agrégation* in Greco-Latin grammar), it appears unlikely that Lamiel did not detect the references, plagiarism, and rewritings in *The Labyrinth of Inhumanity*, which he applauded almost immediately after its publication. He is responsible for the phrase "Negro Rimbaud," which perhaps proves that Lamiel saw but preferred not to mention Elimane's borrowings from Rimbaud and many others, notably authors from the period that was his area of expertise. He reportedly even said to one of his colleagues: "That African has read everything, from Homer to Baudelaire, absolutely everything."

Shortly before his suicide, Lamiel published his final article, dedicated to *The Labyrinth of Inhumanity*, in *L'Humanité*. A bitter Lamiel laments that readers did not understand that Elimane was playing with his references more than he was plagiarizing them, given that the rewritings were too obvious not to have been deliberate (incidentally, he offers this ambiguous observation: *You'd have to be blind not to see them*).

A few days before Christmas, he killed himself by swallowing a cyanide capsule. He had reportedly been having apocalyptic visions, the likes of which Saint John would have recognized. In his final letter, he wrote: *War will come again from Germany. It's inevitable. But this time, I won't do it the pleasure of suffering through it.*

Lamiel's mortal enemy was Édouard Vigier d'Azenac, one of the sharpest tongues at *Le Figaro*, and with whom he crossed swords for many years through his articles. The two men, former friends, even dueled on two occasions, at the end of the nineteenth century. Ultimately, they disagreed on everything: politics, ideology, literary taste, their conception of humanity. But it would appear that the cause of their mutual and robust hatred was romantic. Meaning that they had been lovers before coming to hate one another or that love for the same individual had caused their rift? I found nothing conclusive on the matter.

Albert Maximin (*October 16, 1900–July 4, 1940*): Got mixed up in this terrible business by chance. Scant information about his life. Son-in-law of Professor Paul-Émile Vaillant. Hence why. Publishes his father-in-law's revelations about *Labyrinth*. His article = fairly neutral. Merely enumerates Vaillant's discoveries. Divorces Vaillant's daughter in February 1939. Less than one year of marriage. No real writing talent. Output gradually declines. A hunter. Weapon = double-barrel rifle. Used to take his own life, which is increasingly solitary and darkened by the trauma of the French defeat. Not yet forty years old at his death.

Jules Védrine (*June 11, 1897–June 13, 1939*): At the end of his article about the Elimane scandal that appears in *Paris-Soir*, Védrine implies that the truth of the matter has yet to be determined. In this remark about a truth that remains to be established, we can recognize in Védrine the lover of detective novels. At *Paris-Soir*, he reported on true crime and human-interest stories and occasionally penned reviews of crime novels. He wrote two himself, under the pen name Hector J. Frank. It is difficult to say what he thought of *The Labyrinth of Inhumanity* or its plagiarized content, in literary terms. He appears to have mainly covered the lawsuit. Nonetheless the tone of his article suggests that he was delighted that the official literary milieu (in other words, the milieu that viewed crime fiction with disdain, deeming it common and good for nothing, apart from entertaining the uncultivated masses) had been briefly shaken up by Elimane, even though the affair had ended badly for him. I learned that Védrine had been planning to conduct an investigation into Elimane's true identity. Sadly, a soured love affair stopped him in his tracks. Two days after his forty-second birthday, he threw himself in the path of a Paris subway train. His editor published a manuscript he had submitted one month prior, under his real name. It is, in my opinion, Védrine's best book.

Édouard Vigier d'Azenac (*December 14, 1870–March 9, 1940*): Édouard Vigier d'Azenac's father, Captain Aristide Vigier d'Azenac, died with honor during the Sedan disaster of 1870. A few months later little Édouard came into the world. From childhood, he harbored both a dream of a brilliant military career in homage to his father and a deep hatred for the republic. But the call of literature proved stronger than that of the sword, and D'Azenac, at a young age, wrote biographies of Charles X and the Count of

Chambord that attracted attention. A staunch Legitimist, his motto was reportedly *I live by the light of two eternal Truths—Religion and Monarchy*, a phrase borrowed from Balzac, though he changed the verb.

In 1898, virulent anti-Dreyfusard though he was, he published an article in *Le Figaro* denouncing the simplistic anti-Semitism of most of his friends, which he considered an affront to Christian values.

That text earned him the friendship of a radical Dreyfusard, Auguste-Raymond Lamiel, who found it courageous and honest. The camaraderie between the two young men was as impassioned as it was tempestuous. They frequented one another for one year and professed their mutual admiration, despite the ideological chasms between them. In 1899, something or someone caused their falling-out and ended a friendship that, though beautiful, was untenable in the long term. The pair are said to have faced off in two pistol duels, neither of them with a winner after a total of twelve shots were exchanged. In 1914, at the start of the war, Vigier d'Azenac enlisted for France as a humble stretcher-bearer. The horrors he witnessed and experienced put him off the sight of blood forever. Upon his return from the front, he continued to write books and publish in *Le Figaro*, where he soon became a regular contributor. He submitted his candidacy to the Académie Française on several occasions, without success.

On his final attempt in 1938, Vigier d'Azenac failed to obtain even a single vote for seat 16, to which Maurras was elected that same year.

A keen literary critic, a reader of Taine, and a formidable polemicist, he was a rabid supporter of the colonial enterprise in Africa. Édouard Vigier d'Azenac—and this was visible in his articles during the Elimane scandal—considered blacks subhumans (or sub-apes) who merited only servitude and consequently could not aim to rise to the level of humanity (and even less so of writing). "The Jew is still tolerable, the Negro, not at all!" he wrote in a letter to one of his mistresses. His hatred of *The Labyrinth of Inhumanity* and Elimane is clear, forthright. He proclaims it vigorously and unabashedly. He is the one to publish Bobinal's article. Was he aware it was a confabulation? I don't know.

Apparently, the news of Lamiel's suicide saddened him, and he didn't utter (or write) a word for two days. In the summer of 1939, he was struck by multiple fits of madness. He was eventually committed in an asylum outside Paris. That was where, in March 1940, in a flash of restored lucidity, in his bedroom, he slit his wrists with a razor blade, after carefully blindfolding himself so he wouldn't see his own blood.

———

That's it.

I don't believe the report's implications because I don't believe in mysticism. But as a child, I heard many supernatural stories. And as I was thinking about this string of suicides committed by literary critics with no common link, apart from their profession and the fact that they had written about *The Labyrinth of Inhumanity*, one of those accounts came to mind.

Let me roll a joint before I tell you this story. I'm not going to offer you any: this strain is strong. It's from the high seas, and you're not ready for the high seas yet.

When I was a child, people used to say that back in the day—before I was born—a man named Mbar Ngom, who lived in a Serer village in our region, had been struck by a terrible, unknown illness that caused him horrific physical, psychological, and mental pain. At night, his moans would ring out across the town, and their sinister echoes earned Mbar Ngom a reputation founded partly on commiseration, partly on terror. People took pity on him, while also fearing that the evil eating away at him was contagious. His family, of course, tried to treat him, but in vain: traditional medicine, to which they turned first, struggled to identify the source of his suffering, and several of the diagnoses contradicted each other. As for Western medicine, it quite simply proved incompetent before this unfamiliar pathology. The family visited dozens of healers, menders, sorcerers. None were able to heal him. Some succeeded in alleviating his pain, by stuffing him with drugs and drowning him in malodorous occult fumigations; but their effects would only last a few hours before Mbar Ngom's suffering returned, even greater. Soon, before the unbearable sight of the man's decline, people began to hope, through whispers or tear-dampened looks, that death would deliver him and bring relief to his family. But even death didn't appear to want anything to do with this patient. So Mbar Ngom continued to suffer and scream into the night like a tormented ghost, an unappeasable madman.

His situation troubled and saddened everyone. One night, the village elders gathered in a consuetudinal council of sorts, which was attended by Mbar's family. They discussed how to proceed. A decision was quickly reached. Only one solution, a single chance to help Mbar, remained.

This is where my father, Ousseynou Koumakh, makes his entrance. An emissary from Mbar Ngom's village came to see him one night. Ta Dib is the one who told me this when I was a child. She said that the emissary found my father in front of the house, as though he'd been waiting for him. And before he could even state the reason for his visit, after the exchange of greetings, my father announced:

"I know what brings you."

"In that case, will you help us? Will you help Mbar?"

"Come back in seven days," urged my father.

The emissary left. My father Ousseynou Koumakh, I already told you, was renowned in our region for his mystical knowledge, his soteriological powers, his clairvoyant abilities. When it came to the most complicated or the most desperate cases, he was the man people went to consult. And to be sure, the case that had just been presented to him was not only complicated and desperate but also urgent. Mbar Ngom's illness no longer concerned the man alone: it had been taken on by the community.

Seven days later—it's still Ta Dib telling me all this—the emissary from Mbar Ngom's village came back to our home and spoke with my father, who told him that Mbar Ngom couldn't be healed by any medicine of any kind in this world. The emissary, who knew how to interpret veiled words, immediately understood that Mbar, if he was to recover, could only do so in the other world, the ancestors' eternal land, on the other shore of the great river in which the waters of life and death mix.

"Will he agree to follow you?" inquired the emissary.

My father was silent for a moment, then replied:

"I don't know yet. My sight can't penetrate his will, which is as dense as the forest of spirits."

"Will you come with me?"

"No. I no longer need to physically move. It will happen tomorrow night."

At that, Ta Dib told me, the visitor bowed at my father's feet, as though his final words had revealed a dimension to his knowledge that the emissary hadn't suspected; a dimension that no longer demanded mere respect, but also deference, perhaps fear. Then the visitor left.

The following day, at nightfall, my father's spirit left his body. The villagers say they sensed a powerful wind gusting through the village. The wisest ones knew that Ousseynou Koumakh's spirit was out, and told their families to go inside their homes and stay there. At that moment, my father's body was with us, in the courtyard, clearly visible to his wives and his children. That night he remained still for many hours, sitting on his folding chair, eyes open, as if he had suddenly regained his sight. But we knew he wasn't there, that his spirit had left its corporeal husk and that it was imperative we not address or approach him.

During this time the gust was whirling around the mango tree across from the cemetery. It remained there a few seconds, briefly enveloped, like in a lover's embrace, the absence of Mossane; then it continued its journey. A few minutes later, it passed over the river, caressing the water; the water shivered; large circles formed on its surface and expanded into multiple, regular waves, all the way to the riverbank. Then the gale swept across a vast *tann*, its gusts reverberating, doubled by the loud echo the barren plain made in response. Finally, it crossed into an ancient forest said to be the home of spirits. When the gale passed above their heads, they recognized it and hailed it as one of their own. That is how, at the hour when the ground begins to turn cold, my father's spirit, carried by that wuthering wind, reached Mbar Ngom's village.

As usual, Mbar was screaming from madness and from inexplicable pain. My father's spirit entered his hut. He called to him. I mean that he called to Mbar's spirit, not his body. They say that Mbar, as soon as he heard the call, went quiet. His family knew then that my father had arrived. Everyone held their breath. Mbar's spirit rose as his body remained stretched out in his bed. Frightened, he looked at himself below and tried to cry out; but my father's presence shut his mouth, enveloped him, and led him out of the hut, to somewhere more peaceful. Then my father removed the invisible gag he had placed over the mouth of Mbar Ngom's spirit and told him:

"Don't be afraid. I'm here to free you."

"Free me? Who are you? And what are we?"

"Who I am doesn't matter. But you know what we are in this exact instant. We are what we truly are deep down inside: spirits. Living energies."

At that moment, in the courtyard of our house, Ta Dib told me, my father was talking, voice low, eyes bulging, and body still motionless in his chair.

"Why are you here?"

"You know why, Mbar Ngom. It's time to die. There's no more life for you here. If you continue living, the worst thing that can befall a man on earth will happen."

"What's that?"

"You'll continue to suffer. But that's not the worst part. The worst part is that your diseased soul will detach, while you're alive, from your body. Which will still be alive, but in torment. As for your soul, it will wander as well, through the spirit world. Here or there, you'll be alone and lost."

"I'm already alone and lost."

"That's true. Here, at least. If you agree to willingly enter the other world, the spirits waiting for you there will give you a chance to heal. A new life in a community awaits you. The spirits know that the life of the soul is much longer than that of the body. It's the soul they treat. There's time to care for it on the other side. You can become someone again, take the time to find yourself. There's nothing left for you here. Nothing but suffering."

"What if I'd rather suffer than accept your offer? What if I want to live, even sick?"

"I'd accept your choice. But in that case, you'll die anyway. And at that moment, your soul will already be so damaged by its premature separation from its bodily protection that nothing, not even all of eternity, will be able to save it. You're holding on to your life here despite your pain. But it's on the other side that life truly begins. Come, and you'll see."

Mbar's spirit remained silent. My father's encouraged him to think about it, then took him back to his hut, where he returned to his body. My father told Mbar that he could contain his pain in the palm of his hand for two days, the time for him to make a decision. Mbar thanked him. My father made his way back to his own body, in the courtyard of our home.

When he awoke, Mbar Ngom remembered everything. They say that on that day, for the first time in years, he didn't appear to be suffering. Two days went by, during which he regained an inner peace. He spent time with his children, his wife, his parents, his friends. But everyone knew what that meant.

As he'd promised, my father-spirit returned two nights later. Mbar Ngom was waiting for him.

"Well?" said my father.

"Release me," said Mbar Ngom.

They say that my father opened the palm of his left hand, the one holding the pain, and placed it on Mbar's face. He died immediately. His spirit rose into the sky. My father escorted it to the other shore of the great river of death and life.

———

That's it, Diégane. You know the story of Mbar Ngom.

Now, let's suppose for a moment—emphasis on *suppose*—that it's true, and that my father could in fact enter people's minds and convince them of the necessity of their death. Let's suppose that by promising people an other-world that was joyful, calm, and pure, he had the power to steer them into choosing euthanasia, suicide even. Let's suppose that he might have shared that knowledge with Elimane. You see where I'm going. Of course you do. In his final confession, lying on that shitty mattress, my father said that he taught many things to Elimane Madag, other forms of knowledge. Maybe that mystical knowledge was among them, and maybe Elimane, driven by anger and shame, used it against the literary critics, against Bobinal, against everyone who hadn't understood *The Labyrinth of Inhumanity* or who had hurt him. Again, all this is mere supposition. An unlikely supposition. Those suicides were just coincidences, tragic coincidences. That *The Labyrinth of Inhumanity* was the link between them can only be pure chance. Brigitte Bollème would have told me that chance is simply fate whose writing we can't see. Maybe she believed in mysticism. I don't.

Here, smoke a little, *als het erop aan komt*, smoke the high seas, just one hit, slowly, there, there, *bine-bine*, you got it. Now open your eyes, the sea is yours, sailor boy.

———

It would be terrible if Elimane had actually driven those poor French critics to suicide using his magical powers. But within that nightmarish possibility, I see something comical. Don't you? A writer who believes himself misunderstood, poorly read, humiliated, critiqued through a lens other than literature, reduced to his skin, background, religion, identity, and who begins killing the negative critics of his book out of vengeance: it's pure comedy.

Are things any different nowadays? Do we talk about literature, about aesthetic value, or do we talk about people, about their skin color, their voices, their age, their hair, their pets, how they decorate their houses, whether their carpets match the drapes? Do we talk about writing or about identity, about style or about media buzz that eliminates the need for any, about literary creation or about sensationalist personalities?

W. is the first black novelist to receive such and such prize or join such and such academy: read his book, it's fantastic, obviously.

X. is the first lesbian writer to publish a book written in gender-neutral language: it's the major revolutionary work of our era.

Y. is a bisexual atheist on Thursdays and a cisgender Mohammedan on Fridays: their account is magnificent and moving and so true!

Z. killed her mother while raping her, and when her father comes to see her in prison, she gives him a hand job under the table in the visiting area: her book is a punch in the face.

It's because of all this, all this lauded and rewarded mediocrity, that we deserve to die. Everyone: journalists, critics, readers, publishers, writers, society—everyone.

What would Elimane do nowadays? He'd kill everyone. Then he'd kill himself. I'll say it again: It's all just a comedy. A grim comedy.

———

And what about Denise, right? I'm getting there.

Five days after my visit to her apartment, I got a call at the Vautrin a night that I was dancing. It was the hospital. A doctor told me to come as quickly as possible: Denise wanted to see me. I cut short my performance with Andrée and Lucien's permission, then rushed to the hospital where Denise had been admitted. I found the only family members I knew Denise to have: her uncle, her aunt, and two cousins. Standing in the hallway, they told me that it wasn't your basic fever but a "crisis" related to her disease. What disease? Sickle cell anemia, her aunt informed me. Which she inherited from her father, my brother, who died from it when she was ten. Her mother died a few years after her father, in a maritime accident.

I didn't know any of that, Denise had only confided in me that she'd lost both her parents, but she never mentioned how they died. She also hadn't told me that she sometimes had sickle cell crises.

She's waiting for you, said her aunt. I entered the room. And Denise was waiting for me. She was already looking at the door when I walked in, like she knew I was coming, or had heard my voice in the hallway. I'd prepared myself to find her in a weakened state, unconscious perhaps, surrounded by countless wires that would form an unsettling spider's web, fitted with a catheter slowly draining a translucent or yellowish liquid, connected to tubes themselves connected to machines, oxygen, IV bags. Instead, the space around her bed was empty and bare and hieratic, as though she'd recovered and would soon be discharged, or the opposite: like they knew she wasn't going to make it and had halted all treatment. She was sitting up, legs covered by a white sheet. She was smiling. I went closer and took the arm she held out to me.

"I'm reading this and I really like it. I'd like to find an elegant epitaph in it."

She showed me what she was holding in her other hand: *Philosophical Fragments*. I didn't have the heart or even the desire to sugarcoat the truth or to console her. She knew better than anyone how close to death she was, maybe she could already see its gaze. Telling her those eyes weren't real, telling her they weren't coming for her, would have verged on the kind of arrogance that sometimes colors the hopes of the healthy when confronted with the ill. I simply squeezed her hand.

"Usually," she said, "I sense when a crisis is coming. I know how to prepare. I've learned, over time. There are signs. But this one surprised me, it knocked me on my ass. There was nothing I could do."

"You don't have to talk about it, Denise. We can chat about something else."

"Don't be an idiot, hon. We have to talk about it, and you know it. It happened when I was in room 6. Or rather: it happened after room 6. Or because of it."

She let a brief pause go by. I said nothing. Her hand, when I squeezed it, gave a feeble response.

She said:

"He hasn't come back to the Vautrin since that day, has he?"

"No."

"Maybe he already did it."

"Did what?"

Denise looked at me intensely for a few seconds, then she said:

"When I joined him in room 6, he was sitting in the armchair, in the dark. There was just the night's bright halo coming through the window, which he'd opened despite the cold. But it didn't bother me, I was a little warm. He took off his wide-brimmed hat, but because of the gloom, I couldn't see his face very clearly. I said hello, and I asked if he wanted me to turn on the light. He said no, that the darkness suited him just fine. Then he asked why I was alone. I told him that you hadn't wanted to come. He went quiet, like he was disappointed, and there I was, standing in front of him, not knowing if I should go closer, undress completely, begin dancing, spread out on the bed, or simply wait for him to tell me what he wanted. Finally, after a long pause, he said there was no point, and that on my own I wouldn't be able to relax him enough for what he was planning to do in the coming days. I didn't say anything, and he continued: You're not going to ask me what I'm planning to do? I answered that I had wondered but that I had no right to ask him the question, after all it was his business, and I was just a dancer who was supposed to be pleasuring him. He paused again, before telling me that at one time, before the war, there hadn't been any dancers here. Before I could ask him any questions, he went on: You see, I knew this place, at least, I knew it the way it used to be, it had another name and I would come here sometimes, a long time ago, with friends, or on my own. It was one of the best spots in Place Clichy. Then he asked me to massage his shoulders. I approached him, and for the first time I could see his face in detail. He must have been around seventy, I think. I stepped behind him and started to massage his shoulders. After a moment he began singing a tango by Carlos Gardel. I continued massaging him, hoping that he would sing tangos all night long, because it was very beautiful and he sang well. But he stopped. That's when I began to be afraid, the fear slow but undeniable. I didn't understand where it was coming from. I suppose that's what they call a bad feeling. I began to tremble. I told myself, for reassurance, that I was getting cold because of the open window, even though I knew deep down that it had nothing to do with the chilly air coming in. I still asked the man if I could close it. He stood and closed it himself. Then he came back toward me. He appeared gigantic and I felt defenseless, completely at his mercy. In the chair, he had looked like an elegant but weak old man. Standing, he was a different person entirely: strong and very tall. The fear was still there, weighing in my stomach like a heavy stone. The man must have noticed, and he told me not to be afraid of him, that he wouldn't hurt me, that people his age were mainly preoccupied with what kind of coffin they would have and the type of flowers they wanted at their funeral. I smiled. You can go, he said. I said: Already? He said yes. I took a few steps toward the door, relieved: he sat back in the chair. Then I did something

I never should have done: I stopped and I asked him: What are you planning to do in the coming days? I saw him smile, the stone in my stomach moved. He answered: You're sure you want to know? I nodded. He asked me why. I answered that I had the feeling he wanted me to know. He whispered: Maybe, then paused, before continuing: Okay, I'm going to tell you, since you want to know and maybe I want you to know as well, but whatever you do, don't repeat it, it can't leave this room, otherwise...He didn't finish his sentence. I felt like he was playing with me, and he was playing, but it was a game of life or death and he was the only one who knew the rules. But like an idiot I promised, I won't tell anyone, I promised him that, scared to death, but with a smile. Then, with that terrible sneer, he said: I'm planning to do what I've been doing for many years: kill; I have one person left to kill in the coming days, and then I'll be done with it, it will be finished. He stopped talking, and I just laughed idiotically. But he wasn't smiling anymore. He put his index finger over his lips. I did the same and then left wondering whether the whole thing had been disturbing or comical. When I went back downstairs to get changed in the dressing room, Andrée and Lucien came looking for me. They handed me a bunch of cash. The man had left me a big tip. They hinted that it must have gone really well in room 6 for him to pay me so much. I should have shut my mouth at that point, but I couldn't. I told them what we'd done in the room. I mentioned the massage, the tango, I even mentioned the window. And to finish I suggested that he was a nostalgic and lonely old man who had invented a thrilling life to ease his solitude, and before I left him, he had confessed to being a dangerous murderer who was planning to kill yet again. Andrée responded: How disappointing, and here I thought he had something, but he's just a sad, bored old man who gets by on massages from young women while he sings Gardel; aging... talk about a cosmic void, promise me you won't let me get old, Lucien. Lucien remained serious, like always, and silent. After that I went home. The whole way I felt like I was being followed, but every time I turned around nobody was there. I started to feel the rock in my stomach again. I went to bed, and I slept with it weighing inside me. The next day, the rock was gone, but the first symptoms had appeared. At first, I didn't make the connection with room 6. For three days, I didn't think about it. Or rather, I refused to think about it. I only started to grasp what had happened the day you stopped by. That's why I was acting so strangely. It wasn't because of my disease. It was because I had just realized that all this was happening because of the secret I hadn't kept. I know it's implausible. For that matter, I haven't mentioned it to anyone. No one would believe me. Even you, I can tell, you don't believe me. The doctors can't explain the violence of this sudden crisis. I've been taking all my medication. Things were fine. Until that night, at least. You might not believe it, but I know in my gut that the reason I'm here is because I talked. Since that night, room 6, I've felt like the old man is everywhere around me. Sometimes I hear his voice singing an Argentinean tango, but I don't see anyone. Maybe I'm the one singing without realizing it. Or else he's on the inside. He's in me. He's the ghost of the rock inside of me. They think I'm delirious. But I'm not. And now, he's somewhere in this massive city, killing someone as we speak, or maybe he's already killed that person, and there's nothing to be done."

Denise stopped talking and closed her eyes. I thought she was delirious too. After a few seconds she opened her eyes and said:

"I'm not delirious, Siga. I know I'm not delirious. You have to believe me."

"Do you know his name?"

"He didn't tell me. He didn't tell me anything else about himself, other than that he knew the place before it became the Vautrin, and that he liked that tango song. And that he was a murderer. I don't know anything else. But, hon, I wanted to tell you all this, just in case..."

She paused to take a deep breath. She seemed very weak. I said I was going to leave and that I'd be back to see her soon. She grabbed my hand again.

"...in case I don't make it, and in case he comes back to the Vautrin. Watch out for him. Whatever you do, don't approach him. Or if you approach him, don't ask him what he's going to do."

She closed her eyes again. Talking had cost her. I kissed her goodbye and I left the room.

———

For the rest of the night, I thought about what Denise had told me. I thought about room 6. I mostly thought about the impression I'd had when I went to visit my friend; that there was a human presence hiding behind the Japanese screen. And I thought about the song I was almost sure I had heard when I was standing in front of her door and which I hadn't recognized. And yet none of those thoughts shed any light on the events in room 6 or on Denise's delirium. All I had was a flimsy and muddled web of half feelings, vague impressions, unfounded assumptions. I dropped in on Hafez, my dealer, and asked for his "rough high seas" bud—a special, and powerful, substance that he reserved for his most loyal customers. Myself included. Hafez explained its very specific dosage, which he advised me not to ignore, except in case of emergency. He emphasized that: in case of emergency.

I smoked a little that night and wrote furiously and energetically until dawn. I had started working on *Elegy for Black Night* again. The next day, early in the afternoon, I received two pieces of news in a row that put me in an excellent mood. The first came from the Haitian poetess. She had written to tell me she was coming to Paris in a few days. She was going to spend a week there before going to Argentina on vacation. She told me she missed me. You can imagine the emotions I felt when I read that. I hadn't seen her since Senegal, and the idea that we would be reunited soon made me happier than I'd been in a long time.

The second piece of news came from the hospital. I had called to find out how Denise was doing. She was sleeping, but her aunt told me that her condition had improved overnight.

That evening, I went to the Vautrin in a cheerful mood, certain that Denise would be back soon and happy to be seeing my poetess again in a few days. I had forgotten about the rest. My shift ended around two, and on the way home, I smoked more of Hafez's high tide, increasing the dose. After dancing, I used to stop at a public park sometimes, I liked the silence and the solitude at night. I went in with my joint. I'd taken a few steps when I noticed, a little farther off, the man from the Vautrin. There was little doubt, it was him, enveloped in the purple and green aura.

We were alone in the park. As soon as he was sure I'd seen him, the man advanced rapidly between two rows of trees. I remained frozen for a few seconds, then walked after him. I stepped onto the path but didn't see anyone. Soon I was worried that I'd lost his trail; then, as if he wanted to reassure me, he began singing. I immediately recognized the melody of a famous tango by Carlos Gardel. I heard it distinctly. The man couldn't have been far. I followed the singing.

It was at that moment, I think, that I noticed that I didn't really recognize my surroundings, the path behind me, the things around me. In place of the park benches I'd walked past, there were now trees, but foreign trees, taller than the species typically found there. Their branches were longer and their trunks more imposing; as for the foliage, the leaves were so densely packed that they resembled spheres of compact black resin. I glanced up: the very clear sky that I'd been looking at a few seconds earlier was no longer visible, except through gaps in the thick canopy that had woven itself above me.

Soon I was struggling to make out any familiar markers. The only one remaining was the voice of the invisible man. I listened more carefully, for a long time, while I tried to suppress the crushing wave building inside my chest. I couldn't see the man, but the sound of his voice led me to believe that he was only a few steps ahead. So why couldn't I see him? It was simple: because around me, the park as I'd known it no longer existed. This was another park, a park that belonged to a different world, a different city. My surroundings had completed their silent and invisible metamorphosis: everything had changed without appearing to, as if, without my realizing, without anything moving even, the park had become a jungle, or had been transported into a jungle, or had absorbed part of a jungle; and all that had happened before my eyes, though they saw nothing; I was blind.

Obviously, I told myself: You're out of your mind, it's Hafez's high tide special doing this to you, soon enough you'll see metaphysical tigers crouching behind carnivorous Amazonian bushes, or the reincarnation of your village's legendary crocodile, the one that devoured your grandfather Waly! I laughed and downplayed the situation. I attributed all the extravagant strangeness to the fatigue of the previous days, combined with the effects of the psychotropic. I wondered whether I was having a good trip or a bad trip, a pale copy of a dream or the prelude to a nightmare, but I couldn't decide, probably because what I was having wasn't, for the time being, one or the other: it was a strangeness not yet tinged with anything. I stopped and rolled another joint with the highest possible dose. Case of emergency.

The voice was still singing its tango somewhere ahead of me. So I continued to make my way through the tall trees, guided by the melody. Then, at that point, as if I'd been struck by a bolt of clarity, I saw myself walking in the night, in that park, in pursuit of a man with a purple and green aura. I started to giggle, and my giggling swelled and transformed into a full-blown river of laughter that swept away everything in its path. The noise of that unhinged laughter even managed, for a time, to block out the words of the tango; I was laughing at myself and at my madness, hiccuping partial sentences or words I couldn't finish, and this went on for a lapse of time that seemed long and joyful to me, at least until the moment I realized that what I had taken for a burst of hysterical laughter was in reality a cascade of frightened sobs—or had become so. I stopped and leaned against the trunk of a magnolia tree to calm down and pull myself together. The song, as though it was accompanying me, or had sensed my situation, became a gentle consolation.

By then I was really spooked, and I understood why my laughter had turned to crying a few minutes earlier: my body innately knew that it had no desire to laugh, and that its dominant feeling in that moment was an archaic fear, the sort you feel while waiting for an imminent and unavoidable catastrophe or for the horror to appear. It was the fear of a child convinced, despite their parents' words of reassurance and their verifications, that the monster is under the bed and will inevitably come out; the fear of the investigator who knows that beneath the next shovelful lies the first corpse of an enormous mass grave.

I began to jog after the singing, whispering: Enough already. I couldn't tell you how long I followed that tango, but I do remember the intersections, the forks in the road, the zigging and zagging, the curves, the never-ending straight lines, the paths that popped up at the end of other paths and turned off into new paths, all lined with trees like the ones I've already described and all devoid of streetlamps, though I could see clearly enough, as if light was emanating from invisible particles suspended in the air. Doubt started to soak my bones: What if I was in fact lucid? If I didn't have the recourse of hallucination? What if this tango on the high seas had nothing to do with Hafez's drugs? Nothing is more terrifying than the interference of strange phenomena in your reality, while you're in a rational state, that you then have to make sense of without the crutches of irreality and insanity, those easy resorts that not only spare us from looking at reality's every face, even the most hideous, but have yet to accept the idea that reality has many faces. Is this what Hafez meant when he said that reality has no opposite, that everything that happens is reality?

I was venturing deeper into the park labyrinth, but also into the labyrinth of my life. An easy metaphor, but true. A pirogue high on drugs and lost at sea, following a nighttime tango sung by elusive sirens. And that's all my sad life was: the life of a stoned Ulysses, but a Ulysses with no way home, a Ulysses for whom Ithaca is, can only be, the sea, and the sirens' song, and ruses, and tears beneath the rain, and Cyclops, and the sea again, forever the sea.

I knew I wouldn't be going back to Senegal, Diégane: the rupture was too great, and I could tell that it wouldn't ease with time. On the contrary, the rift would only intensify. It would be necessary for the writer in me to be born; and it would be what remained, after that birth, for me to write. I knew, before I wrote a single one of my books, that every one of them would be about that rupture with my country, with the people I'd known there, with my father, with Mame Coura, Yaye Ngoné, Ta Dib, my stepmothers, with all the men and women encountered in the streets or at school for a single night. I would write about that and no one would understand, everyone there would hate me for a very simple reason: not only would I have betrayed through writing, but I would have compounded that betrayal by writing somewhere else. But so be it, I thought, so be it: I'll write as if I was betraying my country, meaning as if my chosen good earth was not the motherland but the mortal land, the homeland for which our most profound self has always destined us, the inner homeland, the homeland of warm memories and icy shadows, of earliest dreams, of fears and shames streaming, intermingled, down the slopes of the soul, the homeland of primal wandering on petroleum-colored nights, along white streets, through cities deserted even by the ghosts, the homeland of crystallized visions of love and innocence, but also the homeland of gleeful mad-ness and piles of skulls and merciless lucidity that eats away at your liver, the homeland of all the solitude possible and all the silence available, the only homeland I found *livable* (and by livable, I mean impossible to lose or loathe, impos-sible to expose to sentimental and superficial nostalgia, impossible to use as a pretext or take hostage in order to pin the shiny little trinket of exile to your chest, and finally, the homeland impossible to defend, since it can defend itself just fine, with its unassailable buttresses, and it demands no sacrifice apart from our idleness and our desires to make love all the time). So what is this homeland? You know it: it's obviously the land of books. Books read and loved, books read and despised, books we dream of writing, insignificant books that we've forgotten and can't even remember if we ever opened, books we claim to have read, books we'll never read but that we still wouldn't relinquish for anything in the world, books waiting for their hour on a patient night, before the dazzling twilight of dawn readings. Yes, I said, yes: I will be a citizen of that country, I will swear allegiance to that kingdom, the kingdom of the bookshelf.

Lost in thought, I hadn't noticed that the singing had stopped. For how long? I reached the end of the park. There was a small, brightly lit esplanade, a children's playground. I thought the man from the Vautrin would be waiting for me there, that this would be the moment of truth. But the man I found sitting on a bench wasn't him. He was old as well, but on the short side, modestly dressed, no hat. He was wearing black glasses. I went closer. He turned his head toward me, didn't appear surprised. I said hello. He responded with old-fashioned courtesy.

"Excuse me," I said, "but…did you…did you happen to see a man with a fedora, very well-dressed, go by? An African man…Just now…Very tall. He was singing a tango."

The old man was still for several seconds, like I'd spoken too quickly, and he'd needed a little time to understand everything. Then he responded:

"I'm blind, ma'am. That's why I'm wearing these glasses. There was a man here a few minutes ago, but I don't know if he was tall or short, well-dressed or badly dressed. All I can tell you is that he had a calm, reassuring voice, a voice that was supremely confident."

"Where did he go?"

"Do we ever know where people go? He left, is all. The night is a vast land."

"You mentioned his voice. What did he say to you?"

"He thanked me for singing the way I was. Because it wasn't him singing. It was me. The tango was me. The man liked my voice. It brought back memories for him. He thanked me again and wished me a good night. And two minutes later, you arrived. Are you with the police? Is that man wanted?"

"I'm not with the police."

"Do you know him?"

"No, I don't know him. I . . . I don't think I do."

"That's not a very clear answer. Do you know him or not? Is he your lover?"

I didn't respond. I finished my joint and said goodbye to the old man as he began singing again. I wasn't able to sleep that night, so I wrote. The effects of high tide dissipated at dawn. That morning, the hospital called again. I went there. I understood what had happened as soon as I saw Denise's family members' faces. I stayed with them until midafternoon, then I went home and I cried. For all that I rejected it, that I denied it with all my strength, a certainty was growing inside me: the man from the Vautrin had killed Denise, and the man from the Vautrin was Elimane. It was him from the start. It had always been Elimane.

Two days later, Denise's body was taken back to Martinique. As I was preparing to visit the morgue to say my goodbyes, I learned, from the radio, of Brigitte Bollème's death. The president of the Femina jury had just died, at the age of eighty, of a heart attack.

———

In the days that followed, Andrée and Lucien told me to take some time off. I didn't want to stay home, so I drew from my savings to pay for a room at a budget hotel. I fled my tiny studio so Denise's memory wouldn't come back to ask me: Why didn't you go to room 6 with me? I fled my copy of *Labyrinth of Inhumanity*. And I fled the photo of Elimane that hung above my desk, the one Brigitte Bollème had given me. During the day, I would go to cafés to write. But as soon as night came, I returned to my hotel room and stayed put, like a frightened hare in its burrow. The hunter was prowling outside. I could hear his boots. He was coming for me. His footsteps were near. Every night, for a time, was a night on the lookout.

I only dared return home five days later, once the poetess had arrived in Paris. Wrapping my arms around her was an immense relief. I was no longer alone. When we entered the bedroom, it only took her a few seconds to notice the photo of Elimane above my desk. She went pale, and I thought she was going to faint. She sat on the bed for a while, and asked me, after a glass of water, to tell her about the man in the photo.

I sat down beside her. All the emotions of the previous days churned together inside of me, before violently erupting. I cried for a long time, then I told the poetess my history with Elimane, with the ghost of Elimane, the dream of Elimane, the visions of Elimane, with *The Labyrinth of Inhumanity*. I shared everything, from what my father had told me to the most recent events with the man from the Vautrin, including my discussion with Brigitte Bollème. Everything.

When I stopped talking, the poetess took me in her arms. She didn't cry, but her voice shook as she told me she finally understood the origin of and reason for our meeting. "I know that man too," she continued. "Not only through stories, accounts, legends, theories, or his one book. I knew him in the flesh, in real life. I met him. I lived with him. I might have loved Elimane. I went looking for him and you're who I found. But it was he who brought us together. I finally understand that now."

In the Amsterdam Dawn

———

"That's everything? Really?"

"Yes, that's everything. Were you expecting something else?"

Siga D. stood and disappeared into the kitchen, where I heard her preparing coffee. A few minutes later, she came back with two cups, handed me one, then turned off the lights, leaving the first hint of dawn as our only illumination.

She sat back down.

"I was expecting more... What about the man from the Vautrin?" I asked.

"He never came back. In any case, I never saw him again. I quit the Vautrin a few days after the night in the park. I didn't return to the club. But in retrospect, I don't think he had anything to do with Elimane. How could he have?"

"I don't know... I thought the Haitian poetess..."

"... would shed some light on him? That she would tell me that it was Elimane? That she would paint me a clear picture? Impossible. There's no clarity to be found. Anyway, there'd be no point: we can't see the whole picture. Its meaning, its beauty or ugliness, its mystery and the key to its mystery can only be found in the details. The poetess spent a week with me in Paris, after that epic night we told each other everything. She was there when I finished *Elegy for Black Night*. When the first draft was ready, she printed a copy and brought it to Argentina, which is where she planned to spend her three remaining weeks of vacation. I went with her to the airport. We hugged, and the last words she said to me were beautiful words of friendship and love, because that was the sentiment that linked us, the most perfect balance of friendship and love. One week later, there was the car accident. She was on her way back to Buenos Aires after visiting some friends—a couple who used to run an independent movie theater—who lived in a different city. She was driving too fast. She always drove too fast. Do you know what she used to say? *What's the point of having an automobile if you never let yourself experience extreme, dizzying speed?* Her car swerved off that road in Argentina. She died instantly. Her friends let me know. When she died, my draft, which had all my contact information, was among her things. That's how I found out. A few hours after learning of the Haitian poetess's death, as I was drowning in sorrow in my bedroom, I received the first positive and enthusiastic response to my manuscript. I tore up the letter. I hated my manuscript. I hated that coincidence of absolute tragedy and a reason to be happy. I wanted to die, but I no longer had the strength. Writing had already nearly killed me. Denise's death, and more than anything, the poetess's death, had already killed me.

Siga D. paused, and I respected the mournful silence. But she quickly resumed, as if she didn't want to let sadness make her lose the thread of her story:

"At the time, I didn't have the means to go to Argentina. I only made it two and a half years later, in 1988, once my book had been translated into Spanish and published there. The poetess had been buried in Buenos Aires, beside her parents. I stayed at her grave for a long time, not praying, not thinking about any specific moment we'd shared. I was simply there, near her. I tried to hear her voice again. I heard nothing. There was only silence, but it was a peaceful silence, a beautiful, peaceful silence. I left the cemetery and crossed Buenos Aires on foot, with no destination. It was then that I sensed the poetess walking alongside me. All my memories resurfaced during that aimless wandering. I continued walking and I cried in silence. It was finally hitting me that I was in the poetess's city, her last home, but also the city where everything had begun for her. In the end, she couldn't have been buried anywhere else, because even though she was born in Haiti, it was in Buenos Aires, near her prestigious literary teachers, that she was born to literature. Buenos Aires was her city. I sat in a café, thinking that maybe she'd had a drink there, with Elimane. I told myself I'd been lucky to see the poetess one last time, to talk to her, to hold her in my arms, to sleep beside her, to feel her touch. That thought eased the pain of my stay in Buenos Aires. It comforted me. That trip also lightened Elimane's weight in my mind. When I returned to Paris, I stopped looking for him. I reread *The Labrinth of Inhumanity*. I think of him often. I still dream about him, hazy or not particularly interesting dreams, but also dreams where we have long conversations. Meaningful, premonitory dreams that tell or show me something. Erotic dreams too, sometimes just me and him, but more often it's the three of us, with the Haitian poetess, dreams of frightening power and intensity, from which I always emerge trembling, near dead. But after that trip to Buenos Aires, I told him goodbye. I welcome him when he comes back to me. But I no longer seek him out."

"Why?"

"Because I know that finding him wouldn't mean understanding him, and even less so knowing him. That's why I stopped looking for him. In Buenos Aires, I'd suddenly grasped that I shouldn't make the same mistake as Brigitte Bollème and the Haitian poetess: trying to reach the boundaries of Elimane's soul. Who was he? A pure writer? An abashed plagiarist? A brilliant impostor? A mystical assassin? An eater of souls? An eternal nomad? A refined libertine? A child looking for his father? A simple, unhappy exile, who lost his bearings and himself? What does it matter, in the end. What I love in him is something else entirely."

She stopped talking, and so did I. Finally, the Spider-Mother said:

"Let's go for a little walk. Amsterdam at this hour is worth seeing."

We left her place and strolled along the canal, where glimmers of the new day were sliding across the water's surface, wavering between vermilion and silver. I read this as the promise of glorious hours. We walked in silence, yielding, after an entire night spent talking, to the call of our inner citadel. A few stars lingered in the firmament, as if they'd lost their way during some cosmic pilgrimage. Still, they had found an unrivaled stage in the void left by their comrades already embarked on another path through infinity. The lost stars shone there with all their fire before being swallowed by the day. The celestial bodies have their swan song too, which the eyes alone can hear. The world truly is mysterious, I thought, looking at the sky: for starlight, the shadows come in the guise of day.

"And the photo?" I said abruptly. "The photo on the beach. The one Brigitte Bollème gave you along with the letter from July 1940, and that you hung over your desk. You told me you don't have it anymore. Where is it?"

"I gave it to the Haitian poetess. I saw how she was looking at it, when she was with me in Paris, the way she was looking at Elimane's face. So I gave it to her. It was also among her things when the accident happened. Her friends told me she was buried with the photo."

We had just taken a few steps across a small bridge, which led to a jetty of tourist boats, when Siga D. stopped. I turned toward her. The streets were nearly empty. We had only seen a few solitary individuals, either early risers or night owls lingering outside, like the last stars in the sky.

"I don't think I have anything else to tell you, Diégane. I went on with my life, I left France to live here, I decided not to go back to Senegal because it's a lost country (interpret that however you like), I wrote my books and accepted everything they bring me: admiration, hatred, suspicion, lawsuits. What I think about this story no longer matters, except for the writing. Everything I've told you tonight is waiting to be written. A book. Or several. I'll write mine one day. I don't give a damn about the rest. Elimane died a long time ago. Elimane is alive and a hundred and three years old. Elimane left something behind. Elimane left nothing behind. Elimane is real. Elimane is a myth. I couldn't care less. What I mean by that is that Elimane exists inside me, and that life is more powerful than all the other ones, even the life he actually lived. So yes: I don't care about reality. Compared to the truth, it's always lacking. If the same doesn't go for you, if you don't not-care the way I do, you know where you have to go. You know what to do. But like I said, I don't give a damn."

I stepped closer to Siga D. I thought she would back away. She didn't budge. I kissed her. She took my arm, we went back to her place, and for the remainder of that Amsterdam dawn, until the sun's light pulled away from the night and spread through the house, we made love and I didn't think of a single sentence. It was only that evening, as I boarded the train that would take me back to Paris, that I remembered my night vow. Was I free of it, if only temporarily? Had I finished mourning for Aïda between the Spider-Mother's legs and breasts?

Ultimately it didn't matter. What mattered was that, contrary to what I had feared the night I saw her for the first time, that night in Paris, in her hotel room, Siga D.'s touch hadn't obliterated me. And that simple fact brought me enormous relief, made me irrationally happy, even.

Book Three

$$\text{Friendship} - \text{love} \times \frac{\text{literature}}{\text{politics}} = \, ?$$

D – 5

The tragedy had occurred two days earlier, on September 7, shortly after ten. By noon, the boundaries of decency were already being crossed, trampled, in fact. And yet the earliest remarks had all been very dignified: sadness was expressed, shock and dismay too, prayers were offered, hopes shared. But immediately after the prayers, the buck-passing commenced: each and every one washed their hands of all responsibility for what had happened. The spectacle reached its climax during the eight p.m. news, when the prime minister, voice imprecatory and chin high, facing the camera, addressed those who "brought about this morning's horror by systematically sabotaging, for their own vile interests, the government's every effort to emerge from this crisis intact. Your hands will be stained with the blood of many more innocents, whom you'll send to their deaths."

Cynical as it was, this political cliché of the industrial slaughterhouse and sacrificial manipulation went almost unnoticed. That night, the country was holding its breath (and its bile), still transfixed by the memory of the morning's images. Everyone was thinking about the life whose fate would be determined by the skills of a few doctors.

These had fought all day long to save Fatima Diop. But shortly after the prime minister accused the opposition and the activists of having stoked the fire, and despite the doctors' desperate persistence, the young woman succeeded in finishing what she had started: she died.

No one, except her perhaps, knew yet that her suicide would mark not the beginning, but the final act of a long social and political crisis whose epilogue could only be written in a language of chaos, a language of wounded, furious titans.

I landed in Senegal late on September 6, the night before Fatima Diop's suicide. I was still asleep when she died, but was spared nothing upon waking. Like everyone, or nearly, I saw the images. And like everyone, or nearly, I followed everything that came after that ominous video with a mix of emotion and worry.

Fatima Diop's death was announced by a physician from the hospital. Visibly exhausted, he stepped before the television cameras massed at the hospital entrance and stated, with modest and touching simplicity, that he and his colleagues had been unable to save Fatima. That's exactly how he said it, Fatima, like she had been a loved one, maybe his daughter, maybe his niece; like she had been a loved one of all the Senegalese people. He went on to offer his condolences to the young woman's family. Then, when one might have expected him to provide details on the attempts made to save her, the doctor looked at the camera for several seconds without a word, tears in his eyes, then he said sorry, before going back inside the hospital. I think that sorry broke the heart of every person watching. It was an admission of powerlessness and desperation and rage felt not only by the physician but by the entire country.

Fatima's family buried her the next day, on September 8, in Touba. It was a private affair, despite some government figures' calls for a state funeral. The family had refused, preferring to grieve with a minimum of modesty, the only pomp required by the dead.

That afternoon, a citizen's movement, BMS, an acronym for Ba Mu Sëss (let's translate it as "See It Through"), reacted. Meaning it held a press conference, standing room only, the tension palpable as was, according to certain somewhat-operatic journalists, the smell of revolution. The spokesperson of the See-It-Throughers also began by offering his condolences to Fatima's family. He then reminded everyone that she had been an activist with BMS for two years, and swore, tears in his eyes, that the collective would continue the fight. In conclusion, he called for a march on September 14, when, he promised the government, every incensed citizen would raise hell in the streets and thereby hasten the infernal descent of all those who had betrayed their trust and sacrificed their hopes. He ended his brief speech by declaring that the members of BMS, and all patriots, would be the doorkeepers of said hell.

Here, the opposition political parties saw a godsend. Late into the night of September 8, their leaders, despite the accusations of indecency the government tossed at them like rotten eggs, gleefully declared, one after the other, their solidarity with the September 14 march in homage to Fatima Diop. These opposition figures didn't care that the immediate response was that the march was against them as well, seeing as how it was intended to condemn the practices of a political class to which they had long belonged (some among the opposition had even held power once). Truly, they couldn't have cared less. The most important thing, they said, was something else entirely. People gladly believed them.

Faithful to his reputation as a great sphinx, the head of state let his prime minister declare three days of national mourning, while he remained silent. An attitude entirely coherent with a definition he had given for politics a few years prior, when he was seeking power, in a minor and now-forgotten interview: the art of waiting, of making others wait, then appearing suddenly, like a messiah or a prophet or a thunderclap, to regally address the people at a moment when they are so worn down by their suffering that saying to them "What ails you?" will echo in their ears as "I am the sole possible remedy to every imaginable ailment." What did that mean? That timing is everything. Yes, but what else? That in his mind, politics was merely a well-oiled capitalist machine running on well-understood disappointments.

Everyone agreed, however, that he shouldn't count on tensions easing. The march's main leaders swore that apart from shooting bullets into their heads, stacking them up like cockchafers in the repulsive cells of Rebeuss, or funneling tear gas directly into their mouths, no one could stop a pure and fraternal people's homage to Fatima Diop, their comrade in arms, from taking place on September 14.

My sudden return on September 6 had come as a surprise. Four years without going back to Senegal and then, one random day, without warning, I was there. I'd felt a little ashamed to confess the true reason for my presence to my family. So that night I said nothing about it. I claimed homesickness, a need to see my younger brothers and get to know them better, my desire to return to the house, to breathe Senegalese air again. No one, I told myself, would have understood the real purpose of my visit. My father asked me why I hadn't let anyone know, so that they could have thrown me a party. I replied that the best parties were spontaneous, and that the one we were having was making me incredibly happy.

My mother was less credulous, or simply more anxious, and despite her joy at seeing me again, asked me even more questions. Are you having issues with your papers? Did you get kicked out? Did you do something bad in France? The current situation in Senegal, tense even before the tragedy of September 7, led her to think that I had come back for political reasons. She believed that the opposition, or the BMS youth movement, among whom I counted a childhood friend, Chérif Ngaïdé, wanted to recruit me. I denied it and told her I was there to recharge my batteries.

My mother wouldn't drop it. That night, she brought up the political crisis a few times, and asked me what I thought. I told her I didn't think anything—which was the truth: I'd lost all interest in what was happening in Senegal nearly two years prior. My response shocked her: she told me she'd been reading my blog these past few years; I had thoughts about everything and wasn't shy about sharing them. And now, given the circumstances, when it was my own country, I had no opinion? I didn't cave; I maintained that no, I didn't. My mother let up a little. Clearly, she had her opinion about the political crisis that the young people of Senegal had been protesting about for several months. I listened. Then she told me, with the voice of an oracle: This will end badly, young people will die and mothers will cry, the government will open investigations with one hand and shut them just as quickly with the other; only victims, no one at fault, nothing will change, there you have it.

I had smiled at my mother's political discourse: concise, critical, catastrophizing. I told her that she was conservative out of worry. My father, however, was revolutionary out of regret. He was hoping to witness the great political rupture that his generation, as politically active as it was, had failed to accomplish in its juvenescence.

"We thought that the independence movements were the start of that radical break. We realized our mistake too late..."

He was almost apologetic for having believed. I had no interest in putting him on trial. In any case, this country, which incidentally he had helped to build, was taking care of that, offering him daily reminders of his generation's failures. Since retiring, my father had been reeducating himself in politics. I found him much more radical. Simply less naïve, he always corrected me. That night he had said he was waiting for young people to take matters in hand. He wanted to go with them, to take to the streets.

"We'll see about that," said my mother. "If you think I'm going to let you walk out of here when your back pain is only getting worse..."

My father downplayed. My mother exaggerated. I watched them act out this old sketch as funny as it was touching. I had felt simultaneously happy and sad to see them again. Though at least I'd been expecting that.

I'd expected him to leave one day or another, Siga D. said to me, recounting what the Haitian poetess had said to her on the last night they spent together. I never forgot him. Our relationship was like a never-ending storm, but every lull was worth enduring the thunder. I eventually realized that I enjoyed the thunder too. He didn't spend much time within

Argentina's artistic and literary circles. Of course, every once in a while, when he wasn't given a choice, he would make an appearance. He had few friends. He admired Borges's work, but he was closest with Gombrowicz and Sábato. I think he must have slept with every beautiful woman, and every ugly one, among the Buenos Aires intelligentsia. I'm convinced he slept with Victoria Ocampo, but also with Silvina Ocampo, maybe the two sisters at the same time. He was quite the paradoxical hermit. He wasn't a regular at the places to be. But when he did show up, he exuded powerful charm, without seeming to, without effort, even while giving the impression that he was embarrassed or annoyed by the effect his presence had and for which he appeared to be sincerely apologizing; this charm wasn't only physical, it was spiritual, I would even say *mental* if that meant anything. And yet he wasn't very talkative. He didn't make a spectacle of himself. He didn't try to dazzle with his wit, and distrusted all the rhetorical artifices, all the pretensions, all the seductions of intelligence. And still he seduced. He was a black star, but nothing shone brighter than him. I don't think it came from the allure of his mysteriousness. Not just, in any case. That kind of psychological explanation would be too simple. There was something else, something deeper. One day, I heard a friend of my mother's say, looking at him with desire and horror: Surely there's only Satan who can seduce like that man.

I met him in 1958. I was eighteen, and had spent ten of those eighteen years in Haiti, and the other eight split between the United States (my father's country, where he convinced my mother to join him) and Mexico, where my parents had worked as bureaucrats for the young UN starting in 1952, before moving to Argentina in 1957. They loved poetry and art. My mother used to recite the pages Césaire had dedicated to Toussaint Louverture. Those were the first verses I ever memorized.

My father made friends with Argentine intellectuals, some of whom soon began to drop by the house. That was how I encountered Elimane. He was—apart from my mother, and myself, who was mixed—the only black person in those circles.

In 1970, after working in Buenos Aires for a few years, I got a job in Europe, at UNESCO. Since 1966, Argentina had been once again swallowed up by the darkness of a military dictatorship. Civil revolts began in 1969, during what was called the *Cordobazo*. Even I actively participated in the resistance after the junta took power. But I was suffocating amid all that violence. By the end, I was a shell of myself; I wanted to see something different. Elimane had left Argentina a few months earlier.

When we said our goodbyes, he told me he was going to continue his travels, but that his final destination would be his starting point. By then, I knew better than to ask him to clarify his enigmatic statements, which may have been metaphors or not, you could never really tell (you see, I'm not the only who thought so, Siga D. said to me in an aside, then she continued the poetess's account): I simply got used to them. We made love again like we each wanted to imprint the other's skin or soul on our own skin or our own soul.

Then he left. I left the country too, soon after. I knew it was possible that I wouldn't see him again. But I also knew that he needed to leave and do what he had to do. I hoped it would be his last trip through Latin America, and that he would then find peace and the way back to his country. I never could forget him: not the man or the writer. How could I? He'd had me read *The Labyrinth of Inhumanity*, which left a dramatic impression on me, and after which I was long incapable of penning a single line of verse. Later, I went back to writing with a new perspective on things, as though someone had opened my eyes. My poetry became stronger and more personal.

On the last night we spent together, he read me the first pages of a book I'd never read or seen. I don't know whether it was his book, the book he had been working on for all those years. But it was one of the most beautiful beginnings to a book that I had ever heard. Maybe I went looking for him to hear the rest. We all want to find him. Oh, Elimane... You know, *Corazón*, I even wonder if my mother was one of his mistresses. It wouldn't shock me. My mother was very much in love with my father. She was religious, and fidelity mattered to her. But Elimane...

I fell asleep thinking about everything the poetess had told Siga D. I hadn't dared admit to my parents that I had come back for Elimane. I promised myself I would tell them the next day. But the next day was September 7, and I didn't want to bring up the subject when Fatima Diop had just taken her own life and the country was raw with emotion.

We were two days after her death. Her photo was omnipresent, as was the memory of her public suicide. The September 14 march was to take place for her. To pay tribute or avenge her, I didn't know; but it would be for her.

D – 4

Fatima Diop's suicide offered a perfect example, in the press and on social media, of the way human emotions generated by the same event could be both violent and contradictory, not only from one individual to the next, but within the same person. Sadness was mixed with anger, restraint with rage, prayers with insults, and yet all those impulses appeared legitimate. A few hours after her death, Fatima Diop had become a concentrating mirror in which every Senegalese citizen saw their own hideous reflection or projected their daily woes, their too-long-suppressed frustrations, their fear of committing the same act at the end of a day of misery. People looked at her photo, they remembered the images of her death, and immediately thought: that could have been my daughter, my sister, my niece, my cousin, my wife, but mainly, that could have been me.

I spent the day of September 9 reading and listening to the reactions, from all over. A maelstrom of indignation, criticism, terror, shock, the desire to come to blows, to mete out justice, to be heard.

BMS activists talked a lot of talk, rallied lots of troops, created countless combative hashtags and slogans: *dox mba dè*, "walk or perish," *ñaxtu wala faatù*, "speak up or lie down." At times this frenzy verged on one-upmanship, imposture, even; and I suspected some activists of wanting to prove, with a kind of virtual reality–augmented narcissism, that they were the most patriotic, the most radical, the most torn up by Fatima's tragic act. Alone in front of their screens, everyone was debating, judging, talking *urbi et orbi*. In the race for an apt quotation, Fanon ("Each generation must, out of relative obscurity, discover its mission, fulfill it, or betray it") and Sankara ("...the slave who is not able to take charge of his own revolt deserves no pity for his lot") tied for first.

The revolution, finally, was going to happen, and Fatima was its figurehead. Those who dared call for a measured and responsible march became double agents and eventually shut up or deactivated their accounts after grousing about the lack of tolerance afforded them (this was another form of virtual narcissism). Then one wise individual started pointing out that what mattered was being present on the fourteenth, and that all the energy expended blathering on digital *fora* (this sage knew the basics of Latin grammar) should be conserved for D-Day; observations that, most of the time, were applauded. But some reproached the sage for trying to tell people what they should do, both with their Internet connections and their emotions following the young woman's death.

That night, to a get a better sense of what was coming, I called Chérif Ngaïdé, a friend I had studied with at military school. He taught philosophy at the university and had been a BMS activist for some time. He was one of the movement's official theoreticians in a way, and had written many texts that gradually, over the years, came to form the group's intellectual backbone. The activists respected him, appreciated the exactitude of his analyses, the intransigence of his criticism of those in power, his impressive grasp of history, philosophy, and politics. Still, despite all those theoretical accoutrements, he maintained a strong grip on reality, a sensitivity to the hardships of everyday life, and I think it was that, more than anything else, that made him so popular.

I called him *Maas es*, "big brother" in Serer, my mother tongue. He called me *Miñelam*, "little brother" in Peul, which was his. Chérif was happy to hear I was in Senegal. I could sense the exhaustion in his voice—with everything going on, he had to have been in high demand. He invited me over for dinner the next day, and I accepted.

A few hours later, without discussion, I also accepted the price the taxi driver said it would cost to take me to Médina. I hadn't wanted to borrow my father's car. The driver took his time, and the whole drive, my thoughts were pulled in opposing directions: at times toward my current destination, at others, it was Elimane on my mind.

Everyone who'd gone looking for him had been largely trying to dispel the mystery of the man. I was still focused on the mystery of his unpublished work. Elimane, in his roaming, had continued to write. The Haitian poetess had been granted the privilege of hearing a few pages, but she claimed not to remember what they contained. A memory lapse that contradicted the strong impression they'd left on her. How can you forget something that's affected you to such a degree? In my opinion, even if she didn't want to tell Siga D. everything, the Haitian poetess remembered every word.

And yet: No, the Haitian poetess had told her. I can't remember those pages, *Corazón*, but I tried to find them again. Mostly I wanted to find Elimane. I missed him. After ten years in Paris, I made up my mind and requested a transfer to Senegal. That was Elimane's country, and as I already told you, he had said that the final destination of his travels would be his starting point. Maybe, I thought, that statement should be taken literally. Maybe after all those years of wandering, he missed his country and he'd gone back. Or maybe he'd even understood that to finish his masterpiece he had to go home. I was assigned a post in Dakar, where I arrived in 1980.

I didn't have a single clue to his past. Elimane had always been very secretive about where he came from. He had merely shared one day that he grew up near a river and had attended a Catholic missionary school. Nothing about his family. Nothing about his village. I had no last name. So for two years, I combed the valleys of the country's two major rivers: the Senegal River, in the north-northeast, and the Gambia River, in the central west, in the region of Sine Saloum. But without any details, it was an impossible task.

I proceeded more or less at random, on my own, on weekends and holidays. Sometimes I would head north, other times, the central region. I drove without a guide, without a map, just me and that vast landscape. I drove fast. I always drove fast. What's the point of having an automobile if you never let yourself experience extreme, dizzying speed? Now that I was searching for Elimane, that impulse felt even more justified: I wanted to find him as quickly as possible. Though I realized the stupidity of my endeavor on my first excursion. I knew I would never find Elimane's trail this way, unless divine chance was to intervene. Going to a village and trying to ask people who don't understand your language and are curiously staring at you if they know a writer named Elimane...It was as comical as it was futile. After that I asked some Senegalese coworkers for translations of the word writer, or poet, in the country's various languages. Equipped with the words they gave me, I set off again in search of Elimane. In every new village, I would ask what language was spoken. And once I could establish what it was, I would rummage in my knapsack for the translation of poet or writer in said language, and add Elimane. Then, through gestures, I tried to make it clear that I was looking for this poet man. Most often, the only response would be laughter or perplexed expressions that then made me laugh. On occasion, someone would give a long answer while gesticulating directions, and I would eventually understand that a poet or the equivalent of a poet or an individual they considered to be a poet lived somewhere in the village or the region, farther on, that way. I would go. Obviously it never was Elimane, but other poets, other wordsmiths, *aoidos*, magicians and mages, word-bearers, linguistic maieutologists, royal griots, creators of rhymes, speakers of gymnastic poems, other shepherds of silence. Though maybe, quite simply, they were all possible, alternative, faces of Elimane...Sometimes I spent an hour or two with them. We would each speak in our language, without an interpreter. Sometimes they would sing. Sometimes I would recite a poem. I was certain we were talking about the same thing.

This went on for two years. Those expeditions, and the encounters they led to, were how I got to know and love this country. I'll say it again: I knew straight away that I wouldn't find Elimane or where he came from like that. Maybe there were other rivers, other arms of the rivers. Maybe Elimane hadn't told me the truth and grew up in Dakar or Ndar. But I continued my expeditions. In their way, they represented a poetic adventure. Knowing how to say poet or poetry in every language spoken in a country you're discovering is a poetic gesture, isn't it? Isn't it the very birth of the poetic interaction?

In 1982, I stopped the excursions. It was at that moment precisely, when I stopped looking for him, that I found him. Or that he found me. The first weekend I spent in Dakar after my many trips around the country, Elimane came to me. What I mean is that I dreamt of him. It wasn't the first time I'd dreamt about him since we had said our goodbyes in Buenos Aires. Even in Senegal, I'd dreamt about him at times. But this dream was different, because Elimane told me that he needed me. And when I asked him what he wanted, he answered in a language I didn't understand. I told him I didn't speak that language. He repeated in French that he needed me. I again asked him what he wanted. He again spoke in the strange language. And so on, until I woke up.

The dream was also strange because it took place somewhere I recognized immediately. A small fisherman's shack on Ngor Beach, across from the island. I'd go there sometimes after work, to be alone. There were a few shelters like that along the shore, though nobody used them anymore. I'd stop there to read or contemplate the sea. In the dream we were in one of the shacks, in fact, I think it was my favorite one, the farthest from the crowd of swimmers.

When I woke up, I went straight there. No Elimane. The dream wasn't a rendezvous. No one was there, but those sentences were. They covered one of the walls, and I was sure they hadn't been there before. I read them and reread them. I liked them. I made my way down the length of the shore and entered every one of those makeshift huts. And every single one, on some part of the wall, bore your writing, your poetry. After that I started looking for you, everywhere and anywhere, in Dakar. You had left fingerprints all over the capital and yet remained invisible. I looked for you while I read you. Your verses written in black charcoal both guided me through the city and lost me in it. And then one night, finally, I found you.

What brought us together from the start was poetry. It's true; but more than anything, he was the one who brought about our meeting. It was Elimane. But we never spoke about him. We each kept him hidden like a secret, not knowing the other already knew. What would have happened if we'd confided what we were each carrying deep down? I should have taken that dream seriously. Elimane led me to that hut where your sentences were written, and your sentences led me to you. The signs were right in front of me. I didn't know how to understand them. Or maybe I understood them deep down, but didn't want to accept them. And yet, *Corazón* . . .

"Where in Médina?"

"Sorry?"

"We're in Médina. Where should I drop you?"

"Are we far from Marché Tilène?"

"No, it's still a ways up, but not far. Should I take you there?"

"Yes. Actually, a little farther. Across from Ida Mar Diop Stadium. That'll be perfect."

A few minutes later I was outside. Médina was beating like a massive heart in the throes of love at first sight. Life was seeping from every pore of this working-class neighborhood, and that deluge of shouts and arguments and laughter, of cars honking and sheep bleating, of religious chants and exhaust fumes and the smell of trash, the smell of meat grilling, that glorious and miserable deluge had finally taken up every last inch of space, visible or otherwise; then, not knowing where to go, it spread, offering itself, waiting to take or be taken. Here it wasn't death but life that threatened to snatch you at any street corner and smother you until it left you gasping for breath. I had before me the proof that the sight of the most ordinary street in this city rendered any novel futile. Attempt at exhausting a place in Dakar? Perec can come back and try. I skipped my turn and checked the GPS on my phone. The address wasn't far. I took a deep breath, crossed Avenue Blaise-Diagne, and started down Rue 11.

I'm in Dakar for work, since yesterday. Which makes me think about you. I told myself it was worth ending this long but necessary silence. I'll understand if you don't want to respond. It would be normal after all this time. Maybe desirable even. xoxo Aïda.

I'd found the message one hour earlier, on WhatsApp. I went ten minutes not knowing how to respond, eyes glued to the screen. A few times, I began typing idiotic sentences that I immediately deleted.

Aïda had to have sensed my embarrassment and surprise, since the app had been indicating, for several minutes, that I was "typing." The reality was I had no idea what I should or could say to her. Aïda...I didn't need to ask her what she was doing there. I immediately guessed the connection to the political crisis, Fatima Diop's suicide, the September 14 march.

Finally, after comical prevarication, I wrote:

I hope the heat isn't too much for you. Welcome to DK...Crazy thing is I'm here too. I arrived a few days ago. I was happy to get your message, Aïda. All's good with me.

That "crazy thing," intended to sound casual but which carried all my anxiety, was spotted immediately, its forced nonchalance gleaming in the thick of night. I could already see Aïda's cruel and amused smile at my clumsiness. I waited, trembling, for her reply. It came a few minutes later. She didn't beat around the bush but got right to it, not unironically, of course:

Crazy thing...here we are in the same city. Now what?

As I pretended to think for a few seconds, I was lying to myself more than to her. Then I typed on the screen holding my breath. I used the conditional tense, which I hold to be the most useful tense in the French language when it's a matter of disguising fear as prudent wisdom, to feign advancing as you retreat:

We could meet up...

We could. But it's obviously a terrible idea. It'll end badly.

That future tense gave me an indication of her state of mind. I clung to it.

It'll end badly...I've heard that expression a lot lately.

That's because most things end badly. And most people know it.

They don't know anything. It's disillusionment without depth, facile pessimism disguised as insight, heedless cyni-

*cism hidden behind the wisdom of fatalism, a fear of life
dolled up as the philosophy of inquietude.*

I was showing off, but Aïda knew me. Her response
effortlessly rained on my charade.

*You haven't changed—you're still thinking in tidy little
phrases. Catchphrases that maybe not even you believe.
That's the true fear of life right there. It will lead you astray.
Don't say I didn't warn you.*

And to avoid the blathering speech I was preparing, she
sent me the GPS location of the Airbnb where she was staying, in the center of Médina. I told her I'd be there within
the hour. My parents were already asleep. Still, I left a message for my mother telling her I was going out, and that I
might sleep over at a friend's house.

And now I was there, in the beating heart of Médina, and
Aïda was a few minutes' walk away, at the end of Rue 11.

Every revolution begins with the body, and Aïda's body
is a city rising up, a city on fire that will never turn to
ash, and my fight is here, because the fight, the struggle,
is what elevates man, and this cause is worth it, my fight
is here because there's nothing more beautiful than wag-
ing battle in a city that you love even if you feel like you
don't always know it, but it's often because a city keeps
secrets from us, and always because it offers us the chance
to lose ourselves, that we truly love it, and those who say
this city holds no secrets from me, I know it like the back
of my hand or like my mother's belly, those people are
saying something different than I love this city, but I do, I
love this city, because it doesn't surrender entirely, with the
same movement it leans in and pulls away, it's home turf
and foreign soil, I love its narrow and dark long streets,

its open and luminous wide avenues, its imposed stopping points, its fringes and its secret spots, its historic monuments (note the sumptuous Gothic cathedral on your right), its no-man's-lands, its parks, its historic center, its rough neighborhoods, where I try to walk like a top dog (it's obvious I'm not a top dog, but a small-scale pusher who deals in grams), its mysterious underground passages I'm forever discovering, its stubborn dead ends, et cetera, et cetera, still, remember that this city isn't standing or lying down, it's—like I said—a city rising up, it says no and yes at the same time, it knows what it no longer wants, it knows what it yearns for, and it moves in a way that leaves no choice to whoever finds themselves here but to go along with it, to trust with eyes closed, to follow along a trajectory that appears to be aimless but never is, that resembles the rambling of a mad person but is in fact the initiation of the revolutionary, the only true revolutionary there is—the lover—who, at the end of the journey, will discover that they're not ready, because you're never really ready for this kind of thing, but they will have understood the meaning of great sacrifices for just causes.

We made love to try to make up for a year without love. We made love in memory of nights long gone. We made love for the bench in the square on Boulevard Raspail. Then we made love again to build up some reserves, since it was possible that our future would be measured in the eternity of a new silence. The last round drained us. It must have been six a.m. In the waiting room of day, the first noises were growing restless. I wasn't sure you could say that Médina was waking, seeing as how it hadn't slept, or only with one eye open. The other had watched our night uprising.

"We need to get some rest," she said. "At two, Ba Mu Sëss (she said this in clean Wolof) is putting together a protest coordinating committee ahead of September 14. I need to be there."

"Who told you what's going on here?"

"Friends, news correspondents, activists. Lots of journalists are covering citizen movements on the African continent. After Algeria, I went to Burkina Faso. I met powerful, determined people, revolutionaries. Worthy sons of Sankara. When I heard about Fatima Diop's suicide, I immediately understood that something was brewing in Senegal too. It was inevitable that the wildfire would spread to Dakar. I boarded the first plane. There's hope for all the outraged young people of Africa and the world. And I'm not romanticizing rebellion, if that's what you're thinking. I know what these struggles can sometimes cost. That's why I respect them. That's why I want the world to see them how I see them. There's a fire in people's eyes. It moves me. I see it in Fatima's face. It's a fire of anger and humiliation, but also of intense dignity."

I said nothing and wrapped my arm around her. She didn't push me away. I even thought I sensed a slight movement in her thighs and shoulders to bring our two bodies closer. There were a few seconds of silence.

"And you?" she said. "What are you doing in Dakar?"

I stayed silent. Should I mention Elimane and *The Labrinth of Inhumanity*? I was afraid, the same way I'd been with my parents, that Aïda would find me shallow or indecent. Better to lie than admit an obsession that the circumstances had suddenly rendered shameful. Given what had been going on in the country for the past few days, what value, what importance, could my search have? What did the question of writing matter versus that of a society suffering? The quest for the essential book versus aspirations for basic dignity? Literature versus politics? Elimane versus Fatima? So I lied to Aïda. I told her I was there on vacation, to see my family.

D – 3

When we finally said goodbye, in the middle of the street, Aïda and I had hesitated: A kiss on the cheek? The mouth? A handshake? A little wave? The whole street was holding us back, plus the culture, plus the looks, plus our skin color, plus her long hair pleated into one long braid that seemed to catch all the light and midday behind her. Though more likely we were holding each other back, crushed by our past, exhumed for a single night. We tacitly settled on a kiss on the cheek—but only one (and very close to the mouth). I made sure to rub off the scarlet mark near my lips before returning to my parents' house. And she headed off to Université Cheick Anta Diop, a.k.a. UCAD, where the BMS coordination meeting would take place. We promised to write.

When I got home, my mother gave me one of those looks that seemed to say, I'm your mother and I know everything you did last night. Still, she didn't ask any questions, and neither did my father. I spent the afternoon at the house with my younger brothers, and tried to reaccustom myself to a daily rhythm that my life in France had erased down to its very memory.

Text from Aïda: *I admit it—I missed you. I wouldn't let myself write you this whole past year. I didn't want to lose*

face. I didn't want to complicate things. But things get com-
plicated all on their own. I still miss you. My every sense is
begging for you. My body wants to recognize yours. It wants
to be recognized by you. And yet I still think seeing each
other is a bad idea. I know it's contradictory but it's true.
What do YOU want?

You probably want me to tell you what kind of man
he was, don't you? the poetess had said to Siga D., who
then told me. There's no simple answer to that question,
Corazón. He'd been coming to my parents' literary gatherings for several months before I heard his voice for the
first time. He didn't talk much. He listened; and it was as if
people were hoping that at the end of his silent contemplation, all of a sudden, and with a single word, he would rip
the invisible veil that no one saw but everyone sensed, and
which we all divined was separating us from some essential
truth.

He never contributed to the intellectual or political discussions that dominated the gatherings. But no one reproached
him for it, as if he were exempt from verbal participation.
Though that tacit accord was more snobbery than anything
else, the kind to which you don't admit: *Ah, yes, yesterday*
we spent the evening with that mysterious African, Elimane,
who doesn't speak and yet is quite profound, his silence
is spiritual, really. For that matter, no one ever asked him
any questions, even when the conversation turned to topics
related to Africa. I'm not saying that his Africanness gave
him more legitimacy to talk about his continent, but I think
that everyone would have liked to hear what he thought, as
an African, about certain events happening there. This was
the eve of the 1960s. The independence of African nations

was prompting heated debate across the world, and in our living room. But the only African in the group said nothing.

Then one night in 1958, yes, it was October 1958, I got fed up with that respect verging on deference. We were discussing the resounding no that Guinea-Conakry had just given, via referendum, de Gaulle's proposal to include the countries of French West Africa in a "French community." I abruptly stood and I called him out: And you, our African gentleman, what do you think of this decision by the Guinean people? Or maybe you don't have an opinion, maybe all it inspires in you is indifference, and this contemptuous silence you've maintained for months. Maybe you think we're not worthy of what you have to say. But maybe the Guinean people, whom I find magnificent, are worthy, don't you think?

You should have seen the guests' faces, *Corazón*. I stopped the gathering cold. I still remember the look in some of their eyes. There was fear there. But in a few, I saw curiosity, amusement. Gombrowicz, I noticed right away, was champing at the bit, as if he was thinking: Finally, things are about to get interesting! Sábato, Elimane's other good friend, was as serious as ever, but I think he was just as curious to see how Elimane would respond. To be honest, I think that everybody, even those glued in place, was waiting for his reaction. He was sitting in an armchair, off to the side. I had brazenly stepped into his sight line, ten feet away, one hand on my hip, the other holding a glass of wine. I was very young, I wore my hair short, and, that night, big hoop earrings and a long blue dress that had garnered me more looks, compliments, and indecent, unspoken propositions than usual. I was challenging him. He slowly looked up at me. I'd promised myself I wouldn't drop my gaze, something I'd systematically done before, whenever our eyes met. Elimane remained still for several seconds, staring at me. I took one step closer and I said: Maybe you didn't hear me? I asked you what you think about Guinea. I'd like to hear your opinion about their independence, and about their leader, Sékou Touré.

After many heavy seconds, he stood up—he seemed even taller than I'd thought. With one stride he was in my face. I didn't move back. I lifted my chin so I could keep looking him in the eyes. I was eighteen, I'd just begun my law studies. He was already a grown man. I didn't know how old he was. It was only later that I learned that he was forty-three, the same age as my father.

Separated from him by mere inches, I had the confusing impression that I was facing a wall but also a vertical sea, a standing wave of sorts, whose raging inner swells I could hear. For a moment, in his eyes, I thought I saw a glimmer of hate, like he wanted to hit me or kill me. But the glimmer faded quickly. It was followed by a calm, almost amused demeanor. Then he smiled briefly—though I think I was the only one who saw that shadow of a smile—and he walked out of the room without a word.

The silence lasted a while longer. Gombrowicz was the one to break it. He said: Bravo, young lady. You have balls. But I recognized the way the African was walking when he left. You recognized it too, Sábato, right? He was moving like a hunted animal. A wounded beast. He's going to disappear for a while. He always does that when someone gets too close. And when he's preparing to disappear, he walks the way he walked when he left this room. Sábato and I have gotten used to it. You'd be better off getting used to it too. In my opinion, you won't see him back here for some time. But bravo, young lady. He needed to be confronted, and you were the only one here who could do it.

Gombrowicz was right: in the months that followed, Elimane didn't come back. The next time I saw him was nearly one year later, in August 1959. In the interim, Gombrowicz and Sábato occasionally showed up at my parents' gatherings. I would always ask them if their friend was still mad at me. One of them would invariably respond that Elimane wasn't angry. He was simply absent, traveling. Where? Across Latin America. Sometimes it was Chile, sometimes Brazil, Mexico, Guatemala, Uruguay, Colombia, Peru. But neither Gombrowicz nor Sábato knew the reason for those frequent trips. He's traveled a lot for as long as we've known him, Sábato told me one day. But I don't know what he's looking for, or even if he's looking for something.

I chose Sábato and Gombrowicz as my literary teachers. Or rather, they chose me as their protégée. They were already well-known in the world as writers. Although I was studying law, I'd felt deeply drawn to poetry. Gombrowicz and Sábato weren't poets. They were powerful and magnificent prose writers gifted with minds of superior intellect. Even without creating poetry, however, they read and understood it. The discussions we had about poetry were crucial for me when I was starting out.

I subjected my first poetic attempts to their scrutiny; rigorous scrutiny, without indulgence or easy encouragement. If I took literature and poetry seriously, if I wanted to write, Gombrowicz used to tell me, there was no path but rigor, the pure gift of oneself to creation. He would quote Vladimír Holan, the Czech poet: "From the sketch to the work one travels on one's knees." Then he would add: And the voyage is never-ending.

Gombrowicz was the tougher one, but also the most cheerful and the most fantastical. He was always around young people, and there was something rebellious and ironic, almost nasty, about his genius. Sábato was a more taciturn man. He could be merciless in his literary judgments, but exercised great restraint regardless of the circumstances. It was also clear that he was navigating a vast and deep inner universe in which he confronted the great metaphysical questions that permeated his books.

Elimane came up often in our conversations. One night when I was dining alone with Gombrowicz (Ernesto was sick and had been unable to join us), I once again asked him about Elimane. Like you now, *Corazón*, what I wanted to know, ultimately, was the kind of man he was. And so I questioned Gombrowicz at length.

How and why did the African end up here? said Gombrowicz. What a strange question…How and why did he end up here? How and why does anyone end up anywhere? I can't even remember how I got here and why I stayed after the war. And yet I miss the streets of Poland, that cursed country. Maybe the reason I stayed was to find the secret of Warsaw's streets in those of Buenos Aires. To truly see my country by looking at it in the mirror of another country. Maybe…But Elimane? I don't think he ever really told me. Not because he was hiding it, but because I never asked. He and I don't talk about that sort of stuff. Elimane is an exile, like me. The first time we saw each other we understood that, we recognized each other as such. He and I like talking about everything, except exile. In any case, there's nothing to say about it. I can't think of a more boring subject in the world. Though go ahead and ask Sábato, once he's feeling better. Maybe he knows how and why Elimane found himself here. But I'd advise you against questioning Elimane. You might annoy him, and upset him. Most exiles hate that question. And it never really held any interest for me. So there you have it. Now, my dear young girl from the beautiful and fiery island of Haiti, shall we fuck? Or make love, if you prefer. Everything can wait, Elimane can wait, death can wait, actually it's been waiting for us since always, everything can wait, but not the body, not desire, not sex, which I haven't had—and this is unforgivable at my age—since . . .

Four days. Four days after Fatima Diop's death, as a red tide was swelling, the president of the republic finally decided to address the nation on the eight o'clock news. I reached Liberté 6 around seven.

Chérif had been living there alone, in a very nice building, since his divorce two years earlier. We were happy to see each other again, as always. Though I noticed that his face looked drawn, like he hadn't slept in a while.

As we sat down to eat (an excellent *dibi*), the president of the republic's address began.

"He's going to ruin my appetite," said Chérif.

The president spoke forcefully and with solemnity for forty-five minutes. He started by expressing his profound sadness at Fatima Diop's death. Then he philosophized about the cruelty of fate and the tragedy of dying young. Finally, he offered his condolences to the family of the deceased. It was only after this that he ventured onto political terrain, where the people were waiting for rapid, tangible, and effective solutions to the crisis. The sphinx announced a myriad of measures, changes, and reforms. It was time to implement critical projects, he'd heard the anger and the distress, there couldn't be any more Fatimas, his priority was the youth, et cetera.

He was reaching the speech's conclusion when Chérif muted the television. For a few minutes, we watched the president talk on-screen, without hearing his words. His lips were vigorously chewing the air, opening and shutting over the silence.

"This is exactly what's happening in our country," Chérif observed. "Our leaders talk to us from behind a screen, a sheet of glass that no sound can penetrate. No one hears them. It wouldn't change anything if we did. We don't have to hear them anymore to know they're not telling the truth. The world behind that glass is an aquarium. Which means that our leaders are not men but fish: grouper, cod, catfish, swordfish, pike, sea bream, sole, and clownfish. And lots of sharks, of course. But the worst part, when you look at their fish faces, is that they seem to be telling us: In our position, you wouldn't do any better. You would disappoint just like we disappoint."

I read (or thought I read) on the president's lips: "Thank you. *Vive le Sénégal.*" Chérif turned off the TV just as the nation's flag floated gloriously before us.

"Same fuckin' shit," he said. "Every time there's flames, he shows up with his little buckets to fight a fire he started himself. It's an old trick—the pyromaniac firefighter. But we know, and he knows, that it won't put out the fire. His bucket is empty. Meaning filled with his lies. And the idiots swallow it up."

"After the stick comes the carrot..."

"No, no, *Miñelam*. That right there is the fatal illusion. It's statements like the ones he just made to calm people that screw those same people over. There's no longer any difference between the carrot and the stick, no alternating between them: our carrot is also our stick. We're satisfied with so little in this country. We don't have real standards for anything. Not even our own lives. Do we deserve them?"

He didn't give me time to think and continued:

"I've always been critical of anyone who takes the easy way out of saying people have the leaders they deserve. Or the variation: leaders are made in the people's image. That always struck me as easy contempt for the people and unforgivable indulgence toward certain selfish and cruel leaders. 'The crimes of those who lead are not the fault of those who are led,' Victor Hugo wrote somewhere, I can't remember where. But now I'm starting to think that people who claim mediocre leaders are a reflection of their subjects aren't wrong. I look at our compatriots and I ask myself: Do we really deserve better? We're fish too. A school of sardines. What are we doing, either individually or collectively, to deserve better than immoral political figures, better than a kakistocracy?"

"I don't know that word. I assume, based on the context, that it's pejorative. I'll look it up. But how do you answer your own question? As individuals and as a people, do we deserve something different?"

His phone rang just then. Chérif looked at it but didn't answer.

"BMS held a coordination meeting today at the university," he said. "I didn't go. That's why they're calling me.

I'm guessing they want me to write an op-ed. But I don't really feel like talking to them. I don't want to write op-eds and analyses for them anymore."

"Why not?"

"I don't really see myself in what BMS is doing anymore. The movement is getting bogged down in an expected, pointless face-off. Their activism is critical, necessary, and brave. But essentially pointless, unfortunately. It won't change anything. Our actions maintain the political status quo, the illusion of a clash of ideas with those in power. But the status quo always benefits those in power. We need to go further. We need to do more."

"BMS should transform and establish itself as a political party... is that what you call going further? Enter the arena and get your hands dirty, instead of playing at untarnished democratic sentinels?"

"No, that's not what I'm saying. In the end, the game of politics always forces us to play by its rules. It's a millstone, we're the seeds, and the seeds will never change the millstone, which will keep grinding and pulverizing them. Transforming things from the inside is an illusion. On the inside, we end up transforming ourselves. Not politics. Not things. Things never change. Not that way, in any case."

"What way, then? Do you have another suggestion?"

He said yes but backtracked right away, like his idea required further reflection:

"No... I'm not sure. I don't know. I'm looking for a third path. Everything that's happened in the past few days has me convinced we need to do something different. Protest, fight the riot police, endure the batons and the tear gas, scream, throw stones at the National Assembly, the courthouse, or the presidential palace, yell Fatima Diop's name beneath the sun with tears in our eyes, fine. But after? And after that?"

I couldn't think of an answer. Chérif went quiet, and eventually continued:

"Anyway...Let's talk about you, *Miñelam*. What are you doing here, exactly? Research for a new book?"

"Yeah, kind of."

"I hope I'll see more of you in this one. My criticism of the BMS goes for writers too. They need to do more. I'm not saying literature serves no purpose. I have a sacred fear of and dedication to literature, which is why I'll never become a writer. All I'm saying is that if, at the very least, your goal isn't to shake people down to their core, you're better off not writing. Don't write me another book like *Anatomy of the Void*. I'm begging you. The only person that book was speaking to was you. You're better than that. You need to do much better than that. Write us a great book, *Miñelam*. A great political book."

I smiled. This wasn't a surprise: Chérif had given me the same speech after the publication of *Anatomy of the Void*. He had reproached me for abandoning social issues in favor of egocentric preoccupations. He hadn't shared this criticism like the others, morons who thought they knew more of reality, of true life, of concrete things. No: he simply spoke to me with the sincere dismay of a man who no longer recognized his friend.

And true, there was a time when we shared similar ideas. I could even say that, of the two of us, I had been the more radical. But nothing remains unchanged. Would we even want it to? Fidelity to a self that has ossified over time is not simply an illusion; it also strikes me as a blind spot laughed at by life: life, its unpredictable current, its uncertainties, its circumstances that, at times, destroy the values and principles we believed (claimed) to be immutable.

Every so often I'll hear someone say you should remain faithful to the child you once were. Which is the most futile or ill-fated ambition you could have. It's certainly advice I'll never give. The child that once was will always look cruelly or with disappointment at what they've become as an adult, even if they've achieved their dream. That doesn't mean that adulthood is by nature cursed or rigged. Simply, nothing ever lives up to a childhood ideal or dream experienced in all its guileless intensity. Becoming an adult is always a betrayal of our most tender years. But therein lies all the beauty of childhood: it exists to be betrayed, and that betrayal is the birth of nostalgia, the only sentiment that allows us, one day perhaps, at the other end of life, to rediscover the pureness of youth.

Chérif wasn't convinced. He wasn't talking about my childhood, but about the eighteen-year-old me. He acknowledged that life's challenges change us, but didn't understand how a person could turn their back on misery. For him, that concern for others was an invariant of having a conscience. He didn't find it contradictory with the creation of beautiful works of art. Chérif had an especially hard time understanding my "metamorphosis," since he'd known me at a time when I would become incensed at the slightest sign of misery or injustice. The *Miñelam* he'd known, as engaged as I was enraged, had changed so quickly, so abruptly...

"I'll try," I responded. "A great political novel."

Then we discussed more pleasant topics, in appearance at least: books, women, travel, our tragicomic memories of military school; but I could tell Chérif was struggling to maintain the lighthearted mood. There was something deep in his eyes that belied his smiles, whenever he attempted one. Shortly before midnight, I asked for "the way home," the customary way of telling your host that you're ready to leave. He walked me to my car.

"Did you know Fatima Diop?" I asked him. "They say she was a BMS activist."

"Yes."

Before that yes, five or six seconds of silence went by. I intuitively understood that they had smothered or uncovered a pit of memories and pain inside Chérif. His voice, which never shook, had trembled. I told him I was sorry and that I regretted bringing it up. He said thank you and assured me it was nothing. Then there was the silence and the darkness and the sand and the maze of streets.

"That girl had real heart," he suddenly added, as we reached the car. "A beautiful soul. She was one of my philosophy students at UCAD, before we started spending time together at BMS, and then in private. I knew her well. And it's because I knew her that I don't feel like I can go to the September 14 march."

I'd wanted to hug my friend, but an instinctual reserve held me back: we weren't in the habit of giving physical displays of affection or consolation; he would have told me that I *really* had changed, so I merely repeated that I was sorry. He told me that he was too. I advised him to get some rest. He promised he would. We said our good nights and I left. I drove for a few seconds before glancing in the rear-view mirror. Chérif hadn't moved, and I knew that it wasn't me he was watching disappear, but Fatima Diop. I thought: Maybe one day he'll tell me what happened between them, I'd like him to tell me one day, even if it ended badly.

I turned off Liberté 6 and headed west to get on the VDN. Direction Médina. That night, once again, Aïdaville, the capital of orgasmic uprisings and material ecstasies, was calling me, and that imperial summons was directed at my deepest foundations, at my boundless, unconditional desire.

See you tonight, desert poet. Come back and prove it, she'd said after my response to her text that morning: *All I want, for now, is to let our desires guide us...my desire for you is never-ending, it's one year in the making, and every night I think about quenching it. I still thirst for your skin too. I've been walking through the desert for one year, and it will take more than one night for me to slake my thirst. My every sense recognizes you, but recognition isn't enough: you still need to prove it. I want to prove it to you again, even if you believed me.*

D – 2

This morning, owing to the tensions and violence feared on September 14, the country's most widely read newspaper asked the burning question on its front page: *What is to be done?*

The leaders of various religious communities called for cool tempers. They said that the Senegalese people were a community of believers, united by their faith in the same God. The country needed to pray for Fatima Diop and her family. The thing to be done, imperatively, was make peace.

The members of the presidential majority insisted that Fatima Diop's suicide not be politicized or exploited. It was a true tragedy that didn't call for anger, but responsibility. The thing to be done, between now and then, was reopen the dialogue and remain united in spite of political differences.

The veterans of the political opposition railed that the government needed to hear the people's cry and take responsibility. The president should resign and initiate new elections. Therefore, the thing to be done, no matter the cost, was good old-fashioned politics.

Amid the media barrage, good citizens hesitated. They wanted peace, but did peace nourish? Wasn't it better to have a crisis that might bring about greater dignity and social justice than a fake peace that would keep the worse-off right where they were? Stuck in this tragic dilemma, the people hesitated. The thing to be done was to toss and turn over the matter.

For the BMS leaders, there was no room for hesitation. September 14 had to be the first page of a new history book. Not writing it would be betraying Fatima Diop's memory. *What is to be done?* Lenin, in 1902, had published a political tract whose title was that very simple question. His response was equally simple, and the See-It-Throughers borrowed it: for a true revolutionary, the thing to be done was revolution.

And as for me, the writer, the young promising writer, one of the supposed jewels of our august nation's literary future, what was to be done? Someone on the Internet, a radical BMS activist, had called me out on my Facebook page. *What do you think about all this? What are the writers doing? You are the voice of the voiceless! Why so quiet? Don't betray us! The whites talk about you in France. But what do YOU have to say for your country?*

I was tempted by a few responses. *Use your own mouth and speak for yourself, comrade.* Deleted. *But can all the voiceless come together in a single voice?* Deleted. *Speaking for the collective always means betraying individuals.* Deleted again. *Shut the fuck up.* Erased. I didn't feel I had the legitimacy to talk for anyone whatsoever. My own words were already too heavy, and it wasn't my uncertain status as a writer that was changing that. The time of guides, visionaries, prophets, mages, Pythia, and other sublime Hugoisms is over. You can't say which path to take anymore, you just have to follow strangers down theirs, all the way to the end, meaning to the depths of their soul, or your own.

After long hesitation, I decided not to respond to his message. He wrote me again privately to tell me that I was an example for many young people and that they needed me, my words, my engagement. I didn't respond to that one either. Then he went back onto my public profile and left the following message, beneath his first one, in all caps: *Ever wonder why you'll never be a big deal here? Because you act like you're better than us. The whites can celebrate you as much as they like, give you all the prizes they want, talk about you in their fancy papers, but here, you're nothing. Nada. And when you're nothing in your home country, you're nothing everywhere. You're a traitor, a castaway, a house Negro. You'll never reach the caliber of . . .* Then he listed the names of seven or eight intellectuals and writers that he considered to be the people's worthy consciences.

I "liked" his comment and feigned the haughtiest of ironies. But deep down, I could tell he'd wounded me. I was annoyed with myself for giving any importance to the whole thing. To think that a few days earlier I'd been with Siga D. (included by that day's prosecutor, who had no doubt never read her, in his list of model writers), whose entire body of work was built upon the betrayal, the murder even, of the "us," of the native country, of the culture of origins, of the expectations of "your people," of belonging. That was the price of her work. I tried to imagine Elimane in my position. How would he have responded to this guy?

The Haitian poetess, when I asked if she had questioned Elimane about the reasons for his presence in Argentina, told me: Of course I did, *Corazón*. Of course I eventually asked him what brought him to Argentina and what was keeping him there. But that bravery only came to me years later. When I finally asked him the question, contrary to what Gombrowicz had said to me, Elimane didn't become angry. But the steely impassivity covering his face in that instant terrified me more than outright rage. He stared at me. Beads of sweat gleamed on his forehead, a few fell into his eyebrows. Seventeen seconds—I silently counted them thanks to the noisy second hand of the clock hanging above his bed—seventeen seconds passed between us without a word, then he said: You're back at it. I thought you knew why, but I was wrong. You didn't ask Sábato and Gombrowicz about me while I was gone, or simply when you see them without me?

This was in the beginning of 1964, one evening in late January or early February. I remember it had been very hot that day. We'd spent it in the tiny apartment where he was living, shades drawn, to preserve a bit of coolness while waiting for night to come. When it finally did and the temperature dropped a little, we had opened the only window in the room. The air was more bearable, but there wasn't a puff of wind. Cool relief remained suspended in the sky, prevented from falling by a thick, invisible cloak of humidity that soiled everything and glued our clothes to our skin. I'd known him for five years, and it was only that night that I dared ask him the question that had been burning on my lips since I'd seen him again after our confrontation in my parents' living room.

To be honest, his response didn't surprise me. I knew, before asking the question, that he would respond with another question. That was his specialty; after all those years, I'd come to understand him. Do you remember that he had spent several months traveling through South America, after the incident at my parents' house, in 1958? He returned to Buenos Aires in August 1959. The first night that he dined with Sábato and Gombrowicz, the two of them invited me. That was my first time seeing him again since our confrontation in my parents' house. But unlike that evening, when I'd challenged his silence in a surge of rebellion and insolence, I was terrified the night of our reunion. Though I saw right away that he wasn't trying to intimidate me. I found him pleasant even, almost gentle. He was simply spending time with his only friends, and though he wasn't very talkative, in the span of a few minutes he said more words than I'd ever heard him utter in the entirety of his contributions to my parents' artistic gatherings. Maybe that's what terrified me: I was seeing him as I'd never seen him before, as a new man.

It was starting then, on the eve of the 1960s, that I began spending more time with him. At first, it was always with Sábato and Gombrowicz, one of them would invite us over, or we'd meet in a café. Elimane and I also used to cross paths at the homes of other artists, poets, and patrons of Buenos Aires. My parents no longer held their gatherings, but the city certainly wasn't lacking in them at the time. Victoria and Silvina Ocampo's salon was all the rage. You'd see Borges there, Mallea, Bioy, and all the other Argentinean literary figures who orbited around the magazine *Sur*; you might also, at times, run into European intellectuals and writers like Roger Caillois or Aldous Huxley. Elimane would show up on occasion. Though, like his two friends, he preferred smaller, less flashy groups. In the summer, he liked to sit in the city's cafés, his back to the large fans that, back then, all those places usually had. He liked the circulating air that hit the back of his neck and shoulders. He would drink while listening to tangos, especially Gardel's tangos, or banal conversations, political debates, arguments about soccer or boxing, a clamor that would eventually lazily slip away, across the estuary. It was hard to tell if he was happy or sad in those moments. But he seemed at peace, at the least.

It took several months before I felt less intimidated by him; three years before I spent time with him one-on-one. Meanwhile, at regular intervals, he would go on his mysterious trips across Latin America, sometimes for a few days, other times for several weeks. Regardless, I would be desperate to see him whenever he came back, to talk to him, to listen to him, even though he didn't say much. It was like every word counted for him, or against him; like every sentence had a price, and was only spoken after due consideration. Like his acolytes before him, he became my literary mentor of sorts. Being initiated, read, corrected, critiqued, discouraged, and encouraged in my poetic vocation by Sábato, Gombrowicz, and Elimane remains the greatest source of pride in my life, *Corazón*. My teachers were masters.

I've already told you about Gombrowicz and Sábato, about their respective personalities and styles. I guess I should try to tell you about Elimane, even though that's the hardest.

He had rented a spartan two-room furnished flat in the neighborhood of Barracas. It was in terrible condition, like every other apartment in the barrio. The first time he invited me there, he told me I was the first person he'd had over. Not even Gombrowicz or Sábato had set foot there, which they confirmed later when I told them about my visit. Indeed he and I had grown closer in 1963, over the several months we spent alone, meaning without our two friends. At the invitation of a rich and prestigious foundation, Gombrowicz had returned to Europe, to Berlin, for the first time since 1939. Sábato was on a tour of several countries in Latin America, where the publication of *On Heroes and Tombs*, his masterpiece, had made him famous.

In their absence, Elimane and I saw each other more often. I would go to the university during the day, and meet him in the evening at one café or another. We would talk about literature. I asked him very few questions about his personal life and his past; it was a sort of pact between us; and yet the better I got to know him, the more I came to feel that I would never truly know him if he never surrendered the key to his past and his coming to Argentina. But I had no idea how to cross the ice (or the *bolgia* full of alligators) standing between his history and any outside observer. He could be charming, and in fact always was around me, but I quickly understood there was a price for that amenity. He was accessible yet remained unattainable. On several occasions, I tried to steer him into sharing a fragment of his past life, but I was so clumsy that he would guess my intentions before I could ask a single question.

The only breach in his fortress opened thanks to him, that evening when he invited me over for the first time. That was also the first time that he allowed me to read *The Labyrinth of Inhumanity*, which, in Argentina at least, only Gombrowicz and Sábato had read. I sat down on his bed as he read and edited the most recent poems I'd written; I began *The*

Labyrinth of Inhumanity. The clock above his bed sounded like it was breathing its last breath every time its needles moved. Each second that passed elicited a wheeze. But that evening, not even the asthmatic pendulum could tear me away from the pages of *Labyrinth*. It was an extraordinary book, despite everything Elimane told me about it afterward, concerning the plagiarism and what it had cost him in France. Yes, he told me everything. The instances of plagiarism—which I didn't really consider to be plagiarism, incidentally—scarcely mattered, since they had woven together a masterpiece. That's always been my opinion on the matter. That night, the first night I spent in Elimane's home, I asked him many questions about *The Labyrinth of Inhumanity* and how it had been received in France. His answers were measured, guarding what he considered needed to remain in the shadows. But still, I learned a little about his past. Elimane wasn't confessing or complaining: he told me about that part of his life with modesty, without affectation, though it was obvious it still pained him. On two or three occasions, a brief silence, or a quiver in his voice, betrayed an emotion that was still raw—a mix of anger, shame, and bitterness.

At the end of the night, before drifting off to sleep beside him, I understood: Elimane had willingly told me the reasons for his presence, thereby appeasing the questions he sensed I still had about him. I deduced this on my own: he had come to Argentina to recover from the bitter experience of his fall from grace in the French literary world. Or to forget it. It was a satisfying explanation: there was pride, vanity, self-respect, dignity, honor; there were all the values that, when trampled, could drive a man to leave. In

Elimane's case, the explanation was all the more convincing since the book that had brought him dishonor as both a man and a writer was a great book. He never said so, but at the time, this is how I understood it: his coming to Argentina was a question of distance, by which I mean, the way we take our distance when our pride has been wounded. I think that was the night I fell in love, *Corazón*, not with him, but with the permanent wound that he was. Yes, that's what Elimane was: an open wound, from which blood was somehow flowing toward the inside. An internal hemorrhage. An inverted geyser. I didn't want to heal or save him. I had no desire to do either and for that matter didn't think myself capable. His shadows had seduced me; that was it. He became my lover, like Gombrowicz before him.

For several months, I stopped wondering, since I believed I'd gotten my answer, or part of it. I was content to enjoy our time together, his advice, his experience. He completed my literary and sexual initiation, begun by Gombrowicz and Sábato.

Upon his return from Berlin, Gombrowicz told us he was going back to Europe for good. He was moving to France. We threw him a small party, attended by all the Polish maestro's friends, mostly the young poets and poetesses of Buenos Aires, who came to tell him goodbye. Gombrowicz asked me to sleep with him one last time before his departure. By which I mean before my death, he said. I agreed; we spent the whole night making love (my God, was he filthy and lewd and funny and gentle in bed!), then, somewhat oddly, while we were drinking coffee in his kitchen the next morning, he wanted to know if I'd asked Elimane the reason for his presence in Argentina. Which surprised me, since Gombrowicz himself had advised me not to bring it up. I pointed out the contradiction.

I still advise you not to ask him why he's here, he said, ever the contrarian, but I also advise you to demand the truth. Don't give up. I don't think the scandal over the plagiarism in his novel is what brought him here. At least, that's not the only reason. There's something else.

"You think so?"

"Think? How terrible! No, I don't think: I feel."

That was all Gombrowicz would tell me. Then he left for France, where he met the woman who would become his wife, Rita, and they loved each other dearly.

His leaving deeply affected Sábato, of whom we saw less and less, especially once he began to write the final opus of his extraordinary trilogy of novels. And so, yet again, I found myself alone with Elimane most of the time, in cafés or at his apartment. Gombrowicz's comments during our final night together had rekindled the doubt in my mind. Elimane continued, from time to time, to leave Buenos Aires for periods of varying length. Those repeated absences, about which he said nothing, intensified the questions I had begun asking myself again as to the true reason for his presence in Argentina. Where did he really go? What did he do? What was living at the center of his labyrinth? The man was a stranger. Even Sábato, who was his oldest friend in Buenos Aires, knew nothing of his private life.

Some days, I deemed my preoccupation pointless. Was it that important to uncover the secrets of a person you loved? After all, you don't love a person because of what they keep out of reach, right? Isn't whatever connects you far more important than anything you may think they're hiding? My connection to Elimane, before desire or love even, was literature. Or so I would tell myself whenever the subject came up. But the feeling never lasted; as soon as Elimane slipped back into the enigma of his secret life, my suspicions would return and gnaw away at me. And then Gombrowicz's final words would echo once more. Something else...

I couldn't live with the doubts anymore. They were ruining my relationship with Elimane. I admired and hated him for drawing a ring of fire around himself. So one night, when he returned from a four-day trip to Uruguay, I stepped inside the ring and braved the flames. I asked him what he had really been doing in Argentina all this time. You already know his response:

"You're back at it. I thought you knew why, but I was wrong. You didn't ask Sábato and Gombrowicz about me, when you saw each other while I was gone?"

"I did," I said. "But Gombrowicz told me that he didn't know, that he wasn't interested, and that, for that matter, I should avoid asking you the question so as not to upset you."

"I'm not surprised he said that. Even though I'm also sure, knowing him, that he encouraged you not to settle for my answers."

"You know him well."

"And Sábato?"

"Ernesto said both the opposite of Gombrowicz and the same thing as Gombrowicz: he told me that I should ask you the question directly if I wanted to know."

"That doesn't surprise me either, coming from him."

"I want to know. Why did you *really* leave France to come live in Argentina?"

"You're sure you *really* want to know?"

"Yes. Why don't you ever talk about it? Are you running away from something or someone?"

Elimane looked at me very intensely—I got that same sensation of standing before a wall—before calmly responding:

"I'm not running away from anything. I'm looking for someone."

Though caught off guard (I didn't think he was going to answer) I kept going and directed a volley of questions at him, in the hope that my spontaneity would surprise him and prolong the conversation:

"Are your absences and trips across the continent linked to this person?"

"Yes."

"And for all these years, you still haven't found them?"

"No."

"Who is this person?"

That time I knew Elimane wouldn't answer, but I wanted to see his face, the look in his eyes, the moment I asked him.

"Is it a woman?"

He looked at me, unblinking, and his features were illegible.

"What did she promise you? Or steal?"

He said nothing, impassive.

"Or maybe I'm wrong and it's not a woman, but a member of your family. Is it your brother? Your child? Or maybe your father?"

His face remained closed, and the key lay at the bottom of the river. He rose from the bed and went to the open window. He lit a cigarette, leaned his elbows on the ledge, and smoked in silence as he watched something outside, or watched nothing at all, simply the night. Then again, maybe he closed his eyes. He was so tall that, leaning over like that, there was something absurd about his body, something albatrossesque, the famed albatross forever encumbered by its wings. Still, I sensed his power: in his broad back sticking to his shirt, I saw all the harm he could inflict if he were to relinquish control of his movements. The reason he wasn't spreading his wings, that he was holding them tightly against his soul, was because their span would have filled the room, knocked over objects, created an imbalance, a breach into which the whole room could have fallen, with no hope of return or of crashing against a bottom. Without intending to he could have struck a vital organ, disemboweled the night itself. He knew that, and in a way, I knew it too. He couldn't let go, say anything, unburden himself with a confession. The only reason he was alive and keeping others alive was because he was keeping his secrets.

His wide shoulders filled nearly the entire window frame. Outside, we could hear kids hollering as they played soccer in the streets, garbage lots, and *potreros* of Barracas. The games were held at all hours, in the middle of the night even; impassioned, rugged, violent matches, with nothing at stake but honor, which at that age is the most important and perhaps only thing worth playing for, apart from the occasional prize of two jars of milk for which all the children had chipped in. A tango melody entered Elimane's bedroom from the upstairs apartment, whose window must have been open too. Amid the screaming and shouting by the boisterous soccer players, we were able to make out a few words. And yet we didn't need to hear the song clearly to know that like all great tangos, it spoke of the solitude of man's greatest depths, of the impossibility of keeping and even more so bringing back loved ones, of moments of innocence and joy, of the faint imprint of true beauty. From the window we also saw the silhouette of La Bombonera. If there had been a match taking place, we could have heard the Boca fans' frenzied whoops and chants of love escaping the stadium.

I tried one last time to get the truth out of him:

"What do you want from this person?"

I don't know what his face looked like, *Corazón*, I could only see his back. I didn't see his eyes. But his body, in any case, remained motionless; and for one second—one second, not more, a single second—I had the certainty and the physical sensation that everything around us had stopped moving: the hands of the wall clock, the trajectory of the ball in the road, the tango mid-verse, the blood in my veins, and even the smoke from Elimane's cigarette appeared to freeze in the night around him. A single second not outside of time, but *beneath* time, and then everything returned to normal. Elimane stayed at the window a while longer. He smoked a second cigarette. Then he turned toward me.

When I saw his face I understood that not only would he give me no further answers, but also that I wouldn't find the courage to ask him about his past again. He smiled in a way I'd never seen and would never again see a human being smile. The loud clock coughed out ten p.m. from its ravaged lungs. Elimane still had that terrible smile on his lips, and I felt incapable of the slightest movement, frozen, despite the ambient heat. Relief flooded over me once the smile faded from his face.

"Let's dine, shall we?" he said. "I'm hungry. I know a few restaurants near the docks that are still open. Maybe a breeze will come in from Río de la Plata. I'd kill for a gentle, cool wind. The mortal coil is so heavy...I'd have loved to be air; to forever be a light, pleasant wind, gracefully gliding above things and beings."

D – 1

There's no calm before the storm.

Last night, as we were making love, I peered inside a droplet that was trickling along Aïda's body. I was under her. I tried to get a look at her face, but her position hid it from view. She was bucking so hard that her chest went taut, violently propelled forward, and I was able to see the sensual arc of her back. Her long hair was stroking my thighs and caressing the top of her buttocks, the small of her back. I distinguished the outline of her rib cage, the pleats of her stomach, the two domes of her breasts. Her chin jutted out between those two dunes of flesh, like a small pyramid. It was there, on the tip of her chin, that the drop appeared.

It slid down slowly and soon resembled a small stalactite hanging from the chin ceiling. I waited anxiously for it to fall. Aïda thrust her hips even harder, the motion precipitating the drop onto her throat, and its odyssey across her body began. When the drop set out between her breasts, I began to discern hazy visions inside it, like in a fortune teller's orb. A man was following a woman down a street where they were alone; and the man was calling to her, but the woman didn't turn around, though I didn't know if she was ignoring him or didn't hear him.

The drop passed the plexus. I watched the man run, slowly at first, then faster and faster, after the woman. The man, while running, while continuing to shout, in the silence of the street, the name of the human form that still didn't appear to hear him or want to answer him, began to cry, and the scene was so hopeless, it made me so sad, that for a moment I thought I would cry too, and surely would have if I hadn't shaken it off and restrained myself.

The belly button was now approaching after the drop's trek through a forest of beauty marks on Aïda's stomach; her movements were growing longer, more patient, precise, essential, which, I well knew, always signaled her climax. I felt her vagina's slow spasms around my phallus, and the spate swelling inside her, and the white star inside her that would soon explode and shatter the universe all the way to its farthest reaches. In the droplet, in the street, the woman finally turned around, and her face was beautiful, though she looked surprised to see the man running after her shouting her name. The man had nearly caught up to her. But instead of slowing down to stop, he continued running and shouting a woman's name.

The drop slid close to the edge of the naval chasm but didn't fall in. It was now gliding toward the pubis. Aïda leaned forward and brought her head near my face, which was covered by her brown cloud of hair. Her body tensed in a violent contraction, she pressed her forehead to mine, clasped her hands behind my neck, squeezed it, and the cry that erupted from her at that moment, the cry that erupted not from her throat, not from her mouth, not from her chest or her stomach, but from every part of her, was accompanied by an exhalation that reminded me that I was and would forever be barred from understanding it, and allowed merely to form its cortege or its shadow.

Aïda's head was resting on my shoulder, her face glued to my cheek. It seemed like the bedroom, too, was attempting to slow and lengthen its breathing, falling into our rhythm. The woman in the street continued on her way. Ahead of her, the man was still running and chasing and calling a woman whom only he saw: his illusion.

There's no calm before the storm. The real storm always precedes itself, acts as its own emissary; the wind wails in silence, as noiseless as a drop of water embarking along a woman's body tensed with pleasure or pain. Then it passes, the way everything passes, in an illusion of eternal motionlessness. Nothing was destroyed and yet nothing is really left standing.

Aïda told me she wasn't free the next day, meaning today. She had to prepare for her coverage of the big march.

"Maybe we'll see each other there, if you come. We could plan to meet somewhere. Place de l'Obélisque, for example. That's where the march will begin. The obelisk is on top of a large stone pedestal. There's a lion painted on the pedestal. We could meet on the fourteenth, at ten a.m., under the lion's stomach."

We kissed goodbye. I went home. That morning, when I woke, I wrote her:

I'll be at the march. But you won't find me under the lion's stomach today, Aïda. I thought I was satisfying my desire for you, but no: it's my vengeance. What I took for a desire one year in the making is in fact a desire to make you suffer, to make you pay for leaving me. I realize now how much that hurt me. It's over. I came here to find a writer who'll teach

*me who I want to be. He's my illusion. It's better that we stop
now, before I start chasing another illusion—rekindling my
love for you, when in truth, all I'll do is destroy its memory.
I'm sorry.*

I waited for her answer all day long, but it didn't come.

I reread *The Labyrinth of Inhumanity*, and for the first
time the book's ending made me cry. And yet I know it by
heart; I'd read it dozens of times and always walked away
feeling emotional; but never, before that afternoon, had I
cried. Outside, all is calm. It was the calm before the storm,
or more precisely, the storm of September 14.

In late June 1966, said the Haitian poetess to Siga D.,
who later, at her home in Amsterdam, told me, the Argentine Revolution ousted Arturo Illia. General Ongania took
power and established a new military dictatorship. The university, the cafés, the bars, the movie theaters, the clubs, the
concert halls: those places were the first and most heavily
damaged by the moralizing wave to which the new government subjected the country. Young people were of course
the ones whom the military was trying to control. At the
time, fresh out of college, I'd found a job in the legal department of the biggest publishing house in Buenos Aires. At
night, I would assist a couple I'd befriended at school. They
ran a small independent movie theater, where I helped out
by working as an usher. We used to show avant-garde films.
One night, in 1967, we showed *Blow-Up*, the Antonioni
film adapted from a short story by Cortázar, who was very
popular among the Argentinian youth at the time. Soldiers,
alerted by an infiltrated informer, showed up, arrested several people, including my friends, seized all the movie reels
they found, and ordered the small theater's closure. That

same night, I openly joined the fight against the military regime.

I was arrested on several occasions because my hair was cut short, which the junta viewed (along with short skirts) as a sign of female depravity. I refused to wear a wig. For two years I participated in clandestine political meetings. I organized a few myself, in secret locations. I put up signs, hijacked regime ones, signed petitions, contributed to anti-government publications, handed out leaflets, ran from patrols with fear in my belly, spent a few nights in prison. My parents always bailed me out, but never forbade me from resisting. My mother had known political oppression in Haiti. She always told me that hoping that a dictatorship would become less violent because you didn't fight back was a suicidal illusion coupled with cowardice.

For all those reasons, I saw Elimane less and less. He seemed indifferent to the political situation, or worse, bored by it. All that interested him, all that had ever interested and obsessed him, I told myself at the time, was to find the person he was looking for. He continued his quest and would periodically leave Buenos Aires. Suddenly I found Elimane selfish, cowardly almost. His raison d'être was neither love nor friendship (had he ever considered Sábato and Gombrowicz friends?). All that mattered to him was his secrets. Everything else, including me, was a mere backdrop, shallow and artificial, that he could adjust, move around, remove as he pleased, like on a theater stage.

We weren't even good, I told myself, for alleviating or staving off his solitude. On the contrary, we enabled him to sink deeper into that solitude he so loved. He only saw us to measure how precious it was to him. We represented the opposite of solitude, its foil, which he used to remind himself (and teach us) that he didn't need us. That's what I believed at the time.

I thought it only fair to tell him. He told me he understood. And then I stopped seeing him. Between February 1968 and September 1969, I only ran into him once, by chance, in the street. He waved at me. I pretended not to see him. That night, when I thought back to it, I initially told myself I'd done the right thing; but that certainty gradually changed, and became regret, then intense sadness. I still think about it now, *Corazón*, and the pain of having ignored him is always there.

The political struggle continued. There was violence, but it continued; disfigurements, mutilations, torture, but it continued. There were casualties. We kept fighting. Like for many other young people across the world, the year 1968 was my political education.

And yet, in May 1969, when the uprisings were growing and the dictatorship showed the first signs of wavering, I began to feel less engaged with what was happening. I was overcome by a sudden wave of exhaustion at the very moment I should have been my most combative. The whiff of rebellion was spreading, those who had been fighting for the past few years found a reason to hope in that surge of support, the *Cordobazo* had demonstrated the resistance of the humiliated Argentine people in spectacular and violent fashion, and meanwhile I was languishing. I stayed inside my apartment, doing nothing. I kept up with the demonstrations, I was there in spirit, but I no longer participated. The desire to fight hadn't left me; it was simply missing an ingredient that I used to have and no longer did. But I didn't know which one.

I fell out with most of my comrades in arms, who accused me of desertion. They reproached me for pretending to fight alongside them to expiate the guilt of a bourgeois birth. Some brought up my father's status. "Coming from the daughter of an American diplomat, a betrayal like yours isn't much of a surprise. Actually we're wondering why it came so late." My only remaining friends were the couple who owned the avant-garde movie theater. But they had been forced to leave Buenos Aires two months earlier, out of fear of being arrested and tortured.

One evening in September 1969, as I was making dinner, Elimane showed up at my apartment, in the Núñez barrio. I wasn't surprised to see him. In fact, I think I sensed, before opening the door, that I was about to welcome an old acquaintance whom I had invited over. He was holding a bottle of wine. I looked at him without saying anything for several seconds. He didn't speak either. I can't remember what was going through my mind. Maybe: How sad that we're not saying anything, or: How beautiful that we're not saying anything, or, more likely: Here we are and there's nothing to say. I stepped aside and he entered. A military patrol was coming up the street. I closed the door. When I turned around, Elimane hadn't moved, and he was so tall that his head nearly touched the hallway ceiling. I walked past him and preceded him into the living room. He gave me the bottle: "It needs to breathe a little."

I had the odd sensation that his voice had remained the same, and yet it struck me as already different. That sensation that Elimane hadn't changed, but that he was also a stranger to me, stayed with me the whole evening. It was the first time he'd come to that apartment. I had moved there in March or April 1969, shortly after I stopped seeing him. His gaze went from the bookcase to the paintings hanging on the walls, from the lampshade to the piano, from the television set to the sideboard, from a basket of fruit to a mask representing the god Legba. I let him finish his silent inspection and motioned to one of the armchairs.

"It wasn't Sábato who told me where you lived. It was your mother."

"I figured," I said. "Ernesto hasn't come over yet, though he knows I'm living in this neighborhood now."

"You see him less often too?"

"Yes."

He said nothing and sat down. I sat in the facing chair and took a better look at him. The sensation returned: physically, he was just as I remembered him. But there was something ungraspable that had moved in his soul, imperceptibly, the way you might shift the placement of a vase by a few centimeters or adjust a frame on the wall by a few degrees.

I invited him to stay and dine with me. We moved to the table with his wine. He asked me if I was still involved in the resistance against the military regime.

"Not as much."

"I think you're in need of some rest. You seem tired."

I didn't respond.

He continued: "I think I found the person I've been looking for here for the past twenty years. I'm going to take one more trip, to make sure. Then, it will be finished, truly finished this time, and I can finally go home. That will be my last trip, the big homecoming. I came to say a few things, read you a few pages, make love to you if you want it as much as I do, and tell you…"

"Goodbye," I murmured. "I know."

D

Aïda's response didn't come until the evening of September 14, after the day's events. I was smoking in the hospital courtyard when I got her message:

They say revenge is best served cold... Hot or cold, it's difficult to digest. The kind of meal you vomit back up. That's what you did. I hope you feel better. You already got your revenge, Diégane. You returned the slap in the face I gave you more than a year ago. We're even. Now I know how it feels: watching the other person leave when you wish they would stay. A little longer. Forever. Finding you again made me understand that I'd never really lost you. Your memory was deep inside me, stubbornly hanging on. And more than your memory, there was the hope that one day, maybe, we... How stupid. But people are always stupid.

I'll be in Dakar for three more days. I want to see the aftermath of this extraordinary and promising day. I hope you won't ruin everything by trying to see me again. I hope you're far away, already out of reach, on the trail of that writer who'll show you the path of the person you want to become. I also hope that you'll have the class not to respond to this message. Not to explain. Not to justify yourself. If you did, if you were to be that emotionally weak, the gratitude and tenderness I feel for you in this moment, all my

*love for you, would transform—and I would never forgive
you for it—into profound contempt, a feeling contemptible
in itself, sullying both the person who expresses it and whoever's on the receiving end.*

*I don't think I've ever written a sentence as long as that
last one. Just goes to show. Goodbye and good luck.*

I read the message a few times in the poorly lit hospital courtyard. Several minutes went by, I tried to restrain
myself, but couldn't stop myself from writing:

*I know how proud you are, Aïda. You're one of those
people for whom consolation is a reminder that they're in a
position to receive it, like a poison. But I don't want to console you. What I want to do, even if you wish I wouldn't, is
explain. I'm not seeking revenge. I'm trying to avoid seeking
it in the future. I'm saving us from self-destruction. I . . .*

*Everything I've been holding in for one year wants to come
out. Aïda, I want to tell you everything: how much I missed
you, how much I ached every time I thought of you, how
much I, how much you, how much we, etc. What I mean is
I want to write you a great story, but I don't know where
to begin. All the sentences are jostling together in my head.
I've tried every register, every style, every tone, every turn of
phrase.*

*But it feels like every sentence, every word, is missing its
target. I try harder, I demand more: more depth, more preci-
sion, more accuracy. The words elude me, or elude themselves, shying away from their own truth. Subjected to my
relentless tyranny, they tire and fade. Every new attempt
deepens the chasm between what they're truly capable of
and the reality of the inner experience. But it's not so much
me they're betraying as themselves. The words are suicidal.*

And soon, out of fatigue or despair, but perhaps also simple nostalgia for solo navigation, I stop clinging to you and watch, from my unmoored block of land slowly floating toward the center of the ocean, or a new island, your shore drift away, or what I took for a shore but that was no doubt merely another piece of land, an atom in movement among other atoms' movements, and which is setting off, same as me, on a course without coordinates. I'm not taking my revenge, Aïda. I'm trying to preserve what...

I deleted it. Too long. Too ridiculous. Too pretentious. The truth was I wasn't in the mood. The day had drained me of any desire to speak. Aïda was right: it was time to shut up.

Just then, Amadou, Chérif Ngaïdé's brother, joined me in the courtyard. I called him first. He was the only member of Chérif's family whose contact information I had.

"He has several years of recovery and rebuilding ahead of him. He'll never be the same. But he's alive. Thanks to you. The whole family is grateful. I'll keep you posted. Nobody could have imagined that a man like Chérif could have..."

Amadou didn't finish his sentence, but I understood. He shook my hand before going back inside the hospital. I stubbed out my cigarette against a wall and listened to the city. After belching fire for the last few hours, it was strangely silent. It smelled of hot metal, melted tar, gunpowder. After being stifled by tear gas and smoke all day long, Dakar was seeking a breath of fresh air. September 14 had happened. The turnout matched the predictions: nearly half a million people took to the city's streets. There were clashes in several neighborhoods, over one hundred critically injured, including three people in a coma, but no deaths. BMS had already called for people to assemble again the next day, to make those in power yield once and for all. The government appeared to be overwhelmed by the scale of events, and had invited multiple social actors and the leaders of BMS to participate in negotiations that very night. It would be a long one. Nobody knew what would come of it.

I'd been lucky. First, to read Chérif's message immediately after he sent it to me. And then, lucky that my intuition was right. I'd had a few seconds to decide. And I was lucky that time had played in my favor.

This morning, around nine, as I was about to head out to join the protests, he'd sent me a long message via Facebook: *I'll be protesting today after all. I'll protest to atone, because it's all my fault. I'm the one who gave her the idea. We were at my apartment. We'd just heard on the news that three hundred young Senegalese had died at sea while trying to reach Europe in pirogues. Setting out under those conditions, knowing you'll probably die—it's suicide, she'd said. I was so outraged by how terrible, how careless our politicians were that I got carried away, I spoke irresponsibly. I said that in a country like ours, suicide was a horrible but effective method of political action, effective because it was horrible, and maybe the only form of protest still audible to our leaders. Sometimes suicide changes history: look at Mohamed Bouazizi in Tunisia in 2011, look at Jan Palach in Czechoslovakia in '69, look at Thích Quảng Đức in Vietnam in '63, and I won't get into, not here, the legendary suicide of the women of Nder, who chose to burn to death in a hut rather than surrender to the slavers. All those suicides had an impact, grabbed people's attention, carried political significance. Maybe that's all that's left for the populations of our desperate countries. Maybe that's what young people should do: commit suicide, since their lives aren't lives at all . . .*

I tossed those words out without really thinking, because I was emotional, but Fatima took them seriously and didn't forget them. The day she went through with it, she called me a few minutes before and told me I'd been right: this, meaning sacrifice, was the alternate path we'd been searching for: not a metaphorical or partial sacrifice, but a concrete, conscious, willing, absolute sacrifice: the sacrifice of life. I didn't understand what she was trying to tell me. I only understood when I saw the images of her death. And you, Miñelam, do you understand? It was me. Directly or indirectly, I'm the one who inspired her act, or fanned the flames. It's because of me that Fatima committed suicide after making sure her immolation by fire would be broadcast live on social media. A phone wedged into the right spot, video turned on, and the horror. Over these last few days, I've tried to tell myself that I'm not to blame. But it's too hard. I see Fatima every night. I can't sleep anymore. It's unbearable. I am to blame. There's only one way to pay for it. Which is to do exactly the same thing. Goodbye, my brother. One day you'll become the talented writer you need to be. I know so. I hope so.

After I read that, I remained frozen, at my parents' house, for several seconds. Then I tried to call Chérif, but of course he didn't answer. So I took my father's car and raced to his apartment, on Liberté 6. In the moment, I'd thought that with the number of police officers and people that would be in the streets that day, Chérif wouldn't try to set himself on fire in front of the National Assembly, like Fatima Diop, but at home.

I had to have broken countless rules of the road. I still don't know how I didn't run anyone over. A little over a mile from where Chérif lived, the crowds beginning to gather to march toward Place de l'Obélisque became too dense for me to continue by car. I parked haphazardly and ran as fast as I could the rest of the way. When I arrived, roughly ten minutes later, the building concierge refused to let me in at first, but he quickly understood that I wasn't messing around. He opened the door and followed me as I bolted up the stairs. Chérif lived on the fourth floor, but by the second I could hear his cries and smell the terrible odor of burnt flesh. It took the two of us, the concierge and I, to break down the door to the apartment, as his neighbors began to emerge, alerted by the shouting, the smoke, the smell.

Chérif was rolling on the ground, body ablaze. He was making deranged screams that I hadn't thought could come out of a human being's chest; screams that were no longer only expressing a specific physical suffering, but the pure essence of suffering, its boundless, blind, senseless essence, for which Chérif was merely, as in certain possession or trance rituals, the convulsing medium. After a few seconds, the screams were conveying such a level of horror that I separated them from Chérif's body. They couldn't be coming from him. It wasn't he we heard screaming but the pain itself; the pure pain whirling inside him, roaring like a wild animal caught in a trap or an offended deity at the bottom of an ocean. The suffering was no longer content to ravage Chérif's flesh: it wanted to escape him, as if from an oppressive prison. My friend's body had become too cramped for those screams, whose only wish was to grow, spread, explode, and strike everything within reach.

The carpet beneath him caught fire. I rushed to the bedroom, tore the sheets and blankets off the bed, and threw them over Chérif, whose harrowing cries had roused the entire floor. Meanwhile the concierge had had the presence of mind to run into the hallway to grab one of the building's fire extinguishers. I was attempting to cover my friend's body entirely with the blankets when he came back into the room and activated the extinguisher, spraying a wave of cool foam over Chérif and me. The neighbors jumped in to help with buckets of water. In a few seconds, the human torch was extinguished.

The body lay there. The screaming had stopped, but a far more unbearable horror swelled in that sudden silence, from which it was soon seeping like a purulent liquid from a wound: the smell of burnt human flesh. The air buckled beneath it, and we buckled beneath the air, throats tight and chests constricted. The body lay there. Charred bits of skin were stuck to the rug. Smoke was burning our eyes. I moved away from the body and called for an ambulance. I was told they had all been mobilized for the protest in progress. Because of the terrible traffic, the firefighters couldn't come quickly either: they had their hands full too, with all the fires that would inevitably break out across the city throughout the day.

That was when one of the neighbors, amid the general panic, said there was a private clinic a few minutes away. Since we didn't have a stretcher, three men attempted to lift Chérif, whom the blankets thankfully shielded from view. One man volunteered to grab him by the armpits; the second to support his waist; the third to carry his legs. When they began the maneuver, I imagined, in a brief, vivid glint of a nightmarish vision, his body so damaged, so decomposed, that the three men couldn't hold it; that the flesh would crumble beneath their fingers and be impossible to get out of the rug. I closed my eyes to escape that revolting eventuality. Thankfully it didn't come to pass. The three men were able to lift Chérif off the ground and immediately exited the apartment. I followed them. None of us knew if he was still alive. His inert arms hung down on either side as they carried him. I saw the flesh seared raw, repulsive, red and black...

He was admitted for treatment as soon as we arrived at the clinic. I immediately contacted Amadou, who had also attended military school and whose number I had. He arrived a half hour later, accompanied by his parents. Then began a long and silent wait, during which Amadou informed me that Chérif had filmed himself, and that his suicide attempt had been live streamed on his Facebook page, which was very popular, since my friend regularly posted texts and videos of his political and philosophical analyses. Amadou had been able to get the live stream deleted, but some web users had already saved it, and were sharing it on various channels with little regard for human decency. Amadou told me that you could see the concierge and me (though it was hard to recognize us amid the chaos) break down the door and come in. Before dousing himself with gasoline and lighting his body on fire, Chérif, apparently, had uttered one sentence, a single sentence in Wolof: *Fatima lay baalu, na ma sama njaboot baal*, "I beg Fatima's forgiveness, may my family forgive me." I didn't try to watch the video.

I waited at the clinic with Chérif's family. Three hours later, we were told they were going to transport Chérif to the hospital, to a unit designated for severe burn victims. He was hanging between life and death, and had suffered nearly third-degree burns. The tissue structure on the bottom half of his body was almost entirely destroyed.

All the same, in the streets of Dakar, the big September 14 march had the city on its knees. Most of the protesters were as yet unaware of Chérif's act. Some, when they found out, made it into an act of desperate bravery, a martyr's act. Few imagined it was an act of guilt, though it also takes bravery to embrace your guilt and carry out whatever it commands you to do. That's the lesson my friend, through his tragedy, left me with: to be brave and do what you have to do.

And what I needed to do, beyond the search for love, and political legitimacy, and the disappointment such quests can bring, was continue to follow Elimane's trail, his book's trail. My life, like every life, resembled a series of equations. Once their degree was revealed, their terms written, their unknowns established and their complexity set down, what remained? Literature; all that remained and would ever remain was literature; indecent literature, as solution, as problem, as faith, as shame, as pride, as life.

I had just understood that, or rather, accepted it, when Aïda's farewell text arrived.

D+1

My father agreed to lend me his car for a few days. He didn't ask me where I was going. My mother didn't ask either, as if they had guessed that I now wanted to focus on the real reason for my return. I hoped to arrive before nightfall.

He read me the beginning of that mysterious book that night, the Haitian poetess had told Siga D. Yes, it was that same night, *Corazón*. We made love, or rather he made love to me, made love until I felt like there was nothing left, of love, or my body, or my soul, which were one and the same at that moment, nothing except what he knew and made me know. Then he read me the first few pages. I think that moment was both the most beautiful and saddest of my whole life. It made our goodbye a reality. Listening to Elimane read me those pages was as enjoyable as it was difficult. I felt like he was reading me his will. For the first time since I'd met him, I sensed he was ready to tell me everything if I so desired, and it was precisely that sudden openness that saddened me. I sensed he had come to apologize for what he is, for being the way he'd been. I had hated his nature, his silence, his past shrouded in mist and his secrets. More than anything, I had wanted him to open up to me. But not that night, not like that. A man so attached to his solitude wouldn't have left the shadows unless he'd heard their call, a final summons drawing him deeper into night. And so he ventured out one last time, he showed himself. But those close to him weren't fooled and knew the truth: he already belonged to the shadows that he was preparing to rejoin for good. I didn't want to take advantage of his weakness, to benefit from that moment when he willingly dropped his guard to empty him. He was at my mercy; I mean to say: his soul was at my mercy. A simple question would have sufficed to find out what he was doing there, and the object of his long quest. But I said nothing. You're surely wondering why. I wondered too, for a long time. And I think it was simply basic decency, *Corazón*, before one man's truth. Or his pain. Maybe it's the same thing.

"So you didn't ask him any questions?"

"I did: a few. I know that he arrived in Argentina in 1949, by boat. I know he spent the war in France, first in Paris, then a village in the Alps, where he was part of the Resistance. I know that he returned briefly to Paris during liberation, and that after that, for three years, he traveled through various countries in a Europe weakened by war: Germany, Denmark, Sweden, Switzerland, Austria, Italy. I assume the years he spent roaming Europe after the war marked the beginning of his search, which he continued in Latin America for twenty years. He took his time telling me this, always giving me a chance to ask further questions. I stayed in his arms all night. When the sun came up, we had our coffee early. He kissed me and told me not to give up on literature."

"And then?"

"He left. He left, and a few months later, I was offered a job in Paris, and I left too. That's when I understood: that night marked the end of his chapter in Argentina. Mine too.

When I think back, there's only one question I regret not asking him, perhaps the only one I should have: whether he missed his country...I wish I could have asked him, but I never saw him again. It wasn't for lack of trying, in the years that followed. First, whenever I went on a trip. I would leave Paris, go back to Argentina, and comb Buenos Aires, its tango bars, its docks, its poor neighborhoods. The building where he used to live in Barracas was demolished in the mid-70s. I visited the capital cities of other South American countries too. I would always stop in on my old teacher Sábato, and we would talk about the past, the literary soirees where we got to know each other, about Gombrowicz (whom I never got a chance to see in France, since he died in 1969, a few months before my arrival). We would also, inevitably, talk about Elimane. But Sábato didn't know any more than me. They had said their goodbyes the night before we did. But Elimane hadn't given him an address, or any hint about where he was going or might have ended up. Sábato never saw him again in Buenos Aires. When I asked him whether he thought it strange that Elimane entered our lives for all those years and then exited so easily, Sábato responded that it was very strange, then added that not all men require company. You know the rest: I eventually requested a transfer to Dakar, to continue my search, and I met you there, *Corazón*, my little angel..."

Once she had concluded the Haitian poetess's account, Siga D. said:

"As the poetess was telling me all this, I was thinking about the people Elimane could have been so obstinately looking for. I can only come up with three, Diégane: Charles Ellenstein—his friend and editor—Assane Koumakh—

his father—and, finally, though it's unlikely, Mossane, his mother. I think the most credible lead is his father. Assane Koumakh. No one knows whether Elimane found his grave. Maybe Assane Koumakh didn't die during World War I, and he moved to Argentina, for a reason known only to him. Maybe Elimane learned that and followed him. Maybe this whole mystery is one man's long search for his father. But it's also possible that Elimane went to Argentina in pursuit of someone unknown to us, why not a woman, for example, a beautiful woman he met during the war, or after the war, and with whom he fell in love. It's worth considering, Diégane. One big question remains, however: Why didn't Elimane continue writing to his mother and my father? I have a theory: he continued writing to them during his exile, but my bastard of a father destroyed the letters, the same way he destroyed the one that came with the copy of *The Labyrinth of Inhumanity* that Elimane sent him in 1938. After Mossane's disappearance, he had to have blamed Elimane for her madness and for their suffering. So he destroyed the letters without answering them. Elimane might have never known that his mother had disappeared. Obviously I could be wrong on that point too. Maybe Elimane stopped writing because, quite simply, he wanted nothing more to do with his past. Maybe he wanted to forget everything. But I think that it was my father who destroyed the letters he sent. There you have it, Diégane: now you know everything I know."

"That's everything? Really?"

"Yes, that's everything. Were you expecting something else?"

Then came the Amsterdam dawn.

I left Dakar around three p.m., as the protesters were heading to Place Soweto, in front of the National Assembly, where Fatima Diop had killed herself. My only luggage was a few changes of clothes, a notebook, *The Labyrinth of Inhumanity*, and my album of Super Diamono's greatest hits. I hoped to arrive before nightfall.

Fourth Biographeme

The dead letters

Paris, August 16, 1938

Dearest Mother and Uncle,

It's been over a year since I've sent word, and you must think I've forgotten you, like everyone from our corner of the world who, once they leave, erases their past, their land, and their families from memory. By all appearances, I'm guilty of the same, but nothing could be further from the truth. And so I hope that, after reading this, you will forgive me this long silence. Not one day goes by without my thoughts turning to you, or one night without seeing you in my dreams. You are with me everywhere I go. Especially you, Mother. I hope you will understand me by the end of this letter.

Paris, April 13, 1917

Mossane, my love,

More than two years have passed since I left. Why have I never written? Because I didn't want to make you cry. Because I didn't want to cry myself. What's happening here would make anyone cry. That's war. I believed I would return soon. I promised you. Now, I don't know if I will return at all. It's cold here. And wet. There are lots of Africans. They call us the tirailleurs. *We talk amongst ourselves. We huddle together for warmth. But at night, we're each alone again with our memories, our regrets, our fears. Every one of us knows we might never see our country again.*

You were with me a little over two years ago, when I set out across northern France with the only true friend I've made here, in search of my father. These last two years, it's him I've been searching for. This search was for me; but it was also for you. His absence left a hole inside both your hearts, a pit of love or bitterness that I could never fill, and I was its innocent victim. There's a hole in my heart too, dug by my father's ghost, but mine is full of questions. The things you told me about him should have made me hate him. I did hate him. But you can never truly hate someone you don't know; even less when it's your own father. And that residue of hate is giving way to a feeling, I couldn't say what, now that I've read his words.

I miss you and I miss our child. He must be two years old by now. I say he, but I don't even know if it's a boy or a girl. What if I die here…what image will he or she have of me? A father who abandoned his child? A hero who died in battle? A coward who left his family? What will you tell him (or her)? And what will my twin brother, who hates me so? I don't know. That uncertainty, more than the fear, more than the war, is what's killing me right now.

I don't hate my father. Rather, I no longer hate him. Because I had a father, and it's you, Tokô Ousseynou. I never missed my birth father, but I wanted to know what kind of man he was, what he did, what happened to him; I wanted to know what lay deep inside him. Now I know:

fear. He was therefore a man. He made choices, and his final days were spent in fear, like a child, as he wrote that letter. He was simply a man. At the end, he thought about you both, and about me.

I wish I could hold you and the child in my arms. I wish I could tell you both that I love you. Please forgive me. Not for leaving, but for believing that it's an easy feat to survive a war. I was wrong. You don't survive war, even if you don't die in it. Whether I survive and return or die and remain here, there's already something dead inside me. The only thing still alive is your image, Mossane, and the image of our child, whom I don't know. And yet I dream of him. Tell our child that I dream of him every night, every day, even during battle. In Verdun, amid the fire and blood, I dreamt of him.

The friend who accompanied me is like a brother to me. He also lost his father during the war. That's why he understands me. His name is Charles. He helped me in my quest. He's the one who insisted we keep looking for traces of my father. I was hopeless, and he said to me: Let's try another village, Elimane, let's try another village, farther out. That's how we got to a small village in northern France, in the department called the Aisne. It's not far from where the Battle of Chemin des Dames took place. There was a military cemetery in that village. But there was also a small war memorial. That's where I found this letter.

In a few days, a major battle is set to begin. Many Africans will be sent to the front. The white officers are promising a great victory, a victory vital for France. The colonial troops can hear the call of glory. The Negroes hear it even louder. Call of glory, in their language, means the call of death, I think. I'm preparing myself, even if it is impossible to prepare yourself for anything. I wanted to write you this letter before...before what?

There's no doubt in my mind: it's my father. I don't know why he wasn't able to send the letter. Maybe he simply wrote it for himself. I hope that Father Greusard can faithfully translate his words for you. As for me, after I read them, I cried for a long time. Then I returned home with my friend, and I began to write the book that accompanies this letter. It took me a long time to finish. It's my first book, and I'm planning to write others. If Father Greusard doesn't have time to translate it for you, I will upon my return. Because I hope to return soon and make both of you proud of me. You will be, I promise. I won't return a dishonored or disgraced man. I'll return as somebody: a writer. Pray for me.

All my love, my beloved Mossane. All my love to the child. All my love to my brother, whatever he may think of me. Forgive me. Pray for me.

Elimane Madag

PART TWO

Madag's Solitude

I

In Mbour, before getting on the highway to Fatick, which leads inland and toward Elimane's village, I stop to grab some food, fill the tank, and rest a bit. I buy a cup of Café Touba from a street vendor and check my email. Between a message from Stanislas asking how I'm doing and an electricity bill, I see this email, sent last night:

Faye,
I'm writing you from the place from which all my books emerged, though I've always rejected that idea: an unfinished well. I didn't think I would find it here. I believed, out of hope or fear, that it had been destroyed years ago. Everything else was destroyed, or forgotten. The house collapsed. All that remains of it are sorry-looking walls that not even a ghost would bother to go through. But the unfinished well, the well of torment, is still here. If I were a mystic, I would say that it's been waiting for me, that it knew I would come back, and that certainty enabled it to resist the build-up of sand and all the human wickedness it must have seen since that night. But I'm not a mystic. The well is still here, that's all, and so am I.
I'm writing you from inside, seated, like I was back then. It doesn't matter that my head sticks out over the edge of

the hole, it doesn't matter that I've grown, I still feel like I'm drowning in here, and in my fear. This is where I stopped being a child (which doesn't actually mean that I became a man, the opposite in fact: I understood later that it was on that night, in the well, that I lost all chance of truly becoming a man). This is where I became an animal, a beast dripping with sweat. This is also where, without a doubt, I became a writer. The last time we saw each other, you asked me if I knew why I started writing. I told you yes without going any further. I'm going further today.

For a long time, I believed that the reason there were always deaf characters in my books was the same one that explained my calling (what an obnoxious word) as a writer: I thought I was writing to burst my eardrums, which I was unable to do, twenty years ago, inside that well. Until recently, I wrote using loud, sonorous words, so they would cover the horrified clamor of my memory, and so I wouldn't hear anything more.

The thing is my parents didn't die before my eyes. They died in my ears. Their deaths echo there every night. My father had begun digging the well two days earlier, when the regular army crossed our village in a hasty retreat. And yet they had promised us, when they'd come through a few weeks before, that there was no need to worry, that they would win the battle against the shepherds of death. Up until the previous night, the radio had been saying that our soldiers were not only holding their ground but gaining more every day. And we, naïve idiots already fucked, believed it. We believed it until the day a hundred ragged, weakened, tattered, and disarmed soldiers filed past us again with their tails lost between their legs. Some were running, others packed into old Jeeps that then sped away. A few, incapacitated, were hanging over donkeys like wet laundry on a line. The villagers understood that meant defeat and began packing their bags. Get the hell out, and quick.

One of the fleeing soldiers approached our house, walking like he no longer felt the ground beneath him. I still remember his face. Fear wasn't the reigning emotion, more like a hint of horror: a calm and unhurried shadow spreading in a diagonal slash from temple to chin. Gash and burn! Raz(or)ed to the ground! He passed by our house a mere ghost. He wasn't even pretending to run. As though he knew it was pointless, lost from the start, seeing as he was already dead-standing. My father asked him if they were still far, if we had time to get away. The soldier looked at him like he had spoken in some satanic language. He said nothing for several seconds, and I think that my father, looking at that ghost of itself, understood before the soldier responded in his language:

"Better off killing your family and then killing yourself. Better that than letting them take you. They boil you like agouti or corn. They'll be here tomorrow morning, maybe tonight, maybe in an hour. They chop off your hand and shove it up your ass. Better that. I don't know. They were right behind us. Better that. They deal in death. Better that."

He stood there repeating "better that." I was behind my father, clinging to him. I was all of eight. He steered me into the courtyard. He crouched down, grabbed my shoulders, and gave me that look adults give when they know they're about to lie to a child, when they know the child will understand they're lying but lie to them all the same (eventually we'll reach the point of admitting that children, before life or priests or pedophiles and varied other perverts get to them, are first violated by their parents, who lie to them). My father said to me: "Don't worry, he doesn't know what he's saying." Boom went my little kid brain. If this man, who was crazy, but only because he so clearly saw the horror, didn't know what he was saying, who on earth knew what he was saying?

My father went back outside. There was a scream. My mother, who had been preparing our bags for our escape, immediately ran out, in a panic. I peeked through the open doorway. I saw the soldier's body at my father's feet. I also saw, before my mother covered my eyes with her hand, that he had slit his throat and blood was spurting out, boiling hot on the ground. My father closed the door and told us to go into the house. My mother pushed me inside before doing the same thing my father had a few moments earlier: she crouched down and looked me in the eyes. But she told me something different than my father: what I mean is she said nothing, and her whole heart came through in her gaze: You'll need to be brave.

My father returned. Outside, we could hear the sound of fleeing. There wasn't any shouting; only the loud pounding of hurried steps, which were sometimes interrupted by short, brusque words that got straight to the point, like the speakers wanted to save every last bit of breath. My father and my mother looked at each other, and I think that in that look they told themselves there wouldn't be time to run, or that we wouldn't get far. The closest city was four hours away by car. It had a military garrison. But maybe that one had also begun to evacuate. My mother's younger sister lived in one of the villages behind the hill, roughly two hours away, to the west.

We could have tried to get to her, but there was the risk of run-
ning into the killers, who had surrounded the whole region
and knew the hills better than anyone. My parents conferred
privately, as if I wasn't concerned, as if I didn't understand
what was happening. They were wrong: I understood every-
thing. When they came back, they told me we weren't leaving.

"We're going to hide you in the hole your father started
digging," said my mother. "We're going to cover it up so they
don't see you. You have to stay there. You can't make any
noise. You can't come out unless your father or I come get
you. Do you understand?"

"Yes, Ma."

"Are you sure?"

"Yes."

"Not a sound. No crying. Total silence. Don't come out
under any circumstances. Until I come get you."

"Okay."

"And if there are people, if you hear voices that you don't
recognize in the courtyard, plug your ears. Plug your ears
until you can't hear anything. Got it?"

"Yes, Ma."

"If you don't do as I'm telling you, it's me you'll have to
deal with. I'll give you the hiding of your life, you'll be raw
by the end. You got it?"

"Yes, Ma."

"Again!"

"Yes, Ma."

"Yes what?"

"Yes, I got it. I won't make any noise. I won't move. I
won't speak. I'll only come out if it's you who comes to get
me. Or Papa."

"And your ears?"

"I'll plug my ears if I hear voices I don't recognize."

"You'd best not forget."

She wanted to appear terrible and threatening, but she was crying. Her words didn't scare me because of what they were ordering me to do (begging, in reality). They terrified me because I sensed the despair and love with which my mother was saying them. I started to cry too, without making a sound. She hugged me tightly, my father joined our embrace, and we stayed like that for two or three minutes, without a word. Two or three minutes, to collectively live an entire life that we would never live but that we could have; two or three minutes to relive what we had shared until then. That embrace connected the two directions of our time: through memory, it summoned our past; through hope (though that hope was crashing into a wall of blood and bones), it imagined our impossible future.

Then my mother put me in the unfinished well with some food to eat (in silence) if I got hungry. She also gave me a flashlight; it was dark in there. We hugged each other again; we had stopped crying; but that embrace, much shorter and quieter than the previous one, was even more painful. Then my parents climbed out, covered the hole with a sheet of metal, and everything went black. I didn't move and I waited. After a while, not long maybe, or maybe an eternity, or maybe even outside of time, I heard the sound of cars, voices, laughter, machine-gun fire, screams. Night thickened in the well. I plugged my ears.

Death entered the courtyard escorted by its children, and said:

"If anyone lives here, they better come out."

I heard his voice despite my plugged ears. Death was with me in the well. I saw him clearly, standing in the middle of our courtyard, surrounded by his sons. And I saw my father come out of the house and walk toward him. He stopped a few feet from the group.

"Do you live alone?" asked death.

I plugged my ears even harder. I didn't hear what my father said. Maybe he didn't answer.

"If there's anyone else here," said death, "if you have a wife, for example, she better come out. We're gonna look, in any case. And we'll find her, even if she's hiding up her own ass. Or yours. Or God's. So I'll ask again: Do you live alone?"

"No," said my mother, and I saw her—I saw her—come out and join my father in the middle of the courtyard, as death's sons cackled loudly, before death's stony gaze.

"Are there children?"

I dug my fingers into my ears as hard as I could.

"No," said my father. "We don't have any children."

"We'll see about that," said death. "The woman standing in front of me has the belly of someone who's already given birth. But if you say so, my brother, all right, for now. We're going to do this quick. We have lots of worthy candidates. Here are your choices: you kill yourself or we kill you. The decision is yours. But if you choose for us to kill you, we'll do it our way."

"Please," said a voice, but I didn't know if it was my father's or my mother's or one of death's sons, sarcastically begging.

"Choose," said death.

There was silence, then my mother shouted "No!" and that shout was followed by a gunshot. I understood that my father had tried to attack death, who immediately shot him down. He had to have known he didn't stand a chance, and had launched himself at the death sowers in the hope of perishing.

"Your husband chose. Now it's your turn. Choose."

My mother said nothing, and after a long pause, death said: "So you've chosen to let us kill you our way. You probably think you'll have a chance at surviving if you let us at it. You're right to think that. It's best to always think there's a chance you'll escape death. Otherwise, there'd be no point living. We'll take care of you. We're going to kill you."

I had dug my fingers as deep as I could inside my ears and yet I could still hear. And so I heard the cruel laughter of death's children, I heard the sound of their belts being unbuckled and dropped on the ground, I heard what they said about my mother, about her ass, her breasts, her vagina, her mouth. But I didn't hear my mother. Then I heard men moaning, primal cries, obscenities. But I didn't hear my mother. Time passed, then death said:

"That's enough. Go on. I'll finish."

I heard belts being rebuckled, weapons being picked up, the final wave of insults flung at my stubbornly silent mother, the gobs of spit. Then the sons of death left and only my mother and death remained.

"I know why you're not crying out," said death. "I know this strategy. It's the strategy of a mother who wants to protect her child. There's a child hiding somewhere in this house. I'll find him or her. But first, you're going to scream. You're going to beg me to kill you. I'll kill you after I make you scream. Then I'll find your child."

"I'm begging you," I heard my mother say.

"It's not the child you need to worry about or beg for, but yourself, for your life. What I'm going to do to you," said death, "will be more painful than a bullet in between your legs. You're going to scream. They'll hear you all the way in hell."

And death got to work. My mother's screams began as well, and they were so violent and inhuman, they echoed so loudly inside my head, that I passed out. When I came to, the screams had stopped but they were still ringing in my ears. I think that was the moment I understood that they would torment me forever, and that the only way to lessen the pain would be to have even more deafening voices, even wilder screams, inside my head.

I opened my eyes. I wasn't in the well anymore, I was in the courtyard. Beside me lay two lifeless human forms: my parents' bodies.

I closed my eyes. I began to silently cry.

"She almost killed me," said a voice behind me.

It belonged to death. I turned around. I had imagined someone terrifying, a gigantic, monstrous man. The man I saw was short and puny, so unremarkable it was almost comical, but I didn't doubt for a single second that this was death. I looked at him, unable to speak.

"Your mother almost killed me, but at the last minute I saw the blade of the kitchen knife she pulled out of her hair, even as I was making her scream. She struck one second too late. I had already rolled onto my side. She looked at me and understood it was over for her. Before I could finish her off, she slit her throat. That's how she died. Then I searched the house, and I found you in the unfinished well, passed out. What's your name?"

I didn't answer.

"It doesn't matter, son, your name isn't important. Did you hear your mother's cries before you lost consciousness?"

I nodded yes.

"Then I won't kill you. You're nearly dead anyway, and your misery is going to last a long time. So long, orphan boy. I was an orphan too, and I wasn't even as old as you yet. It created a rage inside of me that nothing can extinguish. It's what keeps me alive. Do the same. Hate me, be angry, be strong, become a warrior, become a killer, spill blood, find me when you're grown, and make me pay for the horrific suffering I inflicted on your mother. She suffered at my hands like I've rarely seen a person endure suffering. Goodbye, son, till we meet again."

Death said all that in a gentle voice. He crossed himself like a Christian and then, simply enough, he walked out and left. I stayed alone in the courtyard all night, between my parents' bodies. When the sun rose, I climbed back inside the unfinished well and I waited. I waited for death to return and release me. Or a miracle: my mother. No one came back. So I climbed out of the hole, I was hungry, I left the bodies in the courtyard, and I walked alone to my aunt's village, the village behind the hill; I knew the way.

I didn't encounter anyone on the road. All I saw, all I felt, was the vast harmony of the hill and the peaceful whisper of the forest. Death had paused in the shadow of all that beauty, and the beauty had neither slowed nor tempered it. On the contrary, death had never, I think, flourished the way it did there. Amid the beauty, death showed off its skill. Amid the beauty, it reached its apotheosis. That beauty is where death revealed its true genius. So what does that tell

*us? That perhaps the defining theorem of the human con-
dition is this: the more beautiful the setting, the purer the
horror. So what are we? A spool of blood within a tapestry
of light—or the opposite. And the devil picks up his needle
with a snicker.*

*My aunt's village had been attacked too. That was clear
once I got there. Escape was still fresh on the ground; fear,
thick in the air. But people had stayed, or returned after fleeing, like human boomerangs with nowhere to go. I found my
aunt in her house. I rushed into her arms. She understood. I
understood too: my uncle: dead; their two daughters: dead
and dead. We returned to my parents' home three days later.
Their bodies were gone. There was nothing left but brown
stains of their blood on the sand. We never found out where
they had been buried (and by whom?), or even if they had
been: rumors in the region spoke of black mages gathering
corpses, their grisly but lucrative services in high demand
given the carpet of dead bodies covering the Zairean ground.*

*And so my aunt became my sole family, and I hers. She's
who I fled the country with, for Europe. Though that's a
stubborn illusion: people like me never leave their country. It never leaves us, in any case. I never climbed out of
the unfinished well. All this time it was being dug inside of
me. I'm still there. There's where I write from. That's where
I've always written from. And the screams echo still. But
I stopped plugging my ears. For a long time, I wrote so I
wouldn't hear. Now, I know that I write or must write in
order to hear. I simply couldn't find the courage to admit it.*
The Labyrinth of Inhumanity *gave it to me.*

*It taught (or reminded) me this: the place of greatest evil
always retains a fragment of truth. For me, that place is also*

a time: the past. My intention is to go through it from every possible direction, and to let it go through me like a volley of arrows; my hope, by moving around in this way, is to see the past from multiple angles, to expose it to the harsh light of both day and night. I don't think we should chase ghosts; I think we should join their dance around the fire and, soaked in fear down to our bones, teeth clattering, shitting our pants, take our place and our piece of the past, every last crumb. Fuck calls for resilience! A term I loathe the second it becomes a buzzword. Resilience! Resilience! To hell with them! I want the truth of the long fall, the truth of the infinite fall. I don't repair. None of what was truly destroyed strikes me as reparable. I don't console, others or myself. The most effective amulet against Evil dangles from my belt: the desire for truth, including when the truth is death. I seek the ruins of ancient buried roads. A path can still be made out. It's not on any map. But it's the only one that matters.

I know you know that Wittgenstein quote, at the end of Tractatus: *"Whereof one cannot speak, thereof one must be silent." But staying silent, not telling, doesn't mean you shouldn't show. We're not here to heal ourselves, or to mend, or console, or reassure or educate; we're meant to stand tall in the sacred wound, to see it and show it in silence. That there is the point of* The Labyrinth of Inhumanity. *Everything else is a failure.*

Elimane wanted to write a sort of last book? Failure. The world is full of last books. All the great works are potential epitaphs to the world. The last book in history is always and forever the next book; it therefore has a long and already old past ahead of it.

He wanted to show the creative potency of imitation? Failure. His attempt turned to artifice, a construction that though brilliant and erudite was pointless in the end, tragically pointless.

He wanted to pay homage to all the literature of the centuries that preceded him? Beyond failure. People took what was an extended literary reference for a pitiful act of plagiarism, and no one saw that it was rich in and of itself before borrowing a thing.

But all that disillusionment can teach us a lesson, Faye. Who was Elimane, really? I don't know where your search has taken you these past few weeks. But I see one possible answer: Elimane was the person or thing we mustn't become and that we are slowly becoming. He was a warning that fell on deaf ears. That warning told us African writers: invent your own tradition, establish your literary history, discover your own forms, test them in your spaces, nourish your deepest imagination, have a land of your own, for it's only there that you'll exist not only for yourselves, but also for others. Who was Elimane, really? The most accomplished and most tragic product of colonization. He was its most dazzling success, more so than the paved roads, the hospitals, the Sunday schools. More so than the purebred and pureblood Gaul! Poor Jules Ferry! But Elimane also symbolized what the innate horror of that colonization had destroyed within the peoples subjected to it. Elimane wanted to become white, and he was reminded that not only was he not, but that he never would be despite all his talent. He brandished every card of whiteness, culturally at least; these were simply used as reminders of his negritude. Maybe he understood Europe better than the Europeans. But how did he end up?

Anonymous, disappeared, erased. You know this: coloniza-
tion sows despair, death, and chaos among the colonized.
But it also sows—and this is its most diabolical triumph—
the desire to become one's destroyer. That was Elimane: all
the sadness of alienation.

And Faye, I think that's the fate that awaits us if we keep
chasing Europe, keep chasing the vast Western literary
canon: we'll all be Elimanes, in our own way. Maybe we
already are, in which case let's stop before we're destroyed.
It's time to get out of there, Faye. We should all clear the hell
out. Asphyxiation is coming. We'll be gassed without mercy,
and our deaths will be all the more tragic since no one will
have driven us into the chamber: we'll have rushed in, hop-
ing we would be celebrated. They'll turn us into black soap.
Then our executioners will wash their hands with it, and
become whiter still.

Elimane didn't disappear because he was viewed as a
plagiarist; he disappeared because he harbored a hope that
wasn't possible, that wasn't allowed him. Or maybe he dis-
appeared out of bitterness; but I also hope he eventually
realized that his death in French literature was the best thing
that could have happened to him if he wanted to dedicate
himself to his true work: the work he did only for himself.

I reached a decision over these past few days, Faye: I won't
be going back to France. Not right away, at least. Maybe
never. What I need to write can only be written here, near my
well. The fact that it's unfinished is my existential metaphor:
my inner tragedy but also the meaning of my future. I have
to dig this well until it's done. I have to continue and com-
plete my father's well. Which means I have to turn inward,
seeing as how my true self has yet to take form. Everything

I thought was "me" was in reality merely the substance of others. It's time to drag myself out. I won't go back to Paris, where they feed us with one hand and strangle us with the other. That city is our hell disguised as heaven. I'll stay here, write, teach young people, form a theater troupe, stage outdoor plays, recite poetry in the streets, say and show what it means to be an artist here, maybe starve to death like a pitiful street dog, crushed by real life disguised as an old jalopy missing its brakes; but it will be here. For that, I'll always be grateful to you for letting me read Elimane.

I know you won't agree with what I'm saying: you've always believed that our cultural ambiguity was our true space, our home, and that we should inhabit it the best we can, as assenting tragic figures, as civilizational bastards, bastardy begot by bastardy, bastards born from the rape of our history by another murderous history. Except, I'm afraid that what you call ambiguity is just a ruse for our ongoing destruction. I also know you'll think I've changed, as someone who used to believe that it's not where writers write that determines their worth, and that they can be universal, anywhere, if they have something to say. I still believe that. But now, I also think that you can't discover what you have to say anywhere. You can write anywhere. But knowing and understanding what you truly have to write can't happen everywhere. It was while rereading the manuscript of The Labyrinth of Inhumanity *that I understood that.*

Wherever you are, Faye, I hope you found what you weren't looking for. Whatever you pull out of all this will be beautiful, I'm sure of it. Don't forget to send it to me here. I'll give you my new address soon. Sending all my best, old friend, from my well, with a special thought for my savior, who might also be yours: thank God for Elimane, and for his brilliant fucking book.

Musimbwa

By the time I finish reading, my coffee is cold. I can see Musimbwa, sitting alone in the unfinished well. I promise myself that, when all this is over, I'll write him. Not to respond to any specific point in his email; simply to tell him that what he's doing is stupid, crazy, radical, and brave. Musimbwa is challenging me through his letter. He's telling me: Here's what I was and here's what the book made of me. Your turn now: show us what you have in your gut. I get back in the car and get back on the road.

II

A few miles from Fatick, I head southwest, into Serer country, and enter the heart of Sine. A laterite path cuts across the landscape. My parents' village, which is also my traditional home, isn't far. I'll stop on my way back to see the family I still have there.

Driving down this narrow road, I wonder what might have been written somewhere, long ago, so that today I find myself on my way to a village that neighbors my own, and where Elimane once lived; a village from which emerged, perhaps, *The Labyrinth of Inhumanity*, a book I discovered and read far from here, in the way you discover something of great consequence, something whose importance comes less from the certainty that it will matter in your future life than from the intuition that, in reality, it's always mattered, even before you encountered it, maybe even before your birth, like it's been waiting for you, drawing you near. Because that's just it, the feeling I had the first time I read *The Labyrinth of Inhumanity* that night after I crept out of the Spider-Mother's web. Ever since, I've kept the book close. It's led me across ridges and gulfs, through space and time, among the dead and amid the survivors. And now here we are or here we are again in the land of our origins.

Children, men, women, astride donkeys or horses, in carts, on foot, on motorbikes, bowls or straw hats on their heads, get off the road, stop, watch me pass. Some raise their hands in a friendly wave, but most often, they remain impassive. At the town exits or just beyond, dogs race alongside me, playful or threatening. Thickets of dead branches separate plots of peanut plants from stretches of grass where a few heads of cattle are still grazing before being taken in for the night.

The rainy season was late and short-lived this year: several fields of millet have yet to be harvested—this though we're just past mid-September. The rows of plants extend all the way to the roadside, their panicles dangling. These make a dry thud as they whip against the windshield, sounding just like certain fat insects when they crash into a window midflight. Childhood memories well up from a time when I used to impatiently wait for this wall of suspended flora, as if it were the portal to a fairy-tale land.

Then the landscape transforms: fields and pastures give way to salt plains. The horizon expands in every direction, breaking free from its habitual straits, and swells with all the beauty within reach. It's impossible to look away, the setting obliges, dares you to take everything in. In vain. Beauty's intention, around here, is to overwhelm the eye, which invariably notices it too late. On either side of the road a few watering holes glimmer, offering the sun a final reflection before its departure. I'm nearing one arm of the Sine Saloum river. I'm nearing the village. In ten minutes, I'll be there. All of a sudden that idea takes form in a concrete, measurable, visible reality. I brake abruptly. Dust rises, and when it falls, I find the stillness terrifying. The fear of dereliction: I feel like I'm alone on earth, being watched by the eye of the world. I close mine in the way of a frightened child.

I open them and look down at the book. I contemplate it for a long time, and this silent inspection tells me not to keep going, to turn back and return home. What am I afraid of: discovering something or discovering nothing? An inner voice hopes that Elimane came back here, that he wrote and left something behind; another prays that the opposite is true, that he never returned to his village, never wrote anything after *The Labyrinth of Inhumanity*, and that he met his end in anonymity, the way a star burns out one day amid a thousand others, in the farthest reaches of the cosmos, with no witnesses apart from the silent celestial bodies that surround it, escort it, bury it among them. I remain like this for a while, seemingly frozen, spinning on the inside.

To my right, twilight descends as if being filmed in slow motion. First, the sharp line of the horizon sliced the sun's iris horizontally, precisely through the middle, à la Buñuel; then it spread, from that radiant punctured eye: a sea of cinnabar bestrewn with small flecks of rich indigo and blue, almost black, that grow and then morph into large tumors on the body of the sky. Night falls gently upon the world, like a leaf on the surface of a lake.

III

—

The third person I meet after entering the village on foot, a young woman in her twenties, tells me the same thing as the previous inhabitants I encountered:

"Sorry, but I don't know where anyone named Ousseynou Koumakh Diouf lives."

"Are there any Diouf families around here?"

"Several. I'm a Diouf myself. Ndé Kiraan Diouf. But I've never heard of an Ousseynou Koumakh Diouf. Maybe if you keep going someone will be able to help you."

I thank her, wish her a good night, and walk away. A few seconds later she calls me back. I turn around:

"Is this man still alive?"

"No. But I was told I would find his house if I said his name."

"Did he die a long time ago?"

"Yes, well before you were born. And me too, for that matter."

"In that case my grandmother might know him. She'll tell you. Come with me."

I thank her again and follow her down a few unlit streets whose obscurity is tempered by the glow of electric and solar lamps inside courtyards, or in their outer windows. Ndé Kiraan, still a teenager yet already a woman, walks slowly. Her every step heavy and graceful at the same time.

"My name is Diégane Latyr Faye."

"Welcome. You're the one who arrived by car earlier?"

"How did you know?"

"Everyone in the village must know by now. We heard and saw you coming from far away. And I also know which Serer village you come from. Your accent is easy to recognize."

"Which village?"

She turns to me and smiles, amused by the challenge in my tone.

"You'll leave me your car if I guess?"

"I doubt you know how to drive it."

"Who said anything about driving? I'll sell the thing."

Before I can respond, she says the name of my parents' village. I smile.

"*Laya ndigil*, you're right."

"Better get my car keys ready," she says.

There's something gentle and teasing in her voice. The immediate easy rapport between us alleviates my anxiety.

A few minutes later we reach a house at the entrance to which an old woman, in the way of a night watchman or an indefatigable busybody, appears to be standing guard or spying on the street. Ndé Kiraan introduces me to her grandmother. I say hello, perform the required courtesies, inquire after her health and that of her loved ones. Only then does my hostess ask what she can do for me.

"I'm looking for the house of Ousseynou Koumakh Diouf, a man who lived here a very long time ago. I asked your granddaughter, but she's never even heard the name."

"How could she have?" she interrupts. "Back when Koumakh Diouf died, if it's the Koumakh Diouf I'm thinking of, and I think it is him, at the time of that great man's death, Ndé Kiraan's mother—may Roog welcome her in their hands—wasn't even as old as her daughter is now. You are talking about Ousseynou Koumakh Diouf, the full-head, aren't you?"

"Yes, that's him."

"He died a long time ago, a very long time ago. He was quite a man...A true full-head. Everything he did for this village...He even healed me, when I was expected to die."

"Who was this man, exactly?" asked Ndé Kiraan.

"I'll tell you his story one of these days. Meanwhile, take this handsome young man to your grandmother Dib Diouf *fa maak*."

"Her house?" said Ndé Kiraan, looking at me. "You should have said so, instead of talking about that man the whole time."

"It is a little strange," said the old woman. "Few people still know who Ousseynou Koumakh Diouf was. Only the oldest can remember. Back then, we used to say *Mbin Kou-makh*, Koumakh's house. But we don't call it that anymore."

"What do you call it?"

The old woman smiled.

"The next time you get lost in the village, my child, and you're not lucky enough to run into my beautiful grand-daughter—she is beautiful, isn't she?—say: *Mbin Madag*. Everyone will know that. Even Ndé Kiraan would know. Madag...He was a full-head, too. Maybe even fuller than the full-head of the man he replaced. Anyway, I'll let you go. Accompany him, dear, and come back for dinner. It'll be ready soon. Goodbye, Diégane Faye."

IV

——

"My mother is finishing her prayers. But I told her someone was here to see her. She kindly asks that you wait. She'll join you here after."

The young woman who welcomed us, who appears to be friends with Ndé Kiraan, offers me a seat beneath an imposing kapok tree. Ndé Kiraan tells me she'll be back later to get the keys to her car. The deal sealed, the two friends leave in peals of laughter, the kind through which, around here, a woman's beauty is suggested and heard. The tree dominates the center of a vast courtyard, at the back of which four large huts form an even diamond. A two-story building painted white, from which also escape the everyday sounds of a home, occupies the entire right wing. To the left, set apart from the other dwellings, is an immense hut, and tucked beside it, a long and slender form. I stand up and go closer. It's an old fishing pirogue: lightweight, average size. In the dark, I can't make out the symbols painted on the exterior. Two thick wooden logs, at the fore, support and stabilize the hull. Navigational tools—a paddle and a long rod—rest in the aft, leaning against the stern. The inside of the boat is cluttered with fishing nets.

My inspection of the pirogue reminds me that I'm also in a house of sailors. Then, for a few seconds, I think about

Tokô Ngor, and his brother Waly, about whom I know little, other than that he was, so they say, killed by the giant crocodile while fishing. I also think about Ousseynou Koumakh, who planned on being a fisherman before he lost his sight and became a maker and mender of fishing nets. Maybe the ones piled in the boat are his, nets that he made himself . . .

A hearty "*Ngiroopo!*"—the evening greeting—interrupts my speculations. A slight figure is standing beneath the tree and looking in my direction. It must be Maam Dib *fa maak.* It's only then, as I walk toward her, that I make the connection: Maam Dib must be the woman Siga D. called Ta Dib in her account, one of her stepmothers, one of Ousseynou Koumakh's three wives (Mame Coura and Ya Ngoné were the other two, if I remember correctly). I reach the tree, respect the long but essential ritual greetings, and sit when she invites me to. Her voice is soft, almost a whisper. A veil covers her head, and in her right hand she holds a rosary whose beads sparkle in the dark.

She asks me if I've eaten. I say no, that I'm not hungry, which is true. My stomach is in knots in fact. Still, she offers me milk, which I accept. She summons one of the children, who comes running immediately, then heads into the structure on the right, from which he emerges holding a small calabash. He hands it to me. I thank him and bring the calabash to my lips. I'd almost forgotten the raw taste of fresh, still warm, cow's milk, which is probably only one or two hours old. As a child, whenever I spent a few vacation days in my parents' village, I would milk the cows bred by one of my uncles, squeezing the liquid from their teats and then immediately, greedily, drinking it. Now, I grimace—did she see me? I let a short pause go by, to gather my thoughts, before telling Maam Dib the purpose of my visit. But she beats me to it:

"I know why you're here, Diégane Faye. I won't keep your hopes raised any longer: the man you're seeking is gone. He left us last year. One year ago, as of last week."

She stops talking and looks at me, or listens to me. I betray no emotion. In truth, in the first few seconds that follow her words, I feel none; at least none that affect me strongly enough to overflow from my heart and surface on my face. Not only am I not disappointed, but I'm not even disappointed not to be. I had prepared myself for every situation and possibility: everything I discovered over these last few weeks had inclined me to. But I have to admit that this exact configuration, that Elimane was, for some reason, *absent*, remained the most likely. And therefore the one that surprised me the least. The opposite actually: it felt natural in a way, reassuring almost. After all, Elimane had been absent, elusive, this whole time. And so, finding out he was dead and that I wouldn't see him makes perfect sense, and even obeys the same logic that this man's fate, or my relationship to him, does.

After a few seconds, however, that matter-of-factness fades, the news I've just been given hits me, and with it a wave of heat rises in my stomach: so then Elimane did go home. Though I haven't been very interested in this aspect of his life before now, learning that he died at home, as an old man, after searching for decades, elsewhere, for something I don't know, almost moves me to tears. Both of us remain silent. The leaves of the kapok tree shiver as a breeze gently sweeps the large courtyard.

"He knew you would come," said Maam Dib, judging that she could resume. "He also knew that you would never meet. He told me so. Before he died, he told me that a stranger, a young man, would come for him one night. I knew right away that it was you. I won't say that I was expecting you tonight. But I knew you would be here soon. He saw you such a long time ago."

"Saw me?"

"Yes, saw you. That's one of the things he had inherited from Koumakh: seeing. Not always, of course. And occasionally he'd get things wrong. But he could see. It's something he relearned when he came back here, to his home. Do you know what Madag means, in Serer?"

"Yes, I do. But I thought that..."

She cuts me off: "So you also know that in our tradition, no name is given at random, or for how beautiful it sounds. A name means something. That's common in our traditional societies. But for some, a name doesn't stop at simply meaning something. It's not just a symbol, it's also a sign, for life. The name says something about the being, not just the person but the being who bears it. It guides them. It shows their path. It signals their trajectory or their abilities. Madag's the one who explained all this to me one day, in his words, which I'm repeating now. Madag: the seer. That's what we used to call him here. He refused to be addressed by anything but his traditional name. For that matter, apart from Coura, Ngoné, me, and a few of the village elders, nobody knew his Muslim name, Elimane. He was always Madag, not Elimane. This house we're at is known throughout the village, throughout the region, by the name..."

"*Mbin Madag.*"

"Yes."

We go silent again. Of course I think of Rimbaud, his famous letter of the seer, and the nickname Auguste-Raymond Lamiel, the critic for *L'Humanité*, gave the author of *The Labrinth of Inhumanity*: the "Negro Rimbaud." Now that I know about Madag's long wanderings after the publication of his book, the comparison with Rimbaud takes on seductive resonance. But I immediately reproach myself for reducing him to a kind of Rimbaldian equivalent or African alter ego, for relying on my literary references to interpret everything, when every being possesses their own solitude, sinking ever deeper. That solitude is what needs to be seen: Madag's solitude. I take another sip of milk. The taste is still as strange in my mouth and faint in my memory.

"Maam Dib…I have a question to ask you."

"I'm guessing you have many. Go ahead."

"In Europe, I met someone you knew."

"Siga."

"Yes."

"She rejected us. We loved her. I was very close to her, more so than Coura and Ngoné. I never would have believed she could leave like that one day, and never reach out again. I refuse to hear another word about her. She never came back. Not even when the two other mothers who raised her with me passed away. And yet I had someone write to her. She never replied. She chose to forget us. It's over. I'm not angry at her for what she wrote. It's just writing. I can't read. I can't understand what she wrote. I'm angry at her because she's selfish and ungrateful toward her family. If she's who you want to talk to me about, I'd rather you didn't."

"It's not her specifically I want to talk about. But a song she sang to me one night. She says you're the one who taught it to her. It's the legend of the old fisherman who goes out to sea to confront the fish-goddess…"

I trail off. A horse whinnies in the night. The silence between us is heavy, and all the more somber because I can sense the bitterness, anger, and sadness overwhelming Maam Dib in this moment. She's remembering Siga D., their past, their rift. I feel guilty for reopening the wound. I'm about to apologize when she starts singing the old lullaby. I listen to it again with reverential attention until the end of the last verse, when the pirogue crosses the horizon, as God alone looks on. Then Maam Dib trails off. After a brief pause I ask her whether there's a final verse.

"A final verse…?" says the old woman, in a tone that betrays more amusement than surprise. "If there was," she continues, "what do you imagine it would say, Diégane?"

I think for a second, then respond:

"I imagine that the fisherman comes back one day, much, much later. But he's no longer the same. People claim he's half-mad, destroyed on the inside by what he saw beyond the ocean's horizon. People say that his battle with the goddess inflicted wounds on him that nothing can heal. He has nightmares about it. He barely says a word to his wife and his children. That's what I imagine."

"And then?"

"Then he disappears one day."

"He dies?"

"No, he says he's going back to the fish-goddess."

"Why? Because he fell in love with her? Or because he lost the first battle and wants to take his revenge?"

"I don't know...Both are possible. But it's also possible that he simply wants to return to sea. Maybe the fish-goddess doesn't actually exist. Or no longer exists. The fisherman simply wants to leave."

Maam Dib is silent for a moment, then she says, with what I take to be mocking laughter in her voice:

"You're spinning tales, Diégane Faye. Madag saw that too. He told me: the young stranger who comes will be a storyteller. But no, there's no final verse. I'm going to tell you what I would imagine, if there was another verse. I imagine that the fisherman comes back years later. When he returns, he tells his children about his victorious battle with the goddess. And all ends well. Things don't always finish badly. Nowadays, people always expect sad endings. They don't just expect them: they want those sad endings. Do you know why that is? I don't have a clue."

I respond that sadness better prepares us for life, meaning death, and that most people understand that early on. Or I only think that, in reality. In any case Maam Dib says nothing. A moment of silence, then she asks me if I'm hungry yet.

"I'm starting to get a little hungry, but don't trouble yourself. I have food in my car, which is at the entrance to the village. I can go fetch everything and..."

"You'll offend me if you don't accept my dinner. And my hospitality for tonight. You'll sleep here. So go get whatever you need for the evening from your car, and come back to eat."

"I'll fetch my things later. I'll have dinner first. Thank you, Maam Dib."

"Someone will bring you a plate. I'm going to perform my final prayer while you eat. After your dinner, we'll finish this conversation. And then I'll go to bed. I'm an old lady now. And old ladies go to bed early."

She stands up and slowly heads to the back of the court-yard, toward the diamond of huts. A few minutes later, one of her granddaughters brings me a bowl of *sàcc fu lipp*.

V

He returned in 1986, six years after Koumakh's death. The three of us, Coura, Ngoné, and I, were at the cemetery, praying at our late husband's grave. He entered and we immediately knew it was him: he was the image of Koumakh. Koumakh had told us that Madag was his nephew. But you'd have sworn he was his son. That Madag was old only made the resemblance even stronger. He was seventy, and his wrinkled face looked just like Koumakh's in the final years of his life. The only difference was the height. Madag was much taller than his uncle. He greeted us, and prayed beside us at the grave. Then, he said he needed to talk to us, to tell us who he was. But Coura, the oldest and the first wife, told him:

"We already know who you are. Koumakh—may Roog keep him at their side—spoke of you before he departed. You're Madag."

Before his final sleep, Koumakh had gathered us in his bedroom and told us the story of Mossane. I was the youngest of the three wives. I had heard stories that dated back to before I was born, or to when I was just a child. Stories about a love affair, about rage and madness and jealousy, involving Koumakh, his twin brother, who had disappeared, and Mossane, the madwoman who lived beneath the mango tree by the cemetery. I grew up with that story. The elders used to tell it in the village. But there were many versions. Sometimes they contradicted each other. Some said that Mossane had been married to Koumakh, but had betrayed him one day with his twin brother. Koumakh then supposedly killed his brother, after which Mossane went mad. Other versions claimed that it was Mossane herself who had killed Koumakh's brother to keep him from telling his twin about his wife's adultery. There were still more rumors that maintained that Assane Koumakh, our Koumakh's twin brother, went off to war and never returned, which drove Mossane mad because she was in love with him and not his brother. But all those versions had a common element: at one point or another they mentioned the existence of a child. A child who hadn't survived and had caused the madness and the rift between the three of them. Sometimes people said Ousseynou Koumakh was the father. Other times they said his brother was. I heard those accounts throughout my childhood.

Koumakh asked me to marry him in 1957. I was twenty-one, he was sixty-nine. He was a respected and feared man. A full-head that people consulted about everything. Becoming his spouse was a privilege. I was his third wife. Coura, the first one, was thirty. Ngoné, the second, was twenty-four. After me, he married Tening two years later, in 1959. But Tening died in 1960, while giving birth to Marème Siga. I'm telling you all this so you'll realize something: all of Koumakh's wives came into his life once he had already passed the halfway mark of his voyage here on earth. He had a life before all of us, and in that life, there was one woman, Mossane. Nobody knew what had really happened. Even

Coura was too young to have been around when the whole business between Koumakh, his brother, and Mossane took place. She didn't know any more about it than we did. There had only been rumors, until that night when Koumakh told us things. He didn't give us the details of his relationship with Mossane. But he told us that he had loved her and that Mossane had preferred his brother. She got pregnant with Assane's child shortly before he went to Europe to fight. He must have died there, because he never came back. The child was born. It was Madag. Elimane Madag Diouf. Koumakh raised him like his son, with Mossane. Then, in 1935—I wasn't born yet—Madag went to France too, for his studies. But soon enough he stopped sending word, as if he wanted nothing more to do with his family. Or as if he was dead. His silence drove his mother mad. After living beneath the mango tree for years, she vanished. She left the mango tree all of a sudden and no one ever saw her again. That was the moment the second part of Koumakh's life began, when he found himself alone. That's the first thing he told us from his deathbed.

Maam Dib falls silent. I don't tell her that Siga D. already told me all this, and that I probably know more details of the story than she does. Still, I don't want to interrupt her. I want her to tell me everything at her pace, in her way. She resumes a few seconds later:

Then Koumakh told us he had had a vision the previous night. He saw that Madag would come back. "He'll come back several years after my death," he said. "I want you to welcome him, and let him guide you. He'll be older than all of you. He'll even be older than you, Coura. Follow him, and listen to him, because I believe that his head is even fuller than mine. As for me, I'll speak to him through paths that aren't accessible to you, when I'm in the other world. Whatever you do, don't ask him any questions about what he did, where he was, why he never came back. As long as he doesn't tell you things himself, don't ask him anything." That's what Koumakh told us about Madag. And during the night, he departed.

After his death, Siga left too and never came back. Sometimes we'd hear rumors about her life in Dakar. Terrible, shameful rumors. We wanted to go get her. But Koumakh had forbidden us, it was one of his final wishes, to try to bring her back. She needs to return on her own if she wants to. I don't know if he saw Siga's future, but when it came to her, Koumakh's words and attitude had always been tough, and very harsh. Siga never came back. And here in the village, we kept on living our lives, waiting for Madag's return, which Koumakh had predicted.

Six years went by after his death. Then that day, at the cemetery, Madag returned, dressed very simply, like all the elders here. His only baggage was a leather bag slung over his shoulder. Coura told him we knew who he was, and that we'd been expecting him. We didn't ask him anything. He thanked us, then said he would meet us at the house (he remembered the way to this house, where he grew up). We came back here. The whole walk, none of us spoke. But all three of us were wondering what would happen, what Madag would do, what he would ask of us, what he would say, what we would learn.

He returned two or maybe three hours later. He asked if his uncle's bedroom had been left as it was. We told him yes: that had also been one of our husband's final wishes: no one was to touch anything, we were only to enter to clean occasionally, but all his things had to remain where they were, until the day Madag returned. And then he moved into Koumakh's room, it's the large, secluded hut you see over there, next to the pirogue where you were standing earlier. That became Madag's room. From that moment on, he began another part of his life too, the part with us. I didn't know if it was the second or hundredth part. Maybe Madag had already had several lives before returning. None of us had the faintest idea.

At first we feared that he would be a difficult man. We were wrong: life with him was simple. He gained everyone's respect very quickly. Of course, rumors about his past resurfaced in the village. But by and large, everyone treated him like an exceptional man. He was a full-head. His knowledge, his understanding of the world, his experience with the visible and the invisible, his gifts... all that raised him to the rank of a spiritual authority. He was Koumakh's worthy descendant. Our children, who were his cousins by blood, called him Maam. And true, he was old enough to be their grandfather. He quickly took over his uncle's activities. In the morning, he would hold mystical consultations in his room—after a few miracles in the village (healings mainly), he quickly made a name for himself, and his reputation spread. In the afternoon, here actually, beneath this tree, he would mend or weave fishing nets for the fishermen in the village.

He wasn't a very talkative man, but he reassured us. Still, we could see that he himself wasn't always at peace. In his silence, I heard great pain. Bitter memories. All three of us sensed it. But none of us ever dared question him. We remembered Koumakh's words. But mostly, we saw, just by looking at him, that asking Madag about his disappearance would have hurt him. We didn't know what he had gone through. He had remained in exile so long—half a century!—that we told ourselves he must have left a part of himself behind. Everyone he had known or loved before he left was dead. Asking him where he had been all that time would have been a reminder of what he had lost in his absence. Maybe it would have been taken as a reproach for that absence. So we said nothing.

There were only two things that he explicitly forbade us from doing. The first was to enter his room when he was inside and the door was closed. The second interdiction concerned books. He didn't want to see any in the house. He acknowledged that there were some, but not a single one should be left in his eyesight. Anyone who wanted to read was to do so in their bedroom, or outside the house, or while he was gone. The whole time he lived here, he never went near the school, because he was fearful of seeing books.

One day, in a moment of inattention, Latew, my youngest daughter—the one who greeted you when you arrived with Ndé Kiraan—forgot two books she was meant to read for school here, under this same tree. Madag came out of his hut and saw them. I was a little farther away, at the back of the courtyard. I quickly realized what was happening when I saw him beside the chair where my daughter had left the books. Madag was shaking. Before I could react, he grabbed a book with one hand. With the other, he pulled out a small knife he always carried at his waist. He would use it to mend fishing nets. So, he drew the knife, and then he slashed at the book he was holding. He could have ripped it apart with his hands but he chose to use the knife. He stabbed the book, he eviscerated it. The inside pages and the cover. He did this slowly, in no rush. But pure savagery surged from his every gesture. And what made it so terrifying was that he didn't make a sound. He destroyed the book in utter silence. All you could hear was the pages tearing. Quick enough, the courtyard filled. The children came out, Coura and Ngoné came out. But no one dared intervene. We were all stunned. All we could do was watch him do it. That was the first time we'd seen him like that. But he didn't see us. His blood-rimmed eyes were fixed on the books. He destroyed the first one, then he grabbed the second. He dealt with it the same way. Scraps of paper fell on the ground like leaves from the tree. They formed a rug so white at Madag's feet. He was shaking, but his movements remained precise, violent. It lasted at least an hour.

After slashing the last page, he paused, head down, for several seconds. His breathing was loud, like after you've exerted strenuous effort. Then he lifted his head and saw us, and we saw that he was crying. Without a word, face distorted by rage or pain, he slowly returned to his room, hardly able to walk. He closed the door and didn't reemerge for almost two days. And since he had forbidden anyone from going near his room when he was inside and the door was closed, we didn't check on him, not even to bring him food.

When he reemerged, he was himself again and life went back to normal. Latew wanted to apologize, but he pre-empted her and told her he wouldn't hear of it. In fact, he was the one to apologize, before giving her some money to buy new copies of the books he had destroyed. Of course, no one ever left a book or even a single page outside again. Nor did anyone ask him where that hatred of books came from. We knew it had something to do with his long, fifty-year journey through the white man's land.

Every night, he went to the cemetery. First, he would stand before Koumakh's grave. Then, he would sit beneath the big mango tree, where they said his mother had sat during her madness. He would stay there a long time before returning to the house. But there were nights when he slept there, in the cemetery or across from it, beneath the mango tree. Which, as you can imagine, fed the gossipmongers, who would whisper that he was a black mage, or that at night he transformed into an eater of souls.

One night, when he had returned a little earlier than usual, he found almost the whole family here, in this courtyard. He walked over, sat down, and spoke to us. I've never forgotten and will never forget what he said. I still get shivers when I think about his voice as he revealed his secrets.

He said: I know you're wondering what I do at the cemetery at night. I'm going to tell you: I pray for my uncle, for my father, for friends I've lost, and for my mother. I pray for my mother most of all. That she'll forgive me. I can't see her. And yet I've looked for her everywhere: in the places you can see and the places you can't. I've looked for her through time. But I can't find her. I haven't found her. It's as if she never existed. I hope she hears my prayers. I need her to forgive me. I ask that everyone here pray for me. Pray that Mossane forgives me.

That's what he said. I understood then that even if he was a full-head, Madag wasn't a god. He was a man. He was living with painful memories and questions without answers. You could have felt pity for him. That's all man is: a creature you can feel pity for.

Maam Dib falls silent again. I'm guessing that, in this moment, she's praying for Madag. It abruptly occurs to me, as I watch her, that this woman knew—understood— Elimane Madag far better than me. Not only because she met him and spent many years with him (the number of years is immaterial), but because, for a single moment, she had access to everything: his guilt, his weakness, his desire, his solitude, his anguish. Since the beginning, because I read Elimane, I've thought that his secret has something to do with literature, that it's necessarily related to *The Labyrinth of Inhumanity* and the book that was meant to follow. I've connected all the mystery around the man to his writing, interpreted the silences in his life with the obsessional lenses of a writer. But have they left me nearsighted? Maybe there's nothing to be found within literature. It presents itself as a suspicious casket, gleaming black, but it's possible there's no corpse inside. Over the past weeks, Siga D., Musimbwa, Béatrice, Stanislas, Chérif, Aïda, and now Maam Dib told me as much, or implied it, each in their own way. And perhaps Elimane Madag himself has been trying to tell me, too, since I began following him. But if he has, it's with obscure signs, through the thick fog of time that separates us. Suddenly I feel incredibly sad. Maam Dib resumes:

Coura died seventeen years ago, Ngoné followed her seven years later. And then I was alone with Madag. People who didn't know the story thought he was my husband. We used to laugh about it. The last ten years of his life, he stopped mending and making fishing nets, and merely held his mystical consultations in the mornings. In the afternoons, he would go to the river and walk along the water's edge. But until his final day, he still visited the cemetery and the spot beneath the mango tree. One month before his death, thereabouts, he told me about you. He said that one year after his passing, someone would come and want to talk about him. He didn't know the name of the person. He simply asked me to welcome them.

"He didn't say anything else?"

"He didn't know how many days you would stay. But he asked that I offer you hospitality for as many days as you wanted, to do what you needed to do here."

"He didn't tell you what that was?"

"No. I think that I didn't need to know. But I'm guessing that you do, that you know."

I remain silent for a second and then respond:

"Yes."

"Then I'm done."

"Wait: How did he die?"

"How? The gentlest way you can: in his sleep. He set his affairs in order, performed his final prayers, healed his last patients. He blessed the house and all the houses in the village. Then he fell asleep, at the age of over a hundred, I believe. He was buried in the village cemetery, next to Koumakh's grave. They look like twin graves."

She pauses for a few seconds before continuing:

"We didn't even have to announce Madag's departure for the kingdom of ancestors. Around here, everyone knows that when a spiritual light goes out, it manifests physically. The day of Koumakh's death, it rained from morning till night even though it was the height of the dry season. The day after Madag's death, a veil of black clouds covered the sky and hid the daylight. Some even claimed that the sun didn't rise that morning. At noon, it was very dark, like the night had kept going. We washed and buried him in late afternoon. There were lots of people at his funeral. The whole village, but also many inhabitants of the nearby villages. They had all understood, when they saw night in the middle of the day, that it was Madag, one of the region's last remaining full-heads, leaving. So they came to accompany him. The sun didn't rise until the earth had covered his body, around five o'clock."

She stops a beat, I wait for her to continue, but she doesn't continue. Maam Dib stands, looks at me, and, as though she can guess how I'm feeling, says:

"I don't know what you were imagining, little storyteller with the boundless imagination. I don't know what Madag's life was before his return. I'm assuming it wasn't exactly blissful. But he had a simple end. Not completely happy or at peace maybe, but simple. And I think that's already a lot for someone like him."

Just then, in the distance, we hear Ndé Kiraan and Latew's voices.

"The girls are coming back," says Maam Dib. "That's my signal to go to sleep. They'll keep you company for the rest of the night. *Boo feet ndax Roog*, Diégane Faye. *Ngiroopo*."

"*Bo feet*, Maam Dib. Good night. Thank you."

She heads to her bedroom. A few seconds later, the two young women enter the courtyard. The three of us relax, chat, bond, as we sip tea prepared by Latew. When, much later, I get up to fetch my things from the car, Ndé Kiraan offers to accompany me part of the way. She's ready for bed too and tells me she wants to make sure I don't make off with the car she won in our bet, a few hours earlier. Latew says she's going to prepare my room.

"It'll be that one," she tells me, pointing to the large hut beside the pirogue.

I'm not surprised. In fact, I think I already knew that, inevitably, that was where I would be sleeping.

"My mother must have told you that was Maam Madag's room," continues Latew. "I'll say good night now, in case I'm already asleep when you get back."

Ndé Kiraan and I set out. I turn on my phone flashlight to brighten the path. On the way, I ask her where the village cemetery is.

"The cemetery?"

Her astonishment is clear in the abrupt, astonished, tone of her voice. A few seconds pass, and since I don't answer, thereby reiterating or confirming my question, she tells me:

"It's not very far from the entrance to the village. You can't miss it. When you reach your car, raise your head and look to your left. You'll see high branches and leaves. That's the old mango tree. The cemetery is across from it."

I sense, as I thank her, that she's wondering, but doesn't dare say it, why I asked her that question.

"I want to pray over Madag's grave."

"Tonight, you mean? Aren't you afraid?"

"Of what?"

"I don't know... You know, Maam Madag wasn't like us... In any case, his grave is easy to find. As soon as you enter the cemetery, take the first path on your left. At the end of the path, the grave will be on your left, beside the wall."

I walk her home. We say good night. I can see the worry in her eyes when we part ways. She's still thinking about the grave. It's on both our minds, but for entirely different reasons. I go to the car and fetch my few belongings, plus the book. Then I raise my head: unmoving in the night, to my left, the crown of the mango tree.

VI

How long did you stay beneath Mossane's mango tree, sitting on the ground, in the same spot where she once sat? And how long, in the cemetery, contemplating the twin graves? You have no idea, the same way you have no idea how to articulate the furthest reaches of your emotions. Is this the moment you give free rein to your disappointment and finally allow yourself to think: All that for this? That long road, those long nights of insomnia, those nights spent reading and questioning and dreaming, those nights spent listening and drinking and despairing, to end up at this banality—death? So it's death, then, and nothing more, that is the disappointing truth of every life?

Standing before the grave, you read your favorite pages from *The Labyrinth of Inhumanity*, an adieu of sorts. You went back to the text, meaning to the essence of what's truly connected you to its author these past several weeks. This was how you bid him a final goodbye, and you finally asked yourself what the relationship between story and author was. Now that you knew some bits and pieces, how did you connect Madag's life to his book?

The hypothesis you came up with was the most obvious one—simple transpositions and analogies. The bloodthirsty king is Madag. The power the king desires is the equivalent of the book that Madag wrote: *The Labyrinth of Inhumanity*. To obtain that power, the bloodthirsty king must heed the prophecy and tear down the old world, embodied by the elders of his kingdom. In Madag's destiny, that old world is the world of his childhood and all those who inhabit it: Ousseynou Koumakh, Assane Koumakh, his mother. To become more powerful, the bloodthirsty king has to kill the past. For the sake of his book, Madag forgot his.

It's very clear in your mind: The formal composition of *The Labyrinth of Inhumanity*, the plagiarism, the borrowings, none of that should obscure the heart's truth. And the truth of Madag's heart, you tell yourself, the truth of his book, is the story of a man's ultimate sacrifice: to attain perfection, he kills his memory. But killing it isn't enough to destroy it; and that man, regardless of whether he's the novel's bloodthirsty king or Madag, had forgotten this: Souls who try to flee the past are in fact running behind it and eventually, one day or another, in their future, they'll catch up with it. The past has plenty of time; it waits ever patient at the crossroads with the future; and that is where it collars the man who thought he'd gotten away, locking him inside its five-celled prison: the immortality of the departed, the permanence of forgetting, the inevitability of culpability, the company of solitude, the salutary malediction of love. Madag understood this after all those years on the run. He not only understood that *The Labyrinth of Inhumanity* hadn't brought an end to his past, but also that it was forever leading him back to it. So he came home.

At least that was your interpretation.

You shut the book and cast a weary look at the cemetery, drenched in shadow. For a moment, you envied the dead. Then you walked out and returned to *Mbin Madag*.

The courtyard is still and silent. Latew undoubtedly went to bed a long time ago. You head to the bedroom reserved for you. Standing on the hut threshold, you think about Siga D., decades earlier, preparing to go inside to receive Ousseynou Koumakh's last will and testament. You remember how she described this hut to you in Amsterdam: its stink, its grime, its rot. You wonder if that's still the case, before realizing the idiocy of such a thought. You enter.

Two solar lamps, one set on the ground beside the bed, to the left, and the other on a small desk, to the right, offer some light. Needless to say, no stench greets you. The opposite, in fact: you detect a delicate scent whose censer must have been removed several hours ago, but whose gentle and tenacious imprint lingers in the air. You look up at the straw roof, supported by tall beams converging toward the structure's peak. Beside the entrance, a large water jug welcomes you. A tinplate pot is upside down on its lid. You have another idiotic thought, that maybe it's Ousseynou Koumakh's spit jar. Hanging on the terra-cotta walls are what you guess to be divination instruments belonging to the previous tenants: you see horns, cowrie necklaces, a machete, the hide of an unknown animal, a satchel tied shut with a red string, amulets dangling at the end.

You approach the desk, on top of which there's only a small wooden box minus its lid. It contains large needles, spools of fishing rope, rolls of wire, a few blades, two small knives: the essentials for weaving and mending fishing nets.

Then you sit on the bed and take a long look around the room, thinking: I'm looking at what he looked at every time he sat on his bed. You remain silent for several seconds, waiting for a sign. But nothing happens. You rise and rummage the room, in search of something, any sign whatsoever that you could cling to. You don't find anything under the bed; nothing in the desk drawer or the wardrobe either. All that's left is the satchel hanging on the wall. With trembling hands you untie the red string keeping it shut. A large leather notebook with a broken clasp is waiting for you inside. There's your sign. You open the notebook and find several folded pieces of paper. You unfold them.

It's this letter.

I'm writing you this tonight, before I go to sleep for the last time.

The words you've just read don't really surprise you, even if you stop for a few seconds to think about me. You hesitate to continue reading this letter, which you understand predicts your future and also your immediate past. You also understand that I'm sending it to my future.

In the end, you keep reading.

Inside this large notebook you're holding, there is part of the book that I was never able to finish, despite the many years that have passed. I never gave up on writing. I tried as hard as I could. But I didn't have the strength of absolute silence. It wasn't that The Labyrinth of Inhumanity *and all the problems it caused me spared me from the weakness that is writing. I simply couldn't do it anymore. Hence my growing bitterness, these last few years, at any completed book. They reminded me of my powerlessness to finish my own.*

I can see from here that you now understand what I desire and expect from you.

I wish I could know if you will accept my humble prayer, the prayer of a ghost from the past. I wish that you would publish this manuscript, at least what can be published. I wish I could see the end of my story, but I'm tired. As I write to you, I'm reaching the limits of my vision. It grows hazy the second you finish this sentence.

I'm writing this sentence a long time after that last one, a heaviness in my heart.

For years, in my visions, I saw myself the way I am in this moment, in this room, old, but writing at this table, with a feeling of slight sadness. I interpreted that vision as the sign that I would one day succeed in finishing my life's work, the book to follow The Labyrinth of Inhumanity. I thought my sadness was the kind that overwhelms some creators when they finish a work that required they exhaust every part of themselves. I was mistaken. In reality, and I'm understanding this at this very moment, that vision wasn't showing me finishing my novel, but this letter. The sadness now growing inside me doesn't betray my emotion at completing my book, but at not completing it. I won't finish. I'm a hundred and two years old and I didn't have enough time. The future was too short. Thus it ends for every diviner: nostalgic for the days ahead. Thus it ends for the seer: melancholic for the future.

But that melancholy can still be joyful. It all depends on you. I'm leaving. What consoles me, as I prepare to step into the shadows, is the idea that someone, you, whose name I don't know but whose face is familiar, will read this book, and perhaps draw something from it. I don't want to disappear completely. I want to leave this trace, incomplete though it may be. It's my life.

Epilogue

Dusk fell, and little by little the river took on the sheen of old copper, as if the sun were dissolving in the water. I waded in slowly, deeper.

I've read Madag's manuscript several times over the last two days. The text isn't a sequel to *Labyrinth*, but an auto-biographical account closer, on certain pages, to a diary. The beginning is glorious. I was convinced I was holding the genuine masterpiece I had been seeking. But after a few pages everything changes: the book strays and never finds its way back, as though Madag, after all the years gone by, all the happenings, all the wandering, had no longer been able to keep the promise of those first moments. I read some of the chapters with immeasurable sorrow: I could sense in them the agony of a once-great writer steadily abandoned by his faculties and his talent. I think that he very quickly understood what was happening to him, but persisted. At times, yes, amid erratic paragraphs, I read a few pages, a few sentences, I saw an image, a painting, I heard music; and in those moments, Madag swept me violently off the earth and reminded me what substance made the man. But those flashes of brilliance merely illuminated in crueler fashion the depths of the surrounding literary night, before going out.

The last truly written pages are dated September 1969. Madag, in Buenos Aires at the time, was preparing to go to Bolivia, where he believed he had found the man he'd been chasing across Latin America for twenty years: a former SS officer with whom he'd had dealings, a certain Josef Engelmann. This Engelmann, before fleeing to South America after the war, had met Madag in the 1940s. Madag writes that in 1942, in Paris, Engelmann arrested and tortured his friend Charles Ellenstein before sending him to the camp in Compiègne, after which he was deported to Mauthausen.

Between 1969 and his death last year, a period of nearly fifty years, Madag is irregular in his writing. He makes multiple brief notations, some of which are illegible. He believes he'll quickly track down Engelmann in Bolivia. But the Nazi eludes him for many years to follow. Madag doesn't find him again until 1984 in La Paz. Without going into detail, he writes that the pair put an end to their old history in a "repugnant and ruthless" fashion. He then returns to Paris, where he lives for nearly two years, before going back to Senegal in 1986. He doesn't say much about that second Parisian interlude. He does mention a bar, in Place Clichy, where he would "sometimes return [a]lone, to catch a glimpse of the past." He never names the bar. It could be the Vautrin. But it could also be any other bar in Place Clichy between 1984 and 1986.

One thing is clear: Madag didn't run out of time, as he says in the letter he sent to his future. He simply never got past the *Labrinth of Inhumanity*. He probably should never have tried. Maybe he only had a single book in him; a single, masterful book. It might be that every writer, in the end, only contains a single essential book, a work that demands to be written, between two voids. That night, everything quietly clicked in my mind: there was only one thing to do for *The Labrinth of Inhumanity*, for Madag, and for the manuscript he left behind.

I'd brought it with me. The water was up to my waist. The notebook was already tied to a heavy stone. I tried to think of something solemn, an epitaph, or the final sentence of a will and testament. Nothing came, and I finally threw the stone as far as I could. It sank right away, dragging Madag's notebook down with it. The silence returned, pure to the point of insolence. I tired myself out swimming for a few minutes, then returned to the bank and collapsed directly on the sand and shells. I caught my breath as I watched the Sine's maternal night, unsure whether I felt sad or relieved.

Tomorrow, I'll return home and enjoy some time with my family. I'll pay Chérif a visit. I'll think about Aïda and be tempted to write her. I won't. I'll call Siga D. and promise to visit her when I get back, because unlike Musimbwa, I'll be going back to Paris. Stanislas will ask me how the people's revolution in Senegal is going and I'll tell him the truth: it's well on its way to being suppressed or betrayed, as happens all too often. I'll try to see Béatrice Nanga again.

Then, at last, I'll wait for Madag to come. I couldn't grant his request. Publishing the contents of that notebook would have destroyed his masterpiece, or the selfish memory I want to keep of it. And one night, Madag will pay me a visit, to bring me to account, or maybe to take revenge, I know that much; and his ghost, as it approaches, will whisper the terms of the terrible existential choice that was his life's dilemma; the choice that breeds hesitation in the heart of every person haunted by literature: write, don't write.

Acknowledgments

Thank you to Felwine and Philippe for their trust, their tough but kind feedback, their constant encouragement, and especially their friendship. I'm also grateful to the entire editorial team: Benoit, Mélanie, Marie-Laure.

My thoughts go to my family here and there: Malick and Mame Sabo, my parents and role models; all my brothers, of whom I'm very proud; Franck and Silvia, for taking me in like a son (and feeding me all those Sundays).

Thank you to all the stars in my constellation of friends, whose readings, suggestions, generosity, and simple conversation took this book apart and then put it back together, better than it was: Sami, Annie, Elgas, Laurent, Lamine, Anne-Sophie, Aminata, Aram, Khalil, Ndeye Fatou, Yass, ndeko Philippe, Fran, Abdou Aziz. You each left a piece of yourselves in this book, by which I mean that precious something that is friendship.

I'll end with Mellie, my compass, and that of this book, which, without your presence, would have been lost in the Night.

MOHAMED MBOUGAR SARR was born in Dakar in 1990. He studied literature and philosophy at the École des Hautes Études en Sciences Sociales in Paris. *Brotherhood*, his first novel, won the Grand Prix du Roman Métis, the Prix Ahmadou Kourouma, and the French Voices Grand Prize. The president of Senegal named him a Chevalier of the National Order of Merit. In 2021 Sarr won the Prix Goncourt for *The Most Secret Memory of Men*, becoming the first sub-Saharan African author to do so.

LARA VERGNAUD is a translator of prose, creative non-fiction, and scholarly works from the French. She is the recipient of the French-American Foundation Translation Prize and the French Voices Grand Prize, and has been nominated for the National Translation Award. Her translation of *The Most Secret Memory of Men* was long-listed for the 2023 National Book Award for Translated Literature. Her other recent translations include Fatima Daas's *The Last One* (Other Press, 2021) and Mohamed Leftah's *Demoiselles of Numidia* (Other Press, 2023).